THE
DIRTY
SECRET

BRENT WOLFINGBARGER

BRENT WOLFINGBARGER

SMALLRIDGE PUBLISHING
P.O. Box 13652
Silver Spring, MD 20911-3652

Smallridge Publishing
P.O. Box 13652
Silver Spring, MD 20911-3652
202-450-5910

Smallridge Publishing can bring authors to your live event. For more information or to book an event, contact Smallridge Publishing at 202-450-5910 or visit our website at www.smallridgepublishing.com.

ISBN: 0-9852205-0-3
ISBN-13: 978-0-9852205-0-1

LCCN: 2012904107

This book is dedicated to:

My grandfather, Herman Wolfingbarger, who was the best storyteller I have ever met.

My grandmother, Wilda Wolfingbarger, who shared with me her passion for learning and her love of the written word.

My dad, Wade Wolfingbarger, who has taught me by example what it means to be a good father and husband.

My mom, Deanie Wolfingbarger, who has always shown me unconditional love and support.

My grandmother, Beulah Mann, who continues to embrace life with a smile and a positive attitude as she approaches her 91st birthday.

My wife, Karen, who loves me despite my considerable faults and who gives me strength and comfort on a daily basis.

And my children, Reagan and Titus, who fill my heart with unimaginable love and pride.

BRENT WOLFINGBARGER

ACKNOWLEDGMENTS

First and foremost, I have to thank my wife, Karen, for patiently enduring all the long nights I have spent editing and polishing this book since it was first completed several years ago. I never could have completed this project without her love and support, and I truly thank God for bringing her into my life.

Thanks to those who spent time reviewing early versions of this manuscript, helping me streamline the story, including Craig Dean, Tammy Lowers, Kathy Elder and others. I also thank Jennings Miller, who helped me crystallize my ideas for this book when I represented him in an election law dispute back in 2000.

I thank my editor, Rob Bignell, for his thorough service and constructive criticism. Kudos to Ranilo Cabo, who designed the beautiful cover art for the book, and the folks at 99designs.com who helped me partner with him. Likewise, I am indebted to Tom Kubilius, Chanin & Chris Krivonyak, John Mullins, Ed Duffey, Tracy Keener, Ken & Terri Gould, Steve & Keri Ellison and the inimitable "Son of Tempus" for helping me evaluate the various design proposals that were submitted for this project. Thanks also to all my friends who enthusiastically shared their passionate opinions on that subject by voting in my online polls.

A debt of gratitude is owed to Chuck Sambuchino, Jane Friedman and all the folks at Writer's Digest who provide a wealth of information to aspiring authors with their seminars, blogs and conferences. I am also grateful to the Ramlal clan for all the encouragement they have given me in this endeavor.

Thanks go out to Stephen Coonts, for demonstrating that a lawyer from West Virginia who knows how to spin a good yarn can somehow find his niche in the publishing world. I'd also like to thank Barry Eisler and Joe Konrath for generously sharing their keen insights into the revolutionary ways the publishing world has changed, and how it is likely to continue to evolve in ways that are largely beneficial to authors like me.

Lastly, I thank Neil Clark Warren for broadening my horizons and forever changing my life for the better. Reagan and Titus extend their thanks to Mr. Warren for his services, as well.

BRENT WOLFINGBARGER

FACT:

The statutes, regulations, judicial cases and constitutional provisions cited in this novel accurately reflect the body of law governing American presidential elections as of February 2012, particularly those which govern post-election legal proceedings in the State of West Virginia.

BRENT WOLFINGBARGER

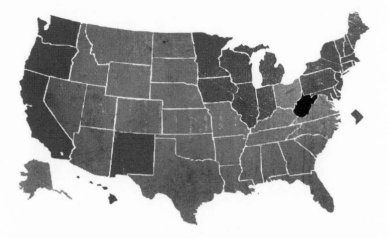

<u>Gov. Jonathan Royal (R-NC)</u>   270*

Alabama (9), Alaska (3), Arizona (11), Arkansas (6), Colorado (9), Florida (29), Georgia (16), Idaho (4), Kansas (6), Kentucky (8), Louisiana (8), Mississippi (6), Missouri (10), Montana (3), Nebraska (5), Nevada (6), North Carolina (15), North Dakota(3), Ohio (18), Oklahoma (7), South Carolina (9), South Dakota (3), Tennessee (11), Texas (38), Utah (6), Virginia (13), Wyoming (3), West Virginia (5)*

<u>Sen. Melanie Wilson (D-CA)</u>   268

California (55), Connecticut (7), District of Columbia (3), Delaware (3), Hawaii (4), Illinois (20), Indiana (11), Iowa (6), Maine (4), Maryland (10), Massachusetts (11), Michigan (16) Minnesota (10), New Hampshire (4), New Jersey (14), New Mexico (5), New York (29), Oregon (7), Pennsylvania (20), Rhode Island (4), Vermont (3), Washington (12), Wisconsin (10)

* Based on initial returns only; canvass is pending.

BRENT WOLFINGBARGER

CHAPTER 1

VIENNA, VIRGINIA
WEDNESDAY, NOVEMBER 5, 10:45 P.M.

A solitary streetlight shone through a copse of barren oak trees on the far side of the empty park. It illuminated a patch of cold, hard ground about fifty yards from the bench where the two men sat.

"Plausible deniability is a must."

Yuri Petrenko sighed wearily, slowly unwrapped a watermelon Jolly Rancher and placed it in his mouth. "Certainly," he replied, as the hard candy rolled over his tongue.

A breeze blew past, carrying with it a foretaste of winter's approaching chill. A mini-cyclone of brittle fallen leaves danced drowsily in a circle, rustling softly as it passed to their left, bathed from behind by the streetlight's glow.

"We deeply appreciate your firm's efforts in this matter," his companion continued, absent-mindedly running an olive-skinned hand through his thick black hair. "We have full confidence in

1

your competence. The precise *means* you use to achieve our shared goals, we'll leave to your discretion."

A forced-looking smile etched itself on Petrenko's face. His teeth were agonizingly bright, as if subjected to whitening treatments around-the-clock. Beneath his short-cropped blond hair, the streetlight revealed that the bottom half of his left ear was missing.

The Russian pulled up the collar of his black greatcoat to shield his neck from the breeze. Pinching the empty Jolly Rancher wrapper between the fingertips and thumb of his right hand, he coiled it into a ball. Standing from the bench, he tossed the wrapper into a green metal trash can a few feet away. "We'll keep you apprised as necessary," he said.

His dark-haired companion extended his right hand for a farewell handshake. Casually ignoring the gesture, Petrenko strolled past the trash can toward a silver Audi convertible that was parallel-parked across the street.

He never looked back.

CHAPTER 2

ROYAL FOR PRESIDENT
NATIONAL CAMPAIGN HEADQUARTERS
WASHINGTON, D.C.
FRIDAY, NOVEMBER 7, 11:30 A.M.

Every time he looked at the map of West Virginia hanging on the War Room wall, Dave Anderson felt his stomach churn. Small towns and obscure counties he had studied back in middle school tauntingly glared at him. The backwoods byways of his home state twisted and turned obscenely, following routes preordained by its mountainous terrain. His fertile mind imagined potential disasters seemingly everywhere.

"Two hundred fifty-nine votes don't leave a whole lot of room for error, Hoss."

Dave glanced over his right shoulder. The booming voice behind him had been burned into the American consciousness for the past year. It belonged to Governor Jonathan Royal, his friend and putative President.

"Not at all," Dave replied, returning his gaze to the map. "Especially since Luke Vincent knows this state like the insides of his own eyelids." He sighed and shook his head slightly. "He could probably generate that many votes just from bodies buried in his family cemetery."

Even though Dave had worked inside the Beltway most of his adult life, his undiluted native twang was a constant reminder of his West Virginia roots. Ordinarily, his childhood home merely made for interesting conversation with the lobbyists and policy wonks who shared his professional world. But with the Electoral College apparently hinging on what happened in West Virginia, all that had abruptly changed.

Royal guffawed heartily and slapped Dave on the back. "Probably, Hoss! Prah-buh-blee. And that's why I've got somebody as smart and as devious as *you* working for me: To keep an eye on that slippery son-of-a-bitch and make sure he doesn't steal the Oval Office from me!"

Royal edged closer to get a better look at the map himself. "So how do you think it's going to play out?" he asked. He ran his hand across the back of his neck, along the base of his mostly-salt-but-sporadically-peppered hair.

Standing just under six feet tall, Dave was a good four inches shorter than the candidate. He touched his index finger to the state's Eastern Panhandle jutting out between Maryland and Virginia. "From what I can gather, we're looking pretty good in the Second District." As he spoke, he moved his finger southwesterly across the thick middle part of West Virginia, coming to a halt over Charleston. "That area leans our way, and it looks like we did well there on Tuesday. Plus those counties aren't known for a whole lot of vote-counting chicanery."

Royal's eyes narrowed and he nodded. *He probably already knew that much*, Dave realized, mentally chalking it up as yet another example of the man's phenomenal memory. The North Carolina governor's mastery of such esoterica unquestionably had aided his rapid political rise.

"The problem is *this* part of the state," Dave continued, moving his finger southward from Charleston. "There are a handful of southern counties that have been locked down by the Dems for a hundred years, and there really isn't even a two-party system to speak of down there." Squinting his green eyes, he paused for a moment. "In places like Boone and Mingo Counties, voter fraud has been turned into an art form over the years. That's where Jack Kennedy's dad bought him the state's primary in 1960, and that's where they could jump up and bite us now."

Royal pursed his lips and nodded, then smoothly transitioned into the storyteller mode that served him so well on the campaign trail. "My dad always told me a dog's less likely to bite you if you keep your eyes on him." Lilting an eyebrow, he shot Dave a conspiratorial grin. "Sounds like pretty good advice right now, if you know what I mean."

4

"Yep. And that's why we've had video cameras poised on every courthouse in the state since the polls closed on Tuesday."

Royal laughed again. "I knew there was a reason I kept your paranoid ass around here!"

Dave grinned. "Just because I'm paranoid doesn't mean they're not out to get me."

CHAPTER 3

ST. MARYS, PLEASANTS COUNTY, WEST VIRGINIA
MONDAY, NOVEMBER 10, 8:45 A.M.

An expansive collection of brownies, cookies, cupcakes and donuts sat arrayed upon a folding table in the back of the room. Examining the caloric cornucopia, Sarika Gudivada pursed her full lips and briefly contemplated declining the temptation to start her day off with a torrent of sugar.

She quickly dismissed that thought, hoisting a German chocolate brownie, two white chocolate macadamia nut cookies, and a big white frosted cupcake onto a Styrofoam plate. Clutching a tall mocha latte from the local coffeehouse in one hand, she balanced her decadent breakfast in the other and returned to her seat; silently promising to make up for her weakness by running a few extra miles in the days ahead.

"Are you sure you don't want a couple of donuts, too, Rikki?"

Sarika heard her nickname at the precise moment she bit into a cookie. The unexpected jibe caused her to bite down harder than intended. A few wayward crumbs slid past her lips and onto the front of her black suit jacket. Looking to her left, she saw State Senator Jack McCallen casting his trademark shit-eating grin her way.

Sighing softly, Rikki brushed the cookie debris from her chest with the side of her right hand. "Why do you ask, Jack?" She drew her long black hair behind her right ear as she spoke. Her light green eyes sparkled mischievously, starkly contrasted against her smooth, mocha-hued face. "Are you calling me fat or something?"

McCallen wagged his finger at her. "You know I'm too smart to call my own lawyer fat. I'm sure I'd pay for that one way or another."

Rikki laughed aloud. It was a contagious laughter that turned heads her direction and brought smiles to the faces of three older women clustered around the cookie table. "You're a smart man, Mr. Senator!" Rikki moved her plate from the folding metal chair to her left and placed it in her lap. McCallen took the cue and sat down beside her. "So how've you been?" she asked.

"Sleeping better now that the election is over. How about you? Was your first time on the ballot as bad as you thought it'd be?"

Rikki paused to finish a bite of her cookie. "Piece of cake. My opponent wasn't nearly as popular as yours."

"Everyone in this county knew the guy you ran against was a no good piece of crap," Jack interjected. "Everybody knows he knocked that little high school girl up, regardless of what he says. I, on the other hand, had the pleasure to run against a retired middle school principal with a rap sheet cleaner than Mother Theresa's. She scared the hell out of me!"

Rikki grinned broadly, her magenta lips parting to reveal perfect white teeth. "Better you than me, Jack. That's why I ran for prosecutor: *Easier pickings*."

McCallen sat silent for a moment, his face the picture of envy. "You chose a good race. Only lawyers can run for prosecutor and it's not like little ol' Pleasants County is crawling with them. Best of all, it's a part-time position, so you can still run your practice on the side and make a little money keeping people like me outta trouble in civil cases. Sounds like a good gig to me."

"Keeping you out of trouble, Jack, is a *full-time* job," Rikki said dryly. "If I have to keep handling your stuff, I don't know if I'll have enough time to be prosecutor."

McCallen squinted his left eye and nodded slightly, apparently conceding the point. "Speaking of which, I need to talk to you soon about that Schoolcraft lease cancellation suit. I about died when I saw all the stuff their evil lawyers sent you last week."

"They're not evil, Jack. They're just doing their job."

"Easy for you to say," he grumbled. "They're not trying to destroy your business. I say they're evil, greedy, blood-sucking assholes."

"Of course you'd say that. You're a Republican. You have a congenital hatred of lawyers who sue businesses even when they deserve to be sued."

"And you're a bleedin'-heart Democrat who just managed to get elected prosecutor because the only lawyer we could put up against you was a bigger waste of oxygen than the bottom-dwellers who're suing me."

Rikki reached over and playfully patted his hand. "Maybe. But I'm also the best oil and gas lawyer in the state, and that's why you put up with my granola-crunching politics."

Jack rocked his chair back on its hind legs and belly-laughed. "Ah, hell, Rikki ... Granola-cruncher or not, I'd still vote for you. As long as you weren't running against me, that is."

The county commission's hearing room was about twenty feet wide by thirty feet long. A large, well-worn oak desk sat atop the twelve-inch-high platform from which the commission would conduct its post-election canvass. An old cloth American flag bearing oversized white stars was suspended from the ceiling behind the middle of the desk.

The room's décor was much like that found in any other rural courthouse in America: Hanging prominently on one wall was an oversized map of the county with boundaries depicted by broad black lines while thinner red and blue lines identified the locations where engineers imagined new water and sewage lines would be laid. Large aerial photographs taken in the 1970s hung elsewhere around the room, depicting both long-gone businesses as well as empty fields where new subdivisions now stood. A litany of framed certificates from local organizations like tee-ball teams and the March of Dimes also lined the walls, tokens of esteem to the commission from the grateful recipients of its largesse.

Hanging on the back wall above the table of brownies and cookies was a large color photograph of the three commissioners and other local honchos clad in yellow construction helmets. They were plunging shiny ceremonial shovel-heads into a large chunk of dirt along the Ohio River where a Japanese company was building a new factory. Rikki snarkily decided the picture should be entitled *Jobs Being Created by Politicians and Alchemy*.

A pen-and-ink drawing of the county's Depression Era courthouse, accurately depicted in its fortress-like position atop a hill overlooking the rest of St. Marys, hung next to the politicians' large, self-aggrandizing picture. It looked both outsized and out-of-kilter by comparison. *I may be a politician now*, Rikki noted silently. *But I will never stoop so low as to wander out into*

8

a field full of mud with a yellow plastic helmet on my noggin just to score a few votes.

Rikki realized her pediatrician father would roll over in his grave if he knew his only daughter had spent the past two months trudging up every holler in the county, knocking on doors in search of votes. Her decision to become an attorney was one he had eventually stomached. But a *politician?* Rikki snorted, knowing all too well what the man locals had called "Doctor G" would have thought about *that* career trajectory.

Pleasants County had a reputation as a relatively open-minded place where people voted for individual candidates based on their perceived merits regardless of party affiliation. Thus, the courthouse was populated by office holders from both parties, and it was largely (although not entirely) devoid of the political posturing and backbiting that was common elsewhere.

Staring toward the open door at the rear of the room, Jack flipped Rikki's arm with the back of his hand. "Speaking of rock-ribbed Republicans," he announced dramatically. "Here comes the sheriff."

A barrel-chested man about six feet three stood in the doorway with a broad-brimmed deputy's hat atop his buzz-cropped head. Clad in a button-up gray shirt with black epaulettes, he had a silver badge clipped to his left chest pocket. A small paunch crested the waistband of his black Sansabelt trousers as he crossed the room toward Rikki and McCallen. "Mornin', Senator," he said. Then he nodded curtly her way. "Mornin' to you, too, Rikki."

"How's everything goin' today, Sheriff?" Jack inquired.

Doug Vaughn shrugged. "We busted a meth lab up on the Pike last night. City boys had a DUI down by the Wendy's. That's about it."

"Pretty quiet night then, huh?" Rikki asked rhetorically.

"Yup," the sheriff replied. Then an awkward silence developed.

No wonder they call him "Silent Doug," Rikki thought. She had initially suspected that Vaughn's quiet demeanor would be an impediment on the campaign trail. But his reputation for diligence and integrity had helped him win re-election by the widest margin on the ballot.

"So how long do you think we'll be here?" Rikki asked, hoping the question would breathe some life back into the conversation.

"Coupla hours at most," Jack answered. "There's only 18 challenged ballots, so there's not a whole lot of fighting for the lawyers to do here." He motioned with his head toward the front of the room, where two men were sitting at separate tables facing the commission's platform. Apparently oblivious to the discussion around them, their faces were buried in thick green books. From the looks of their virtually identical black pin-striped suits, Rikki surmised they must have gone shopping together at Peckerheads R Us.

"Good," Silent Doug said. "I need to get the paperwork done on that meth lab anyway."

Rikki stared at the sheriff and struggled to remember which one of his eyes was the "good" one. For the life of her, she could never remember whether it was the right eye or the left that had been replaced with a glass orb after some hideous incident in Vietnam. She had heard a variety of stories over the years about what supposedly cost Silent Doug his eye, but she had no idea if any of them were true and her sense of decorum dictated she not ask him about it directly. After a few moments of intense scrutiny, Rikki detected the tell-tale inch-long scar beneath the sheriff's left eye. Thereafter she directed all of her attention toward his right eye, feverishly trying to devise a mnemonic to burn that detail into her brain for future reference.

"All right, folks," a raspy female voice called from the front of the room. Rikki turned and saw Alice Snyder, the sole Republican on the county commission, taking her seat on the platform as her two Democrat counterparts followed suit. "Let's get this show on the road."

Rikki took a bite of her brownie and hoped "the show" would be over soon.

CHAPTER 4

CHARLESTON, WEST VIRGINIA
MONDAY, NOVEMBER 10, 12:45 P.M.

Luke Vincent could not imagine what Tabatha must have looked like at twenty, because staring at her now – as she approached *forty* – she was simply stunning. Standing five-ten in her bare feet, her long legs were smooth and carved, leading up to the spectacular ass that first caught his eye the previous year at a Christmas party. Her stomach was flat as a washboard, and although her breasts filled D-cups, they simultaneously felt soft *and* firm, seeming to defy gravity as she rode herself to climax again and again.

After Tabatha satisfied herself, she slid off the bed and knelt in the floor. Governor Vincent recognized the cue and stood before her, weaving his fingers into her long, silky red hair. Vincent gently guided her as she took him in her mouth. The long, slender fingers of her left hand gingerly cupped his balls while her full lips gracefully slid up and down him, working their magic.

Vincent gripped her hair tighter, pulling her toward him with increasing force. Tabatha moaned with excitement and stared up at the Democratic Party's vice-presidential nominee. Her blue eyes were ferocious and determined, and she worked him like an engine piston.

After rolling around with Tabatha for a half-hour, West Virginia's fifty-three-year-old governor could take no more. His breaths grew shorter as the expectation rose. Sensing the moment of truth was nigh, her pace quickened and her muffled moaning grew more urgent. At last, Vincent let loose and cried out in ecstasy. His legs felt jelly-like, and his eyelids fluttered spastically, mimicking the synapses firing in his brain.

At his release, Tabatha emitted one last moan then began chuckling softly. Although Vincent had seen this reaction before, it still unnerved him. As she consumed the last drops of his discharge, staccato bursts of laughter somehow escaped her full mouth and Vincent silently scolded himself again for his carnal weakness. *I've got to stop doing this! She's a demon in bed, but crazier than a rat in a coffee can!*

Finally spent, the governor closed his eyes and shook his head from side-to-side as if clearing out cobwebs. "Whew!" he exhaled, leaning away from Tabatha as if to detach from her mouth. His progress abruptly halted when he felt her fingernails digging into his butt cheek.

Vincent stared down and saw displeasure burning in her blue eyes as she unwrapped her lips from him. Squeezing out the last of his essence with her right hand, she dabbed it off with a fingertip and inserted it between her pouted lips. "I wasn't finished," she declared. Her voice was sonorous, sensuous and gravely serious.

"Sorry. I must have forgotten how thorough you are."

Tabatha stood and casually brushed her hair from her face. Standing naked, her statuesque figure glistened with sweat. She ran her palms across the governor's chest. "Of course you have. You haven't seen me in almost three months."

Vincent sighed. *I knew this was going to happen.* "The press has been all over me since the convention. There's no way I could risk seeing you."

Softly illuminated by a brass lamp sitting beside the bed, Tabatha's face turned chilly. "The press can't do anything that even compares to what *I* could do to you, Governor."

Doused by an icy blast of reality, Vincent's mind reeled. The campaign's rigorous pace had pushed the power Tabatha wielded to the periphery of his awareness. Now it was staring him square in the face once more, and he hated it more than ever.

The governor tried to assume a conciliatory tone. "I know. But think about what that would do to my wife and kids."

Tabatha's laughter rose out of her belly in billowing waves before slowly fading away. "You should have thought about that before you fucked me, Governor." Caressing the side of his face with her right palm, she stared at him, seemingly amused. Then she stood up on her tiptoes and gently kissed his cheek before walking into the bathroom. Chuckling again with her back to him, she called over her shoulder, "Yeah, you should have thought about that *before* you fucked me." Then she pulled the bathroom door shut.

Vincent retrieved his black boxers from the foot of the bed and clumsily slid them up his legs. Collapsing on the bed, he silently cursed his weakness – his abject *stupidity* – for getting involved with the dangerous succubus named Tabatha McCallen.

CHAPTER 5

ST. MARYS, PLEASANTS COUNTY, WEST VIRGINIA
MONDAY, NOVEMBER 10, 6:00 P.M.

Sitting at her mother's dining room table, Rikki stared at the aging framed pictures that adorned the room's walls. The familiar aromas of ginger and garlic wafted from the kitchen, reminding Rikki of her childhood and contributing to the strong sense of nostalgia that the old family pictures evoked.

The largest framed photo in the room was an 11x17 studio portrait taken when she was seven years old. Her father had just moved the family from Chicago and opened his pediatrics practice in St. Marys that summer, prior to the start of her third-grade year. An only child, Rikki wore a white sundress with her long black hair hanging over her mocha shoulders. Smiling broadly with a mischievous glint in her pale green eyes, she was flanked by her obviously adoring parents clad in their now dated Sunday best.

Positioned slightly above and to the right of that portrait was an informal 8x10 photo taken the night of her high school graduation ceremony. Wearing the distinctive purple robe and mortarboard donned by generations of Pleasants County High School students, Rikki was blossoming into womanhood. One of her classmates – a slightly taller young man with white skin, brown hair and green eyes – stood to her left with his right arm draped around her neck. Her mother stood smiling in a dark blue silk dress to the boy's left while her irrepressible father, Dr. G, was positioned to Rikki's right in a black three-piece suit.

Like so many times in the past, Rikki felt a pang in her stomach as she stared at that graduation snapshot. She had asked her mother to take it down, suggesting other photos that could be hung in its place. She had argued with her mother, passionately insisting that its prominent position was inappropriate, and she eventually <u>demanded</u> that the picture be removed from the dining room wall. Her efforts were to no avail. Madhani Gudivada insisted that she liked the graduation photo and steadfastly refused to put it away. Knowing that her own stubbornness was but a poor reflection of her mother's pigheadedness, Rikki finally gave up and just tried to ignore the picture whenever she visited.

"Dinner's ready!"

Rikki tore her thoughts from the past and glanced over to see her mother carrying a white Corning dish filled with *khorma* into the dining room. The distinctive smell of garlic, ginger and paprika filled the room, and the sight of steaming cubes of lamb mixed with fresh whole potatoes and baby carrots made Rikki smile.

"Could you bring the *roti* out of the kitchen, honey?" Madhani asked in strongly accented words that reflected her Gujarati upbringing. Rikki nodded and walked into the kitchen, returning quickly with a plate of warm *roti* shells in her hands.

Placing the *roti* on the table, Rikki watched her mother scoop a small helping of *khorma* onto her plate without taking a seat. Rikki stared at her quizzically, as her mother habitually insisted they eat at the dining room table even though it was only the two of them now. "Aren't we going to eat in here?"

Her mother seemed surprised by the question. "Oh, no," she responded, donning a shy grin as she slid past Rikki. "I saw the Channel Five van at the courthouse and thought they might show you on the news." Pride and a touch of excitement were evident in her voice, as she turned and walked into the living room carrying the plate. Two small black folding tables were already situated in front of the burgundy couch, facing the television.

Rikki chuckled softly. *God, Mom is cute*, she thought. It reminded Rikki of her grade school trip to the regional spelling bee when her mother had planted herself in front of the TV just hoping to catch a glimpse of her little girl on the local newscast.

After helping herself to some *khorma* and *roti*, Rikki carried her plate and a glass of ice water into the living room and sat down on the right side of the couch. Her mother nibbled at her food while gazing at the television, seemingly enthralled by coverage of a tractor-trailer accident on I-77. Rikki swirled a torn piece of *roti* in the *khorma* and took a bite. As always, her mother had used the precise combination of spices that Rikki felt perfectly accentuated the tender lamb meat.

After an excruciating segment about two women who dressed their dogs up for a make-believe wedding, the coverage turned to the election. "County courthouses all over West Virginia are struggling to cope with a deluge of reporters from around the world as post-election canvasses kicked off today," said the smiling blonde anchorwoman. "Melissa Dotson was in Pleasants County this morning, as the county commission tackled this important task."

The screen flashed to a shot of the courthouse's front portico and the four white Doric columns that were its most prominent features. An attractive brunette in her late twenties held a microphone emblazoned with WTAP's logo in her left hand. "Although the stakes are high, the atmosphere here in Saint Marys was low key as county commissioners conducted the official canvass of last Tuesday's election returns."

The video switched to a prerecorded scene inside the commission's hearing room. Alice Snyder's mouth moved silently while the reporter's voiceover continued. "With only eighteen challenged ballots up for grabs here, the results from all of the county and legislative races remained unchanged. But the presidential campaign of Senator Melanie Wilson garnered a net increase of three votes, raising her supporters' hopes that similar results elsewhere might swing West Virginia's five electoral votes into the Senator's camp and ensure her election."

Rikki smiled and softly clapped her hands. Her mother's attention remained fixed on the television.

"What do you have to say about these results, Senator?" the reporter asked, directing her microphone toward Jack McCallen's face.

"Well, it really wasn't surprising, Melissa. Senator Wilson carried Pleasants County on Tuesday night and she picked up a few more votes here today. But historically, canvasses don't change an election's results because challenged ballots tend to break along the same percentages as the initial returns. So we expect Governor Royal to pick up additional votes in the counties where he ran strongest – like Kanawha, Putnam, Berkeley and Jefferson – with the final result being the same as it was on Tuesday night."

As Jack finished his statement, Rikki's face briefly appeared onscreen as she walked across the room behind him. "There you are!" her mother exclaimed, reaching over to pat her left forearm.

"You look so beautiful and ... *professional*, honey. Your father would have been so proud of you."

Rikki looked at her mom and grinned, but said nothing. Even though he had been gone almost fifteen years, she still missed her dad immensely. Nothing in the world had bucked up her spirits like hearing Dr. G tell one of his engaging stories or let out a heartfelt laugh, and his death from cancer at the age of fifty-two continued to strike Rikki as exceedingly unfair.

Lost in her own thoughts, Rikki missed the end of the report from Pleasants County. "Meanwhile," the anchor continued. "Another area native is continuing to make headlines around the world through his work on Governor Royal's presidential campaign. For more on this story, we go to Brad Billingsley down in Madison. Brad..."

An immaculately dressed black man appeared on-screen with a microphone in his hand. "That's right, Emily. The proceedings here in Boone County were far more contentious than those Melissa covered. There are 112 challenged ballots at stake here, and it looks like every one of them will be intensely scrutinized and hotly debated by the lawyers representing the two presidential candidates. And coordinating the efforts of Governor Royal's team on the ground here in Madison was none other than Saint Marys' own Dave Anderson."

Rikki's stomach dropped as she heard his name. Her mother's smile vanished, and she glanced over at Rikki, gauging her reaction.

The station began broadcasting images from inside Boone County's impressive, cavernous old courtroom. Standing behind three lawyers with his arms crossed, Dave closely followed the arguments unfolding before him as the reporter continued speaking over the video feed. "The salutatorian of his class at

Pleasants County High School, Anderson has been a prominent advisor to Governor Royal for years, and he's leading the campaign's post-election efforts in West Virginia. Today, he was here in Madison monitoring the canvass in this crucial county with a colorful history of creative electioneering."

Rikki bit her lip and stared at the screen, studying Dave's face. Part of her wished he had grown prematurely old and grotesquely fat. *Maybe balding with a bad comb over, too.* But he looked fit and trim in his dark blue pinstriped suit, his broad shoulders filling it out nicely. His dark brown hair was streaked with gray, but his eyes still burned with an intensity she knew she would never forget.

"So how are things looking, Mr. Anderson?" the reporter asked in a prerecorded interview. The open-domed, golden belvedere of Boone County's courthouse hovered over Dave's left shoulder.

Dave smiled and arched his left eyebrow. "Well, we've been tradin' punches pretty good in there," he said in his mountain twang. "Governor Royal is still standin' tall right now, but it's only about the third round. Ask me again in a few weeks."

Rikki briefly cracked a grin despite herself. Noting her reaction, Madhani smiled, too.

"So how does it feel to be back in West Virginia?" the reporter asked.

Dave paused, looking thoughtful for a moment, and then his smile widened slightly. "You know, I grew up in Pleasants County and some of the most important people in my life still live there. I'm deeply honored to have the privilege of workin' for a man like Governor Royal, but West Virginia will always be home to me, and it feels good to be home again." Then Dave emitted a quick, loud chuckle. "The next time I come home, though, I hope it's under less stressful circumstances."

The interview ended, and a live shot of the reporter standing in front of the dingy white limestone courthouse returned to the screen. "The canvass will continue here in Boone County tomorrow morning at nine. From Madison, this is Brad Billingsley reporting."

The newscast kept rolling, but Rikki remained silent. After a few awkward moments, her mother broke the silence. "I saw David's mother at the store on Wednesday. She said he had asked how your election went and told her to congratulate you for him."

Rikki's eyes flamed but her voice was cold. "Tell Ellen I said, 'Hi,' the next time you see her."

Madhani Gudivada sighed deeply. "It's been a long time, daughter," she said softly, placing her hand on Rikki's left thigh. "I think you would be happier if you could find a way to forgive him. You two were so close for so long, and it breaks my heart that you cannot at least be *friends* again."

Rikki breathed in, gathering her thoughts. Throughout her life, she had tried to think before she spoke, heeding her father's admonition that words cannot be taken back once they are spoken. Seconds later, her voice sounded calm, though distant. "It broke *my* heart that when Daddy got sick, Dave decided to stay in school in Charlottesville. He *knew* I had to come home to help you take care of him. I *begged* him just to take a semester off to come home and support me and he told me, 'No.'"

Sadness filled Madhani's eyes, and she shook her head lightly. Rikki knew her mother probably could not count the times she had heard similar sentiments. But the passing of 15 years had not changed her feelings. Asked to choose between his high school sweetheart – and best friend – on one hand, and finishing his last three months of law school on the other, Dave had opted to graduate on time. He gambled that Dr. G would be fine until summer.

But the cancer ravaging the doctor's body had spread faster than predicted, and Dave lost that wager. Dr. G passed away the last day of Dave's final exams. Rikki never forgave him for leaving her alone during those difficult days, as she watched life slowly ebb from her father and as her mother watched the love of her life inexorably slip away.

"Yet you refuse to acknowledge that your own *father* told David to stay in school," Madhani stated. "He would have forfeited his full scholarship if he did not graduate on time, and he listened to your father's advice. After all these years, Sarika, hasn't he been punished enough?"

Rikki looked into her mother's pleading dark eyes and felt the foundation underlying her pain and rage soften just a little. It *had* been a long time. But she remained silent as she grabbed her half-finished plate and walked to the kitchen, privately contemplating her response.

CHAPTER 6

GOVERNOR'S MANSION
CHARLESTON, WEST VIRGINIA
TUESDAY, NOVEMBER 11, 12:15 P.M.

Luke Vincent stood in the living quarters of the Governor's Mansion, staring blankly at the Kanawha River. The television was tuned to CNN where self-important talking heads blathered about the myriad ways the ongoing election drama might play out. The governor paid them no attention. Standing silently with his back to the TV, his gaze remained fixed on the broad expanse of water flowing north toward its confluence with the Ohio River.

"Penny for your thoughts."

Vincent turned and saw his wife, Donna, staring back at him with a wan smile. Her graying hair was cut short and layered, neatly framing the soft angles of her porcelain-hued, cherubic face. Drab rays of daylight permeated the room through bulletproof windows that adorned all three of its exterior walls. An air of dreariness infused the room, broken only by the fresh-cut white and pinkish flowers that the First Lady was placing into a vase atop the mahogany Pembroke table situated along the east wall.

The governor turned from the window, walking toward his wife. "What kind of flowers are those? I don't think I've seen them before."

The First Lady's hazel eyes twinkled as she used her fingertips to daintily tuft up the flowers. "They're Japanese anemones. They just started blooming around Halloween."

Strolling behind his wife, Vincent draped his right arm around her neck. Bending almost a foot, he kissed the crown of her head. "They're beautiful, Donna. Really brighten up the room. Lord knows we all could use a little cheer around here."

The First Lady turned and nuzzled the side of her face against his chest. "You need to stop worrying about everything and put your trust in God. As the Bible says, 'If ye have faith as a grain of mustard seed, *nothing* shall be impossible unto you.'"

Luke Vincent felt his stomach tighten, but his face remained plastered with a calm smile. Shamefully recalling his recent encounter with Tabatha McCallen and the lustful thoughts she always invoked, he wasn't optimistic The Big Guy would be moving mountains for him anytime soon. *Wanton disregard for the Seventh and Tenth Commandments doesn't strike me as the modus operandi God rewards with high office and public acclaim. The examples of Bill Clinton and Newt Gingrich notwithstanding.*

The governor's train of thought was interrupted when Marshall University's fight song, the "Sons of Marshall," erupted from his cell phone. Vincent glanced at the screen and was greeted by his running mate's smiling campaign headshot and home number. He smoothly exited his wife's embrace. "I gotta take this. It's Senator Wilson."

Donna smiled, patted him lovingly on the cheek, and dutifully returned her attention to the flowers.

"Hello, Senator. How are you doing?"

"Well, I'm drinking more Pepto Bismol than vodka, so I guess I'm holding up pretty well," Melanie Wilson replied. Her voice was pleasant, although utterly bereft of any regional dialect. Whether that was the result of deliberate effort or merely the happenstance of an Ivy League education combined with her Midwest upbringing, Vincent had no idea. "How are things looking over in West Virginia?"

Vincent knew Senator Wilson had all four fingers and her thumb wrapped competently around his state's wrist, monitoring its pulse from her campaign headquarters in D.C. Nevertheless, he respected the fact that she *acted* as if his insight warranted a personal call.

"I think we'll pull it out," Vincent declared. "Gobs of ballots down south weren't counted Tuesday night. You know ... a few glitches with machines here, a few overlooked boxes there. Those things add up pretty quickly."

"Not *too* quickly, I hope," Wilson interjected. "But I'll sleep better knowing *all* the votes are being counted."

"Absolutely. There's no way we're going to let a bunch of Republican thugs steal this election." *Not as hard as our thugs are trying to even the playing field.*

"That's what I wanted to hear, Luke. Keep up the good work."

"Will do, Melanie. You worry about New Mexico and Iowa and everywhere else. We have West Virginia well under control."

The phone died as Senator Wilson hung up. Vincent pressed a button and returned the phone to his belt clip, hoping he could live up to that promise.

CHAPTER 7

PLEASANTS COUNTY, WEST VIRGINIA
TUESDAY, NOVEMBER 11, 6:30 P.M.

State Senator Jack McCallen slumped over his cherry desk with his face cupped in his hands. The discovery requests were stacked upon virtually every flat surface in the office. His temples throbbing, Jack struggled to control the anger and anxiety rising in his chest.

Jack felt the lawyers were burying him in an avalanche of paperwork:

They demanded he recite the details of every conversation he – or any of his employees – ever had with any of the mineral owners about the lease that gave his company the right to extract the property's oil and gas.

They insisted he turn over copies of every royalty check his company had given the mineral owners during the past ten years.

They wanted copies of the production logs reflecting every drop of crude oil and every cubic foot of natural gas extracted from the 2,500-acre Schoolcraft property during the past decade.

They commanded he provide them copies of any bank statements and invoices reflecting the money generated from sales of the property's mineral resources to third parties.

Jack's father, Duke McCallen, had returned from World War II and used his GI Bill money to obtain a geology degree from Marietta College. After three years working for Quaker State, Duke had quit his job and used his life savings to start McCallen Resources. Three wells drilled on his first 50-acre lease in Doddridge County hit big, and the resulting cash flow helped turn his company into one of the state's biggest independent oil and gas companies. Over the next forty years, Duke had expanded operations whenever possible while riding out the inevitable bust cycles as best he could.

Jack learned a lot watching his dad over the years: How to put suspicious landowners at ease with a joke and how to earn their trust by honoring the terms of a handshake deal. How to maintain organized records and keep the local bankers happy. And how to take off the gloves and fight like hell when another operator tried to screw you over. If someone tried to place a wellhead capable of stealing oil or gas from under your leasehold, it was war. If someone instigated mineral owners to attack the validity of your lease, it was war.

When you're at war, you use *nukes* if you have to. You do whatever it takes to win.

Although the issues in the Schoolcraft case were the same ones Jack had litigated with other mineral owners, the stakes were much higher this time. First, the sheer size of the land involved dwarfed any other leasehold the company held. Secondly, if the test results his geologists had reviewed were accurate, a wide swath of the gas-rich Marcellus Shale was situated about 6,500 feet beneath the entire tract. There also appeared to be a colossal pocket of natural gas lying untapped in the sandstone another 2,000 feet below the Marcellus. In all, McCallen Resources stood to make a fortune extracting gas from the property, but only if he and Rikki could fight off this lawsuit.

"So did that camel jockey lawyer of yours squeeze any more money out of us today?"

Jack looked up and saw his wife standing in the doorway. She was sneering at him with her arms crossed, dressed to kill in a black business suit. Black hose covered her sculpted legs and she tapped the toe of her two-inch-high black heel twice on the reddish-gold hardwood flooring. The sound resonated like gunshots against the office's paneled walls.

Jack slowly removed his hands from his face and took a deep breath. Long ago, he might have cared enough to explain that Indians were more likely to ride elephants than camels. Now, he just sighed and gritted his teeth without even addressing her ignorant and gratuitously nasty comment. The look on Tabatha's face was the very definition of smug.

"I don't know what you have against Rikki. She can't work for free and we'd be sunk in this case without her."

Tabatha's blue eyes flashed. "That's what you keep saying, Jack. But I haven't seen her do anything except send us *bills!*"

The senator felt his face flush. It was tough enough fighting this lawsuit. If he lost, all the money he had invested in geological reports and test drilling would go up in flames, and his most lucrative leasehold would be reopened to other bidders.

Developers with much bigger pockets were slobbering at the thought of drilling wells on that land if his lease fell through and these constant battles with his wife were grating his nerves to no end.

"Damn it, Tabatha!" The scream rattled his chest and strained his throat. His face twisted with rage, he hurled two high stacks of papers from the desk onto the floor with one quick backward sweep of his left hand and stood to face her. "Why can't you get off my back, shut the hell up, and *support* me for a change?"

Tabatha's pupils widened and her lips peeled back from her teeth, morphing into an adrenaline-fueled grin. "If you were any kind of a man, Jack, the precious little company your daddy left you wouldn't be on the brink of bankruptcy." Her voice dripped with detestation. "And you'd be able to support your wife and kids the way we deserve."

McCallen knew she was pushing his buttons, but he felt powerless to ignore her attack. He could see in her eyes how much she relished pummeling his self-esteem. For perhaps the millionth time, he wondered how he had fallen in love with such a sadistic, hate-filled woman.

Breathing heavily, Jack balled his hands into tight fists. "You're lucky my dad taught me to treat a woman with respect," he said slowly. "Because if you were a man and tried talkin' to me like that, I'd kick the dog shit out of you right where you stand."

Tabatha stepped out of the doorway, laughing as she stalked toward him. "Don't let that stop you, big boy. Go ahead and try it! You lay a finger on me, and I'll have state troopers hauling your ass out of here so fast it'll make your head spin."

The Senator closed his eyes, struggling to control his emotions. He shook his head in disbelief as he stormed past his wife and out of the office. "Go fuck yourself, Tabatha."

She turned and watched him walk out. "I don't need to fuck myself, Jack! There's a long line of guys just begging to tap this since you're no longer man enough for the job!"

McCallen did not turn around or say a word. Continuing to walk away, he paused just long enough to punch a hole in the drywall before barreling out the front door.

CHAPTER 8

NEW YORK CITY
TUESDAY, NOVEMBER 11, 7:45 P.M.

The relaxing sounds of a string quartet floated through the room like the soundtrack to a dream. In another environment, Yuri Petrenko would have found the music soothing. Tonight, he took another tiny bite of his entrée and hoped he looked like he enjoyed it.

No matter how many times Yuri sat down to his host's table, trying to keep an open mind when faced with yet another dish from the Caucasus, the meal always ended with him slipping into the bathroom to shovel Mylanta into his mouth while praying he wouldn't hurl.

In his heart, Yuri knew this night would end no differently. Nevertheless, he heroically kept chewing. He even managed to emit a few grunts of feigned pleasure.

Dmitri Mazniashvili, on the other hand, loved the food of his homeland. He insisted guests broaden their culinary horizons whenever they joined him for dinner at the luxurious condominium often referred to by insiders as "Cloud Nine." Located atop a building near the corner of East 59th Street and Park Avenue, Mazniashvili spared no expense when he remodeled his home, fully intending to impress even the fortunate few who could afford to own property in this exclusive neighborhood.

Having heard the story more times than he could count, Yuri knew the entire project had been orchestrated by the hottest young designer in town. The rich cherry planks adorning the walls were purchased from a Revolutionary Era mansion upstate, painstakingly refinished and installed here at mind-boggling cost. Recessed lighting imbued the room with a warm, cozy glow. A carefully chosen assemblage of colorful artwork by recognized masters like Matisse and Lievens, as well as up-and-coming contemporary talents, were strategically placed throughout the expansive room. An enormous window stretched floor-to-ceiling the entire length of the western wall, providing the same soothing view of Central Park's green open spaces that Andrew Carnegie and other titans of the Gilded Age had appreciated from nearby mansions over a century ago.

"Would you like some more *muzhuzhi?*" Mazniashvili smiled, gesturing enthusiastically toward a plate of pig legs that reeked of vinegar and looked like they had been boiled. "Niko really outdid himself this time!"

Yuri felt his mouth water. Not in a good way. From his experience with Georgian cuisine, he knew it probably signaled a rapidly approaching visit from the Gods of Angry Vomitation.

Donning his best poker face, Yuri swallowed his food and shook his head negatively. "No thank you, *vozhd,*" he replied, knowing Mazniashvili worshiped Josef Stalin and savored his use of the dictator's intimate moniker. "I'm trying to save room for his dessert."

The host clucked disapprovingly but wore an indulgent smile. He was a good bit older than Yuri, with a shock of white hair and uncontrollable eyebrows perched atop shrewd dark brown eyes. "Very well," he said, grabbing another pig leg for himself. "Fortunately for you, Niko is making his *nigvzis torti* tonight."

Yuri felt his nausea subside. The walnut-raisin torte was by far one of his favorite Georgian dishes, and it would serve as a welcome change from this evening's main course. In the meantime, he reached into his pocket and extracted a watermelon-flavored Jolly Rancher to help remove the taste of the *muzhuzhi* from his mouth.

After savoring his meal a few more bites, Mazniashvili finally turned the conversation to the matter at hand. "The election isn't looking as good as we had hoped."

Yuri nodded crisply. "*Da.* I've been watching the news. No chance of winning Louisiana, so we're just left with West Virginia."

Mazniashvili grunted. "And we still have to hang on to New Mexico. Nine hundred votes isn't a very large lead, but it should be much harder for Royal to gain that many in New Mexico than for Vincent to find three hundred in West Virginia." The determined glint in his eyes bespoke the ruthlessness Yuri knew had made him one of the richest men in the world.

"And what is the news from West Virginia?" Yuri inquired.

Mazniashvili edged the plate away from him and wiped his mouth with a crimson linen napkin. "Too early to tell. Royal's two biggest counties should be finished tomorrow morning, at which point Vincent says we will know how many votes we must *find* elsewhere." He arched his right eyebrow and grinned.

"Sounds like a good plan," Yuri acknowledged. But long years spent in the hard service of the Russian Special Forces – the Spetsnaz – had taught him the need for contingency planning, the absence of which all too often meant the difference between life and a grisly, premature death. "But what if Vincent does not come through with the votes?"

Mazniashvili's smile disappeared. "We will cross that bridge when we come to it," he said coldly, reclining slightly in his black leather chair. "But Jonathan Royal will roast in hell before he has a chance to deport me back to Georgia, as he has promised to do if elected."

CHAPTER 9

CHARLESTON, WEST VIRGINIA
WEST VIRGINIA STATE CAPITOL BUILDING
WEDNESDAY, NOVEMBER 12, 10:15 A.M.

Orange and baby blue flames crackled silently inside the gas fireplace, providing more ambience than heat. Luke Vincent sat in a forest green Queen Anne chair to the fireplace's right, his face bathed in its glow.

Sitting in a matching chair to Vincent's left was a thick-necked bald man in a gray sweater holding a cell phone to his ear. His thick fingers looked like bratwursts, enveloping the phone in his paw. "Well, that's not as bad as I thought it would be," he said. His voice sounded like he had spent his entire life gargling gravel. "I'll let Governor Vincent know."

"Let me know what, Dick?"

Dick Bowen put the phone down. "The canvass in Kanawha County is over. Royal only picked up 24 votes there. Personally, I thought it'd be fifty."

Governor Vincent nodded in agreement. "Me, too. The whole Republican ticket ran strong there. The biggest county in the state ... If he only gained 24 there, his overall number should be within striking distance."

Bowen grabbed a yellow legal pad from the end table situated between the two chairs and scribbled on it. His eyes darted across the page as he silently ran the figures. "He gained 30 in the Eastern Panhandle, which typically leans conservative, and another 19 over in Putnam County. But you and Melanie picked up more votes elsewhere, so his total lead is down to about 190."

Vincent stood up and strolled behind his chair. Resting his hands atop the chair's back, he leaned forward and sighed. "I'd feel better if it was around a hundred. But we'll have to make do. How are our boys down south doing?"

"They're really slugging it out down in Boone County. That Anderson guy from Saint Marys is watching things like a hawk and his lawyers are damn good ones. They're making us work for every vote we get there."

Vincent's heart skipped a beat at the mention of St. Marys. He couldn't think of that town without thinking about Tabatha McCallen. He had not heard from her since their hotel rendezvous the previous week and that made him nervous, wondering what her fevered mind might be concocting to make his life even more complicated.

The sound of Bowen's gravelly voice refocused his attention. "On the other hand, we have everything in place in Mingo County. We're just waiting on the word from you to spring into action."

Governor Vincent glanced down at his watch. It was 10:30 a.m. "Let's crunch the numbers one last time. But go ahead and tell those boys to get ready to roll. I don't think we can wait any longer."

Vincent's cell phone suddenly started buzzing and vibrating. Removing it from his belt clip, the governor saw he had a new multimedia message from a number he did not recognize.

"What you got there, Luke?" Bowen asked.

"Don't know yet. A new message of some sort." Vincent hit a button on his phone to retrieve the message.

The governor stared at the screen as his phone downloaded the message. Its subject line read, "Still Waiting" and there was a video clip attached to it. Clicking the attachment, he watched the blue progress bar slowly advance across the screen, widening from left to right as the download neared completion. Finally, the clip began to play and his face turned pale.

The screen depicted the inside of a Charleston hotel suite he recognized. A close friend owned the hotel and Vincent used the facility on occasions when discretion was required.

"So who do you think is going to win tonight, Governor?"

Vincent felt a cold chill migrate down his spine. The sultry voice blaring from the phone belonged to Tabatha McCallen.

His fingers frantically flew across the phone's touchscreen. Unalloyed fear tore at his heart. *Has someone finally uncovered my lies? Who could have recorded this? How did they get my private cell phone number? And why did they send me this?*

"Definitely Marshall," he heard his own voice declare. "WVU's defense can't stop our three-point shooters."

A quizzical look crossed Dick Bowen's face as he strained his neck, attempting to get a look at the phone's screen. "What was that?"

Vincent shut off the clip and the dialogue abruptly stopped. "Nothing. Just a TV interview I did back in February right before the WVU/Marshall basketball game."

Bowen's visage turned from quizzical to skeptical. "Why would someone send a nine-month-old television interview to your cell phone?"

Think, Vincent told himself. *Think quickly.* "One of our media consultants," he said slowly, attempting to buy some time to make the lie more believable. "He's been complaining about my ties. Says they're too 'flashy' and turn voters off. I guess he decided to send me that clip as an example of a tie he thinks would work better for me."

Bowen eyed him closely, saying nothing. The room was silent, save for the low crackling of the gas logs. The governor felt his palms turning clammy.

"I can't help you, Luke, if you don't tell me the truth."

Vincent knew Bowen had his best interests at heart and truly wanted to help him. They had worked with one another for almost two decades. But to the best of his knowledge, the only three people who knew about his trysts with Tabatha McCallen were himself, the hotel owner, and the siren herself. And even the hotel owner didn't know Tabatha's real name.

"You must think my life is a lot more interesting than it really is," the governor said, cracking a grin. "Sorry to burst your bubble, Dick."

By the look on Bowen's face, Vincent judged the man was unconvinced. But much to his relief, Bowen let the matter drop. "Well, tell that fancy 'media consultant' to postpone his wardrobe recommendations until *after* we get you elected, okay? Until then, we both have far more important things to worry about than what kind of friggin' ties you should be wearing."

Vincent emitted a breezy laugh. "You got it."

Relief flooded the governor's mind. Although he knew Bowen meant well, Vincent fully intended to keep knowledge of his affair as limited as possible. For some reason, one of Benjamin Franklin's most famous sayings invaded his consciousness: "Three people can keep a secret if two of them are dead."

That advice sounded perfectly sage.

CHAPTER 10

MADISON, BOONE COUNTY, WEST VIRGINIA
WEDNESDAY, NOVEMBER 12, 12:05 P.M.

Dave bid the campaign's lawyers adieu and jumped in Ned Hopson's big red Ford F-450 pickup truck. Although there was a chill in the air, the sun was shining down through a bright blue sky unmarred by clouds. Climbing into the passenger side, Dave closed the door behind him and exclaimed, "All right, Ned, you're killing me! Now that we've broken for lunch, could you tell me who in the hell's that old coot you keep exchanging silent glances with?"

The Boone County Republican Party's chairman laughed out loud and turned the ignition key. Shifting into reverse, he gently backed up. "Ever heard of Zeke Crouser?"

"Sure. He heads up one of the two Democrat factions down here. Knows every person up every holler in the county. The guy's a legend."

Hopson put the truck into drive and cut the steering wheel to the left, maneuvering into northbound traffic headed away from

Madison toward the nearby town of Danville. "Well, my friend, that old guy you're so fascinated with is the one and only Zeke Crouser."

Dave's jaw dropped open. "Why would you pay attention to anything *he* has to say? I mean ... Why in God's name would he want to help *us?*"

Hopson chuckled. "The world's a strange place, Mr. Anderson. And no place is quite as strange as southern West Virginia at election time."

"Enlighten me, Ned. I thought I had a pretty good handle on things but you've got me totally lost right now."

"There are two dynamics here. First of all, you're in the heart of coal country."

"I know *that*," Dave retorted. "Coal operators down here contributed piles of money for Governor Royal. You'd expect that. But Boone County is the heart of UMW country, too."

"True, some union miners would vote for Hitler before they'd vote for a Republican, and there's nothing you can do about those guys. But there's plenty of others who know which side their bread is buttered on, and they can't stand Senator Wilson."

Dave's mouth opened and his eyes widened as comprehension began to dawn. "Because of her environmental positions."

"Yep. Global warming and all that jazz ... gets the operators *and* the miners all in a tizzy. They think she's just another bunny-hugging Yankee secretly plotting to regulate the coal industry out of existence as soon as she gets into office."

"Makes sense. So what's the second dynamic I need to know about?"

"Pretty simple," Ned replied. "Lotsa people in the coalfields think Luke Vincent has gotten too big for his britches. He's broken some campaign promises, particularly when it comes to funding new roads down here. More importantly, he helped folks from the northern part of the state squeeze some of our local boys outta leadership positions in the Legislature when he took office four years ago. Including the House of Delegates' *former* Finance Chairman, who is the brother-in-law of none other than our good ol' buddy, Zeke Crouser."

Dave whistled. "Wow. We didn't know there was so much bad blood down here."

"Down here in *Boone County*," Hopson corrected. "Vincent hasn't alienated *everyone* in southern West Virginia. He still has plenty of friends in other places – like Mingo County, for instance. The governor still has a lot of patronage to throw around and plenty of chips to cash in. But two of our three county commissioners are aligned with Zeke's faction, so don't expect Vincent to pull off any funny business here."

A ringing phone interrupted their conversation. Anderson pulled his phone from his right front pants pocket and looked at the screen. It was Jonathan Royal. "Hello."

"How are things looking in Madison?" the nominee's voice boomed.

Dave smiled and winked at Hopson. "Better than we realized."

"Hot damn! Nice to hear. Couldn't have come at a better time, in fact."

A look of concern lodged itself on Dave's face. "Why? What's up?"

Royal sighed heavily. "We just got word from Williamson. There's something fishy going on down there with the voting machines' memory cards."

"What do you mean by *fishy?*"

"They say some of the memory cards aren't working right. The data from the cards was supposedly uploaded on Election Night to servers maintained by the company that sold the machines to the county. Our opponents want to use that backup data for the canvass. Care to guess which vendor's machines the good folks in Mingo County used?"

Dave's stomach sank. "AIS?"

"AIS," Royal affirmed. "Assurant Information Services, which bought the Cicero brand electronic voting system from the civic-minded nerds who developed it. And the venture capital group that owns AIS is headed by your friend and mine ..."

"Dmitri Mazniashvili," Dave moaned.

"The very bastard. Wanna bet which way the votes stored in that backup data are gonna swing?"

"Shit! Who do we have in charge down there?"

"It doesn't matter. I've told them you're taking over as soon as you can get there. Until then, they'll keep the cameras rolling and stall for time."

"Got it," Dave said. Mentally calculating the distance down Route 119 to Williamson, he added, "I can be there in a little under an hour."

"Don't get pulled over – especially by state troopers, ha ha! But get there quick. They're gonna start dealing with this *discovery* about one o'clock."

Dave glanced down at the platinum Rolex watch on his left wrist. It was ten after twelve. "I'm on my way."

Dave hung up the phone and glanced at Hopson. "Can I borrow your truck?"

"Where you taking it?" Hopson asked. "Williamson?"

"Yep. Some of their voting machines' memory cards magically stopped working this morning."

Hopson snorted. "Magic, my ass." He flipped on his turn signal and pulled into the restaurant's parking lot. "I'll jump out here at the pizza place. My wife can pick me up and take me back to the courthouse after lunch."

"Thanks. I'll get your truck back as soon as I can."

Hopson unbuckled his seatbelt and opened the door. "Don't worry about it," he said calmly, leaving the keys in the ignition as he exited the cab. "Good luck and Godspeed, Mr. Anderson." With those blessings, he raised his cell phone to his ear and strolled toward the restaurant's front door.

Dave slid into the driver's seat and put on his seat belt. Throwing the truck's transmission into drive, he started plotting a course of action.

CHAPTER 11

INTERSTATE 79 NEAR BRIDGEPORT, WEST VIRGINIA
WEDNESDAY, NOVEMBER 12, 12:30 P.M.

As State Senator Jack McCallen drove north on I-79 toward Morgantown, his thoughts raced through his PowerPoint presentation. The commercial loan officer had coached him on the points he should emphasize in his pitch to the bank's president, and Jack mentally reviewed those items one last time.

McCallen Resources had friendly relationships with the "gathering" companies that purchased raw oil and the "transportation" companies that purchased raw natural gas from well-head operators like his company. Those companies sold them for a profit to local plants that refined and processed them into products consumers could use. Jack would argue that his company's good relations with those middlemen improved its chances to turn a profit even if prices dropped and times got tough.

Moreover, Jack knew MR had invested wisely during the recent boom, updating and upgrading its wells with the most accurate measuring devices and the most efficient capturing equipment available. Those investments maximized its profits and improved its chances to endure the bust periods that scared the bejeezus out of jittery, conservative bankers.

Mentally reaching the presentation's midpoint, Jack recalled the vivid, full-color pie charts and bar graphs he had generated from stacks of MR's production records and sales invoices. Those graphics showed that over the past five years, MR had significantly increased both the oil and gas it was extracting from its leaseholds as well as its profit margin.

Jack stared at himself in the rearview mirror. *If only that told the whole story. If that were the case, I would sleep like a baby. Instead, I have bags under my eyes and an Elavil prescription that needs refilled.*

Driving between Fairmont and Morgantown, Jack was struck by the barren scenery around him. The rolling hills of north central West Virginia – so lush and green in the summer and painted in fiery reds, deep oranges and golden yellows in the fall – were brown and dead-looking today. As they would remain, Jack knew, until the leaves began to return in the middle of April. Despite winning yet another election last week, Jack felt the aching emptiness of those hills perfectly reflected the despair and loneliness weighing him down.

Jack suddenly realized he had to shake this foul mood, quickly. In only minutes, he would be shaking hands with the banker and he needed his "A" game. He closed his eyes and bent his head sideways like he was trying to touch his ear to his shoulder. First to the right, then to the left, he felt the taut muscles in his neck slowly begin to unknot.

Jack turned on the radio and a few haunting lyrics from Doug Stone's old song, "I'd Be Better Off (In A Pine Box)" poured out of the speakers. Scowling, he jammed his thumb against the tuning button, hoping to find something less likely to make him slit his wrists.

Moments later, the melodic strumming of a single electric guitar began to fill his ears and he pulled his finger away from the stereo controls. Exhaling deeply, he leaned his head back against the seat and closed his eyes as the lead vocalist of the '80s hair metal band, Tesla, crooned the first few lines from *Gettin' Better*.

The guitarist kicked his efforts up a notch and the rest of the band followed suit. Jack tapped his left hand on the steering wheel in time with the music and felt his outlook on life improve. As the song played on, he became more and more animated, banging his head slightly and even balling his right hand into a fist at one point he found particularly uplifting.

By song's end, he was rolling into the bank's parking lot without a trace of the gloom and doom that had earlier gripped him. Turning the volume down, he shut off the engine and grabbed his laptop case after making a mental note to download that old Tesla album soon.

It might come in handy the next time I feel like throttling Tabatha, he privately quipped, cracking a wry smile as he strolled toward the bank.

A stunning woman in her early thirties with long wavy hair the color of cornsilk sat behind a semi-circular stainless steel desk. "Hello," she said with a smile. "How may I help you?" Her words flowed smoothly, sounding melodious, educated, accommodating and sultry.

Jack returned the smile. "I have an appointment with Marty Tharp at one."

The receptionist glanced down at her calendar. "Mr. McCallen?"

"You're looking at him." From years spent making campaign speeches and shaking hands with farmers in the oil patch, Jack felt his comfort level rising as he subconsciously switched into glad-handing mode.

The woman nodded. "Have a seat, and I'll let Mr. Tharp know you are here." She motioned toward a row of burgundy leather office chairs aligned along a glass wall to her right. Jack silently dipped his head in acknowledgment and took a seat.

Magazines half-covered the cherry end table beside his chair. Jack pawed through them before selecting a Smithsonian to pass the time. Less than a minute later, a man called from across the lobby. "Jack?"

Glancing up from the magazine, Jack saw a tall, slightly-built man in a crisply-tailored suit staring back at him expectantly. His rusty-colored hair was thick on top with an emerging widow's peak. Light brown eyes gazed through a pair of rectangular metal eyeglasses, and dark freckles dotted the man's middle-aged cheeks and forehead.

The banker smiled and approached him, extending his right hand. "I'm Marty Tharp. You want to come on back?"

Jack accepted the grip. "Thanks for seeing me. You lead the way."

Tharp whirled on his right heel and headed back across the lobby toward a pair of stainless steel elevator doors. Jack followed suit.

The banker pressed the call button. "So how was your drive over from Saint Marys?"

"Not bad. Route 50 was a little boring, but at least I didn't hit any deer along the way."

Tharp chuckled. A bell rang, and the elevator doors parted, revealing the cabin's rich mahogany walls. "Yeah, it's about that time of the year, isn't it? Are you a hunter?"

"Well, I like to get out in the woods during rifle season when work allows it. But I haven't bagged one in a while, so I hope I'm due for one this year."

The doors shut, and the elevator car began to rise accompanied by the soothing melodies of some song Jack thought was by Kenny G. As the digital screen morphed from a four into a five, the elevator slowed to a stop, and the doors opened. Tharp walked directly across the hallway into an open conference room. Jack mentally steeled himself as he followed the banker into the room with his laptop draped over his right shoulder.

A massive oval table was situated in the middle of the room. Tharp sat in a black, ergonomically-sculpted chair positioned within easy reach of Jack's loan application package, which was neatly spread out in a semicircular pattern atop the table. The banker spun 90 degrees and faced Jack, gently reclining his chair. "I understand you have a PowerPoint presentation for me."

"I figured that would be easier than asking you to dig through all that paperwork like you're looking for a needle in a haystack."

Tharp motioned to a projector stationed in the middle of the conference table, focused on a large white screen protruding from the ceiling. "Go right ahead."

As Jack spoke, he felt like he had been transported from his body. He had memorized the script down to a tee, having practiced at least fifty times. Smoothly transitioning from slide-to-slide, he gave his spiel to the banker with the same polished delivery that had earned him votes for years.

Tharp stared across the room at the projector screen, nodding as Jack used his laser pointer remote to highlight important language from his exploration geologist's report. He pointed out the gas pocket believed to exist about 8,500 feet below the Schoolcraft property, and the likelihood that a thick strand of the untapped Marcellus Shale strata ran through the property about 6,500 feet underground.

"But isn't your lease on that tract tied up in litigation right now?" the banker asked, his red eyebrows furrowed above his eyeglasses.

"We can't actually drill on the property until the lawsuit is resolved," Jack conceded. "But our lawyer thinks the lease will remain valid because the plaintiffs can't prove we haven't 'reasonably developed' those resources. After all, until this new ground-penetrating radar equipment was created, no one could have envisioned such an unusual sandstone formation at that depth. Plus, until recently, no one had devised a way to economically harvest the gas trapped in the Marcellus."

Tharp slowly nodded his head, but the skepticism did not fade from his eyes. "Who's your lawyer?"

"Rikki Gudivada."

The banker's posture loosened, and his eyebrows smoothed out. "She's one of the best. When's the case supposed to go to trial?"

Jack felt his stomach tighten. "The first slot the judge could give us was July 14th. Of course, that's if the judge doesn't grant us summary judgment, and we don't settle the case."

Tharp whistled loudly. "That's what ... eight months from now?"

Jack hoped the glumness in his heart wasn't manifested on his face. "Yeah," he said, trying to sound upbeat. "But the judge will hear our motion for summary judgment in May. Rikki thinks we have a pretty good shot at winning that one unless the plaintiffs can pull a rabbit out of their hat."

"Strange things happen in litigation," the banker observed ominously. "I'd feel a lot better about loaning you 3 million dollars if that lawsuit wasn't hanging over your head."

"If that lawsuit wasn't hanging over my head, I wouldn't need to borrow 3 million dollars. I'd have people lined up to *throw* money at me."

Tharp nodded curtly. "Quite true," he said, tightening his lips and staring at Jack as if taking his measure. Jack stood motionless with the computer remote cupped in his right hand, returning the gaze unwaveringly.

"Hey," the banker blurted, scooting his chair closer to the conference table. "I meant to tell you that I saw your name in the paper this morning."

"Oh, yeah?" Jack asked, his eyes narrowing. "Which one?"

"The Dominion-Post. It was a big story about the election brouhaha. I didn't know you're one of our presidential Electors."

"Well, I will be if Governor Vincent doesn't magically manufacture a few hundred votes for Senator Wilson out of thin air."

The banker's face suddenly brightened. "That's pretty cool. I had no idea how that whole thing worked."

"Most people don't. It only becomes an issue about once a century."

"So how did you become an Elector? I don't remember ever voting for you."

"Nah, it's not an elected office," Jack said. "Each party picks five people from around the state to vote as members of the Electoral College in the event their nominee wins the state's popular vote. I've been shaking hands and kissing babies for the Republican Party for a long time. I guess they figured naming me as an elector would be a nice way to honor my service."

"And what about your wife? Doesn't she have something to do with it too?"

Jack smiled like a poker player trying to bluff a pot with a pair of fives. "The party named her as an alternate. She's put in a lot of time at Republican Women's lunches and working on party fundraisers over the years. The folks down at headquarters kinda look at us like we're a matched set. If they're having me do something, chances are they're roping Tabatha into it, too."

Tharp tapped his fingertips on the table. "Ah, I see. Well, I do think that's pretty neat. I bet your kids will look back on that as a real accomplishment someday."

Jack snorted. "I hope that casting one ceremonial vote in the Electoral College ends up paling by comparison to leaving them a prosperous oil and gas company when I croak."

The banker laughed. "Absolutely," he said, rising from the table.

Jack recognized the meeting had ended and subtly used his remote to darken the projector screen. "So when do you think you'll be able to let me know about this loan?"

"Well, I need to run everything by our loan committee. We're supposed to meet again tomorrow, so hopefully you'll know something no later than Friday."

McCallen clapped his hands together and rubbed them lightly. "Sounds good to me," he said, extending his right hand to the banker. "I hope we'll be doing business together."

Tharp shook his hand. "I'll call you as soon as I can."

Well, that was a pretty non-committal response, Jack silently noted. He pumped the banker's hand up and down twice and then turned his attention to his laptop, disconnecting it from the projector and powering it down.

The banker reassembled the loan application documents into neat little stacks while Jack folded his laptop and gingerly stowed it away. Then the two made a beeline for the elevator.

"I have another meeting I need to get to," Tharp said, lightly patting Jack on the back. "You mind if I stay up here and let you find your own way out?"

"No problem. You have a good one and I'll talk to you on Friday."

Tharp nodded, pressed the elevator's call button and headed down the hallway toward a corner office. Jack stepped into the elevator and hit the button for the lobby, silently praying the bank would give him good news. And *fast*.

CHAPTER 12

WILLIAMSON, MINGO COUNTY, WEST VIRGINIA
WEDNESDAY, NOVEMBER 12, 1:00 P.M.

The hills surrounding the town of Williamson were so steep they made Madison look like Kansas City. If railroad construction in the 1890s had not made extracting the region's vast coal reserves feasible, Dave saw no reason why a town would have developed here at all.

Only sheer stubbornness seemed to explain Williamson's creation and continuing existence. Narrow streets had been painstakingly carved from the hills in strict conformity with the area's unforgiving topography. The Tug River's brown waters coursed through town, serving as the border between West Virginia and Kentucky.

On several instances over the past hundred years, the Tug had done its damnedest to wipe Williamson off the map by overflowing its banks and sending a torrent of floodwater through its streets, most recently in 1977. A small voice inside Dave's head sardonically opined that such a result would have been an appropriate punishment for the town's real and perceived sins over the years. Even though God – *For reasons known only to Him*, lamented Dave – had chosen not to sweep Williamson from its tenuous grip on the planet's surface, the resulting damage was so extensive that documents in the courthouse had been saturated, if not destroyed, by the mud.

By the time Dave arrived in Williamson, there were no open parking spaces on any of the streets wedged around the courthouse between the mountains and the Tug. After making it a block past the courthouse, and a small black building constructed entirely from coal that caught his eye, Dave reluctantly parked Ned Hopson's big truck in a parking garage several blocks away. Much to his relief, he didn't hear sheet metal or plastic scraping against concrete as he did so.

Dave grabbed his laptop case and headed for the courthouse. Exiting the darkened garage, his green eyes momentarily struggled to re-adjust to the bright afternoon sunlight as he strolled toward the clump of humanity clustered around the building's entrance. As he drew closer, the tension in the air became more palpable. By the time he reached the front door, it seemed ready to explode.

A slightly chubby guy in his mid-twenties with unruly blond hair had been watching Dave closely as he walked toward the courthouse. Wearing a chocolate brown sweater and khaki pants, his face was wrought with anxiety. As Dave stepped onto the sidewalk leading to the front door, the young man broke away from the crowd and approached him. "Are you Dave Anderson?"

"The one and only," he replied wearily. *Dear God! How many times have people asked me that question over the past few days?* "I got here as soon as I could. What have I missed?"

The youngster made for the front door, clearing a path for Dave as he went. "The Commission is trying to figure out what to do about these memory cards," he explained, speaking quickly and sounding out of breath. "Mark Monroe wants to use the backup data from AIS and recalculate the votes in the affected precincts immediately. Pete Warner wants to quarantine those memory cards and use the hard copy printouts made on Election Night for those precincts instead. And Ruth Thompson looks like she's about to have a stroke because she doesn't know *what* she wants to do with 'em."

"I assume you're not surprised by any of that are you?" Dave said wryly.

The man glanced over his shoulder as they squeezed through the crowd. "Not hardly. Monroe is aligned with the faction that supports Governor Vincent and Senator Wilson. Pete's with us. And Ruth's not really with anyone ... The only reason she's even on the Commission is because one of her two opponents in the last primary was arrested a month before the election. The other guy died right after that. And although she was the only candidate both breathing and out of jail when the primary was held, she *still* only beat the dead guy by 50 votes."

Dave chuckled. "So tell me everything you know about these memory cards."

"Wait 'til we get past security," the young man replied, holding open the door. "The less the other side knows about our thought process, the better."

Ah! Dave thought. Remembering the setup from Boone County, it stood to reason that the guards manning the courthouse metal detector worked for the county sheriff and that his young tour guide distrusted the sheriff's political leanings.

Dave detected a conspiratorial glint in the man's eye. The younger man stood in front of the security checkpoint and emptied his pockets, dutifully depositing his keys, cell phone and loose change into a circular gray plastic tub. A short, reed-thin man with stringy black hair and streaks of acne across his cheeks grunted and motioned him through the metal detector while sliding the plastic container through an X-ray machine.

Dave was painfully familiar with security protocol from his years in D.C., and he quickly followed suit. The guard, whom

Dave had privately dubbed The Greasy Redneck Goth, marked him as an outsider and eyed him suspiciously. "Is that a cum-pewter in yer case?" the guard asked, tapping the black leather laptop case with his left hand.

No, you moron. It's filled with river rocks and pint bottles of Jack Daniels. But Dave somehow managed to silence his Inner Smartass and simply answered, "Yes."

"I needja tuh take eet outta thuh case, sir," the guard said with a jarring twang that made Dave suddenly feel as if his own voice had no accent at all. "Put eet een that beeg gray tub fur mee and slyde thuh case on through by eetself."

Anderson bit his tongue, trying not to roll his eyes. Obeying seemingly arbitrary orders had never been one of his strong points, but his ability to control those defiant tendencies had improved with age. Unzipping the computer case, he tried to ignore the tightening sensation in his chest and did as he was told.

A minute later, apparently satisfied that an unfamiliar middle-aged white guy in a suit was not going to blow the Mingo County Courthouse to smithereens, the guard begrudgingly nodded at Dave and gave him his laptop back. With lips that looked like they had been sealed shut with Super Glue, Dave returned the nod, grabbed his computer and scurried after his tour guide who was climbing a staircase on the lobby's left side.

Dave's companion turned left at the top of the steps before speedwalking through an open set of wooden double doors. The courtroom was filled to capacity with the same broad mix of curious locals and media types he had seen in Boone County. Mingo County's courtroom was boxy and plain, like some cookie-cutter creation of an uninspired, monetarily challenged architect from the 1960s. Which, in reality, is precisely what it was.

At the front of the room, two well-dressed clusters of people stood separate and distinct from one another. The heads of each group were literally huddled together. A bald man built like an Abrams tank seemed to be serving as the nucleus of the cluster on the right side of the room. He looked like a tightly wound ball of energy threatening to uncoil at any moment. A crisply starched white dress shirt collar was laboring mightily to restrain the man's muscular neck, and even from across the room, Dave thought he could see veins bulging in the man's temples as his bright blue eyes burrowed into one of the minions orbiting around him. As Dave and his tour guide closed on the circle, the bald man diverted his attention to them.

"I got him here as soon as I could," the tour guide blurted half-apologetically.

"About damn time," the bald guy replied gruffly. "The Commission should have been back from lunch five minutes ago."

Dave decided to take the initiative, extending his right hand to the apparent leader of Jonathan Royal's Mingo County posse. "Dave Anderson. I don't think my speedometer dipped below 95 the whole way from Madison. Sorry I couldn't get here sooner."

The bald man's expression softened slightly but he returned the handshake with a grip so firm Dave felt like his metacarpals were shattering. "Mack Palmer. We don't have a lot of time, so quickly tell me exactly what you think these guys want to pull with this memory card stunt."

"Well, I'm no computer scientist," Dave began, "but I have a lifetime of experience working on political campaigns and an encyclopedic knowledge of the ways people have stolen elections in the past. Combine those things with my inherent distrust of people in general, and I think I have a pretty good idea of what's going on."

Palmer's eyes narrowed and he tilted his head back slightly. "Oh, yeah?" he asked, a note of curiosity in his voice.

"It's a two-prong strategy," Dave explained. "First of all, if everything goes well for them, they really do hope to substitute the alleged 'backup data' from AIS's server for the real McCoy that was processed on Election Night twice – initially at the precincts themselves, and then later at the County Clerk's Office. If they convince the County Commission to do that, considering who really calls the shots at AIS, there's no doubt Jonathan Royal loses this election.

"Secondly, even if they can't persuade the County Commission that the 'backup data' is more reliable than the original returns, they hope to discredit the results reported by those disputed precincts on Election Night. Because the memory cards aren't functioning properly now, they will argue, it stands to reason that those same memory cards very well may have not been working properly on Election Night. If that's the case, why should the County Commission – or the rest of the world, for that matter – have any faith that the initial results tabulated for those precincts are accurate either?"

Palmer spoke slowly as he digested the ploy's political ramifications. "So if they can't shift enough votes into Senator Wilson's column by substituting the backup data for the original results, they can still muddy the water enough to confuse the public."

"Yep. And try to create enough uncertainty that would allow the courts to overturn the results and declare that Wilson and

Vincent won West Virginia's popular vote. Considering the fact that four of the five justices on the state Supreme Court are Democrats, I'd say that's not an outlandish possibility."

Mack Palmer's head bobbed up and down once. "Now *that* angle of things," he said. "Twenty years of practicing law in this state has made me well aware of. I know West Virginia election law like the inside of my own eyelids, but I've never claimed to be a politician, and I *certainly* don't know much about computers. That's what Spence here is for." He jabbed his index finger toward the chest of Dave's tour guide.

Dave shook his head rapidly as if trying to sweep haze from his mind. The young blond man smiled sheepishly and said, "Surprisingly enough, they actually trust me to do more around here than just fetch coffee and lost bigwigs from D.C."

Anderson viewed the youngster with newfound respect. "Well, all right. In that case, Spence, why would the vote count from Election Night be more reliable than the backup data?"

Spence adjusted his eyeglasses and paused, pondering the query, as everyone stared at him expectantly. "Although I don't have any personal experience working with this software – since AIS refuses to let outsiders inspect it due to its so-called 'trade secrets' – it's my understanding Cicero has specific safeguards in its code to ensure the software functioned properly on Election Day. According to the Cicero website, these machines are programmed to connect via satellite to the main AIS server every twenty minutes after the polls open for diagnostic testing. If a machine has any glitches, it is programmed to shut down, and voters are directed to use other machines until county officials can bring in a replacement."

Dave stood with his arms crossed, completely focused on the young man's explanation. "So if these machines kept working all day, they apparently weren't malfunctioning."

"Precisely. If the machines were working when the results were calculated on Election Night, any current memory card problems must have arisen after those results were printed."

Seeing a chorus of nods around him, Dave put a hand on Spence's shoulder. "Write down every theory you think their computer experts might use to argue the backup data would be more reliable than the results announced on Election Night. We'll put our heads together and try to poke holes in their arguments as best we can."

Spence nodded, grinning. Mack Palmer sighed loudly. "I can't believe a presidential election might hinge on a bunch of computer geeks arguing over this kind of crap. I thought we couldn't stoop any lower than arguing over how to interpret 'hanging chads.'" He shook his head in disgust. "God help us all."

CHAPTER 13

ST. MARYS, PLEASANTS COUNTY, WEST VIRGINIA
THURSDAY, NOVEMBER 13, 11:00 A.M.

Rikki leaned back in her black leather office chair, scanning Pleasants County's pending criminal cases for the names of any past or current clients. Such conflicts of interest would require the appointment of a special prosecutor once she took office in January.

Noticing a familiar name, Rikki smirked and whipped out her yellow highlighter. "What did Phil Nutter get himself into this time?" she asked aloud.

"Worthless checks," replied the silver-haired woman on the other side of her desk. Clad in a conservative-looking navy blue dress, the eyeglasses atop her nose were also chained around her neck by a beaded lanyard. "That, plus a fraudulent pretences charge, which should be listed on the next page."

Rikki winced slightly and let out a soft whistle. Worthless check charges were misdemeanors, but obtaining money from someone under false pretenses was a felony. "Sorry to hear that about Phil," she said. "I'll definitely need a special prosecutor for those cases. Thanks for pointing out that felony, Martha."

The older woman smiled warmly. "You're welcome, Rikki. Personally, I'm just relieved to know that the office will be in good hands soon. You know Joe just hasn't been up to working lately, and the backlog is too much for me to handle on my own."

Rikki's full lips grew taut and she laid down the list of cases. "How's Joe doing, anyway?"

Martha sighed. "Not good. The cancer has spread to his brain and the doctors don't think he has much time left."

"That's too bad. Joe has treated me like gold ever since I was a little girl. He's been a great prosecutor and an even better man."

Martha smiled sadly. "He was happy you won. I've worked for him for twenty years and he always worried about what might happen to the office after he retired. He told me last week it brought him great comfort to know you're the one who will succeed him."

"Aww ... That was so sweet of him to say. I just hope I don't let him down."

Martha patted Rikki's hand. "You won't, honey," she said, a tone of certainty in her voice. "I *know* you won't. In fact, Joe wants to get you into office as soon as possible."

A puzzled look crossed Rikki's face. "What do you mean?"

"Joe thought about resigning before the election. But he was afraid people would get mad, thinking he was trying to crown his own successor. But now that you've been elected, there's really no sense in waiting until January 1st for you to take office. Especially since it looks like Joe couldn't come back to work even if he wanted to."

"So what does he want to do?"

"Submit his resignation and ask the County Commission to appoint you to finish his term that ends December 31st," Martha replied. "He's spoken with the commissioners and since state law requires any replacement to belong to the same political party as Joe, they have agreed to go ahead and appoint you and let you start transitioning into the office a little early."

Rikki had to admit the plan made sense. *If Joe's too sick to return to work, the backlog will only get bigger between now and January.*

"And the commissioners are on board with this plan?" Rikki asked.

Martha nodded. "Yes. They know Joe's illness has kept him away from the courthouse a lot lately and they want to make it as easy on you as possible. If you're willing to start early, Joe will submit his resignation, and they will put your appointment on the agenda for next week's Commission meeting."

Rikki briefly mulled it over one last time. "Tell Joe I'm honored he has that much confidence in me and if he won't be able to return to work by the end of the year, I'm willing to step in now."

"I'll let him know," Martha said.

After taking a moment to digest the news, Rikki turned her attention back to the list of pending cases. "Well, I suppose we should get back to work now that our local criminals will be dealing with me sooner than expected."

CHAPTER 14

PLEASANTS COUNTY, WEST VIRGINIA
THURSDAY, NOVEMBER 13, 1:45 P.M.

Jack felt his belt buzz. Snatching his cell phone from its belt clip, he saw the incoming call was from the bank. "Jack McCallen here."

"Hey, Jack! It's Marty Tharp from the bank. How are you doing?"

Jack felt his stomach tighten like someone had poured Quikrete into it. "I guess I can't complain. I hope you're calling to give me some good news."

There was silence on the other end of the phone. Then Tharp sighed. "I wish I could say I was, Jack. But I'm afraid the loan committee has denied your application. Your cash flow looks good, but your credit history has taken a hit the past nine months."

Jack felt his face begin to flush. "That's because we ran into solid granite drilling that new deep well near Pennsboro," he half-screamed. "I burnt up a bunch of drill bits, which aren't exactly cheap. Then the whole damn *drill* burned up, and I had a choice: I could buy a new drill and let my bills slide a little in the short term - or I could pay the bills on time, delay buying the drill, and end up losing the lease on that property. I couldn't run that risk."

"I understand, Jack," the banker said calmly. "I really do. But like you couldn't run that risk, we don't feel comfortable risking 3 million bucks on essentially an unsecured loan."

"I put up the Schoolcraft lease as collateral for the loan, damn it! That's 2,500 acres that have never been drilled below 6,000 feet. You've seen the geological reports. You know how big those reserves are!"

"And it isn't worth a plug nickel if your lease gets overturned," Tharp forcefully answered. "Not one damn nickel. I'm sorry, Jack, but that's a chance we can't take. Come and talk to us once the lawsuit is resolved."

"Pardon my French, Marty," McCallen yelled, his face red and twisted with fury. "But your loan committee can go fuck itself! If I can hold everything together long enough to see this bullshit lawsuit get dismissed, I'll have enough money to *buy* your damn bank! And when that happens - not *if* mind you, but *when* that happens - you can bet your ass there will be a bunch of you stuffed-suit-wearing motherfuckers looking for new jobs."

The banker remained silent for almost a minute. Jack was breathing so hard he felt like he had just finished running a five mile race and he held his cell phone in a death-grip.

"I'm sorry you feel that way, Jack," Tharp finally said, his voice laden with stress. "But we're not in the business of losing money, and if my own money was riding on whether or not McCallen Resources will still be solvent come July, I'd bet against it."

"Well, you better hope you're right," McCallen said menacingly. "Otherwise, you'll need to brush up your resume."

Before the banker could say anything else, Jack hung up the phone and hurled it against the wall of his office. Bits of plastic and electronic circuitry flew in every direction as the sounds of his guttural screaming echoed off the walls.

Tharp's bank was the last in the area to look at his loan application, and only the most recent one to turn down his request. He slumped into his chair and struggled to fight back tears, knowing in his heart of hearts that in the absence of some sort of miracle, the company his dad had spent years building from the ground up was about to go down in flames, and there was nothing he could do to stop it.

CHAPTER 15

CHARLESTON, WEST VIRGINIA
THURSDAY, NOVEMBER 13, 2:30 P.M.

Luke Vincent sat in the rear of his limousine. Leaning forward, he clutched his cell phone and stared at it, silently pondering his next move.

His State Police escort stood outside the limo, dutifully allowing him a moment alone. Clad in a long, olive greatcoat, a plume of fog billowed from the trooper's mouth as he rubbed his gloves together, trying to keep himself warm. Secret Service agents hovered nearby.

Vincent took a deep breath, hit "send," and raised the phone to his ear. His heart was racing as the phone began ringing.

"Hello?" said the spectacularly sultry voice which answered his call.

"I didn't appreciate that little stunt you pulled the other morning," Vincent said. "What in the world were you thinking when you sent me that video clip?"

"I don't like being kept waiting, nor do I care for that tone of voice, Mr. Governor."

Vincent felt a pang in his chest. This was not how he had envisioned this conversation unfolding. He was the *Governor* for Christ's sake! Most people wouldn't dare talk to him like that. Knowing she had the power to do so made him both furious and terrified, a combination that seriously hindered his ability to think clearly.

"I'm sorry," he said gently, "but I was in a meeting when your message came through, and I had to make up some cockamamie story I'm sure no one believed. Just think what would have happened if Donna had been there when I opened that message."

"Not my problem, Luke. Make arrangements to see me more often, I'll be a happy camper, and you won't hear from your mistress when you're in polite company. But if you keep putting me off and making me feel like some kind of whore you're ashamed of ..." She paused, letting the threat hang. " ... well, if you keep treating me like that, you can't expect me to keep playing nice. Maybe next time, I'll send the clip directly to Donna's phone."

"I didn't get where I am by being pushed around or threatened," the governor snapped. "You're not the first person who thought they had me by the short and curlies, and don't you ever threaten to drag my wife into this situation again. Because if you do, Tabatha, you're gonna find out real quick that it's not smart to get on my bad side."

Vincent heard Tabatha start sobbing. "I am so, so sorry, baby. I just want to be with you so bad, and it hurts when I can't see you. I don't like feeling like a whore, Luke. I don't like going days and days without hearing so much as a peep from you. It makes me feel like you don't care about me, and that all you want me for is sex."

The most primal part of the governor's brain responsible for detecting danger began flooding his system with adrenaline. *She has let her emotions get involved. I'm skating on thin ice here, and I need to ratchet down the tension a notch.*

"You know better than that," he coaxed. "I love being with you, but I have to be careful. Especially now with the media camped out all over the damn state. I'm just asking you to be patient with me. That's all. Just bear with me a little while and I promise I'll make it up to you."

Sniffles trickled into his ear. "You promise?" she asked, sounding like a little girl who wanted to go to Disneyland but would settle for a trip to the ice cream parlor instead.

Vincent felt a deep sense of relief and the muscles in his neck began to relax. "I promise. Cross my heart, Tabatha. Just give me a little time and trust me, okay?"

"Okay," she said, fighting through sniffles. "I'll try not to freak out on you any more, Luke, I really will. But don't keep me waiting forever, okay?"

"I won't. I'll call you sometime next week, and we'll see what we can work out."

A laugh tinged with sorrow greeted his words. "I'll be waiting to hear from you, baby. I can't wait to see you again."

"Me either," he lied. "Bye, bye."

Vincent didn't even wait to hear what she might have said in response before he hung up the phone and tapped on the window, summoning the trooper. His mind was already in overdrive, trying to figure out how to eliminate this nightmare from his life.

CHAPTER 16

WILLIAMSON, MINGO COUNTY, WEST VIRGINIA
FRIDAY, NOVEMBER 14, 11:00 A.M.

Mack Palmer sat erect in his chair, facing the Mingo County Commission while listening to the opposition's arguments. Dave thought Palmer was gritting his teeth and silently reciting yoga mantras to remain calm while the other lawyer's voice grew increasingly louder.

"There's no question the results reported on Election Night from the precincts using these malfunctioning machines don't add up," Susan Mathis asserted in a strong voice belying her short, petite stature. Her long auburn hair and porcelain skin looked impeccable despite having been under the glare of television lights for over an hour. "Registered Democrats outnumber Republicans in those precincts ten-to-one, yet the initial returns indicate Governor Royal won 70 percent of their votes. Such a switch would be unheard of, especially when you look at the figures from those same precincts four years ago when the Democrat nominee won two-thirds of the votes.

"In light of these facts," Mathis continued, shifting her weight to her right leg as she stood behind the podium, her hands cupped together atop the wooden lectern, "plus the testimony of our IT experts and simple common sense, the Commission must acknowledge that the backup data uploaded onto AIS's server constitutes the most accurate measure of the voters' intent in those precincts on Election Day. Thank you."

A man in his late forties with sandy blond hair and a thick moustache sat in the middle of the County Commission's dais at the front of the room, watching the attorney return to her seat. Over the past two days, Dave had learned the man was Mark Monroe, the president of the Commission who was undyingly devoted to the Wilson/Vincent campaign.

"Thank you, Ms. Mathis, for your enlightening presentation," Monroe gushed. His fawning tone made Dave want to puke. "Mr. Palmer, you may proceed."

Palmer stood up and marched to the podium, tight-jawed with a steely glare in his eyes. To Dave, he looked imminently prepared for battle. He neatly stacked his prepared notes on the right side of the lectern, casually adjusted the left sleeve of his black suit jacket and stared up at the members of the Commission.

"Thank you, Commissioner Monroe," he began. "I must begin by giving credit where credit is due, and acknowledge that the proposition advanced by Ms. Mathis in this case is creative. Without any basis in the law, but creative nonetheless."

The muscular, bald lawyer glanced down at the lectern and gingerly adjusted his crisp stack of papers. "According to section twenty-eight of the West Virginia Code, chapter three, article four-a," Palmer continued, speaking in a slow, methodical manner, "your role as the board of canvassers requires you to 'examine all of the vote-recording devices' and 'determine the number of votes cast for each candidate.' Having conducted such an examination, you must then 'procure the correct returns and ascertain the true results of the election.'" Palmer paused, giving the Commissioners a moment to digest the statute. Monroe's eyes were glazed over, but the other two members of the Commission were listening closely. "Section twenty-nine goes on to say that if it appears 'a vote recording device ... has by reason of mechanical failure or improper or fraudulent preparation or tampering, incorrectly recorded or tabulated the actual votes cast or counted ...' then this body 'shall have the cause of the error corrected and the ballots affected recounted so that the election returns will accurately reflect the votes cast at such election *if it is possible to correct such error.*'" As his voice rose in pitch to emphasize the last phrase of that sentence, Palmer drew the forefinger, middle finger and thumb of his right hand together, using them to punctuate the air in front of him.

"In other words," the lawyer continued, exuding an aura of confidence, "there are a whole lot of hoops you have to jump through to get where Ms. Mathis wants to take you. First off, you have to conclude that the memory cards from these nine specific voting machines malfunctioned on Election Night, *twice*: Once during the initial tabulation at the individual precincts and a second time when they were processed at the County Clerk's Office. And to reach that conclusion, you also must believe these malfunctions went undetected by the so-called 'experts' at AIS during *each* of the *eight* diagnostic tests that were performed on *each* of those nine machines between 7:20 p.m. and 9:40 p.m. on November 4th."

Palmer stopped and shook his head, a mixture of skepticism and sadness reflected on his face. "What are the odds of that occurring? 72 diagnostic tests on those machines during that time frame, and a total of 432 tests throughout the day, yet not one malfunction was identified by the folks at AIS. Not one! If you ask me, I'd say those odds are pretty non-existent."

The attorney lifted the top page from his stack of documents and turned it face down on the left side of the lectern. An underling surreptitiously slid a glass of ice water onto the right side of the table upon which the lectern was stationed. Palmer smoothly grabbed the glass in his right hand and raised it to his lips.

"Nevertheless," Palmer declared. "Even if you determine that all of the stars aligned for those malfunctions to elude the *vigilant* oversight of the folks at AIS, that's not the end of the road." He smirked and raised an eyebrow. "The Code indicates that 'if an error is found, the board of canvassers shall have *the cause of the error corrected* and the ballots affected recounted so that the election returns will accurately reflect the votes cast at such election *if it is possible to correct such error.*'

"I can't stress this point enough. The West Virginia Code does not permit this body to substitute 'backup data' stored on the AIS servers for the actual memory cards used in these nine voting machines. If you can find a way to correct the problems which these memory cards are currently experiencing – if you can find a way to fix their actual *malfunctions* – and then reprocess the data stored on those memory cards, that would be a permissible action under section twenty-nine of the Code. But *substituting* the 'backup data' stored on the AIS servers *does not* correct the cause of the errors allegedly experienced by the memory cards and thus does not comply with the procedures outlined in section twenty-nine."

A murmur swept through the courtroom audience as some suddenly grasped the importance of the distinction drawn by Palmer and attempted to explain it to their neighbors. Reporters furiously scribbled on their notepads while the hot white lights of the television cameras glared down on the lawyer's bald head. A scowl formed under Monroe's thick moustache. Pete Warner, the commissioner who belonged to the faction that had supported Jonathan Royal in the recent election, beamed. Ruth Thompson, the third member of the commission, had the same deer-in-the-headlights look she had worn throughout the proceedings.

"So tell me something, Mr. Palmer," challenged Monroe. "What if we think the memory cards were malfunctioning on Election Night but we *can't* fix the cards themselves to retrieve the data? Are you saying we should *ignore* the perfectly reliable backup data on the server?"

"Aside from the half-baked opinions offered *now* by the same 'experts' from AIS who detected no malfunctions in those machines on Election Day, there is no evidence the data on the server is reliable at all," Palmer retorted. "Moreover, the Legislature specifically addressed that issue when it passed the law authorizing counties to use electronic voting systems in lieu of paper ballots." Palmer pulled a sheet of paper from his stack and read directly from it. "Section twenty-nine dictates 'if the board of canvassers is unable to accurately correct such errors made by said device or equipment and therefore cannot correct the returns to accurately reflect the actual votes cast at such election, the total votes recorded or tabulated on such device or equipment, *despite the fact that such vote may be erroneous*, shall be accepted as the votes cast.'"

Mack Palmer casually but neatly reassembled the stack. Monroe's moustache twitched and his eyes glowered with silent fury.

"All of that being said," Palmer continued. "The fact remains that the evidence before the Commission clearly demonstrates that the most accurate reflection of the voters' will as expressed on those nine machines on November 4th is the printed tabulations from the precincts in question after the polls closed. Those results were confirmed when the memory cards were processed a second time at the County Clerk's Office later that night. The mere fact that the memory cards are apparently malfunctioning now is completely irrelevant to your deliberations in the course of this canvass."

The lawyer stood at the podium, awaiting questions from the three commissioners. Pete Warner ended the silence. "Thank you very much, Mr. Palmer. It's refreshing to hear someone cut through this computerized crap and get to the heart of the matter." Warner then turned to his right, facing his two fellow Commissioners. "Do either of my colleagues have any further questions for Mr. Palmer?"

Monroe shook his head negatively but said nothing. Ruth Thompson was wide-eyed, apparently terrified she might have to speak in front of a wall of television cameras. "Very well," Warner said. "You may have a seat, Mr. Palmer."

As the bald-headed lawyer strolled back to his chair, Mark Monroe shook off his funk. "At this time, I think we should go into executive session to discuss this matter with the prosecutor. Would either of my colleagues care to make a motion to that effect?"

"I'll make that motion," Ruth Thompson blurted.

"I'll second it," Monroe added. "All in favor?"

"Aye," said all three commissioners.

"The motion carries," Monroe announced. "The Commission sitting as the board of canvassers for the general election will retire into executive session. These proceedings are hereby adjourned." Monroe banged his gavel and the commissioners stood and exited the room to the left of the dais, trailed by the county's tight-lipped prosecutor who carried a thick pile of manila folders and two even thicker green legal books.

Dave Anderson sat directly behind the Royal campaign's legal team and Mack Palmer approached him, a broad smile across his face. "Great work, Dave," he said, heartily extending his right hand. "That was some pretty slick lawyering, picking up on that whole 'cause of the error' language in the statute."

Dave smiled and shrugged his shoulders in an 'aw-shucks' manner. "I'm glad you found my two cents was worth something. I haven't practiced law in eons, but even a blind squirrel finds an acorn every now and then."

Palmer relinquished the handshake and slapped Dave on the shoulder. "Say what you want, but Governor Royal knew what he was doing when he sent you down here. I think we might actually pull this thing out."

Dave exhaled. "I hope you're right, Mack. I hope you're right."

CHAPTER 17

ST. MARYS, PLEASANTS COUNTY, WEST VIRGINIA
FRIDAY, NOVEMBER 14, 4:00 P.M.

The cherry conference table in Rikki's office looked like someone had backed up a U-Haul truck and used a forklift to cover it with three-feet-high stacks of documents. With a black ink pen clamped loosely between her full lips, Rikki surveyed the piles of manila folders and papers before her, telling herself that answering these discovery requests was not akin to trying to empty the Ohio River with a teaspoon.

"Okay," she said wearily. "Let's move on to request for production number eight, Jack. They've asked us to produce 'copies of any and all financial records, bills, invoices, statements or other documents pertaining to any expenses which you or any of your predecessors in interest claim to have incurred, whether paid or unpaid, in connection with the development, operation, maintenance or repair of any oil or gas wells situate on the Schoolcraft lease premises during the preceding ten years.'"

Jack McCallen loosened his forest green silk tie and unfastened the top button of his lightly starched white dress shirt. His whole face was coated with a sweaty residue, and the sight amused Rikki in her quasi-punch-drunk state of mind. *He looks like someone sprayed him down with a bottle of diluted pancake syrup*, she thought.

The oilman slowly made his way around the table before stopping at a mangled-looking banker's box directly across the table from Rikki. "Our expenses related to the wells?" he asked, fingering through the folders in the box without glancing up at his lawyer.

"Yeah. Have you found them?"

McCallen navigated through the box and pulled out a folder. "I have all the expenses *we've* incurred on those wells. But anything I got from the people who sold me the lease is either back at my office or in storage. I'll dig that stuff up and get it to you next week."

Rikki's mouth tightened into a frown. "Get it to me this weekend. Wednesday is our deadline and I'll need time to figure out what we have to turn over and what we can object to."

McCallen sighed loudly and began pawing at his iPhone. "Fine. I'll start working on it tomorrow. If the Lord's willing and the creek don't rise, you'll have it by Sunday afternoon."

As mentally drained as she was, Rikki could not help but manage a weak grin. "You and your crazy country sayings! I grew up here, and I *still* have no idea where you come up with some of that stuff."

Jack stretched himself the full length of his six-feet-one frame and smiled proudly. "Well, it's not your fault your folks didn't grow up here, Rikki. I'm sure some of our favorite euphemisms probably weren't all that popular back in India."

"True. Even so, I think you probably have more of those goofball phrases floating around your head than anybody I've ever met. Except for Dave, maybe."

McCallen's eyes widened. "What did you just say?"

Realizing the comparison she had made, Rikki felt her mouth drop open. Her face felt warm, and she knew it would be turning bright red if not for her dark brown complexion.

"It must be something in the water around here," she blurted. "Because I've never seen so many bullshit artists come out of one place in my entire life."

McCallen snorted. "Call it bullshit if you want, but I prefer to think sayings like that are just a good old-fashioned way of making people relax and feel at home."

Rikki's lips tightened, and she folded her arms across her buxom chest. Jack stared back blankly but said nothing. Finally, the silence grew too uncomfortable. "Dear God, Jack! I can hear him using those exact same words. It's like you're *channeling* him or something!"

"Dave always did have a good head on his shoulders," he quipped.

"Yeah, except for that whole 'leaving his fiancé to watch her dad die alone' thing, huh?" Her voice dripped with sarcasm.

The glint in McCallen's eyes faded and softened. "It's a damn shame," he remarked with a shake of his head, tapping a manila folder against the palm of his left hand.

Rikki could feel anger rising in her chest. "What's that, Jack?" she asked brusquely, a tone of defiance in her voice.

"That a good man like Dave could spend his entire life paying for one bad decision," McCallen observed. "And that a good woman like you might never find it in her heart to forgive him for being less than perfect."

Her client's words pierced the bubble of Rikki's anger, leaving a faint vapor of sadness in its wake. She bit her lower lip and rapped her fingertips lightly against the inside of her opposite bicep. "It's not that simple."

Jack smiled like a wizened uncle. "Yes it is," he said softly. "You just don't realize it."

Rikki uncrossed her arms, and her posture slackened. Letting out a sigh, she flopped down in a chair at the end of the conference table. "I hear what you're saying, Jack. I really do. My mom tried telling me the same thing a few days ago when we saw Dave on TV."

Jack sat down in a chair to her right. Leaning toward her, he laced his hands together and rested them on top of the conference table. "So why don't you try *listening* to us for a change? Carrying around that kind of anger can't be good for you, Rikki."

"I know that," she replied edgily. "It's just that I'm good at a lot of things, Jack, but forgiveness isn't one of them."

Jack nodded sympathetically. "Have you thought about counseling?"

Rikki guffawed loudly. "No way I'm letting some shrink start poking around in *my* noggin, Mr. Senator," she said, breaking into a broad smile. "That's fine and dandy for some people and God love 'em for it. But not for me, thanks."

"Well, I can't say I blame ya there. Just thought I'd throw it out there. Lord knows it hasn't done much for me and Tabatha."

Rikki knew all about his marital problems, as Jack had consulted her many times when he had seriously contemplated divorce. "Are things still rough on the home front?" she asked.

Now it was Jack's turn to laugh, and he let out a thunderous one. The bitterness in his expression was apparent, and it made Rikki cringe. "You could say that. It usually feels more like the Western Front than the home front."

"That bad, huh?"

McCallen paused, seeking the right words. "Every night," he said solemnly, "I pray that God will grant me the strength to keep from choking her to death in her sleep."

"Ouch. I'm sorry to hear that."

Jack slumped. "You have no idea how bad it is, Rikki, unless you experience it yourself. Until you live under the same roof with someone you love *and* despise, you just can't comprehend how miserable life can be. And never in a million years would I wish that on you."

Rikki listened to him vent. Years spent dealing with distraught clients had taught her to know when to offer advice, and when to simply listen to their frustration and heartache. Knowing how to distinguish the two separated good lawyers from mediocre ones, and Rikki prided herself on being one of the best.

"I know you two have been through a lot lately. Between your campaign and getting hit with this lawsuit, the stress has to take a toll on your relationship."

Jack shook his head. "Things have been even rockier lately, sure. Things have been bad for years but all we ever do now is argue. About *everything*. It's gotten old, and now I'm pretty sure she's cheating on me."

Rikki tried to look surprised, but she had seen the way Tabatha acted toward other men at political functions and felt Jack's suspicions were not borne from paranoia. "Why do you say that?" she asked, both to gather more information and to let Jack vent a little steam.

"Lots of little things, but if you put them all together, they just don't make any sense."

"Such as?"

"Well, let's see. To begin with," he said, touching the tip of his right index finger to his left pinky finger as he spoke, "I saw her with a new cell phone about six months ago. Not the cell phone I call her on, which is paid for by McCallen Resources, but a *different* one. She claimed that it belonged to her friend, Betsy, who accidentally left it at a restaurant after dinner one evening. But I've seen that same damn phone in her purse on at least three different occasions, and I don't think even *Betsy* is that damn stupid to lose her phone three times."

Rikki chuckled. "Go on."

"Then," he continued, moving his fingertip to the top joint of his left ring finger, ticking off the next item on his list, "she's acted real weird a few times, dropping whatever it is she's doing on a moment's notice, telling me one of her friends is 'having a crisis' of some sort. But before she 'runs off' to help this 'friend,' she'll take the time to fix herself up like she's going out on the town. And sometimes I won't even see her again until the next day."

Rikki felt her stomach drop. "That doesn't sound good. What else?"

"Those are the big ones that I can point to. Other than that, I just have a gut feeling that something's going on. And me and my gut have been together long enough for me to know it's usually right about these things."

"Well, you've won enough elections and bet successfully enough times in the oil patch that I won't argue with your gut," Rikki joked. "But let's assume Tabatha is cheating on you. What does that really change? If you're unhappy, you're unhappy. Why should her infidelity be the determining factor in whether you decide to get a divorce?"

"Ah!" he exclaimed triumphantly, "because my good friend and kickass lawyer, Sarika Gudivada, was watching out for me before I got married, and she referred me to another kickass lawyer in Parkersburg who whipped up a pre-nup for me."

"I remember that. I stay as far away from that family law stuff as I can. So what does your pre-nuptial agreement say about adultery?"

Jack smiled deviously. "The pre-nup takes a very dim view of adultery. In fact, if it were to come to pass that my good wife has fallen victim to temptation and violated the terms of our sacred marital vows, the 'injured party' – meaning *me* – would be freed from paying spousal support. Even more importantly," he continued, growing visibly energized, "infidelity is to be taken into consideration by the court in determining who gets custody of the kids."

Rikki whistled appreciatively. "Wow. That guy did some nice work for you, Jack. I never would have thought Tabatha would agree to something like that."

"She didn't have a whole lot of choice if she wanted a ring on her finger. When I agreed to marry her, I signed up for thick and thin, in sickness and health, and all that other happy shit. I knew I could remain faithful, regardless of what happened. God knows, she has given me a million reasons to stray. But the fact that I respect those vows – and that despite it all, I still do love her crazy ass – outweighs everything else in my mind."

Rikki felt her throat tighten and her eyes began to water. "You're a good man, Jack. I wish I could find someone who looked at love like that. I'd be married in a heartbeat."

Jack stared unblinkingly into her eyes and his expression morphed from anger and pride into a look of compassion. "Not if you threw him away for the sin of being imperfect."

CHAPTER 18

CHARLESTON, WEST VIRGINIA
WEST VIRGINIA STATE CAPITOL BUILDING
SATURDAY, NOVEMBER 15, 12:15 P.M.

Dick Bowen, the governor's closest advisor, grimaced and squirmed slightly in the leather chair facing Governor Vincent's massive black walnut desk. The gas fireplace's flames danced blurrily in Bowen's peripheral vision.

"I'm not a very happy man," Vincent declared coldly. His hard gaze tunneled into Bowen.

"Absolutely, Mr. Governor," Bowen replied, his voice sounding as gravelly as ever despite the tense atmosphere. Ordinarily, he would have referred to Vincent by his first name. Today, circumstances dictated greater deference. "We didn't anticipate the Mingo County canvass would turn this direction."

"Why not?" Vincent loudly demanded. Beneath his thick waves of silver and light brown hair, his forehead and cheeks began to turn pinkish-red.

Bowen sat rigidly in the chair. His fingernails dug through his black dress pants into the tops of his thighs. "Our lawyers misread the statute that covers voting machine malfunctions. They researched the issue and discussed it at length with both national counsel and the geeks at AIS. Everyone thought utilizing the back-up data from the servers would 'correct' the problem, as required by the law. No one foresaw the law might be interpreted differently."

"Except for Royal's lawyers, that is. Right?"

Bowen gritted his teeth. "There's no need to panic. The county commission will make its decision on Monday, and since Ruth Thompson holds the swing vote, we've been going through her life with a fine-toothed comb, looking for something that might ... *persuade* her to vote properly when the time comes."

Bowen sighed and rustled through a stack of papers. "Unfortunately, she may be the most boring person on the planet. Sixty-two years old. Never married and no kids. Worked at a dentist's office for thirty-five years before retiring. She plays piano at the biggest Baptist church in Mingo County, and she has three cats. Which eat Friskies cat food, by the way."

"*What?*" Vincent asked incredulously.

"Her cats eat Friskies," Bowen repeated.

"How the hell do you know that?"

Bowen sighed again. "Because the info our buddies at AIS have systematically accumulated in their database is fucking terrifying, that's how. For instance, every time you use a coupon at the grocery store and pay your bill with a check, credit card or debit card, the register's software – designed by AIS – collects that data. Slowly but surely, their database grows until they know almost everything about you. Your age, address, phone number, spending habits, favorite products, etc. Which they sell to *other* corporations who want to sell you other products you might like, according to your AIS profile."

"Wow. I had no idea."

"That's just the tip of the iceberg. Combined with the other information it has obtained from the public sector like voters registration records, criminal charges, speeding tickets, permit applications and lawsuits, AIS probably has more dirt on American citizens in its database than the FBI does."

"I'm glad they're on *our* side," Vincent quipped.

Bowen guffawed. "No shit. One guy from the old Soviet Union makes a fortune from the communists' oil and gas reserves and then starts buying American companies. No wonder some people imagine there's a New World Order controlling everything behind closed doors."

The governor strolled over to an ornate, antique black walnut liquor cabinet sitting behind his desk and pulled out a fifth of Gentleman Jack and two old-fashioned glasses. Pouring double shots into each, he extended one to Bowen. "Man," he said wistfully. "I wish I had been alive back in the good old days when you could just properly distribute pints of bourbon in the coalfields and wait for the election to be safely delivered inside stacked ballot boxes."

Bowen clinked glasses with his boss and guzzled the whiskey. "Ah, hell, Luke," he said, his mouth twisting sourly. "We had shit go wrong back then, too. You just have to handle the curveballs that come your way."

Vincent licked a trickle of whiskey from his lower lip and placed his glass on the desk. "Speaking of curveballs, I have a little situation on my hands I could use some help with."

"Tell me about it."

The governor edged his chair back. "It's a long story, Dick. And not something I'm particularly proud of."

Bowen's eyes narrowed as he directed his full attention on Vincent. "If you were proud of it, you wouldn't need my help dealing with it. Would you?"

Vincent grinned sheepishly. He paused, trying to describe his problem with a modicum of decency. "Let's just say I have a female admirer I have become a little too intimate with."

Bowen folded his sausage-like fingers together across his belly and leaned back in his chair. "I see. How long has this *intimacy* been going on, and when did it become a problem?"

"About a year, but it wasn't a problem until the campaign heated up around Labor Day."

Bowen nodded curtly, absorbing the information. "Give me the lowdown on your admirer, Luke. I need to know what I'm dealing with here."

"It's Tabatha McCallen."

"*Jack* McCallen's wife? The State Senator?"

The governor nodded. "That's her."

Bowen whistled. "Well, I'll give you one thing, Luke. When you decided to complicate your life, you didn't half-ass it like Clinton by trolling through the trailer parks or the college interns. You went straight to the top of the food chain and picked the hottest, craziest woman in sight. And one married to a prominent Republican with every incentive in the world to destroy you. That takes moxie, or maybe just a staggering degree of stupidity."

"A little of both," Vincent admitted. "In the beginning, I was just letting my little head do the thinking for me. Stupid, I admit. But you've *seen* her, for crying out loud."

"I'd drink her dirty bathwater to nail her," Bowen conceded. "But I'm not the fucking governor, Luke! I'm a crusty old lobbyist whose wife has been dead for ten years. But you…"

Vincent closed his eyes and shook his head sadly. "Yeah, I know. I'm running for vice-president, and I'm a slack-jawed moron. I can't fart without a TV reporter telling the world what it smells like, and yet I'm sneaking around Charleston, cheating on a saint like Donna with a state senator's wife who's crazier than a one-eyed squirrel on acid."

"When you put it like that, it sounds even dumber than I thought," Bowen cracked. "So what is she doing that's got you so worried?"

Vincent stared out the window at the State Capitol lawn, tight-lipped. Groundskeepers busily removed mountains of fallen leaves from the sprawling expanse of grass between his office and Kanawha Boulevard. "She's become awfully needy lately," he said, still gazing outside. "At first, as long as we saw each other once a month or so, she was fine. But now she's getting pushy. Plus she has a sex clip of the two of us she's threatened to use against me if I don't see her more often."

Bowen winced. "That was the message you received on your phone the other day?"

Vincent turned from the window, faced his advisor and nodded.

Bowen's eyes turned cold and calculating. "Who else knows about this?"

"Just Marco Zakarias. He's owns the new hotel downtown where I usually meet her."

"I know Marco," Bowen said. "He's solid. So when are you gonna see her again?"

"I haven't decided yet. I was vague the last time we talked, but I hinted around I might try to see her next week."

Bowen glanced over at a giant fish tank, watching a pair of silver angelfish swim lazily through the water. "We'll get it taken care of, Luke," he said. "Mrs. McCallen will either wise up and realize that screwing you isn't all it's cracked up to be, or she'll wish she'd never tripped and let your dick fall in her. Either way, this problem *will* be taken care of."

CHAPTER 19

VIENNA, VIRGINIA
SATURDAY, NOVEMBER 15, 2:00 P.M.

Yuri Petrenko was peripherally aware that Maryland had just scored another touchdown. He wasn't following the game closely, but the broadcasters' excited voices indicated the Terrapins were pulling away from Virginia Tech.

Yuri glanced up from his papers and saw a kicker wearing a red jersey boot the football through the goalposts. The score at the bottom of the screen rolled over and increased by one, showing the Terps now ahead 34-20. Yuri drained the last swig of his beer and set the empty bottle down on the coffee table.

The longer he lived in America, the more he enjoyed its version of football. At first, he was drawn mostly to the spectacle – the pure *violence* – of the sport. But as he watched the game more, he began to appreciate its strategic aspects: Should the offense run the ball or try to throw downfield? Should the defense stack the line to defend the run or blitz a cornerback into the backfield to disrupt the play? Because so many of the game's concepts applied to the real world, he understood why observers often used military analogies to describe events on the field.

Looking down at the thick dossier of information in front of him, Yuri viewed it as a detailed scouting report on his team's opponent in the national championship game. And Yuri viewed himself as the team's offensive coordinator, looking for weaknesses in the enemy's defense that could be exploited to win the most important game of the year with the highest stakes imaginable – the White House itself.

After two tours of duty with the Spetsnaz in Chechnya, Petrenko spent five years in Moscow with the Federal Security Service handling electronic surveillance and cyber warfare. Then Mazniashvili made him a financial offer he could not refuse, so he finished his term with the military and moved to America.

The front page was embossed with the words "Operation Aristocrates." God only knew why Mazniashvili had chosen that moniker for the project. But since he was fronting all the project's expenses, Yuri supposed he could call it whatever he wanted. After all, "Screwing Jonathan Royal while Keeping My Rich Ass away from a Firing Squad In Tbilisi" may have more precisely described the project, but it gave off no cool, yet sinister vibes. Thus, "Operation Aristocrates" carried the day.

Petrenko waded through the document with a highlighter, highly impressed with the quality of information his boss had accumulated. Unfettered access to exceptionally private and valuable information was apparently one of the privileges Mazniashvili enjoyed in his role as the financier and behind-the-scenes puppet-master at AIS.

Yuri had spent most of the past five days reviewing the voluminous file for "Operation Aristocrates," painstakingly trying to identify the one man or woman best suited for their project. After initially narrowing his choices down to four, Yuri found his focus returning to one particular candidate over and over.

Staring at the photographs for at least the twentieth time, Petrenko concentrated on the candidate's eyes, attempting to probe his soul. Then he closed his eyes and focused his mind.

Yes, he told himself with certainty. *This is the one.*

Yuri lifted his laptop from the coffee table, leaned back and tapped on the keyboard. In his mind, the game had kicked off and he had called his team's first offensive play of the game.

It's game time, boys! Let's put the ball in the end zone.

CHAPTER 20

CHARLESTON, WEST VIRGINIA
GOVERNOR'S MANSION
SATURDAY, NOVEMBER 15, 10:00 P.M.

Arriving home from a fundraiser, Vincent stripped out of his tuxedo and tried to get comfortable. He slipped a green Thundering Herd tee-shirt over his head and pulled a pair of matching cotton pajama bottoms over his black silk boxers. Throwing a pair of slippers on his feet, he headed into the bathroom while his wife completed her own clothing transformation.

The Vincents had been married for 25 years, and his wife rarely deviated from her Saturday night routine. In the absence of some calamity, he knew Donna would crawl in bed at 10:00 p.m., flip on the bedside lamp and watch a re-run of The Golden Girls. When the show was over, she would read the Bible for 20 minutes, turn off the light and go to sleep. In his mind, neither solar eclipses nor the phases of the moon were as predictable as his wife's behavior, and he derived a certain degree of comfort from that predictability.

By the same token, in a self-analytical moment that arrived while he was taking a leak, he wondered whether his own boredom with that predictability had led him to pursue his tryst with Tabatha McCallen. *If you wanted more excitement in your life, you should have taken up skydiving instead of playing 'hide the sausage' with another woman.*

Such self-indictments were not amenable to a good night's sleep. Vincent flushed the toilet, washed and dried his hands, then let out a deep sigh. Opening the door, he saw Donna propped up in bed facing the television with a smile. Sure enough, the four Golden Girls were sitting around the kitchen table, and when Sophia let loose with one of her biting one-liners, the First Lady let out a chuckle that was perfectly on cue with the show's laugh track.

Vincent strolled over to his wife, bent down and gave her a kiss on the forehead. "I'm going to check out the scores online."

Donna looked up, still smiling. "Okay, honey. But don't sit too close to the computer screen or you'll hurt your eyes."

"I won't. Be back in a jiffy."

The First Lady nodded and patted his hand. "Don't keep me waiting," she said with a wink. "You looked awfully handsome in that tuxedo tonight, Mr. Governor."

Vincent grinned back. "You looked quite smashing yourself. Don't fall asleep on me."

"Not a chance," Donna replied. "I'll be waiting."

The governor raised her hand to his lips, gave it a little peck and then walked across the hallway to the extra bedroom that served as his office in the Mansion's living quarters. He crossed the room, sat down at the red oak desk and brought the computer to life with a tap of the mouse. Just as he opened ESPN's website, his cell phone began playing Marshall's fight song. Peering at the viewscreen, he saw Dick Bowen's face and phone number.

"Hello?"

"Good evening, Luke. How was the fundraiser?"

"Just like all the others," Vincent deadpanned. "Dressed-up rich people hobnobbing, writing checks, nibbling on hors d'oeuvres and drinking booze like the plane is going down. What's up?"

"We've made our pitch to Ruth Thompson on the memory cards. She didn't give us a firm commitment, but we've given her some food for thought. I'll touch base again tomorrow."

Vincent heard the phone click before he had a chance to respond. If nothing else, Dick Bowen was astonishingly focused. Give him a task, and he would demolish a brick wall with his skull if necessary to get it done.

I just hope he applies that same tenacity to my dilemma with Tabatha.

CHAPTER 21

ST. MARYS, PLEASANTS COUNTY, WEST VIRGINIA
SUNDAY, NOVEMBER 16, 9:00 A.M.

Rikki slept later than anticipated, so she quickly walked down to the basement and jumped on the treadmill, trying to work up a good sweat before heading to work. Listening to her favorite workout mix via wireless Bluetooth earbuds, her running shoes rhythmically pounded the treadmill belt as the sculpted muscles in her long, dark brown legs stretched and contracted with each step.

The television mounted to the ceiling was tuned to CNN's Sunday morning show. Although the music blocked out the talking heads, she followed the discussion via closed captioning. West Virginia's fifty five counties were depicted on a map, variously colored blue or red and she noted with satisfaction that Pleasants County was depicted in blue. Then one county in the southern part of the state was expanded into a separate graphic by itself.

Rikki pressed a button on her earbuds and the music came to a halt. Grabbing the remote, she turned up the TV to drown out the treadmill's whirring engine. The words "MINGO COUNTY" had morphed onto the screen along with a circle labeled "Williamson" on the west-central edge of the map.

"Mingo County is the only county that still has not completed its post-election canvass," an off-screen male anchor reported. "Technical glitches in the county's voting machines have delayed that process, and the two campaigns have waged a bitter battle over what the County Commission must do in this situation.

"Joining us today from Charleston, West Virginia, is Susan Mathis, the lead attorney for Senator Wilson's campaign in

Mingo County. And from Williamson, West Virginia, we also have David Anderson, Governor Royal's chief legal advisor. Thank you both for being here."

"Thank you for having me," Mathis replied.

"It's my pleasure," Dave added. He stood in front of the boxy-looking county courthouse wearing a light blue dress shirt and a solid silver tie.

"Ms. Mathis," the anchor opened. "Why do you want the commission to throw out the initial election returns in favor of this 'backup data' we've heard so much about?"

"Because it's the most accurate reflection of the voters' intentions. The memory cards in nine machines were malfunctioning when the tabulations were run on Election Night. The backup data was uploaded to the server before the malfunctions occurred. Using that data is the only way to determine how those people voted and we must make sure every vote is counted."

Mathis disappeared and was replaced by a split-screen image of the anchor on the left side and Dave on the right. "How do you respond to that position, Mr. Anderson? Why shouldn't every vote that was cast in this election be counted?"

Dave cracked an amused grin. "We agree that every vote cast must be counted. But there's no evidence this so-called 'backup data' is any more accurate than the calculations which were made *twice* on Election Night ..."

"The computer experts from AIS *testified* that the backup data is more accurate than those initial calculations," Mathis loudly interjected from off-screen.

Anderson chuckled, and the look on his face was one Rikki instantly recognized as the likely precursor to some wickedly disdainful response.

"Ah," Dave said, feigning enlightenment, "you mean the same bozos who didn't detect any malfunctions in those nine machines on Election Night? Whose paychecks are signed by Dmitri Mazniashvili, an indicted criminal that Governor Royal wants to deport to face justice for defrauding his homeland of billions of dollars? Who has given millions from those ill-gotten gains to Senator Wilson's party? You want us to take *their* word for it?" Dave laughed caustically. "For all we know, this 'glitch' is just a scam Mazniashvili dreamed up to cook our election results and avoid extradition for his crimes. Personally, I'll put my faith in the results originally reported on Election Night."

Rikki muted the TV, reactivated the music and continued running, lost in thought as the treadmill whirred along. Although she was a loyal Democrat who had enthusiastically voted for Senator Wilson, the campaign's ties to Mazniashvili made her uncomfortable. Though they frequently clashed on political matters, she had never known Dave to speak untruthfully about anything. He had foibles and flaws, for sure – some of which she found utterly *maddening* – but dishonesty was not one of them.

On the other hand, she hadn't spoken to Dave in almost fifteen years. A good deal of that time Dave had lived and worked in D.C., a town not exactly renowned for truthfulness. Who knew how much he might have changed after a decade and a half in that environment?

But as she stared at the television, intensely studying his face, her heart told her Dave had not changed at all. That self-confident glint in his green eyes. That fiery tone of defiance in his voice as he belittled his opponent's arguments. No, that was not some changed man from her past she barely recognized. The handsome, smiling face she saw staring back at her on TV belonged to the same brilliant, incisive, passionate, articulate, funny, infuriatingly conservative and pigheaded man she had fallen in love with so long ago. She was certain of it.

Red lights on the treadmill's display began flashing and the conveyor belt slowed down. *Have I really been running for 45 minutes?* Her labored breathing coupled with the streams of sweat flowing down her arms, back and legs rendered that conclusion irrefutable.

Rikki's pace slowed, as she caught her breath and lowered her heart rate. Toweling off her face and neck, she turned off the TV and walked upstairs to get ready for the day.

Entering the master bedroom, Rikki kicked off her shoes and socks and stripped out of her sweaty workout clothes. Strolling into the bathroom naked, she pulled back the shower curtain and turned on the water.

Waiting for the shower to heat up, Rikki exhaled deeply. Running her hands through her long, sweaty black hair, she stared in the mirror. Even though she was pushing forty, she thought she had taken pretty good care of herself over the years. Sure, she might not be as perky and tight in certain places as she had been in her twenties, but she knew she still turned men's heads. Her face was unlined, causing most people to underestimate her age, and she knew she had an exotic look that frequently elicited questions about the precise nature of her ethnicity.

Turning away from the mirror, she stepped into the shower and closed the curtain. The water felt wonderful, and she closed her eyes as she stuck her face beneath the showerhead and wet her long hair. As she worked a big handful of shampoo into her hair, her mind ran rampant.

Why am I suddenly so distracted by thoughts of Dave? For years, she felt confident she had put their breakup behind her and moved on with her life. Now she had doubts. Maybe it was the recent conversations with her mom and Jack, or maybe it was because she had seen him on TV so much lately. Regardless, she wasn't happy with the situation.

Rikki rinsed the shampoo from her hair and poured a mass of fragrant orange body wash into a loofah sponge, reflecting as she lathered it onto her arms. She hadn't been a shrinking violet since breaking up with Dave; far from it. She had dated numerous men on a short-term basis and had a few longer relationships as well. She honestly could not remember a time when she had lacked attractive romantic options, including several viewed as "keepers" by her friends. But for whatever reason, she inevitably found her suitors lacking in some way. And then it was just a matter of time before she would end the relationship, much to the frequent exasperation of those around her.

Oh, well. There's no sense getting all worked up about it. If she was destined to fall in love again and perhaps even get married, she had faith it would happen when the circumstances were right. And if not … Well, if that were the case, she thought she would be okay with that too.

Rikki shut off the water and grabbed two thick cotton towels. Drying herself off, she wrapped her long hair up in one of the towels and stepped onto a bath mat before making her way into the bedroom.

Forty minutes later, she was fully clothed in a comfortable baby blue sweater, designer jeans and a pair of snazzy black boots. Sitting alone in her breakfast nook, she sipped on a cup of coffee heavily flavored with cream and sugar as a plate with toast crumbs and dried egg yolk sat in front of her. Sunshine poured into the room through a bay window overlooking her back yard, and the cloudless sky greeting her this morning was a mesmerizing, flawless shade of blue.

Staring out the window, she saw two whitetail deer walk cautiously out of the woods into her unfenced yard. A big, healthy-looking doe and her fawn were enjoying the warm weather, blissfully unaware that the woods would be swarming with rifle-toting hunters in only eight days. Just as Rikki began wondering how the doe would fare, her thoughts were interrupted by her cell phone ringing. She answered the phone without even looking at the caller ID. "Hello?"

"Hey, Rikki. It's Jack. How are you doing?"

"Good," she replied energetically. "I just finished breakfast, and now I'm debating whether I can squeeze in time for church today. What's going on?"

"I need to get those financial records to you. And I was hoping we could get together to go over a few things, including an interesting email I received this morning."

"Oh, yeah? Who was it from?"

"I should just show you the email in person. Let's just say I found it very interesting, and it's very sensitive."

"You've piqued my curiosity, Jack. How does two o'clock at the courthouse sound? I need to start moving my stuff in there because I may be taking over sooner than expected."

"That's what I heard. Sounds smart, especially if Joe's health is as bad as they say."

Rikki shook her head and smiled. *Dear Lord! Yet another reminder of just how quickly news spreads around here.* "So does two o'clock work for you, Mr. Chatty Cathy?" she asked with a giggle.

"Two will be fine."

"I'll meet you at the door facing the refinery," Rikki clarified.

"Gotcha. See you then."

Rikki hung up, finished her java and carried her plate and mug to the kitchen sink. *I wonder what this email is all about? Did he catch Tabatha fooling around? Between politics, his crazy wife and the Schoolcraft lease cancellation suit, it could be anything.*

Two hours later, Rikki opened the heavy glass courthouse door with one hand while clutching a stuffed banker's box beneath the other. After six trips lugging boxes from her hybrid SUV up three flights of stairs to her new office, her breathing was labored.

Maybe I'm not in as good shape as I thought I was!

As she prepared to lock the door behind her, a car horn blared. Glancing up, she saw a gray Durango stopped in the road between the courthouse and a rusting oil refinery. The barrel-chested figure of Sheriff Vaughn was behind the wheel.

"Howdy, Rikki," Vaughn's rich bass voice called. "What're you doing here today?"

Rikki propped the door open with a box and strolled toward the cruiser, her black boots pounding the pavement with each step. Crossing the street fluidly, her light blue sweater and designer jeans tastefully accentuated her figure without clinging to it. "Just moving in some of my things, getting ready to take over. How are *you* doing?"

The Sheriff's lower lip bulged with snuff and he lifted a paper cup to his mouth, spitting a stream of vile-looking brownish residue into it. "No complaints."

As always, a man of few words, Rikki noted.

Squatting down, she rested her elbows on the open window sill while staying safely away from the Sheriff's spittoon. "Sometime soon, we need to go over all of our pending cases.

Make sure we have everything we need for trial and that we're all on the same page with things."

Vaughn nodded, fixing Rikki in the same screwball-eyed gaze that had made her uneasy since she was a kid. Quickly remembering that Vaughn's scar was beneath his left eye, Rikki focused on his functional right one.

Vaughn's good eye flashed. "Sure thing, as long as it's before the end of next weekend. Next Monday is the first day of deer season." He shot her a toothy grin. "Good luck finding me then."

Rikki threw back her head and laughed aloud. "So fighting crime takes a back seat to deer hunting around here, eh, Sheriff?"

Vaughn spit into his cup, nodding and grinning sheepishly. "Something like that. Unless something big breaks loose, I figure it can wait 'til rifle season is over."

Jack McCallen walked around the corner of the courthouse carrying his own bankers' box. "Don't you go distracting my lawyer, Doug! I need her full attention today."

The sheriff set his spittoon down in the cupholder and waved. "No problem, Senator. I need to hit the road anyway. Ya'll be good."

Vaughn shifted the vehicle into gear and Rikki stepped away from the cruiser. Rolling up the window, the Sheriff saluted crisply and drove away.

Meeting Jack on the sidewalk, Rikki tapped his banker's box. "Looks like you're about to get a hernia."

McCallen snorted. "If so, it will be your fault for making me dig through our storage unit for these old records. This lawsuit's going to be death of me!"

Rikki giggled, picked up her own box and held the door open with her foot. "Quit your belly-aching, Jack. This is a painful, but necessary part of the process. If we don't produce these records, we have no chance of winning. And you don't want that to happen, do you?"

"No," he grumbled, trudging up the stairs. "It's just a pain in the ass."

Rikki locked the door and followed suit. "I know. But complaining about it won't make it any better. Do you think I *like* being cooped up inside on a beautiful day like today?"

"All right, all right. You've made your point. I'll keep my griping to a minimum."

They wound their way upstairs and entered the prosecutor's office where half-empty boxes were strewn throughout the place. "Sorry about the mess," Rikki apologized. "I hope to have a handle on things by the time the Commission meets on Wednesday."

McCallen set his box down on an empty patch of table space in the conference room. "Is that when they're appointing you to finish out Joe's term?"

Rikki hefted the box she was hauling onto the table. "Supposedly. But I won't know 'til tomorrow if they got it on the agenda in time."

A few minutes later, the conference table was clear enough to spread out Jack's files for review. Methodically, they pored over the documents and separated them into two piles: One for those that had to be disclosed to the plaintiffs and a second for those that did not fall within the scope of materials covered by the discovery requests or were protected from disclosure due to some sort of privilege. All the documents were run through a "Bates" machine and imprinted with unique identification numbers. For each document believed to be privileged, Rikki made notes regarding why it was not required to be disclosed.

Nearing the end of the process, Rikki hunched over the table and rubbed her temples with both hands. "According to the production logs, when did you last generate any marketable volume of gas from the wells on this property?"

Clad in a black and gold Pittsburgh Steelers sweatshirt, Jack paced along the far side of the table. His hands were buried in the front pockets of his mud-stained blue jeans as he closed his eyes, scanning his memory. "Just a little under two years ago."

Rikki winced. "I thought you said it was *one* year."

Jack shook his head. "The mineral owners' last *royalty checks* were cut about a year ago. But only a marginal amount of gas is reflected in the production logs for the past eighteen months, probably just free gas provided for the mineral owners' homes. Our records don't indicate we've sold much gas from those wells during the past 30 months or so."

"You know what that means, don't you?"

McCallen sighed. "Yeah. It looks like we haven't been fully developing or marketing the gas from those wells for almost two years."

Rikki put aside the folder and nodded. "Not good. But then again, it's been nine months since they filed suit to cancel the lease, and they were harassing your crews well before that."

Jack whirled on his heel and faced her. With his hands spread apart, palms upward, he declared, "How could we get gas from those wells after they shot at us and ran us off the land?!"

"If the jury believes your crew's testimony, that's fine," she replied. "The plaintiffs wouldn't be able to hold that period of time against you. It all comes down to whether your actions marketing the gas from those wells to third parties and exploring the possibility of drilling additional wells on the property were reasonable. But *reasonable* is in the eye of the beholder, which means the judge might deny our motion for summary judgment and let a jury look at the facts for themselves."

McCallen's face turned red. "We're going to have to go to *trial* on this damn thing?"

Rikki stiffened. "If the production logs and sales invoices don't show more gas going through the wellhead meters than the plaintiffs have used in their own homes, I'd say so."

Jack looked dumbfounded. "You've got to be kidding me! That means this suit will still be hanging over my head until July! I thought it all would be wrapped up by May!"

"That's still a possibility. But our judge hates to take cases away from a jury. *Especially* when you're dealing with property rights."

McCallen closed his eyes, slumped his head and leaned forward, resting his hands on the back of a chair across the table from Rikki. "I can't make it that long," he said softly.

Rikki cocked her head, turning her left ear toward him. "What did you say?"

Jack raised his eyes. "I can't make it that long. Between the expenses from this lawsuit, the cost of trying to get other old leaseholds back into production before *they* lapse, and trying to make payroll, I'll be bankrupt by July."

Rikki sat silently for about twenty seconds. "I had no idea things were that tight, Jack. Why didn't you say something to me about it earlier?"

"And what could you have done about it, if you *had* known?!" he half-shouted. "The plaintiffs have made it clear from the get-go their only objective in this suit is to get my lease canceled. Not modified, not broken into a bunch of smaller leaseholds. *Canceled.* And we both know that's because one of the big boys is trying to backdoor me by promising to sweeten the pot if bidding on that leasehold comes open again."

Rikki didn't deny his assertion. "So what are you going to do? Can you get a credit line to make it through this suit and get the other leases back in production?"

McCallen laughed bitterly. "I've applied for loans with every bank within a hundred miles of here. I've even talked to banks in Columbus and Pittsburgh. No takers."

"How much money have you asked for?"

"Three million. The problem is, the bankers all know about this lawsuit because it's disclosed on my application as a contingent liability. Plus my credit scores took a hit last year when I had to juggle some bills to replace the drill rig that blew up."

"I remember that." Rikki's absent-mindedly tapped an ink pen on the table, first one end, then the other, pondering her client's predicament.

"And while we're discussing my financial illiquidity," Jack segued. "I want you to look at this email." He reached into his rear pocket and extracted a piece of paper folded into quarters. "I still don't know what to make of it."

Rikki unfolded it and began reading:

Partnership Opportunity
From: alex.beria@petromica.com
To: Jack@mccallenresources.com
Date: Sat, 15 Nov 2:31 pm
Attachments: mccallen.xls

Dear Mr. McCallen,

In exploring new investment opportunities, our analysts have identified your company as a potential partner. The purpose of this email is to provide you with some information about us, and to gauge your interest in joining forces.

Petromica is a privately-held Bahamian limited liability company focused on energy investments. Over the past five years, our gross revenues and net profits have grown significantly. During the last fiscal year, Petromica's net profits totaled $45 million and our investments' net worth exceeded a quarter of a billion dollars. For more information, including independent financial audits, visit our website at www.petromica.com.

We've thrived by identifying opportunities that more conservative firms might deem too risky and acting aggressively to exploit them. After examining the publicly available information, we believe McCallen Resources offers us a prime opportunity to obtain significant investment returns at a tolerable risk. Moreover, partnering with your firm would allow Petromica to expand its footprint into the Appalachian Basin, which we believe possesses some of the most under-developed natural gas deposits in the world.

Please review the attached spreadsheet our analysts have prepared in the course of their research. If the same accurately reflects your company's current financial condition, please be advised that Petromica would be interested in partnering with McCallen Resources ("MR") along the following general lines:

1. Petromica would invest a total of $25 million dollars in MR for the purpose of fully developing its existing inventory of mineral leases, focusing on drilling new wells at depths exceeding 6000 feet on existing leaseholds and an emphasis on horizontal wells penetrating into the Marcellus Shale.

2. In exchange for its investment, Petromica would get a 49% equity stake in MR.

3. MR's current management team, including yourself, would continue to exercise full control of MR's day-to-day operations for a period not less than 2 years.

4. MR would utilize a portion of Petromica's investment to completely eliminate its existing debt, improve MR's objective net worth and make the firm a more attractive target for outside investors.

5. MR's current ownership would have an option to repurchase Petromica's 49% equity stake in the firm at the end of 2 years for the sum of $31,750,000, which would constitute an annual return on our investment roughly equal to 12%.

Please be advised we are currently exploring other investments in the Appalachian Basin and we intend to finalize a deal to expand into that region as quickly as possible; if not with your firm, then with another. If you can confirm the accuracy of our financial data on MR and would like to discuss this proposal further, please contact me at your earliest convenience via email. Or you can reach me on my cell phone at (703) 925-1420.

Sincerely,

Alex Beria
Executive VP, Mergers & Acquisitions
Petromica, LLC

Rikki laid the email down and looked at Jack. He was staring back at her, tight-lipped and awaiting her response.

"So have you done any research on these guys?" she asked.

"Just a little. Not much on this Beria guy, but Petromica looks like it's the real deal."

Rikki opened her laptop and banged on the keys. "Let's have a look-see at their website," she said. Jack stood behind her, staring down at the screen.

Petromica's easily identifiable black and gold logo was prominently featured at the top left corner of the company's homepage and the entire layout oozed with professionalism. Quickly clicking through the website, Rikki found it easy to navigate and full of detailed information, including financial data and several recent press releases.

Satisfying her urge to double-check the veracity of Petromica's claims, Rikki swiftly ran two of the press releases through her favorite internet search engine. Much to her surprise, the information touted in the releases was consistently reported elsewhere in the mainstream media.

Rikki spun around to face Jack. "Okay. It looks like Petromica is legit and could come up with that kind of cash. The bigger question for me is why would they contact Jack McCallen out of the blue with a business proposition?"

"I have no idea. But they've done their homework: That spreadsheet is identical to the one I've given to banks with my loan applications for the past three months."

"Is it accurate?"

McCallen looked offended. "You think I want to go to prison for bank fraud?!"

Rikki swatted him on the thigh and laughed. "Heck, no, doofus! You'd look downright *awful* in an orange jumpsuit, and I don't think you'd like the food much either."

A smirk emerged on Jack's face and he shook his head amusedly. "Leave it to you to find humor in the thought of me going to jail."

Rikki shrugged, playfully feigning a lack of concern. "That's what friends are for, Jack. So tell me this: From a financial standpoint, does their proposal make good business sense?"

"For them or for me?"

"Both."

Jack paused, mulling the question. "For me, it's a double-edged sword. On the one hand, it would give me a huge cash infusion when I'm teetering on the hairy edge of bankruptcy and have no other realistic options. On the other hand, my dad built McCallen Resources from the ground up. It's always been a family-owned business, and the thought of having outsiders involved in it makes me want to puke."

"But you'd still own a majority interest in the company," Rikki responded. "They're willing to let you run things for the next two years *and* give you an option to buy back their shares. To me, it looks like they're basically offering to give you a twenty-five million dollar loan at 12 percent interest, secured by stock in your company."

"To an extent, that's true," Jack conceded. "But they'd be receiving half the profits we earn between now and then. That could make it pretty damn hard for me to come up with the extra 7 million bucks I'd need to buy those shares back."

Rikki silently digested the information. "You tell me you can't find a single bank willing to loan you 3 million bucks, without which cash your company will go belly-up within six months. So why would this company – from the Bahamas of all places – offer to give you *eight times* that much money for roughly a half-interest in your firm?"

Jack's smile turned positively predatory. "Because if my geologists are right, I'm sitting on a proverbial gold mine worth far more than that."

Rikki leaned back, twisting the chair clockwise, then counterclockwise, deep in thought. "Forgive me for not remembering the details of those big old geology reports, but you're not my only client *and* I've been kinda busy on the campaign trail. Refresh my memory."

Jack grew energetic. "Okay!" he exclaimed, gesticulating with his hands like a Pentecostal preacher at a revival. "Here we go … As you know, few of the gas wells in the Appalachian Basin extend deeper than 6,000 feet underground. It's not been cost-effective to drill wells below that depth."

"You do realize I'm the best oil and gas lawyer in this state, don't you, Jack? It's not like I'm a total idiot here."

He ignored the wisecrack. "But technology has improved and developers are exploring ways to extract gas from deeper deposits. Some geologists believe large deposits may lie as deep as 20,000 feet below the surface, but it's still not practical for us to drill that deep yet. The deeper we drill, the further back we go in time. In some areas, you'll run into seams of coal that were deposited during the Pennsylvanian Period, between 320 and 290 million years ago."

"Did I ask to sit through a freshman geology class, Jack? It's Sunday afternoon, and it's *gorgeous* outside. I've got better things to do than listen to you ramble on like some nerd on the History Channel, so wrap up your lecture and get to the point."

Jack sighed. "Very well," he said sullenly. "Below that level, around 6,000 feet or so, we find even older strata dating back to the Devonian. And at that depth, through a good chunk of West Virginia, you'll find a seam of shale between 15 and 300 feet thick known as the Marcellus Shale."

Rikki wiggled her right index finger in the air, a light of recognition in her pale green eyes. "Oh, yeah! You oil and gas boys get all hot and bothered talking about that stuff."

"With good reason. Because trapped within the black sedimentary rock of the Marcellus lays an enormous amount of natural gas. Maybe 80 trillion harvestable cubic feet of it."

Rikki's eyes widened. "How much?"

Jack smiled. "You heard me. *Eighty trillion cubic feet.*"

Rikki whistled. "Wow."

"And if the horizontal drilling methods prove as successful here as they were in Texas, we may be able to extract that gas from the Marcellus in a very cost-effective manner."

"*Horizontal* drilling?"

"Crazy as it sounds, the well is initially drilled straight down. But once the drill bit reaches the depth of the Marcellus, the equipment can be operated to make a right angle and drill horizontally into the shale. They then use water pressure to create openings in the shale that allows the gas trapped there to pour into the new horizontal well at substantially high flow rates."

"Sounds pretty complicated to me. Probably pretty expensive, too."

The look on Jack's face soured. "Unfortunately, you're right. A conventional well would probably cost about two-fifty, maybe 300,000 dollars to drill. But for a horizontal well, it's more like 3 million bucks."

"Dear Lord! Why would you drop 3 million bucks to drill a horizontal well when you could get eight or twelve conventional wells drilled for the same price?"

"Because there's *so much gas* believed to be trapped in the Marcellus Shale. And after people have spent the past 40 years fruitlessly trying to pull it out of with vertical wells, it looks like horizontal drilling is the only way to do it. And if you bet right and hit a big reservoir of gas in the shale under one of your leaseholds, you'll get a huge return on your investment."

Rikki subconsciously tapped her fingers on the conference table like ocean waves. "Care to give me an example?"

"Similar horizontal wells drilled into a section of the Marcellus in Pennsylvania yielded flow rates around 4 million cubic feet per day," Jack replied. "*Per well*. With gas prices as high as they are now, just one successful horizontal well – if it yielded a similar flow rate – would bring in about…"

"Forty thousand dollars per day," Rikki finished.

"Or about fourteen and a half million dollars in one year," Jack added. "A 500 percent return on your investment, less the one-eighth interest retained by the mineral owners? Sounds sweet to me."

"But if that's the case, why wouldn't a bank around here loan you the money?"

Jack gritted his teeth and a vein in his neck grew visible. "Because bankers tend to be nutless, conservative sacks of crap. They don't have an entrepreneurial bone in their bodies and the fact remains you never know what you're going to run into underground until it hits you in the face. If the geologists are right, I'll be filthy, filthy, *filthy* rich. If they're wrong, the bank will have a gaping hole in the earth to show for the 3 million bucks it lent me and when risks like that go bad, bankers have a tendency to jump off high buildings.

"Hence, the sorry bastards won't loan me any money. Which is a damn shame because even if the wells I drilled ended up as dry holes, at least I would have done the world a favor by reducing the number of bankers polluting its surface by one or two."

Rikki chuckled softly. "Bitter?"

"Just a little."

Turning her head slightly, Rikki stared out the window overlooking the courthouse parking lot. A pair of elderly women wearing sweatpants and lightweight jackets strolled across the lot, wearing guilty grins as if they were eagerly engaged in some juicy gossip.

"So what are you going to do?" she asked.

Jack grimaced. "My instinct is to say I'm willing to listen and see what else they have to say. I hate the thought of bringing outsiders into the company, but I don't think I have a choice."

Rikki nodded sympathetically. "It doesn't hurt to listen. If they're serious, they can put together a formal contract and I'll look it over. In the meantime, we still need to finish these discovery responses."

McCallen's nose crinkled as he sat back down at the conference table. "Bluck," he declared. By his tone, the sentiment came straight from his heart.

CHAPTER 22

PLEASANTS COUNTY, WEST VIRGINIA
SUNDAY, NOVEMBER 16, 9:45 P.M.

Leaning toward the monitor with his hand cupping his mouth, Jack scanned yet another article on Petromica. Printouts of news articles and reports culled from the web were stacked beside him. Everything he found corroborated the picture Alex Beria had painted in his email.

Beria himself was a mystery, however. Petromica's website had no information on the man and a Google search yielded little. One guy by that name participated in a marathon in Shreveport, Louisiana five years ago. An undergrad at North Carolina State with the same name blogged about things only an undergrad would care about. Lots of partial hits that looked both inaccurate and irrelevant (e.g., "**alex** herbal Viagra tits **beria**".) But nothing jumped out and told Jack, "This is the guy you're looking for."

The office was dark aside from the monitor and a small lamp. As Jack returned to Petromica's homepage, he suddenly felt two warm hands brush against both sides of his neck.

"The kids are asleep," Tabatha whispered sultrily, gently massaging his shoulders and neck. "Why don't you come to bed, too?"

Staring up at her, he was struck by how beautiful she appeared in the dim light. Her blue eyes sparkled and her come-hither smile was loving and serene. She bore no resemblance to the combative, spiteful woman who spewed such venom at him just a week earlier, and he struggled once again to reconcile those polar-opposite images.

Jack often wondered if his wife was bipolar or had multiple personalities. He had no other explanation for her bewildering, wildly-fluctuating behavior. Her emotions seemed to turn as violently as the weather in June, when a warm sunny day could be suddenly chased away by the blackening skies and howling winds of an afternoon thunderstorm.

Unlike the weather, however, no barometer could predict when Tabatha's emotional pressure would spike, leaving a wake of destruction in its path. And when that happened it was impossible to secure shelter from the storms that arose, breeding tornados that honed in on him, plucked him up and hurled him around helplessly in their wake.

As her hands kneaded into his tightened muscles, those turbulent thoughts dissipated and his stress evaporated. Closing his eyes, he relaxed and took a deep breath. The unmistakable floral aroma of Tabatha's perfume wafted into his brain, subtly stirring his passions and putting a grin on his face.

"I'd love to, but I can't," Jack replied. "I really need to get some work done tonight."

Tabatha stuck out her lower lip and playfully feigned sadness. "Are you sure? You have something more important to do than *me?*" Batting her eyelids, she ran the fingernails of her left hand along the side of Jack's neck, causing goose bumps to arise on his skin, spreading up to his scalp and down his back.

Jack debated how much information he should share with Tabatha. But the smell of her perfume, the feel of her touch, the echo of her seductive words in his head, and the love and longing he felt in his heart brushed aside his concerns. "I'm doing some research on a company that wants to invest in McCallen Resources." The words sounded surreal to him.

Tabatha abruptly stopped rubbing his neck. "Oh, really?" Resuming the massage, she asked, "When did this happen?"

Jack remained adrift in pleasant sensations. "I received their email this morning."

Tabatha gazed over Jack's head at the monitor. "What company? And what kind of an investment do they want to make?"

"It's called Petromica. They're out of the Bahamas. Nothing concrete yet, but if things pan out, they might invest the kind of cash we need to drill horizontal wells into the Marcellus."

Tabatha gasped. "*Wells? Plural?* I thought those cost millions of dollars each!"

Savoring the massage, Jack's eyelids remained closed. "Yep. Three mil a piece."

"Oh, honey! That's wonderful!" She leaned down, threw her arms around his neck and planted a wet kiss on his cheek.

Her reaction shook Jack from his dreamlike state. Wriggling free, he swung his chair around to face her. "Now hold your horses! There's no contract yet and a deal this big could get spiked by all kinds of little things. So don't go counting your chickens just yet."

Jack watched as anger momentarily flared in his wife's eyes. But her tranquility re-emerged, combined now with an air of giddiness. "Okay, okay. But I can't help being excited. And I just *know* you'll find a way to make this deal happen, baby. I just know it!"

McCallen snorted. "Oh, really? Just a few days ago, you said I wasn't man enough to take care of my family."

Tabatha's lips tightened. Squatting down so that their faces were on the same level, she ran her fingers along his jaw line and kissed him softly on the lips, dropping her gaze. "I am *soooooooo* sorry." After a few moments of silence, she raised her head and looked him square in the eyes. "Why don't we go upstairs and you can show me how wrong I was."

Taking his hand in hers, she slowly pulled her five-feet-ten frame erect. Never breaking eye contact, Jack could feel her simply *willing* him to rise from his chair. His pride screamed at him to defy Tabatha's wishes, but his love for her begged him to accept her apparent change of heart at face value.

It felt like an out-of-body experience seconds later, when Jack stood and followed her to their bedroom. He was an extremely proud man, but at the moment of truth in this battle between his strongest passions, it was love that carried the day.

CHAPTER 23

ST. MARYS, PLEASANTS COUNTY, WEST VIRGINIA
MONDAY, NOVEMBER 17, 7:05 A.M.

After another morning bout with the treadmill, Rikki poured fresh coffee into her favorite porcelain mug, mixing in cream and sugar. Mug in hand, she trudged through the dining room and into her office, where a twenty-five inch television was already tuned to CNN.

"The eyes of the world are turned to Williamson, West Virginia, today," an attractive Asian woman in her mid-thirties declared. She stood beneath an umbrella with the now famous boxy-looking courthouse rising behind her. "At one o'clock, the Mingo County Commission will convene to conclude its post-election canvass and determine whether Governor Royal retains his slim lead in this state, which now stands at only 140 votes."

The glorious weather from the previous day seemed a distant memory. Rikki peered through her open blinds and the dark, gloomy-looking images being broadcast from Williamson were duplicated here. Situated atop a hill overlooking a bend in the Ohio River, the view from her house generally was quite pleasant. But not today. Placing her palm on the window pane brought a cold sensation that made her scowl.

"At issue here are the memory cards from nine voting machines that apparently malfunctioned on Election Night. Sources from both campaigns say they expect the legal wrangling to continue *regardless* of the Commission's decision this afternoon. But according to CNN's legal experts, the future landscape will be framed by this vote because it will determine which side gets to defend its margin of victory, and which side has to bear the burden of proof when this battle shifts to the courts."

Rikki muted the television and focused on her email. The first message that grabbed her attention was sent by Jack an hour ago.

Sheez! He was up and at 'em awfully early this morning!

Re: Partnership Opportunity
From: Jack@mccallenresources.com
To: alex.beria@petromica.com
bcc: OGMLawyer@hotmail.com
Date: Mon, 17 Nov 5:53 am

Dear Mr. Beria,

Thank you for your recent email.

Based on my initial research, I agree that Petromica and McCallen Resources appear to be a good match. My company has the leasehold assets, combined with over fifty years of on-the-ground experience in West Virginia and Ohio, which would assist your company in expanding into Appalachia. Petromica has the financial wherewithal to help us fully develop the properties we currently have under lease. At first glance, pairing our companies' strengths seems a no-brainer for both firms.

The spreadsheet attached to your email accurately reflects our current financial state. Accordingly, if Petromica remains interested in exploring a partnership along the general parameters outlined in your email, I'd be happy to discuss ways we might move forward with such a venture.

Should you desire to discuss this matter in greater detail via telephone, feel free to contact me at the office or on my cell. See the attached vcard for those numbers.

Thanks for your interest in doing business and I look forward to hearing from you.

Very truly yours,

Jack McCallen
Managing Member,
McCallen Resources, LLC

P.S. How long have you been with Petromica? I couldn't find anything about you on the company's website.

Nicely done, Rikki thought to herself. Despite his pressing financial problems, Jack expressed his interest in Petromica's proposal without seeming too eager. Jack sent the email to her via blind carbon copy, so Beria would not know he had involved his attorney so early in the negotiations. All-in-all, a fine performance.

Seeing no other messages of interest, Rikki signed out and headed upstairs toward the shower. So far, this was shaping up to be a very interesting Monday.

CHAPTER 24

VIENNA, VIRGINIA
MONDAY NOVEMBER 17, 8:05 A.M.

Yuri Petrenko reviewed the daily planner on his smartphone. As he took a drink from his cup of steaming hot black tea, he cynically realized all of the tasks cluttering his calendar were best classified under the heading, "Taking Care of Mazniashvili's Shit."

The boss paid him handsomely, however, so Yuri did not complain. But Petrenko did find the sheer *scope* of Mazniashvili's business interests maddening. The man had his finger in everything under the sun and, as his unofficial "fixer," Yuri's energies were necessarily directed across a spectrum of enterprises just as far-ranging.

His phone vibrated and his calendar faded from the screen, replaced by a phone number from the 304 area code.

"Hello?" he asked, recognizing in his own voice the faintest remnant of the Russian accent that once heavily tainted his words. A Bluetooth device was wedged in his mangled left ear, empty space protruding below it where an earlobe should have been.

"Yuri, my friend! It's Dick Bowen here. How's the weather over in D.C.?"

Looking out his living room window, Petrenko saw light gray skies stretching from horizon to horizon over a row of townhouses. His Audi's windshield was covered with beads of water and a fine mist continued falling from the sky. "Shitty. What's up?"

Bowen coughed. "The current project should be completed at half the original estimate. Have your investors wire their money to the account we discussed on Friday."

Yuri manipulated his phone, grumbling beneath his breath. Political code-talk drove him bonkers. Using coded language had been necessary when he ran ops for the Spetsnaz. To communicate otherwise would have subjected him to deadly serious risks like falling into the hands of Chechen rebels.

The mere thought of his two tours in Chechnya made him shudder. Those crazy Muslim bastards were *hardcore*. If a sensitive political communication here in the United States was intercepted by the authorities, he might do a stint in prison for bribery. Probably be deported, too. *Whoopty-friggin-doo.*

If the *Chechens* had intercepted an uncoded message, the repercussions would have been much worse. Being sodomized with a bayonet was just an appetizer on their smorgasbord of torture techniques. Being fed his own testicles after they were pulverized by a sledgehammer (while still in his scrotum, of course) ... Avoiding *that* was worth using code words.

Petrenko shook the image from his mind. "I can do that. But first, our investors need to know their money's not being wasted."

"We still might have to spend the amount we discussed on Friday," Bowen replied. "We don't want to run out of money if our new estimates prove overly optimistic."

Yuri paused, wondering if Bowen was telling him the truth. The boss was not afraid to spend money to accomplish his goals, but he was a stickler when it came to tracking his investments. If Yuri could not account for the money, he knew Mazniashvili's retribution would make the Chechens' treatment of Russian prisoners look like a Sunday School picnic.

"I'll wire the money this morning," Yuri said. "But only after your bank sends me written confirmation the wire is reversible. The funds will be available in that account, but they may not be disbursed without my personal approval."

"What the hell do you mean? You can't do that!"

Yuri took a deep breath, summoning the reserves of patience and willpower that had served him so well in the military. The resolve that helped him learn how to speak English more fluently than most people who learn it as their native tongue. The determination that allowed him to survive the grueling Spetsnaz selection course and all the physical brutality, mental abuse and sleep deprivation it entailed. The patience and stamina required to lie awake, camouflaged in a freezing-ass ditch for almost forty hours, until he finally got the chance to blow out a Chechen rebel commander's brains with one clean shot from his sniper rifle.

"It is *our* money, Mr. Bowen," he said bluntly. "And I'm not going to release it to you carte blanche. Accept our money on our conditions or call someone else who's willing to wire you millions of dollars without strings attached. Your choice."

A full 30 seconds elapsed before Bowen responded. "Fine. I'll have the bank send you a fax. But remember West Virginia is the only state still in play in this election. And if your boy wants to keep Jonathan Royal out of the White House, he better whip out his checkbook."

Yuri smiled. "Mr. Bowen, we are *fully* committed to helping Senator Wilson win West Virginia. Trust me."

CHAPTER 25

MINGO COUNTY COURTHOUSE
WILLIAMSON, MINGO COUNTY, WEST VIRGINIA
MONDAY, NOVEMBER 17, 12:45 P.M.

The demand for seats inside the courtroom was so overwhelming the county staff had worked all weekend trying to fashion a system that would appease as many people as possible. The end result, however, had pleased no one while angering quite a few.

West Virginia media outlets were allotted twenty seats at the canvass, which got the national press corps grumbling about "home cooking." When Williamson's newspaper and AM radio station received two of *those* spots, the rest of the state's media got peeved.

The national TV networks were positioned at the back of the courtroom in a space 15 feet wide by 8 feet deep where they placed two cameras whose video and audio feeds would be shared by the world. Foreign TV reporters, whose viewers were just as interested in the canvass as the American audience, were clustered together in an identical strip of floor space immediately adjacent to their American counterparts. However, that space was occupied by twice as many reporters speaking twenty different languages. Dave had no idea how those people could possibly concentrate with so many conversations taking place in such a small area.

A well-behaved mob of photographers sat and squatted on the floor between the Commission's platform and the tables where the campaigns' lawyers were seated. With their powerful cameras honed in on the platform, the shutterbugs studiously attempted to avoid hindering the lawyers' field of vision while maintaining a clear view of the three commissioners.

Newspaper and magazine reporters, as well as radio journalists, had been assigned all of the seats on the left wall of the courtroom plus many on the right. The remaining fifteen seats were reserved for lucky members of the general public selected in a random drawing the previous night.

Dave glanced down at his watch. It was 12:50 p.m. Ten minutes to go.

"I'll talk to you later," Spence whispered into his cell phone before snapping it shut.

"Who was that?" Dave asked.

"Melissa," Spence replied. "My girlfriend."

"You have a *girlfriend?*" Dave deadpanned.

Spence looked wounded. "I've been known to be popular with the ladies," he blurted.

Dave laughed. "Must not be much competition around here."

Realizing his leg was being pulled, Spence's face relaxed. "Ha ha ha. Very funny."

Ten minutes later, the three commissioners took their places on the platform. Sitting in the middle of the table, Mark Monroe banged his gavel three times. "I hereby call this meeting of the Mingo County Commission, sitting as a Board of Canvassers, to order. Madam Clerk, will you please call the roll?"

Sitting at a small clerical desk at the far right end of the platform, the County Clerk stood up, holding a yellow legal pad. "Commissioner Monroe?"

"Here," he quickly answered.

"Commissioner Thompson?"

Staring out over the courtroom, Ruth Thompson looked petrified and her eyelids twitched. "Here," she responded.

Well, that sounded hesitant, Dave thought. *God only knows how she's going to vote.*

The Clerk scribbled on her pad. "Commissioner Warner?"

Pete Warner, the Democrat who not-so-secretly supported Governor Royal's campaign, cleared his throat. "Present," he replied loudly.

"All three members of the Commission being present, we have a quorum," the Clerk declared and sat down.

"Ladies and gentlemen, my name is Mark Monroe, and I am the President of the Mingo County Commission. I want to thank everyone for their patience this afternoon. We're running behind schedule and I apologize for the delay."

As Monroe continued talking, Dave's attention drifted away. He felt sure the hearing itself would be brief as things could only unfold a few ways. First of all, Monroe personally could not advance any motions during the canvass because he was serving as the Commission's presiding officer. He could *second* a motion to use the backup data to calculate vote totals cast on the disputed machines, but he could not put such a motion on the table. Pete Warner opposed taking that route, so if any such motion would be made, Ruth Thompson was the only person who could do it.

On the other hand, Warner tended to move quickly and aggressively when the Commission was divided on an issue. Under such circumstances, he almost habitually threw a motion on the table hoping Ruth Thompson would second it, because when Warner was at odds with another commissioner, it was usually Monroe.

Warner's voice interrupted Dave's train of thought. "We've gone over this repeatedly," he said, leaning forward with his forearms resting on the desk. "Both sides have their points, but there's no point talking this thing to death. I've been a Democrat my whole life, but I don't buy the argument that the results we got on Election Night aren't any good because these memory cards aren't working now. That doesn't explain why no malfunctions were detected on Election Day. If the cards weren't doing what they were supposed to do, the vendor should have found those problems and alerted us. They didn't.

"Thus, despite my loyalty to my party, my constitutional duty requires me to move that we accept the initial returns reported on those machines and have the final results of the county's canvass tabulated on that basis."

Dave watched the audience literally turn its attention toward Ruth Thompson. She scanned the courtroom and then Dave suddenly found himself locking eyes with her. Leaning back in his chair with his arms folded across his chest and his legs kicked out in front of him, Dave smiled peacefully.

Vote whichever way you think the law requires, he mentally willed the Commission's swing vote. *If God desires it, Governor Royal will win the White House. If not, he won't.*

Dave thought he saw the woman nod. Then she bucked herself up in her chair and said, "I second that motion."

The audience began to hum as it processed her action. Dave felt as if the weight of the world had been lifted from his shoulders. Commissioner Monroe's mouth hung open beneath his moustache and his eyes looked glassy. Ten seconds later he still had not uttered a word.

"I believe the motion has been made and properly seconded," Pete Warner noted. "Will the chair call for a vote on the motion?"

Monroe whirled to face Warner. Ten more seconds elapsed. Then he exhaled softly and rotated his chair ninety degrees to the right, facing the audience. "The motion has been duly made and seconded. All those in favor will signify by saying 'Aye.'"

"Aye," Warner and Thompson declared in unison.

"All those opposed to the motion will signify by saying, 'No,'" Monroe continued. "No. By a vote of two-to-one, the motion carries. The county's canvass will include the initial returns reported by the Gilbert and Matewan precincts, including those from the nine machines with malfunctioning memory cards. Madam Clerk, please calculate our final results on that basis."

The Clerk nodded curtly, rose from her chair and exited the room. For three long minutes, the Commissioners sat silently while the audience murmured to one another in excited but hushed tones and reporters whispered into their microphones.

Finally, the Clerk returned, holding a thin document. Clearing her throat, she spoke into her microphone. "The official general election results are as follows: For president and vice president, 5,886 votes for Senator Wilson and Governor Vincent; 5,107 votes for Governor Royal and Senator Johnstone; 28 votes for the Libertarian nominees and one write-in vote.

"For United States Senator, there were...."

The Clerk continued announcing the results, but the audience was already filing out of the courtroom. A few local Democrats scowled, shaking their heads in disgust.

Monroe banged his gavel once, returning Dave's attention to the platform. "You've heard the final election results," he announced gruffly. "Does anyone have a motion to make?"

Warner said, "I move that the Commission declare these figures to be the official results of the general election, thereby concluding our work as the Board of Canvassers."

"Subject to the right of any candidate to request a recount," Monroe interjected. "Correct?"

Warner's jaw clenched. "Correct. Although I don't see what purpose would be served by having the machines count those ballots again."

The blank look on Monroe's face reminded Dave of an old Hollywood western card shark. Whatever his cards were, they were held close to his chest.

"I just want to make sure we do everything by the book," Monroe replied. "The statute says candidates have 48 hours to decide if they want a recount, and we can't certify the results until then. That's all I'm saying."

"So moved," Ruth said.

"And seconded," Monroe added. "All those in favor?"

"Aye," all three Commissioners declared.

"The motion carries. The Mingo County Commission sitting as a Board of Canvassers will stand adjourned until we reconvene on Friday, November 21st at 9 a.m. for the purpose of certifying the results of the election."

Monroe pounded the gavel three times, pushed his chair away from the desk and stormed toward the exit. Leaning down toward Ruth Thompson as he passed, Monroe's voice was almost inaudible over the P.A. system.

But if Dave's lip-reading was accurate, he would have sworn the man had growled, "You're gonna regret screwing the party like this, I promise."

CHAPTER 26

RALEIGH, NORTH CAROLINA
MONDAY, NOVEMBER 17, 10:30 P.M.

Dave stared vapidly at the logs crackling before him. An icy bottle of Yuengling sat on the table between him and Jonathan Royal, the current occupant of this fine governor's mansion.

Royal had installed the small fire pit soon after taking office nearly eight years earlier. Traditionalists denounced the move, arguing the fire pit clashed with the Victorian ambience of the

Executive Mansion's Southern Garden. A few architecture professors accused him of insufficiently revering the building's history, sniffling that such a trait might bode ill for his prospects in office, when he would have to *compromise* with those who opposed his positions.

Royal gave not a damn about such criticisms. It was *his* house, he argued. If he had to live in the place, he was going to enjoy it. Plus, the fire pit was removable and if the next occupant of the mansion didn't like it, he (or she) could get rid of it.

For the next two months, regardless of the results of the election, Royal could satiate his desire to unwind by the fire at the end of the day. And on a clear, beautiful night like this one, with a cold beer in one hand and a fine cigar in the other, Dave was not inclined to argue with the man's thought process.

"How ya like that stogie?" The fire's glow danced along Royal's face as he awaited an answer. In the distance, strolling atop the red brick wall surrounding the garden, a Secret Service agent aimed to make sure no one offed the candidate.

Holding the cigar lightly, Dave blew out a plume of smoke and gazed appreciatively at the cigar's label. "Cohiba Sublimes. I'm sure some of our friends in South Florida would argue we shouldn't be propping up Cuba's current regime by spending money on these things."

Royal chuckled. "Probably. But what's the point in being President if you can't smoke Cubans every now and then?"

"True, but we're not home free yet. I feel better about our chances now, though I have to admit that when the time came for Ruth to vote today, it took everything I had to smile and look relaxed. Until she actually said, 'I second that motion,' I was scared shitless."

Royal laughed and slapped Dave on the back. "Ain't nothing wrong with that, Hoss. Woody Allen once said 'Ninety percent of success is just showing up.' But personally, I'd say the key is finding that delicate balance between being *gutsy* enough to take risks when opportunity knocks and being *smart* enough to know when it's time to be scared."

Dave smiled and nodded, but said nothing. Staring into the fire, he took a swig of his beer and subconsciously placed the half-empty bottle back down on the table.

Royal looked at his confidant studiously. "So tell me, Dave: Once this election is over, are you finally going to buckle down and find yourself a good woman?"

Dave kept staring at the logs. Wayward pinpoints of brilliant white light flickered and arced away from the fire as logs crackled and popped in the heat. The air was saturated with the smell of burning pine logs mixed with the sweet, pungent aroma of the Cohibas.

"You know," Dave began. "I think I'm in a pretty good place right now. I've accepted the fact that marrying Krista was a piss-poor decision, and getting divorced was the best thing for me under the circumstances."

"Especially before you had any kids," Royal interjected.

Dave turned his face to the governor. "No doubt. But 'finding a good woman' isn't at the top of my priority list right now. Don't get me wrong: I'd be *thrilled* if it happened. But when it comes to women, I've spent most of my life trying to jam square pegs into a triangular hole, and I figure the best thing I can do is to just let things ride for a while.

"If it's meant to be, it's meant to be," he continued. "As hokey as it might sound, I really do believe God has a plan for me. Maybe next year, I'll fall head over in heels in love with some amazing woman who will birth me a big-headed kid destined to cure cancer. But I could just as easily get flattened by an eighteen-wheeler tomorrow."

Dave paused long enough to take another drink of Yuengling. "Who knows? I don't have a crystal ball. All I can say for sure is I'm damn tired of bashing my skull against square pegs. But if God ever gets around to introducing me to a woman who's *really* right for me – you know, the kind I can get along with, be myself with, laugh with and grow old with. Well … If He ever decides to do that for me, I'm ready for it."

Royal eyed his friend closely, blowing two smoke rings toward the fire as he mulled it over. "Fair enough. Lord knows you've had enough bad women in your life over the 15 years I've known you. It's a wonder you don't have a big square hole in your forehead." He raised his bottle. "Here's hoping The Man Upstairs sends you a triangular peg soon."

Relieved that their discussion of his love life had ended, Dave clinked bottles with the politician. "I'll *definitely* drink to that."

CHAPTER 27

PLEASANTS COUNTY, WEST VIRGINIA
TUESDAY, NOVEMBER 18, 5:40 P.M.

"No fair!" the dark-haired boy squealed, thrashing his legs around wildly. His neck was twisted at an odd angle as he pawed at his incapacitated left shoulder.

Sprawled on the plush gray carpet, Jack was smiling but panting as he struggled to fight a two-front war with his sons.

He had inflicted a "Vulcan nerve pinch" on his oldest son while restraining his youngest son with his legs in a scissors grip.

"Quit your belly-aching, Logan," Jack said. "You're eight years old. You should know better than let me get a 'Spock Lock' on you!"

Jack's gloating was rudely interrupted by an excruciating blast of pain from his inner thigh. He screamed and opened his legs, thereby releasing the red-headed boy who moments ago seemed safely ensconced. "How many times do I have to tell you, Brandon? No biting!"

The freckle-faced youngster slithered out-of-reach and smiled up at him triumphantly. *If he feels any guilt or remorse for fighting dirty, he sure doesn't look like it,* Jack thought.

The click-clack sound of high heels making contact with ceramic tile approached from the kitchen. Jack looked up and saw Tabatha standing in the doorway, scowling and holding a phone to her ear. "Knock it off! Can't you see I'm on the phone here?"

Jack clamped down on his rising anger. Half out of breath, he took in two lungfuls of air and counted to three. Relinquishing his hard-won grip on Logan's nerve, he patted the boy on the back and sat up Indian-style in the floor. "Sorry, honey. We got a little carried away and I didn't know you had a call."

Tabatha said nothing but the message in her smoldering eyes came across loud and clear: *Keep those kids quiet and don't bother me!*

At that moment, a loud beep echoed from the office. "Okay, boys," Jack said. "Let's take a break while your mom's on the phone. Go clean up your rooms before dinner is ready."

"Oh, *man!*" Brandon complained. "Just when we had you right where we wanted you!"

Jack chuckled. "In your dreams, bucko. Scoot! We'll finish this match later."

The boys glumly trudged away. Tabatha shot Jack one last cold look before turning back into the kitchen. "I'm back," she said into the phone. "I just had to lay down the law a little bit."

Just as Jack thought his anger would boil over, two little arms wrapped around his neck. Peeking over his shoulder, his mischievous younger son was pretending to put him in a sleeper hold. "We're not finished with you yet, old man!"

Jack couldn't help but laugh. He knew which of his two sons would give him ulcers later in life. "Oh, yeah? Well, we'll just see about that."

As the boys ascended the stairs to half-heartedly clean their rooms, Jack tried to ignore his aching joints and rose from the floor. He headed into the office, sat down at the computer and clicked on the new email:

From: alex.beria@petromica.com
To: Jack@mccallenresources.com
Date: Tues, 18 Nov 5:41 pm

Dear Mr. McCallen,

I've relayed your response up the chain of command. I expect they will want you to provide us with some additional information about MR's operations to help us do our due diligence. I'll let you know when I hear more.

I apologize for not getting back to you sooner, but I've been out of the office and tied up in meetings most of the week. I just started working here last week and I'm trying hard to bring myself up to speed on things. Here is a link to Petromica's press release announcing my hiring.

I'll be in touch. As always, if you need to reach me, feel free to call me on my cell.

Sincerely,

Alex Beria
Executive VP, Mergers & Acquisitions
Petromica, LLC

Jack clicked on the link, opening a press release dated November 12 indicating Petromica was pleased to announce Alex Beria had accepted a position with its mergers & acquisitions department. "Mr. Beria brings a wealth of experience to the table, having previously held leadership positions with several Fortune 500 companies. He will primarily work at the firm's new headquarters for North American operations located in Reston, Virginia, as we seek to expand our corporate footprint into new regions."

A small glamour-style photo depicting the company's new hire was included in the release. His face was positioned so that the right side of his head was most prominently featured, and Jack was immediately taken aback by the jarring whiteness of his toothy smile. His eyes looked to be blue, but the picture was small. He had high cheekbones, a strong jawline and his blond hair was cut short and neatly trimmed.

After reviewing the press release once more, Jack fired out a short response to Beria and forwarded it to Rikki, along with the simple note, "FYI."

The clock on Jack's computer showed it was almost six. Shocked the boys weren't hungry yet, he leapt up and headed for the kitchen, hoping Tabatha had whipped something together for dinner.

Much to his chagrin, his wife was sitting on the couch in the living room, still gabbing on her cell phone. Gingerly approaching her, he mouthed, "What's for dinner?"

Tabatha scowled and tilted the phone away from her mouth. "Can't you see I'm *busy* here? Your hands aren't broken. Fix it yourself."

Jack felt the sudden urge to rip the phone out of her hands and punch her in the face. But remembering his two sons were upstairs helped him resist that impulse. Gritting his teeth, he stormed into the kitchen and tore open the refrigerator door, looking for something he could quickly heat up to feed the family.

As his eyes scanned the fridge shelves, his mind tried to ascertain why he would continue living like this, never knowing with which of his wife's personalities he would have to deal from one day to the next.

CHAPTER 28

McLEAN, VIRGINIA
TUESDAY, NOVEMBER 18, 6:45 P.M.

Senator Wilson's formal dining room was silent as the eight people in attendance waited for someone to take the lead. Although that prerogative belonged to the Senator, Luke Vincent (and everyone else) knew she preferred to ask questions, listen to her advisors' opinions and formulate her own thoughts before asserting control of such meetings.

"Let's get the lawyer on the phone," the campaign chairman said, asserting *de facto* control over the discussion. Several people around the oval mahogany table nodded, including Wilson. Thus, the meeting began.

A black phone sat at the center of the table. The campaign chairman sat directly across the table from Vincent and Bowen, and he activated the speakerphone and dialed the number.

Two rings later, a woman picked up the line. "Hello?"

"Susan!" the campaign chairman chirped. "We're all here. How are you doing?"

"I'm well," Susan Mathis, the campaign's lead attorney in West Virginia, replied. "Still irritated about how things went in Williamson yesterday, but I'm sure we all are."

"Well that's what we want to discuss. To see what we can do to turn things around there."

"Are we out of luck in the other close states?" the woman asked.

"Yes," the campaign chairman answered. "Our only hope of winning the election now is to find a way to win West Virginia."

Mathis paused. "I understand. So what do you need from me?"

"Susan, Tyson Vasquez is here with us. You know he's been overseeing our activities in West Virginia, so I'll let him take over. Tyson?"

Vasquez was one of Wilson's closest advisors. A former congressman from California, Vincent knew the man had made a fortune in the private sector after leaving office by working for a telecom company whose initiatives he had supported while in Congress. His dark complexion and thick mane of coal black hair reflected his Hispanic heritage. Although relatively short at five-feet-seven, he was phenomenally photogenic, having been named to one popular magazine's Most Beautiful Americans list three years running.

Vasquez scooted closer to the table and leaned toward the speakerphone. "Hey, Susan, this is Tyson here. Can you hear me?"

"Hi, Tyson. I can hear you just fine."

"Good. As you know, we filed recount requests with every other county in the state. Those requests were filed within 48 hours after the counties' canvasses ended, as required by statute, and you need to file one in Mingo County no later than noon tomorrow."

"We've already turned it in. We didn't want to take any chances with it."

Vasquez raised his bottled water and took a drink. "Excellent. We don't want to make the same mistakes Al Gore made in Florida back in 2000."

"What do you mean?" Mathis asked.

Vasquez glanced over at the short, bespectacled man with a receding gray hair line who was sitting to his left. "I'll let Evan Rothman explain it. He's a professor at Georgetown's law school and our general counsel. He's also the guy who'll argue this case in front of the Supreme Court if it ends up there."

Rothman cleared his throat. "Good evening, Susan. We requested recounts in every county in the state because we want to follow Bush v. Gore as closely as possible. There were two main reasons why the Supreme Court overturned Florida's recount procedures in 2000:

"First, the Court felt there wasn't any *uniformity* in Florida's recount procedures, which varied widely from county-to-county, and that raised the possibility some citizens' votes were being treated differently than others in violation of the Equal Protection Clause.

"Secondly, the Court bluntly noted that individual American citizens do not have a constitutional right to vote in presidential elections. Under Article Two, Section One of the Constitution, it's the individual *states* that are empowered to *appoint* the 'Electors' whose ballots actually determine who wins the presidential election."

"The Electoral College," Mathis interjected.

"Precisely. The Electors meet in their individual states on the first Monday following the second Wednesday in December to cast ballots for the offices of President and Vice-President. In Bush v. Gore, the Supreme Court said the Florida recounts could not be wrapped up in time for the state's Electors to cast ballots in the Electoral College. Or, more specifically, no later than six days before the Electoral College was scheduled to convene that year."

"I remember that," Mathis said. "It had something to do with a 'safe harbor' provision in federal law."

"Yes," Rothman replied. "That would be Title Three, Section Five of the U.S. Code. The Safe Harbor Provision notes that although the constitution vests each individual *state* with the authority to determine how its votes in the Electoral College will be cast, the states must make that determination no later than six days before the Electoral College meets. If a state's election procedures aren't completed by that deadline, the state runs the risk of losing its right to cast ballots in the Electoral College altogether."

"Wow," Dick Bowen blurted. Senator Wilson and her husband both shot him disapproving looks, and he meekly raised his hand and grimaced in apology.

"I see," Mathis said. "So when does the deadline fall this year?"

Rothman peered down and ran his finger along his notes. "The Electoral College ballots will be cast on Monday, December 15th. That means the deadline for state election law contests to be concluded is Tuesday, December 9th."

"That's exactly three weeks from today," Wilson observed.

"Not a lot of time," Rothman conceded. "So we have to make sure the procedures we follow in challenging the results in West Virginia are both *uniform* throughout the state and *completed* within the next 21 days."

The room was silent for about ten seconds until Susan Mathis's voice emanated from the speakerphone. "So whatever we decide to do, we have to do it quickly."

"Yes," the campaign chairman said. "And since you're our expert on West Virginia's election laws, can you tell us what happens now?"

"Basically, every county's recount must be conducted in accordance with the Secretary of State's regulations. Tyson has assigned lawyers to work in every county courthouse during the recount just like the canvasses. If they think a county commission is not following those procedures, they will immediately call the Secretary of State's office to rectify the situation.

"In order to impose some sort of order on this process," she continued. "The Secretary of State has asked all 55 counties to commence their recounts next Monday the 24th. It is possible recounts have been requested in other races on the ballot, but this process will be focused on the presidential race."

There was a brief pause on the lawyer's end of the line. Vincent figured she was flipping through her papers or getting something to drink. In either event, Mathis picked up where she left off. "Each county's recount will be conducted by teams of two people – one Democrat, one Republican – assigned by the County Clerk. Aside from two counties that still use paper ballots, the other counties all use either optical scan ballots or direct-recording electronic voting machines, which are known as 'DRE' machines for short."

"I'm familiar with optical scan ballots," the nominee interrupted. "That's where you shade in circles like on the old SAT exams. But what exactly are these DRE machines?"

"DRE machines are computerized systems that typically use touchscreen monitors to 'directly' record a person's ballot electronically," Mathis replied. "Instead of using a computer to interpret optical scan ballots and tabulate the votes, a DRE machine cuts out the middle man by immediately processing and storing the votes on the machine's hard drive or memory card."

"Ah," Senator Wilson said, "that's why there was such a stink about the memory cards in Mingo County. Go on."

"Thank you, Senator. So recognizing that 53 of West Virginia's 55 counties use some sort of machine to tabulate their votes, the recount will essentially consist of these teams of two people hand counting the ballots in 5 percent of each county's precincts."

"Optical scan ballots are one thing, but how can you *hand count* votes that are directly recorded onto a machine's hard drive?" Vincent asked.

"You can't," Mathis conceded. "Not exactly, anyway. The law requires touchscreen machines to be equipped with what is called a 'voter verified paper audit trail' or VVPAT for short. Theoretically, every button pushed on the touchscreen while the voter is standing in the booth is printed on a roll of paper inside the machine that looks like what's used in cash registers. When one person finishes voting and presses a button on the touchscreen to submit their ballot, two things happen: One, the data reflecting that person's ballot is imprinted on the machine's memory card. Secondly, the VVPAT is imprinted with a heading that reads 'End of Ballot' before it rolls forward in preparation for the next voter to use the machine."

Senator Wilson's eyebrows creased. "What if a voter presses a button to vote for one candidate and then changes their mind? Wouldn't that mess things up?"

"It's not supposed to," Mathis replied. "The VVPAT would show the voter canceled his first action. Plus the digital data isn't imprinted to the memory card until the voter goes through the entire ballot and *confirms* they want to 'drop their ballot in the box' so to speak."

"Regardless, I still don't understand what a recount of the data on those memory cards is going to accomplish," Governor Vincent reiterated.

Mathis sighed loudly. "Mister Governor," she said slowly. "The recount does not involve the data on the memory cards at all. Instead, the statute calls for the teams to hand-count the individual ballots as they are printed sequentially on the *paper trail.*"

"Ah! That makes more sense. But what happens if the figures reflected on the paper trail don't match up with the computer's calculations that were printed on Election Night?"

"By law, the county would use the paper trail recount figures in its final returns. The calculations printed on Election Night would be thrown out."

Governor Vincent watched Tyson Vasquez lock eyes with Bowen and nod his head once. Bowen smirked and nodded in return.

"So how do the counties decide which precincts are recounted?" Wilson asked.

"It's totally random. Basically, they throw the precincts into a big hat, pull out a number of slips which equals 5 percent of the total precincts in the county and use those precincts for the recount."

"But what about the allegations that African American voters were intimidated into staying away from the polls in certain parts of West Virginia?" Senator Wilson asked. "How does that factor into the process?"

"Unfortunately, it doesn't. Not at this stage, anyway. During the recount, county commissions can only consider evidence 'obtainable from the viewing of the election material as it exists or from relevant evidence from the election commissioners, poll clerks or other persons present at the election in which the recount is being conducted.' So unless you have poll workers testifying the intimidation occurred, testimony regarding issues like voter fraud or intimidation would only come into play, if at all, after the recount is over during a subsequent procedure known as an election *contest*. But for now, they're irrelevant."

"Okay," the campaign chairman said, "we'll take it one step at a time. So for now, we need to focus on the recounts which begin next Monday, correct?"

"Yes," Mathis confirmed.

"Fine. We'll worry about those other issues later. In the meantime, does anyone have any other questions for Susan?"

No one spoke up, and both Senator Wilson and her husband actively shook their heads from side-to-side. "All right, then. Tyson will be in touch with you tomorrow, Susan. Thanks!"

"You're welcome. Call me if you need anything else."

"We will," Wilson said. "Thanks for all your help and keep up the good work."

"Thank you, Senator."

The campaign chairman pressed a button, ending the call. "All right, Tyson. We all know what's going on now. Tell us what you need."

Vasquez tapped his designer pen on the table. "First, we need money to fund this recount. It isn't cheap to pay lawyers to work around the clock in 55 counties."

"Not a problem," the campaign's finance chairman responded. She was a woman in her mid-fifties with a perpetually hard look on her face. "Our base is fired up, and they don't want to lose. Contributions keep pouring in, and West Virginia is where we must focus now."

"Good. Secondly, Mr. Bowen and I need to coordinate some of our more *unconventional* tactics."

"Whoa, whoa, whoa!" Senator Wilson's husband exclaimed. "Stop right there. Melanie, the kids are calling for us upstairs."

"You're right, honey," the nominee replied calmly. "I only have so much time and I must entrust some aspects of this campaign to others. Folks, if you'll excuse us, we'll leave the remaining details in your competent hands."

With that, the senator and her husband rose from the table and left the room without even saying "goodbye" to the others.

"I need to take off, too," the campaign chairman said. Facing the finance chairman and the campaign's general counsel, he added, "I'm heading back to Georgetown, so if you guys want a ride, the bus is leaving."

The law professor and the hard-looking woman stood up and followed the campaign chairman as he passed through the French doors and exited the dining room.

"Personally, I need to hit the head," Governor Vincent added. "Dick, I'll be in the car."

"Gotcha," Bowen responded. "See ya in a few."

The governor patted his advisor on the shoulder as he headed out, closing the doors behind him. "Looks like it's just you and me now," Bowen said to Vasquez.

"What did you expect?" Vasquez quipped bitterly. "Everybody else has their panties in a bunch, worrying about 'plausible deniability.' That just leaves the two of us to get our hands dirty and actually *win* this damn election."

Bowen leaned forward, clasping his bratwurst-looking fingers together like a church steeple on the table in front of him. "Amen, brother. What do you say we get down to business?"

CHAPTER 29

ST. MARYS, PLEASANTS COUNTY, WEST VIRGINIA
WEDNESDAY NOVEMBER 19, 10:00 A.M.

Sitting at a table in front of the judge's dais, Rikki tried to look casual as she glanced over her shoulder at the crowd gathering behind her. Her mother sat directly behind her, wearing a conservative black dress and simple pearl earrings. Watching her mom talk with her aunt and uncle who had flown in from Dallas for the ceremony, Rikki admired how elegant she looked and hoped she would age that well herself.

The courtroom doors swung open, and Sheriff Vaughn sauntered in, clasping a single piece of paper in his right hand. As he approached her desk, Rikki saw an embossed gold seal on the document. Vaughn handed it to Rikki for her inspection. "Here it is. Just as expected."

The document was signed and sealed by the County Clerk, who attested the County Commission had duly appointed her to complete the remaining six weeks of Joe's term as prosecutor. All that remained was for her to take the oath of office.

Rikki smiled, handing the paper back. Vaughn nodded curtly, walked over to the Circuit Clerk's desk, and bent down, whispering something in the woman's ear. The Circuit Clerk grinned and shot Rikki a thumbs up before briskly walking into the Judge's office to let him know everything was ready to go.

Exactly one minute later, the Judge entered the room. The bailiff dutifully directed the audience to stand up, warned them what the judge might do if they misbehaved, articulated a brief invocation of divine blessing on the court and then told them to sit back down.

"Good morning," the Judge opened, a jolly smile on his face. With a gray moustache and largely bald pate, the man looked like he had been born to be a judge (or play one on TV.) "I hear there's something special afoot today."

The Circuit Clerk handed him the appointment. "That's right. The only item on the docket today is the vacancy in the prosecutor's office."

"Very well," the Judge remarked, peering down at the document. "Everything appears to be in order. Rikki ... Would you approach the bench?"

Rikki stood and fastidiously smoothed the front of her sharp-looking gray pantsuit. Satisfied with her appearance, she turned to her mother and motioned for her to stand.

Madhani nodded and rose, holding an old, thick white leather-bound Bible in her hands. Together, the two women walked up to the dais, facing one another. Madhani balanced the

Bible while Rikki rested her left hand on its cover and raised her right hand.

"Sarika Dawn Gudivada," the Judge dramatically intoned. "Do you solemnly swear or affirm that you will support the constitution of the United States and the constitution of the State of West Virginia, and that you will faithfully discharge the duties of the Office of Prosecuting Attorney of Pleasants County, West Virginia, to the best of your skill and judgment?"

"I do."

"Congratulations, Rikki," the Judge declared, extending his right hand. Rikki accepted the handshake and the crowd broke into cheers and applause. Turning away from the bench, the new prosecutor saw her proud mother blinking back tears of joy. Rikki smiled and gave her mom a hug and a peck on the cheek.

"I'm so proud of you, honey," Madhani whispered. "I just wish your father was here."

Rikki rubbed her mother's back softly. "I'm sure he is, Mom. We might not be able to see him, but I'm sure he's here."

Feeling the approach of onlookers, they parted and turned to greet the crowd. Rikki's aunt and uncle were first in line, and she was surprised by the brevity of their congratulations.

Sheriff Vaughn came next. "Looking forward to working with ya, Rikki," he said with a warm smile. Shaking his hand, Rikki remembered to focus on his right eye. Three seconds later, still smiling, he relinquished her hand and walked away, making room for others.

Efficient as always, Rikki noted, suppressing a chuckle as he disappeared into the crowd.

Turning back to greet the next person in line, Rikki's heart skipped a beat. Desperately hoping she didn't look flustered, Rikki put on a smile. "Ellen! So great to see you!"

Ellen Anderson opened her arms and gave Rikki a warm hug. "Congratulations, honey! Everyone's so proud of you. You'll do a wonderful job."

Wrapped in her embrace, Rikki sensed the sincerity in the older woman's words. "Thank you, Ellen. That means a lot to me. It really does."

Ellen stepped back and took a long, admiring look at Rikki. Still holding one of her hands, she gave it a slight tug, but said nothing. Rikki thought the woman was struggling to find the right words to say.

Finally, the words came. "Dave sends his congratulations, too." As the sentence escaped her lips, Rikki saw Ellen's back stiffen. The warmth in her eyes was replaced by anxiety.

Suddenly, a sense of sadness washed over Rikki. *My God. Have I been so cold and unforgiving over the years that this sweet woman — who once was like a second mother to me — is actually afraid of how I'd react to such an innocuous message from her son?*

Rikki sighed. *No matter what transpired between me and Dave, Ellen had nothing to do with it. And she doesn't deserve to be on the receiving end of my unresolved issues.*

Rikki placed her left hand on top of their handshake and looked Ellen square in the eye. "Thank you for passing that along to me. That really means a lot to me, too."

CHAPTER 30

CHARLESTON, WEST VIRGINIA
WEDNESDAY, NOVEMBER 19, 1:45 P.M.

"So what did you find out?" Bowen asked, speaking into his cell phone.

"It pains me to say it," Vasquez replied. "But after talking to Petrenko, you're right."

Bowen nonchalantly shrugged. "I didn't know exactly how many counties used that Cicero system, but I figured it was less than five. Cicero's good software, but it's fairly new. And we West Virginians tend to be a little resistant to change at times."

"But *two* counties?" Vasquez half-shrieked. "Out of the entire fucking state, you're telling me AIS has contracts in only two counties? What the hell?"

"Their main competitor's been doing business here for 30 years, back when everyone used pull-lever systems. They've been greasing the wheels and schmoozing politicians around here for years. They know how to play the game, and if AIS wants to take away that business, they'll have to *fight* for it. And they better pack a lunch."

Vasquez sighed. "I already know all I'll ever care to know about Mingo County. The other county that uses Cicero is Grant County, which I know nothing about, so fill me in on it."

Bowen winced. "Ouch. That's our only other option?"

"Yeah. Why? Is that a bad thing?"

"Well, for starters, it's one of the few counties in the state where registered Republican voters outnumber Democrats."

"You've got to be kidding me," Vasquez responded.

"Nope. Those are some gun-toting, flag-waving people over there, my friend. Royal carried Grant County by a four-to-one margin and all three county commissioners are Republicans."

"Not much chance we'll make headway there, huh?" Vasquez said glumly.

"I wouldn't bet on it," Bowen replied. "The county commission won't be cooperating with us, and if we try to pull too much hanky-panky with the machines behind their backs, they'll drag the U.S. Attorney's Office into it. Lord knows we don't want *those* guys going over things with a fine-toothed comb. They have a tendency to *find* dirt when they go looking for it."

"So we're back to Mingo County. Dear God! That makes me want to hang myself."

"Well, don't go buying rope just yet. Tinkering with memory cards and software code are just new-fangled ways to ... *adjust* an election's results. We still have some old school methods at our disposal."

"Such as?"

"For starters, remember that my good buddy, Sheriff Perkins, is in charge of courthouse security in Mingo County."

"Fair enough," Vasquez admitted. "That could come in handy. What are you thinking?"

"I'm thinking there's fifteen seconds left in the game and we're down by five points. We're all out of timeouts and a field goal ain't gonna help us. It's time to use that sneaky little trick play we talked about last night."

Vasquez grew silent. "That'd be pretty ballsy. Do you think we can pull it off?"

"What do we have to lose?" Bowen shot back. "We know the machines' serial numbers and the precincts where they were used. Hell, they *announced* that information during the canvass to help everyone keep tabs on them! We've claimed the memory cards malfunctioned. If we're gonna lie to win this election, I say we stick to our story and lie *big*."

"All right," Vasquez relented. "I'll get things moving on this front. You handle things on the ground down in that godforsaken hellhole. But just in case those idiots are as worthless as I think, do we have a backup plan?"

"Braxton County still uses paper ballots. The kind where voters actually mark an 'x' beside the names of the candidates they want to vote for. So does Wyoming County."

"Say *what?!* Vasquez asked, incredulous.

"I told you we're resistant to change. And seeing how easy it is for a computer vendor to monkey with election results, who can say those folks are wrong for sticking with paper ballots? People can still manipulate the results, but at least they haven't spent tens of thousands of dollars on computer software and equipment that's just as easy to manipulate but harder to monitor."

"True. But just how many precincts will actually be recounted on Monday?"

"Not many at first," Bowen admitted. "Two precincts in Mingo County initially. Maybe one or two in Braxton. But if we can make up a hundred votes in those two precincts in Mingo, or sixty votes in Braxton, that'll trigger an automatic recount of *every* precinct in those counties."

"That's asking an awful lot, don't you think?"

"That's why I said it's time to lie *big*."

CHAPTER 31

PLEASANTS COUNTY COURTHOUSE
ST. MARYS, PLEASANTS COUNTY, WEST VIRGINIA
WEDNESDAY, NOVEMBER 19, 2:30 P.M.

Less than five hours after taking office, Rikki wondered if she had bitten off more than she could chew.

She had to file three emergency child abuse and neglect petitions within the next 24 hours. Cops kept walking in to discuss cases that had dragged on during Joe's illness. Citizens unhappy with the progress of various law enforcement investigations did likewise. And the county assessor needed help with an ongoing dispute between two brothers over who had inherited their father's property under his recently probated (and hopelessly convoluted) will.

When things finally slowed down, Rikki realized she hadn't checked her email since the previous evening. Whirling her chair 90 degrees, she typed in her password and was aghast to learn she had 50 new unopened messages.

Rikki quickly sorted the messages into two groups: Those that were on fire and those that were not. Seeing a message from Jack caused her to remember (with mortification) that today was their deadline to file discovery responses in the Schoolcraft case. Opening the message, she clicked on the embedded link and hastily reviewed Petromica's press release about Beria's recent hiring. Studying his picture, she noted he was ruggedly handsome though a tad too uptight (*"Nazi-looking"*) for her taste. She saved the photo to her hard drive before turning her attention to their current crisis:

Discovery Responses!!!!
From: OGMLawyer@hotmail.com
To: Jack@mccallenresources.com
Date: Wed, 19 Nov 2:38 pm

Jack,

I got your email from Petromica. Now do me a favor and GET ME THE STUFF I NEED TO FINISH YOUR DISCOVERY RESPONSES!!! :-)

I'm going to ask the other side to give us until the end of the week to turn our answers over, but if they won't give us an extension, you'll need to run whatever documents you have over to me here at the courthouse ASAP, so we can at least get <u>something</u> in the mail to them before the post office closes at 4:30.

Hasta,

Rikki

Immediately after sending the email to Jack, she heard another knock on her door. Looking up, she saw her secretary in the doorway, smiling indulgently. Rikki sighed. "What now, Martha?"

"Delbert Keegan's on the phone. He's upset because his neighbor won't keep his cows fenced in and they're tearing up his property. He says that if somebody doesn't put a stop to it soon, he's 'fixing to go over there and shoot all those damn cows himself.'"

Rikki closed her eyes and dropped her head. "Send the call back, and I'll see if I can get Delbert calmed down."

Martha returned to her desk on the other side of the door. Five seconds later the phone on Rikki's desk rang. The clock on the wall said it was 2:45. Grabbing the phone, she took a deep breath and raised it to her left ear.

"What's this I hear about you threatening to shoot up some cows?" Rikki asked, putting a playful and friendly tone in her voice. "My first day on the job has been rough enough, Delbert, so don't you go causing me any more headaches."

CHAPTER 32

WEST VIRGINIA STATE CAPITOL
CHARLESTON, WEST VIRGINIA
THURSDAY, NOVEMBER 20, 1:05 P.M.

As Governor Vincent reviewed a memo from one of his department heads, his cell phone vibrated. Looked down at the screen, he saw he had a new text message. Using his thumb, he opened the message and noted it was from Tabatha McCallen. His stomach dropped.

"It's been a week since I heard from you," the text message read. "You're making me feel like a whore again."

Vincent's nostrils flared and his mouth tightened. Without taking time to cool down, he blasted on the phone's QWERTY keyboard with his thumb.

"I don't have time for this shit. I have a state to run and I'll contact you when I can."

Vincent sent the message and put the phone down, knowing Tabatha would respond almost immediately. Although he kept staring at the memo, his mind was elsewhere; wondering just how badly she would react to his curt response. When it arrived a minute later, his phone vibrated again and the screen lit up.

"Sorry ur secret little whore has disturbed u, Mr. Governor. By all means, get back to running this shitty state. It's your loss."

The governor pursed his lips and stared into the distance, still gripping the phone tightly. Setting the memo aside, he reclined his chair and silently lamented the poor decisions that had led him to this uncomfortable and dangerous place.

This situation is no longer tenable. So what am I going to do about it?

*   *   *

PLEASANTS COUNTY, WEST VIRGINIA
THURSDAY, NOVEMBER 20, 1:15 P.M.

"That son-of-a-bitch," Tabatha muttered through clenched teeth, staring at her phone hatefully.

"Who's that?" Jack asked.

Tabatha's face shot up and she looked at Jack, wide-eyed. Then the fury faded from her face, replaced with a mask. "Some jackass from American Express. My card was declined at the gas station this morning, and he had the *nerve* to say our credit limit had been cut because we were behind on our payments. Is that true?"

Jack felt his chest tighten. "Probably, honey. I had to let the credit cards slide for a few months to keep a handle on the company's expenses. I'm sorry."

Tabatha squinted her eyes, and Jack braced for another tongue-lashing. But the storm quickly subsided. "That's okay," she said, placing her hand on the door frame. "Once this deal with Petromica goes through, our money problems will be over,

146

won't they?" She tapped on the wood with her red-painted fingernails and gave him an expectant stare.

He swallowed a lump in his throat. "If the Lord's willing and the creek don't rise."

"Good. Then I'll pay off that card and tell them to go fuck themselves."

Jack belly laughed. "Now *that* sounds like my wife! Always ready to even the score."

The statuesque redhead smirked and flitted her eyebrows, then bent down and kissed him on the cheek. "And don't you *ever* forget that." She then wheeled and strolled sensuously through the living room.

Admiring her figure as she walked away, Jack shook his head wearing a half-amused smile. Then he returned to Beria's latest email:

Due Diligence
From: alex.beria@petromica.com
To: Jack@mccallenresources.com
Date: Thurs, 20 Nov 1:12 pm

Dear Mr. McCallen,

As expected, we need more info so our eggheads can do their due diligence. :-) How soon can you get me copies of the last five years' production logs for all your wells? We also need a detailed breakdown of what you've spent the past five years in maintaining and upgrading your well equipment.

If you have any questions, you know how to reach me.

Sincerely,

Alex

Jack cursed under his breath. It was bad enough compiling those records for the wells involved in the Schoolcraft case. *Now I have to do the same thing for all our wells!*

Fortunately, having already sorting through those documents for the Schoolcraft case, Jack thought his staff could gather the additional documentation Beria wanted without too much effort.

McCallen fired off a quick response and got to work.

CHAPTER 33

GAITHERSBURG, MARYLAND
THURSDAY, NOVEMBER 20, 6:30 P.M.

Petrenko stood at the counter, watching workers place two packages inside each of the ten large boxes he had just purchased. He had given them each a hundred dollar tip, and they were carefully encasing the smaller packages in an avalanche of Styrofoam peanuts.

After the large boxes were sealed, Petrenko personally inspected them. They appeared safe. Fully loaded, he lifted one up and estimated it weighed 40 pounds.

"They look good. And you're sure they'll get there tomorrow morning?"

The young man smiled widely. "Damn straight," he said over the register's beeps. "The carrier guarantees delivery by 10:30 in the morning. *Gair-awn-teed.*"

Petrenko extended his credit card. "Very good."

The cashier processed the card and handed it back. "Here's your card, your receipt and your tracking slips."

Petrenko turned toward the door. "Thanks. I'll monitor their progress online."

"You do that. Those packages will be right where you want 'em tomorrow morning."

Petrenko smirked and flashed a thumbs up sign as he walked out the door. A chime announced his departure.

CHAPTER 34

MAGGIE'S DINER
SOUTH WILLIAMSON, KENTUCKY
FRIDAY, NOVEMBER 21, 7:15 A.M.

Bowen gulped black coffee, struggling to wake up. "Why couldn't this guy meet us later in the day?"

"Our schedule's too tight," Sheriff Perkins replied. "He's coming here straight from his shift as is."

Bowen curled his upper lip but said nothing. His back was to the door and Perkins sat across the booth from him. Suddenly, the sheriff stared over his head and gave a quick wave.

A man walked up to their booth. About six feet tall, he wore a brown goatee and tufts of brown hair were visible beneath his baseball cap. Wearing Carhartt coveralls and well-worn steel-toed boots, he lifted his cap and ran his hand through his hair. "Morning, Sheriff."

Perkins scooted toward the inside of the booth. "Good morning, Larry. Care to join us?"

"Sure," the man answered, sitting down next to the aisle.

A waitress approached the booth with an order pad. "What can I get you boys?"

"I'll have the biscuits and gravy," Perkins said.

Bowen's head was bowed as he studied the menu closely. "I'll have the western omelet with wheat toast. Plus an order of home fries."

The waitress scribbled it down. "How 'bout you, Larry?"

Larry absent-mindedly stroked his goatee. "Ham and eggs. Over easy with a side of bacon and hash browns."

"And to drink?"

"A cup of coffee."

The waitress tucked her pen behind her ear. "Coming right up."

Perkins rotated to face Larry slightly. "So how's the power company been treating ya?"

"Can't complain. As far as jobs go, it's a pretty good one."

"Have they said anything about the hearing you have in a few weeks?"

Larry's posture turned rigid. "They don't know what it's about. I told 'em I had to be in court that day, but I didn't tell 'em why. They probably think it's another child custody hearing. God knows I've had enough of them over the years."

The sheriff chuckled lightly. "Makes sense. But don't ya think they'll cut ya loose if ya get another DUI conviction? That would make your third."

Larry winced. "If my lawyer can't get me out of that DUI, my goose is *cooked*. Without a driver's license, I can't drive the company's truck. They'd *have* to shitcan me."

Perkins clucked sympathetically. "Sorry to hear that. Your lawyer called me and asked me to talk to the prosecutor for ya. You know, to see if we could work something out so you wouldn't lose your job, since good-paying jobs like that are hard to come by around here."

"I know," Larry grumbled. "He said you couldn't help me 'cause I blew a point one eight on the breathalyzer."

"That's aggravated DUI, Larry," Perkins emphasized. "Plus, you're a repeat offender! MADD would crucify my ass if I let you off the hook."

The man slumped back in the booth. "I know, I know. It's my own damn fault. I was out with my buddies, shooting pool and got to feeling sorry for myself about the way my ex-wife keeps my kids away from me. The next thing you know, I'm plastered and too damn pigheaded to let anybody drive me home." Larry sighed and shook his head sadly. "Like I said, it's my own damn fault. I'll live with the consequences. But thanks for thinking about it, anyway. I appreciate it."

Perkins glanced at Bowen, who shot him a quick nod. "Well, what would ya say if I told ya there *might* be a way to make that DUI go away?"

Larry's posture straightened. "I'd ask whose dick I have to suck to make it happen. Yours? *His?*" He motioned toward Bowen with his head. "Fuck, let's go out back and you can *both* whip 'em out. I don't give a shit. I need my job!"

The man bit off his next thought as the waitress walked up with a tray. She distributed their plates and drinks and scurried away.

"Relax," Perkins said. "No dick-sucking required. We just need a little favor this weekend. About 11:30 on Saturday night to be precise."

"What do you need me to do? I mean, I was ready to start slobbing on your knobs, man. Short of killing somebody, there's not much I wouldn't do."

The sheriff shot Bowen a look that seemed to say, *It's your call.*

The lobbyist folded his thick fingers together and leaned forward. "We only need about two hours of your time. And after you've done your part, Sheriff Perkins will give you *this* on Monday."

On cue, Perkins slid a piece of paper in front of Larry. Reading the document, his face lit into a smile that ran from ear to ear.

"Exactly what do ya'll need me to do?"

CHAPTER 35

WASHINGTON, D.C.
FRIDAY, NOVEMBER 21, 9:45 A.M.

"That sounds great," Tyson Vasquez exclaimed, flashing Petrenko a thumbs up sign. The Russian was reading the newspaper and barely paying attention to the former congressman's phone conversation. Petrenko half-heartedly returned the gesture without looking up.

Vasquez hung up. "So far, so good. We're just waiting for the shipment to arrive."

Petrenko kept reading the paper. "It will be there before 10:30. *Gair-awn-teed.*" He smirked, mimicking the shipping clerk's pronunciation to a tee.

"Have you checked the tracking numbers?" Vasquez asked.

The Russian exhaled and put the paper aside. "The boxes are heading there as we speak."

Vasquez nervously tapped one finger on the desk. "All we can do now is wait, huh?"

Petrenko unfolded the newspaper again, scanning the sports section for another interesting read. "That's what I told you an hour ago."

CHARLESTON CIVIC CENTER
CHARLESTON, WEST VIRGINIA
FRIDAY, NOVEMBER 21, 10:05 A.M.

Dave stood behind the podium, staring out at the rows of tables arrayed horizontally across the room. With his thumb drive connected to the ballroom's multimedia system, he quickly flashed through the PowerPoint overview of the state's recount procedures.

"How does it look from back there?" he called.

Spence sat in the back of the room, squinting. "A little dark. It's hard to see."

Dave's lips tightened. "That's what I was afraid of. What can we do to fix it?"

"I'll see if they have a better projector around here."

"Whatever you have to do, jump on it. Even if we have to go out and buy one, everyone must be able to follow along when we do this for real tomorrow."

Spence jotted a note and sighed. "Is all this really *necessary*? I mean, bringing in reps from the Republican Executive Committee in every county? Not to mention an army of lawyers. Putting them up in hotels, feeding them, renting this place ... It must cost a fortune."

"Think about it this way," Dave explained. "Between the campaigns and the various interest groups trying to influence the outcome, more than 2 *billion* dollars has been spent on this race so far. That's 'billion' with a 'b.' Now it all boils down to who wins West Virginia. We're up a 140 votes out of 800,000 overall, and literally *every single vote counts*. Our people on these recount teams need to understand the law and be ready to fight like hell every chance they get to pick up a vote for us.

"I don't know about you, but I haven't spent the past two years of my life trying to get Jonathan Royal elected president, just to watch my work go spinning down the crapper because some yahoo in Welch, Weirton, Wellsburg, West Union or Webster Springs was asleep at the wheel when this recount starts on Monday."

Spence grinned mischievously. "What about Weston or Wheeling?"

"There too," Dave retorted. "And of course, nowhere is more important than your lovely hometown of Williamson."

Spence's grin vanished. "Don't remind me. I get ulcers thinking about what they might try to pull down there."

"Me, too."

MINGO COUNTY COURTHOUSE
WILLIAMSON, WEST VIRGINIA
FRIDAY NOVEMBER 21, 10:40 A.M.

"What do we have here, Sheriff?" Mark Monroe asked.

Perkins signed the digital clipboard and handed it back to the delivery driver. "That grant came through. These are ten new dashboard video camera systems for our deputies' cruisers."

Monroe's brow furrowed. "I don't remember hearing anything about a grant."

Deputies clad in black uniforms and baseball caps ferried boxes into the courthouse from a delivery van as they spoke. "Just take those up to my office, boys," Perkins said. "We'll unpack 'em and start getting them installed this weekend."

He faced Monroe once more. "The Proudfoot Family Foundation started a grant program for local law enforcement. It didn't get much publicity, so not many departments applied for it. Made it a lot easier for us."

Monroe put his hands on his hips and nodded. "Good work, Sheriff. Anything that saves the county money sounds good to me."

"Well, you're looking at 30,000 bucks worth of equipment there. Not bad for just submitting a little paperwork, huh?"

"Not at all. And from the size of those boxes, that's some heavy duty equipment!"

"Only the best for *our* boys," Perkins said. "Why settle for less when they're giving away free money?"

Monroe clapped Perkins on the back. "Like I said, keep up the good work."

A devilish grin crossed the sheriff's face as he watched the commissioner walk away. "Bet on it!"

CHAPTER 36

PLEASANTS COUNTY COURTHOUSE
ST. MARYS, PLEASANTS COUNTY, WEST VIRGINIA
FRIDAY, NOVEMBER 21, 2:30 P.M.

Rikki was reviewing a file when it felt like an earthquake had hit her office. The conference table shook violently and a loud thud reverberated in her ears.

Glancing up, she saw Jack grinning at the end of the table. Two bankers' boxes full of documents jostled atop the conference table in front of him.

"There you go," he proudly declared. "Every damn piece of paper those bottom-dwellers have demanded."

"Congratulations. And you're only two days late."

If Jack detected the sarcasm, he did not show it. Resting his hands on a box, he exhaled. "Man, I'm relieved that's over! One big document search down. One to go."

"What do you mean?"

"My staff still has to dig out the rest of our production logs for Petromica. But it'll be a lot easier now that we've dealt with this crap. We've already found the logs; we just have to get 'em organized and copied."

Rikki pushed her chair back and rotated her body to face him. "How long will that take?"

"I'm going home to work on it this afternoon," he replied. "Then I'm taking the boys to the high school playoff game against Williamstown."

Rikki winced. "Ouch. Are you glutton for punishment or something?"

Jack's eyes narrowed. "Why would you say that?"

"Haven't they beaten our football team like 50 straight years?" she gently asked.

"Ah. You mean *The Curse*. Well, what if this is the year we manage to break it? Don't you want to be able to tell your kids you were there to see it in person?"

"Jack, I don't *have* any kids. And at the rate I'm going, I don't see any coming my way."

McCallen shrugged. "Suit yourself. But don't blame me when you're 60 and those rugrats science helped you squeeze out at 50 think you're lame because you missed out on the end of The Curse."

"Consider yourself absolved," Rikki quipped. "And besides, I have too much stuff to do. I'd planned to review some criminal files this afternoon, but I suppose I'll put that off and switch gears so I can finalize your discovery responses. Since you finally brought me the stuff you were supposed to, that is."

"Thanks, Rikki. You're a lifesaver. Even though you're a Democrat, I don't know what I'd do without you."

"Just doing my job, Jack. Now get out of here and go home so you can get some work done and take your boys to the game tonight."

Jack smiled and walked behind her, heading for the door. As he passed her chair, he bent down and gave her a little peck on the top of her head. "Thanks again. Don't work too hard and get home at a reasonable hour. Everybody needs sleep."

Rikki belly laughed. "Not me, Jack. I'm like *Supergirl* or something."

"Yeah, right," McCallen retorted as he marched toward the exit. "Keep telling yourself that and eventually you're going to crash and burn."

Rikki silently stared at the door for a while before setting aside the burglary file. "Hey, Martha!" she yelled. "Can you bring me our draft discovery responses in the Schoolcraft case? I need to get all this stuff copied and mailed out before the post office closes."

The secretary peeked into the conference room and saw the two boxes on the table. "In less than two hours? You really *do* think you're Supergirl, don't you?"

Rikki snorted, rolling up her sleeves. "You don't think I can do it? Well, just sit back and watch me then!"

CHAPTER 37

VIENNA, VIRGINIA
SATURDAY, NOVEMBER 22, 10:45 A.M.

Yuri Petrenko paced across his living room, pressing his phone up to his non-mangled right ear. ESPN's college football pregame show played in the background on mute. "So is everything a go?" he asked.

"For the most part," Bowen replied. "Perkins got it all loaded in his office. He even shoved a dashboard camera in Pete Warner's face when that turncoat came sniffing around."

Petrenko chuckled softly. "Good, good. Anything else you need from me?"

"You wouldn't happen to have access to a squirrel, would you?"

The Russian stopped dead in his tracks. "A *what?*"

"Never mind," Bowen mumbled, sounding dejected. "We probably couldn't get it here in time, even if you did."

Petrenko shut his eyes and rubbed his forehead. He was becoming convinced these West Virginians were insane. "Why in the world do you need a *squirrel?*"

"Don't worry about it," Bowen said curtly. "I shouldn't have even mentioned it over the phone. I'll take care of it."

Petrenko rolled his eyes and held the phone at arm's length from his mouth, as if fighting the urge to scream. Five seconds and one deep breath later, he said, "Fine. If I stumble across a squirrel, I'll let you know. If you need anything else, call me."

"Ten-four. If all goes well, everything will be taken care of by tomorrow morning."

"Keep me in the loop. And good luck with that whole squirrel thing."

"Thanks. We'll need it."

CHAPTER 38

CHARLESTON CIVIC CENTER
CHARLESTON, WEST VIRGINIA
SATURDAY, NOVEMBER 22, 1:10 P.M.

Two huge screens hung on the wall behind the stage, one on each side of the podium, projecting the red, white and blue Royal/Johnstone campaign logo as GOP activists gathered for the recount training. Standing behind the podium, Dave sensed the crowd was growing agitated. He had waited 10 minutes to accommodate late arrivals, and he knew he could wait no more.

"Okay, folks," he said, adjusting the podium's flexible microphone. "Let's get started. For those who don't know me, I'm David Anderson. I'm with Governor Royal's headquarters, and I'll be coordinating our recount efforts. As you can probably tell from my accent, I was born and bred here in West Virginia. So *please* … Don't look at me like I have three heads just because I work inside the Beltway now."

Dave heard some sporadic chuckles, and that laughter helped him relax. As if on cue, the ballroom doors swung open, and Dave saw a familiar face enter the room.

"Well, well, well," he said with a smirk. "If it isn't my good friend and mentor, Senator Jack McCallen. Glad you could finally join us, Jack."

Hearing his name, Jack froze in place. Dave watched the senator gaze up at the stage, trying to identify who had busted him for showing up late. Meeting his eyes, Jack's startled look transformed into recognition. "Dave Anderson, you son-of-a-gun!" he exclaimed with a beaming smile. "You mean to tell me that *you* are the most qualified man Governor Royal could send to oversee this thing?" He shook his head, feigning disbelief. "Man, we're *really* in trouble now."

Dave laughed. "You don't know the half of it. Good to see you again, Jack. Now, if you'd sit down and at least act like you're going to behave, I'll continue."

Jack side-stepped behind a long row of people, making his way to his seat. "Go ahead."

"Thanks. As I was saying, I'm a state native. And unlike most people from Washington who may tell you, 'I'm here to help,' I really *mean* it."

More laughter met the jibe, a little louder this time. "During this seminar, we'll explain the procedures that are *supposed* to be followed during the recounts. As we all know, *some* of the county clerks around the state – all shifty-eyed Democrats, of course – may try to play loose with the rules if they get a chance. But by-and-large, I think the last thing most people want to happen is for West Virginians to look as stupid as the folks in Florida did back in 2000."

A chorus of vigorous nods followed. "And the best way we can avoid looking like idiots is to avoid *acting* like idiots," Dave said. "That's why the Secretary of State *strongly suggested* that all 55 counties start their recounts on the same day – to give everyone time to become familiar with these procedures.

"That's also why the Secretary of State *strongly suggested* county clerks should work closely with the county chairpersons of both political parties: To make sure the people appointed to work on the recount enjoy broad respect in their communities. People will be less likely to criticize the results if they trust the folks doing the counting, and I think it's in our whole state's best interests for this thing to go off without a hitch."

Dave raised a glass of water to his lips. "But no system is perfect and inevitably there will be some bad apples slip through the cracks. And if you're assigned to work with one of them, you need to understand the rules and fight back when they push the envelope unfairly."

Looking down at the audience, Dave saw a collective sense of determination in their eyes. Although a few seemed distracted, most were focused, and that sight boosted his confidence in Royal's chances for success.

"With that being said, I intend to help this process by doing what folks from D.C. should do more often when they venture outside the Beltway, and that's to know when it's time to *get out of the way*. So let me make way for our top lawyer in West Virginia – the man who convinced the Mingo County Commission to do the right thing last week – Mr. Mack Palmer."

As the muscular, slick-headed lawyer crossed the stage to the lectern, the crowd went wild. The forceful arguments he had advanced for Royal in Mingo County had turned him into a nationally recognizable figure, and a cult hero to Republicans in West Virginia. That admiration was reflected by loud whoops, fervent clapping, and a standing ovation.

"Thank you very much," Palmer began. The crowd remained on its feet, continuing to clap, while Dave quietly slipped off stage. "Really, you're too kind."

Dave sat down along the back wall where he could watch the presentation while slipping out to take a phone call if necessary.

He sat down just when the crowd decided that Palmer had been sufficiently showered with adulation.

"As you all know," Palmer said, "Monday's a big day. In order for Governor Royal to hold on to his victory, we must be on top of our game. Although the procedures vary slightly – depending upon whether your county uses optical scan machines, the new DRE touchscreens or good old-fashioned paper ballots – I'm here to give you a general overview. We'll focus on the different voting systems in greater detail during our breakout sessions this afternoon."

Palmer stepped back from the podium and turned toward a projection screen. As he moved, the stage lights glistened off his bald head. Hitting his remote, the campaign logo onscreen disappeared, replaced with a black outline of West Virginia against a light gray background. The symbols "153 CSR 20" were superimposed across the map in royal blue.

"According to the regs," he said, flicking the remote. "Governor Royal can only have one official representative in each county. That person is authorized to 'observe the recount proceedings, including observing each ballot as it is read in a hand-count process. They may view and examine the tally sheets and ballots, but may not handle the election material.'"

"Because the final outcome may turn on legal issues," Palmer explained. "Governor Royal has designated the attorneys assigned to each county as his official representatives. As much as we value the involvement of local officials in this process, when fights start breaking out over the proper application of the regulations – as they inevitably will – we need to make sure the person speaking for the campaign is well-trained for those battles."

Palmer continued through his presentation. "The county clerks will assign two-man teams – one Democrat, one Republican – to work together on the recount. To speed things up, there will be multiple two-person teams in each county working on the recount at the same time. One team examines each ballot individually, announcing the voter's choice, while a second two-person team writes down the results on individual tally sheets. Each pair of two-person teams will work on one precinct at a time, and they are supposed to pause after every twenty votes to double-check the tally sheets. If those don't match, they recount the last 20 ballots and check again. If necessary, they go back and start the whole precinct over."

Palmer returned to the podium. "We'll go over the specifics in the breakout sessions. But regardless of what ballots were used in your county, what you're looking for is a clear expression of the voter's preference on each ballot. Did the voter mostly shade in an oval on an optical scan ballot? What does the VVPAT reflect? If the ballot demonstrates who the voter chose, we want the recount to reflect that preference.

"On the other hand," Palmer cautioned. "We don't want this process to deteriorate into a battle of wishful thinking, where the Democrats claim certain ballots reflect votes for Senator Wilson where none exist, and we respond by similarly imagining votes for Governor Royal."

Palmer hit his remote and a new slide appeared. "If you think a Dem has called a vote for Wilson where none exists, dispute that opinion. According to the rules, 'If a ballot is questioned, the deputized team shall reexamine that ballot and reach their finding. Any ballot questioned shall be marked to provide for its identification at any future contest of the election. *If a majority of the deputized team cannot agree on the intent of the voter's markings on a ballot, it shall remain questioned and the votes for that ballot shall not be recorded."*

Palmer's arms dropped to his side. "No ifs, ands or buts. A majority of the two-person team examining the ballots is *two*. So if *both* workers on the team don't agree on the voter's intention, then no vote from that ballot is recorded. Period. That ballot is marked and identified so we can argue about it later if there's a contest after the recount is over.

"Now we don't want you folks to act like no vote for Wilson counts unless every single microdot on an oval is shaded in," he clarified. "Be reasonable. Follow the Golden Rule and 'do unto others as you would have them do unto you.' Don't hold their voters to a higher standard than you hold ours, because we don't want the Dems nitpicking about ballots reflecting votes for our guy either." Palmer rested his left hand on the lectern. "Questions?"

Dave raised his hand.

"Yes, Dave."

"You're not saying we should just roll over and make nice, are you? What if the Democrats they're paired off with try to question every ballot for Governor Royal? Are we supposed to just sit back and let every vote for Wilson slide by?"

Palmer's jaw tightened, and he shook his head. "Not at all. If someone isn't playing by the rules, trying to void as many votes for Governor Royal as they can, call their actions to the County Commission's attention. They're still presiding over the recount, and they probably don't want the whole world to think they're stupid or corrupt, or both.

"If that occurs," Palmer continued. "Our lawyer should pull the other side's rep aside and try to reason with him. Explain that everyone needs to play by the rules. If they want to throw all our votes into a pile to be dealt with during the contest, we can do the same thing. What's fair for the goose is fair for the gander. We can all look fair and honest, or we can all look mean-spirited and vindictive. Everyone will be happier if the world thinks this is an impartial recount, but we won't let the other side steal this election by acting unfairly, either."

Dave nodded, satisfied. Looking around the ballroom, many others agreed.

"Any other questions regarding the overall process?" Palmer asked. With none forthcoming, he hit the remote and the campaign logo returned to the projector screens. "If not, we'll separate into our individual groups. Those of you from counties using DRE touchscreens will stay here. Folks from counties with optical scan ballots should go to West Virginia Room 105. And the people from Braxton County and Wyoming County will head over to Room 207, where we will discuss the recount of paper ballots."

As the audience headed to their respective meetings, Dave navigated through the crowd to Jack's table. As he drew closer, the senator saw him and smiled. Rising to his feet, he extended his hand. "Dave Anderson! It's been a coon's age since I saw you. How ya been?"

Dave gave Jack's hand an energetic, heartfelt pump. "No complaints. How are the kids and Tabatha doing?"

"The boys are shooting up like reeds. Tabatha is ... well ... *Tabatha*." He chuckled uneasily and shrugged. "What else can I say?"

Dave tightened his lips and nodded. "Say nothing more. I understand. So are you sticking around tonight? Maybe I could take you out and buy you a beer or something. It's the least I could do to thank you for introducing me to our next president."

Jack beamed and let out a loud laugh. "Who could have imagined? You were a young Republican law school grad looking for a job in D.C. I knew Jonathan from our regional state legislators' meetings, and he had just won his first election to Congress. I gave him a ring, put in a good word for you, and the rest is history."

Jack let out a sigh. "Unfortunately, I have to head back to Saint Marys right after the seminar. I have a lot of work to get done and this recount has put me behind schedule."

Dave grinned. "Since when did *you* start working on weekends? The most I've ever seen you do on a Saturday is hit a round of golf."

Jack chuckled. "I can't deny that. But right now, this big firm's looking to invest a chunk of money in my company, and I'm busting my hump trying to hammer out a deal."

"Some big pockets outfit trying to get in on the Marcellus Shale play?"

"Yep, and with big pockets come big expectations. They want me to drop everything to get them the paperwork they need for their due diligence, and with the money they're talking about investing with me, I'm willing to do it."

"Good for you," Dave said. "Well, maybe I'll look you up next weekend. I'll be home for Thanksgiving and it'd be nice to catch up with you and see how big the boys are getting."

"Why don't you swing by on Saturday night and watch the WVU-Pitt game with us?"

"Sounds like a plan. I'll give you a ring."

Jack gave Dave a vigorous pat on the arm as they parted. "I'll look forward to it. Maybe we'll be able to toast the country's next president by then. And I don't mean Melanie Wilson."

CHAPTER 39

MINGO COUNTY COURTHOUSE
WILLIAMSON, MINGO COUNTY, WEST VIRGINIA
SATURDAY, NOVEMBER 22, 10:55 P.M.

Sheriff Perkins confidently strolled down Second Avenue in his black uniform, the white streetlamps silhouetting his figure on the concrete sidewalk. Hoisting a bundle of keys, he swiftly found the one that unlocked the courthouse. Swinging the glass door open, he walked through it like he owned the place before studiously relocking it.

Entering his department's second floor suite, Perkins turned on the overhead lights and walked back to his private office. Using another key, he unbolted both locks and entered the room, quietly shutting the door behind him.

Perkins tiptoed through his darkened office to the windows overlooking Second Avenue. Sure enough, the occupants of that damn black van were scurrying around the building. Peeking through the blinds, he saw four men feverishly training their video cameras on strategic areas of the building, including his office and that of the county clerk.

Turning from the window, he walked across the room and stood in front of the bank vault door guarding his department's weapons. Reaching into his pants, he pulled out the only key in existence that would open the door without a locksmith's assistance.

Still operating in the dark, Perkins ran the palm of his left hand along the door face and located its locking mechanisms. Deftly retrieving a small flashlight from his utility belt, he leaned his forehead against the door and placed the flashlight in his mouth, directing its beam down toward the combination lock. Using his right hand to rotate the dial clockwise, then counterclockwise, then clockwise yet again, he held the key in the keyhole with his left hand. After entering the combination, he turned the key to the right, pulled down on a lever located to the right of the keyhole, and grinned when the tumblers fell into place.

The door nudged open. Widening the gap, the sheriff peered inside the weapons cabinet and saw the means to Melanie Wilson's election lying on the floor, waiting for him.

CHAPTER 40

CHARLESTON, WEST VIRGINIA
SATURDAY, NOVEMBER 22, 11:25 P.M.

Sitting alone on a barstool in the hotel lounge, Dave stared at the television behind the bar, watching college football highlights on SportsCenter. The bartender also watched the highlights while gathering discarded bottles and glasses.

"So what did you think about UCLA knocking off USC?" the barkeep asked.

Dave swallowed a mouthful of beer. "I thought USC was kind of overrated this year. But it ought to help the Mountaineers, anyway."

"If we can beat Pitt next weekend, we should be sitting pretty," the bartender opined, throwing empty bottles in the trashcan. The glass bottles clinked together loudly before hitting the bottom of the can with a resounding clank.

Dave shook his head, wearing an amused grin. "Never bet *on* and never bet *against* the Mountaineers, my friend. They'll break your heart and steal your money every time."

The bartender wiped down the bar with a wet dishcloth, clenching his teeth. "You got that right. I still have nightmares about RichRod costing us a shot at the title in '07."

Dave barked a pain-filled laugh. "Whoever coined the maxim, 'Don't count your chickens before they hatch' would have gotten a kick out of that game." Draining the dregs of his beer, he tapped the empty bottle on the lacquered bar. "Damn bubble screens."

Dave's cell phone rang. Leaning back, he pulled the phone from his pocket. The call was coming from the campaign's national headquarters. "Anderson here."

"It looks like we might have a problem down in Mingo County."

Dave's posture straightened and he put his hand over his open ear. "What's going on?"

"One of our video surveillance guys is on the other line. They said the sheriff unexpectedly walked into the courthouse a half-hour ago."

"Is he supposed to be on duty tonight or something?"

"No clue. It's not like we have a copy of the sheriff department's work schedule. But the video guys are freaking out about it."

Dave sighed and motioned for another beer. Without knowing whether Perkins was slated to work that night, his presence at the courthouse could be completely innocent. "Can you patch their call through to me? I wanna hear what they have to say first-hand."

"Sure thing. Hold on just a sec."

The line went silent as Dave was put on hold. Ten seconds later, a new voice came over the line. "Mr. Anderson!" the man panted. "Thank God we got in touch with you!"

"Calm down. Tell me what's happening."

The man took a few deep breaths. "Sorry I'm winded, but I sprinted down the block to get a stronger cell phone signal, and I've been living off little chocolate donuts and cheeseburgers for the past two weeks down here."

"Take your time."

Silence, interspersed with desperate attempts to inhale oxygen, ensued. "The sheriff showed up about a half-hour ago and walked in the courthouse."

"Is he scheduled to work tonight?"

"He pretty much comes and goes as he pleases. But he *did* work the midnight shift last Saturday, come to think of it."

The bartender slid a local microbrew in front of Dave, who raised it to his lips and frowned slightly. *Not bad, but definitely not as tasty as Yuengling.*

"Okay," Dave said, gently setting the bottle down. "So the mere fact he's at the courthouse doesn't tell us much. Have you seen anything else suspicious?"

"Well, the Sheriff's Department usually doesn't have more than two guys on nightshift at the courthouse. Counting the Sheriff, tonight there are three."

"Odd," Dave conceded. "But not overly so. Anything else?"

"*Holy shit!*" the man exclaimed.

"What? What is it?"

"There was a loud explosion on the hill and every fucking light in town just went off!"

"Say *what?*!"

"Every fucking light in town just went off! Streetlights, the lights from the gas station down the road. *Everything*. It's like the whole town of Williamson just lost power."

Dave's mind began racing. "Where are the voting machines stored?"

"Down in the courthouse basement." The investigator was breathing heavily.

"Are there any windows to that room which are visible from the outside?"

"I'm not sure. We don't exactly have a copy of the blueprints in the van."

"I know that," Dave snapped. "We need to think fast. Try to remember exactly where that room is located."

"It's kind of in the middle of the basement. Along the back wall, on the opposite side of the building from the side that faces Second Avenue. Kinda towards the end of the courthouse that's adjacent to the Coal House."

Dave consciously tried to remain calm. "Okay. Get the cameras positioned on windows that are located as close to that area of the building as possible."

"There *aren't* any windows close to that area," the man answered emphatically. "I ran back down to the courthouse, and I'm looking at it now. There's a wall of black marble four feet high wrapped around the base of the whole building and there are no windows in the basement."

"Then focus the cameras on the glass doors and any windows that might give you a glimpse into the stairwells and call Pete Warner immediately. He has keys to the courthouse and we need him to get in there and see what's going on."

"I'm on it. We'll call you back."

Dave's phone went silent. Slumping forward, he thought he might pass out. He was a hundred miles from Williamson, and he could do nothing but wait and pray.

CHAPTER 41

MINGO COUNTY COURTHOUSE
WILLIAMSON, MINGO COUNTY, WEST VIRGINIA
SUNDAY, NOVEMBER 23, 12:15 A.M.

"What the hell are you boys *doing* out here?!" Perkins yelled. He was standing in the front doorway to the courthouse, propping it open with a black snakeskin cowboy boot.

The two cameramen whirled away from the windows they were monitoring and marched toward him, plainly itching for a confrontation.

"The better question, *Sheriff*, is what have you been doing in *there*?" one shot back.

"Not that it's any of your business, but I've been trying to get paperwork done in the fucking dark. That's what."

A gold SUV barreled up to the courthouse and squealed to a stop. Pete Warner jumped out wearing gray sweatpants and a camouflage jacket, and jogged up to the courthouse door.

"Commissioner Warner," Perkins said with a malicious smile. "What brings you all the way here from Varney this time of night?"

"You know damn good and well what I'm doing here," Warner growled. "What are *you* doing here? You're not scheduled to work tonight."

The sheriff took one long stride toward Warner, still smiling but deliberately invading his personal space. "Bob called in sick. Bad case of the Hershey squirts. I'm filling in for him. You got a problem with that, Pete?"

Warner's chest heaved up and down as he stared at the sheriff, his balled fists clenched to his sides. "What's going on with the power?"

"I don't rightly know. I sent a deputy to check on it but I haven't heard back from him. Hold on." He pulled a handheld radio from his belt. "Fifty-four, you there? Over."

A baritone voice replied through crackling static. "Fifty-four here, Sheriff. Over."

"Have you figured out what happened to the electricity yet?"

Static filled the air for 15 seconds as Warner and the two cameramen surrounded Perkins. The other two video guys came trotting around the corner of the building to join the festivities. The bright lights from their cameras bounced in the dark with each step.

"Roger. Looks like a transformer up here at the substation blew. The power company has a man here working on it. Over."

Perkins nodded. "Any word on what caused the transformer to blow?"

Chuckles echoed out of the radio speaker. "Roger, Sheriff. The guy here says it looks like a squirrel got into it somehow."

The sheriff rocked back on his heels and let out a big laugh. "A *squirrel?* You gotta be kidding me!"

"Can't say I am, Sheriff. Larry's over there, scraping what's left of the sorry critter into a trash bag. That thing looks charbroiled as hell." Then the deputy made a retching noise. "It *smells* like hell, too. I think I'm gonna hurl."

Perkins doubled over laughing. "Don't do that! Think of something else to soothe your stomach. Like a moldy baloney sandwich floating in a dirty ashtray full of spoiled milk."

Full-fledged vomiting noises followed the comment, and the sheriff's laughter grew even louder. "That wasn't nice," the deputy sulked. "Over."

Perkins slowly caught his breath. "I'm sorry, Frank. I just couldn't help myself. Find out how much longer it's gonna take and then head back out on patrol, okay? Over."

"He says he should have everything back up and running in a few minutes."

"All right then. If he doesn't need anything else, go ahead and take off. I'll see you shortly. Over."

"Roger that. Fifty-four out."

Perkins returned the radio to his belt. Grinning broadly, he stood tall with his hands on his hips. "Any more questions?"

"Yeah," Warner replied. "Are the election materials still safely secured?"

"I suppose so. It's not like I've *checked* on 'em or anything, but I'm sure they're fine." Perkins rotated toward the closest cameraman. "I mean, *you guys* had your cameras fixed on the courthouse. Did *you* see anybody sneaking around in there?"

"We couldn't see much. We'll have to wait and see if the night vision cameras captured anything once we review the footage in slow motion."

The sheriff's smile remained fixed. "Well, I was upstairs in my office the whole time. But if you guys didn't see anybody rummaging around in the basement, everything should be fine down there."

Warner cracked a grin. "Why don't we wander down there and check things out? You know ... just to *make sure.*"

Perkins shrugged. "Might as well, while we're here." He took a step backward, away from the cameras and into the courthouse doorway.

"Can I borrow your flashlight, Sheriff?" Warner asked.

The lawman swung open the door and held it open. "Sure. What do you need it for?"

"I need to go down to my office and grab a few things."

Perkins handed him the flashlight. "Go ahead. We'll wait here for you."

"Thanks," Warner replied gruffly. He grabbed the flashlight and turned left down the main hallway. As he strolled into the darkness, following the diffused cone of light, his rubber soles squeaked loudly on the waxed vinyl floor.

Two minutes later, Warner's office door slammed shut just as the streetlamps came back on. The sound of a computer rebooting percolated from the courthouse security station. Green and red lights flashed on the metal detector and the X-ray monitor lit up, as well.

"Well, whadda ya know?" Perkins quipped. "It looks like that squirrel was no match for the power grid, after all."

Warner came around the corner and entered the foyer, holding a stapled document.

"Whatcha got there, Pete?" Perkins asked.

"Oh, just some paperwork," Warner replied. "Which way do you want to go?"

"Let's take the main stairwell, just in case the power goes out again. No offense, but I don't wanna be holed up with you boys in a disabled elevator all night." Perkins ambled toward the stairs and Warner stepped aside, permitting him to lead the way.

The six men entered the stairwell and descended single-file into the basement. Perkins slung open the heavy steel fire door and turned left, hitting a light switch. The others followed.

Fifteen feet down the hallway, Perkins wheeled left and stood before a door. Pulling a retractable key-ring from his belt, he fingered through the keys dangling at his side. Finding the right one, he inserted it into the keyhole, opened the door and flipped on the lights.

Carefully positioned both on top of tables and on the floor beneath them was a sea of transparent, suitcase-sized plastic containers. Each held what looked like a huge gray laptop computer, and they were all fastened shut with red plastic locks bearing serial numbers. Sheets of copy paper bearing individual precinct names and numbers were scrupulously positioned atop various constellations of containers.

Warner brushed past Perkins toward the plastic containers labeled, "Gilbert Middle School #75." Squatting down to get a closer look, he flipped through the document in his hands. Perkins watched, bemused, as Warner's eyes quickly scanned down the page, searching for some particular piece of data.

"Here we go," Warner declared, sounding satisfied. "Gilbert precinct. Five machines. The serial numbers for the locks fastened on the containers after the canvass are 569872, 569714, 381622, 743559 and 381407."

Warner examined the locks on the plastic containers holding the voting machines from Gilbert. That precinct, along with the one in Matewan, had been the focus point of the parties' arguments during the canvass. Holding one of the locks, he studied its serial number and compared it to the list in his other hand. "569714. This one matches up."

Perkins stood behind Warner. "Imagine that," he said snidely.

Warner scowled, but continued his work. "381622. Okay. 743559. 381407. 569872. Hmmph. They all have the same numbers announced at the canvass."

Perkins raised an eyebrow and crossed his arms. "Scandalous, isn't it? You wanna go through *all* the machines from the other 38 precincts while we're down here, Pete? I mean, it's not like I have anything *better* to do right now. You know … Like *do my job* and keep tabs on people who might be up to no good."

Warned raised himself from the floor. Staring up at Perkins, he was tight-lipped. "I suppose not. We'll just check out the courthouse video surveillance footage. That should show us if anyone's been up to any funny business around here."

Perkins grinned. "Suuuuuurrrre," he said slowly. "Let's do that right now. I just hope the power surge before the blackout didn't knock the backup system outta whack."

"What do you mean?" Warner demanded.

"I've been complaining for years that the County Commission keeps short-changing my department," the sheriff replied, a bit defiantly. "With a tight budget, you have to make hard decisions from time-to-time. Do I keep fuel in my cruisers and keep deputies on the road, protecting the community? With the price of gas these days, that's no easy task. Or do I leave a cruiser parked so I can spend money on some fancy battery-powered backup system for the courthouse surveillance system?" Perkins rocked back on his heels, smiling smugly. "What choice do *you* think I made?"

CHAPTER 42

WEST VIRGINIA REPUBLICAN HEADQUARTERS
CHARLESTON, WEST VIRGINIA
MONDAY, NOVEMBER 24, 8:30 A.M.

Dave looked across the cherry conference table at Gil Dean, the executive director of West Virginia's Republican Party, and asked, "Are we ready to begin the conference call?"

Gil nodded. His hand hovered over a speakerphone.

Dave exhaled, flicking his arms to get his blood circulating. "Okay. Let's do it."

Gil hit a button and the speakerphone came to life.

"All right, everybody," Dave said loudly. "The recounts kick off in thirty minutes. Let's do a roll call to make sure everyone's here. Barbour County?"

"Chip Walton here in Barbour County," a young man responded.

"Berkeley County?"

"This is Monica Boley in Martinsburg," a female voice declared.

"Boone County?"

The cattle call was met with silence. "Boone County?" Dave repeated.

"Hey, Dave. This is Ned Hopson here."

Dave smiled. "Glad to know Boone County's in good hands, Ned!"

The roll call continued through all 55 counties. At the end, Dave clapped once. "All right, guys. We've prepared you for this recount. Now, it's all up to you. We'll have conference calls at the bottom of every hour until the recounts are completed. If you're tied up, make sure *someone* calls in with the latest numbers from your county."

Dave paced along the perimeter of the conference table. "During our first call, tell us the *specific* precincts that are being recounted in your county. Five percent of each county's precincts will be hand-counted today, and knowing the identities of those precincts will help us here at headquarters.

"We want four pieces of information from you during every call," Dave said, motioning with his hands as he spoke. "One: We want the total number of votes tabulated for each of the two candidates at the time of the call."

"Two: We want the net difference, at that time, between the votes reported on Election Night and the votes tallied during the recount. If Governor Royal has gained two votes during the recount, say, 'Plus two.' If Wilson has narrowed our lead by two votes, say, 'Minus two.'

"Three: Let us know which precinct in your county is currently being recounted. When a particular precinct's recount is over, let us know that and tell us what the final net vote difference in that precinct was."

"And fourth," Dave stressed. "For the 53 counties that used optical scan ballots or touchscreens, tell us if the net difference between the votes reported on Election Night and the votes tabulated during the recount has exceeded 1 percent of the total votes cast for president in those random precincts. If the net difference from those random precincts ends up being more than 1 percent, then *every* precinct in that county will be recounted. If not, the recount will end once the hand count of the sample precincts is over."

Dave stopped moving and squared his shoulders to the phone, as if facing an invisible audience. He glanced at his watch. The recount was scheduled to start in seven minutes.

"It's almost show time. Keep your crucial phone numbers handy. The video guys need good vantage points, especially if you think the Dems are trying to pull a fast one.

"And finally, remember to be reasonable and play fair if at all possible. But scrutinize *every single ballot* as if the election depends on it, because it very well may. Thanks for all your hard work, folks, and good luck."

As the county reps said goodbye, Gil disengaged the call. "Nice pep talk," he said.

Dave sat down and took in a deep breath, nodding. At that moment, he honestly felt he had done everything in his power to help Royal hold onto his margin of victory. Now, they just had to stay on their toes and react swiftly as developments occurred.

He leaned forward with a sigh, placing both elbows on the conference table, and rested his face in his hands. *This is going to be one hell of a long day.*

CHAPTER 43

MINGO COUNTY COURTHOUSE
WILLIAMSON, MINGO COUNTY, WEST VIRGINIA
MONDAY, NOVEMBER 24, 9:00 A.M.

"Madam Clerk ... Will you please remove two cards from the bowl?"

Mark Monroe's voice jolted the County Clerk from her daze. She glanced to her right. All three county commissioners awaited her next move.

The Clerk rose from her desk and slowly walked across the courtroom, trying not to fall down in the process. A table with a bowl full of cards sat in front of the Commission's dais.

Standing at the table, her right eye began itching terribly. Although she desperately wanted to scratch at it, the thought of drawing any attention to her eyes right now terrified her.

Stay calm. This will be over in two minutes and you'll be 500,000 dollars richer.

The Clerk looked into the glass bowl that was the center of her universe. Staring at the 39 folded slips of paper lying inside it, the sheriff's voice floated through her mind: *"The first card you pull out can be any damn precinct you want,"* he had told her yesterday evening as they discussed his proposal. *"But the second card must be Gilbert Middle School. Precinct Number 75."*

She stuck her hand in the bowl and swirled the cards around. Staring at the cards, she patiently looked for the sign.

Suddenly, she saw the pale yellow dot she was looking for. She abruptly stopped stirring and grabbed one card with her hand while memorizing the location of that *other* card which bore the luminous ink she had dabbed on it this morning.

She pulled out the first card. Unfolding it, she announced, "Tug Valley High School. Precinct Number 41." Turning around, she displayed the slip to Monroe before carrying it to both ends of the platform so Ruth Thompson and Pete Warner could examine it, too.

Monroe absent-mindedly swiveled his chair from left to right, clutching his gavel tightly. "Tug Valley High School is the first precinct we will recount today," he confirmed.

A sudden flash of movement from Governor Royal's lawyers caught the Clerk's eye. One man was smiling and subtly yanking his right arm in a motion that looked like he was repeatedly pulling an oven door toward him.

The Clerk looked away from the disturbing spectacle of happy lawyers and put the first slip aside. It would have been difficult enough to watch without these weird contacts in her eyes. Under the circumstances, however, the whole scene looked discolored and downright surreal.

Now for the tricky part. The cash is riding on this one.

Staring into the bowl, the Clerk blocked out everything around her except for the cards. She returned her gaze to the area she had committed to memory and...

Voila! There it is!

She felt her hand tremble as she reached for the card with a luminous yellow dot on one corner. Grasping it tightly with her thumb and three fingers, she carefully plucked it from the bowl and ritualistically unfolded it before the watchful eyes of the audience.

"Gilbert Middle School," she declared, hoping she sounded subdued. "Precinct Number 75."

The jovial mood of Royal's lawyers evaporated. The man who earlier had impersonated Kirk Gibson looked like he had just learned his blind date was a 70-year-old woman with a beard.

The Clerk again presented the slip for the Commission's review. As before, they looked down from their seats on the platform, glanced at the paper and nodded their acceptance.

"Precinct Number 75 at Gilbert Middle School is the second precinct we will recount. Madam Clerk, please administer the appropriate oaths to our bipartisan recount teams."

"Yes, Commissioner Monroe."

As the Clerk lifted the bowl and turned toward her desk, she spied Sheriff Perkins standing alone with his back against the far wall. Wearing his crisply pressed black uniform, he was grinning like the proverbial Cheshire cat, and he gave her a quick wink.

Placing the bowl on her desk, she turned around and prepared to swear in the recount teams. Gazing through the strange contact lenses the sheriff had given her, she noted the somber looks in her prospective deputies' eyes and tried to ignore the sinking feeling in her stomach.

Anyone else in your shoes would have done the same thing, she told herself. With the passage of enough time, she hoped she would actually believe it.

CHAPTER 44

WEST VIRGINIA REPUBLICAN HEADQUARTERS
CHARLESTON, WEST VIRGINIA
MONDAY, NOVEMBER 24, 9:40 A.M.

Dave had grown weary of the conference calls only 10 minutes into the second one. He sat on the conference table with his legs dangling off the edge. "McDowell County?" he asked.

"The two precincts they're recountin' are Iaeger Town Hall and Bull Creek Baptist Church," a woman replied in a thick drawl. "But I don't have any numbers yet."

"Thank you," Dave stated. "Mercer County?"

"They're halfway finished with Bluefield High School," a squeaky-sounding man explained. "The other two precincts are

Princeton Elementary and Bramwell Fire Department. No numbers yet."

"Very good. Mineral County?"

"They just started Ridgeley Fire Hall. No final tallies yet. The other precinct is Clary Street Learning Center. Talk to you next hour."

"Thanks," Dave said. "Mingo County?"

"Hey, Dave. This is Spence."

Dave grinned. "What news do you have from the People's Republic of Mingo County?"

Spence paused. "I don't have a real good feeling about this. I can't put my finger on it, but I'm picking up some bad vibes."

Dave stopped kicking his legs. "Talk to me, Spence."

"Sheriff Perkins is walking around like he has a winning Powerball ticket in his pocket. Again, it's a gut instinct. No numbers to report yet. The recount team just started digging into the Tug Valley High School precinct. The good news is Wilson cleaned our clock there on Election Day at a three-to-one clip. So they're unlikely to pick up many votes there."

Spence paused again. Dave leaned toward the phone, his eyes wide with anticipation.

"The bad news is that Gilbert Middle School is the other precinct being recounted. We did well there, but it's one of the precincts that supposedly had trouble with the memory cards on Election Day."

"Ugh," Dave spat. "No wonder your gut's churning. Thanks for bringing that to our attention and call us if anything happens."

"Ten-four, boss."

Dave grabbed his coffee and took a sip before resuming the roll call. But his paranoid mind kept racing through scenarios where the opposition somehow managed to generate enough new votes in Mingo County to snatch victory from the jaws of defeat.

CHAPTER 45

WEST VIRGINIA STATE CAPITOL
CHARLESTON, WEST VIRGINIA
MONDAY, NOVEMBER 24, 9:50 A.M.

Dick Bowen reclined in front of the governor's desk, both feet sprawled out. A steaming mug of coffee sat on the table to his left and the latest Charleston Gazette was in his hands.

"Heh, heh," he lightly chuckled. "Get a load of this, Luke."

Vincent looked up from his work. "What is it?"

"The headline on page three reads, 'Wildlife Leaves Williamson in the Dark.'"

"That's rich," Vincent quipped.

Bowen kept reading. "'Power company officials say squirrels are responsible for even more blackouts than lightning strikes. Nationwide, squirrels cause tens of thousands of power outages every year. In 2006, there were almost 17,000 such outages in Georgia alone, usually where squirrels simultaneously come into contact with power lines and adjacent transformers, thereby completing an electric circuit and frying themselves.'" Bowen barked a loud laugh. "Too funny!"

"I have to hand it to you, Dick: That was a slick scheme you cooked up. Great work."

"We had a hell of a time finding a squirrel, though. I ended up paying one of the groundskeepers here at the Capitol five grand to give me one."

"*What?!*" Vincent shrieked.

"Simmer down. I told the guy my granddaughter *adored* squirrels and desperately wanted one for her birthday. Which was yesterday. She'd be heartbroken if I couldn't find her one in time for her birthday party. Blah blah blah."

"You don't even *have* a granddaughter, Dick!"

Bowen shrugged. "He doesn't know that. He thinks he just made some little girl's day and he got an extra five grand just by putting on some thick-ass leather gloves and strolling up to one of the tame little bastards with some peanuts. Two minutes later, old Rocky is chomping on nuts, sitting in a wire rabbit cage on a one-way trip to Williamson. *Everybody's* happy."

"Except the squirrel," the governor pointed out.

"Ah, hell. Quit acting like you're a fuckin' Boy Scout. You don't have any qualms about *stealing an election*, yet your lower lip starts quivering because a damn *squirrel* bit the dust?" Bowen shook his head in disbelief. "That makes as much sense as you sneaking around, banging Tabatha McCallen."

Vincent glowered but said nothing. Then Bowen's phone rang, interrupting their touchy ethical discussion.

"It's Perkins," Bowen announced. "Hello?"

"Hey, Dick," the sheriff opened. "The recount started 20 minutes ago. The second precinct up is Gilbert Middle School, Number 75."

"*Woohoo!*" Bowen cheered. "Great news! I'll pass it along."

"I can't wait to see Warner's face after they count that precinct," Perkins added. "He's gonna look like someone fed him a turd sandwich."

Bowen laughed. "Serves him right. And there'll be more paybacks coming, I promise."

"As always, Dick … It's been a pleasure doing business with you."

Bowen hung up the phone and stretched his arms, interlacing his thick fingers behind his head. "I feel like Hannibal Smith from 'The A-Team,'" he said with a grin. "I *love* it when a plan comes together!"

CHAPTER 46

WEST VIRGINIA REPUBLICAN HEADQUARTERS
CHARLESTON, WEST VIRGINIA
MONDAY, NOVEMBER 24, 10:20 A.M.

Dave Anderson walked into Gil's office holding his phone. He closed the door behind him. "Okay, Spence. I'm alone now. What's up?"

"We ended up *gaining* a vote in the first precinct. But they're working on Gilbert Middle School now, and – pardon my French – the crap is hitting the fan."

"How so?"

"Remember how they made a big deal about Governor Royal winning 70 percent of the vote there? Since the Dems usually win there by a two-to-one margin?"

"Yeah," Dave replied.

"Well, history may be repeating itself. The results are flip-flopped now. A third of the way through the precinct and Senator Wilson is pulling about two votes for every one of ours."

"Son-of-a-bitch! Are we sure those paper rolls are from the same machines that were used on Election Day?"

"The red locks on the plastic containers had the same numbers this morning that were announced after the canvass. The serial numbers stamped on the voting machines match up, too, as do the seals affixed on the VVPAT rolls."

Dave slapped the desk. "Who knows? Maybe those bastards were right. Maybe the memory cards really *did* malfunction after the polls closed. How else can we explain this?"

"Maybe they switched out the whole machines. You know … hardware, memory cards, VVPAT rolls. The whole kit-n-kaboodle."

"That'd be tough to pull off. The county couldn't produce new voting machines with the *same serial numbers* as the original ones. AIS could do *that*, but they don't manufacture the red locks on the plastic containers. Plus, they'd have to know what the *numbers* were on those seals after the canvass. You're talking about a pretty extensive conspiracy."

"Maybe, but aren't you always jabbering about how much money has been spent on this election and how much is at stake here?"

After silently pondering Spence's outlandish hypothesis, Dave admitted it *did* make a degree of sense. After spending a billion dollars on this race – if not *more* – why would the opposition flinch at spending more now? Especially when victory seemed oh so attainable?

"Okay," he conceded. "Maybe you're right. But without any evidence supporting our suspicions, we're hosed. We have *one* elected ally in Mingo County: Pete Warner. And even *he* publicly acts like he doesn't support us. The sheriff's department, the state police, the Williamson city cops ... They're all run by the opposition."

"What about the feds?" Spence asked. "Maybe the FBI would look into it."

"We don't have any *evidence*," Dave repeated. "Suspicions aren't enough. Without evidence, we just look like sore losers. And even if we *did* have evidence supporting our allegations, the feds don't wrap up an investigation overnight. They get their ducks in a row so they can nail your ass to a tree when they *do* come after you. They might put some people away eventually, but it won't be any time soon. Certainly not in time to help us win this election."

"Then what are we gonna do?" Spence cried, exasperated.

Dave sighed. "It looks like there'll be a net difference of more than one percent between the votes reported in those two precincts on Election Night and the ballots counted today."

"Definitely."

"That means the whole county will be recounted. Make sure our folks don't give up. We could still pick up votes elsewhere around the state. Maybe we'll get lucky and the other side's math will be off."

"That's not much to hang our hat on," Spence said.

"Maybe not," Dave conceded. "But right now, that's all we've got."

PLEASANTS COUNTY COURTHOUSE
ST. MARYS, PLEASANTS COUNTY, WEST VIRGINIA
MONDAY, NOVEMBER 24, 11:15 A.M.

"Well, that sure didn't take long," Rikki said.

Jack strolled beside her toward the exit. "What did you expect? The county only has eleven precincts, so we just had to hand count one precinct, and that ended up being Hebron, the smallest precinct in the county. If we couldn't make short work of 140 ballots, that'd be pretty pathetic."

"True," she replied. "In fact, I'd bet we spent more time getting the lawyers to play nice with each other than we did on the entire recount itself."

Jack chuckled. "Yep. And after all that, both sides ended up with the same votes they had after the canvass."

"Sure makes you glad you live in Pleasants County, doesn't it?"

"Damn straight, especially after listening to the crazy stuff happening elsewhere."

Rikki stopped in her tracks. "Oh, yeah? Like what?"

"For starters," Jack began, "a fistfight broke out between two lawyers in Preston County at 8:30 a.m. The Sheriff – who's a good Republican, mind you – saw the whole thing and had the Democrat lawyer arrested for battery."

"You've got to be kidding me."

"Scout's honor. Then one of Senator Wilson's paralegals raised cane, so the sheriff had *her* arrested for obstructing an officer." Jack laughed loudly and shook his head. "The magistrate – who's a stinking Democrat, by the way – released them both on personal recognizance bonds. But when they re-entered the courtroom, the sheriff demanded to see the lawyer's bond papers.

"Sure enough," Jack continued, "the bond prohibited him from having any contact with 'the victim' of the battery, so the sheriff *rearrested* him for violating the terms of his bond by being in the same room as the guy he punched and hauled him back to magistrate court. Long story short: By the time the magistrate amended the lawyer's bond, released him on a second P.R. bond and finished reading the riot act to the sheriff, it was past 10 o'clock and the county hadn't even *started* its recount yet."

"What a circus!"

"You got that right. Those other places can keep their melodramas. Give me good old boring Saint Marys any day of the week."

Rikki chuckled. "They don't call it Mayberry for nothing."

"Yep. And we like it that way."

CHAPTER 47

WEST VIRGINIA REPUBLICAN HEADQUARTERS
CHARLESTON, WEST VIRGINIA
MONDAY, NOVEMBER 24, 11:30 A.M.

With a growing sense of dread, Dave awaited the next conference call. Gil Dean, the state GOP's executive director, looked at the clock and hit the speakerphone button.

"Hello, everyone," he opened. "Gil here. I know things are hectic, so let's jump right on your reports. Barbour County."

"Royal 4,030, Wilson 2,634. Net difference from the canvass is plus two. We're currently recounting Belington. So far, the net difference is less than 1 percent, so we're not looking at a countywide recount."

"Thanks," Gil said. A college student with her brown hair pulled back in a ponytail stood beside five whiteboards mounted on the wall. As the report came through the speakerphone, she scribbled the information down in columns beside the county's name.

"Berkeley County," Gil continued.

A young-sounding woman spoke up. "Royal 21,325 to Wilson 12,223. Net difference is plus five. Falling Waters Post Office precinct is up now. Net difference is below 1 percent."

"Thanks, Monica. And if you would, stay on the line. We need to talk after everyone is finished reporting."

"Sure thing," she replied.

"Boone County," Gil prompted.

"Ned Hopson here. Governor Royal has 4,308 and that Communist floozy he's running against has 6,011. I'm sorry the people here are so thickheaded. Net difference is plus three, though. Lower Hewitt is being recounted now. I doubt we end up with a 1 percent difference when it's all said and done, but stranger things have happened. This is Boone County, after all."

"Heh heh. Thanks for keeping things in perspective for us, Ned. Braxton County."

"Royal 3,012. Wilson 3,023. Net difference is minus four. Tesla Fire Department is up now. We use paper ballots, so we'll be here all day hand counting *all* of our precincts *regardless* of what the percentage difference is."

"That's true," Gil remarked. "Thanks for your hard work. Brooke County."

The team's reps dutifully provided the requested information. Most of the counties were reporting single-digit net differences, plus or minus. Approaching the halfway point, Dave's thoughts became fixated on Spence's upcoming report from Mingo County. His stomach felt like butterflies were having dogfights inside it.

Gil's voice brought matters to a head. "Sounds good. Mingo County." The line was totally silent. "Mingo County," he repeated.

A long sigh issued from the phone. "They just finished Gilbert Middle School. We're over the 1 percent threshold, and the other precincts will be recounted by hand. The score now is Royal 4,701, Wilson 5,889. Net difference is minus 127."

Gasps and expressions of disbelief followed. Dave's head tilted backwards and he stared up at the ceiling, stunned.

"Did you say minus *one-twenty-seven*?" Gil asked.

"Unfortunately, yes. We lost 128 in that one precinct. Throw in the vote we gained in the Tug Valley precinct, and that leaves us 127 in the hole."

"But doesn't that pretty much wipe out the whole lead we had statewide at the beginning of the day?" a female voice asked.

"Not entirely," Gil quickly replied. "But it's going to hurt us, no doubt."

"This is a bunch of bullshit!" a man exclaimed. "What're you guys doing down there? Just sitting with your thumbs in your asses, watching them *steal* this damn election?"

Spence started to respond but was drowned out by Gil. "Settle down, folks! We're all trying to win this thing and we're all in it together! Backbiting will get us nowhere. We have to buckle down and work even harder."

Despite Gil's exhortations, Dave heard a steady murmur of grumbles in the background.

"Okay, Spence," Gil continued. "Keep your chin up and dig in for the long haul. You have 37 more precincts to go, and we can't afford any more like that last one."

"Thanks, Gil. We'll do that."

"Monongalia County."

As the reports continued to trickle in, the intern dutifully scribbled on the whiteboards. But towering over the single digit differences being reported elsewhere was the negative monstrosity from Mingo County. With one fell swoop, it had essentially erased their fragile lead. The effect of that revelation on morale was undeniable.

At last, the cattle call wound down. "Wood County," Gil barked.

"Royal 25,105. Wilson 13,982," a man replied in a deep, authoritative voice. "Parkersburg Catholic High School precinct was just completed and our total net difference at this time is plus four. Mineral Wells Lions' Club is next on the list. Call me crazy, but I doubt if we end up having to recount the whole county."

"That's a shame," Gil retorted. "With a margin of victory like that, I'd think we might be able to pick up a few votes if the recount extended countywide."

The caller snorted. "Maybe if we had those magic, reprogrammable machines like the ones down in Mingo County. No offense, but I'm not going to wait around to be chastised for being negative. I'll call back in an hour." He abruptly hung up.

Gil shook his head sadly. "Wyoming County."

"Royal 5,024. Wilson 3,687. Oceana Senior Citizens' Center just ended and our net difference is plus two. We have to recount the whole county like Braxton County because we still use paper ballots. Talk to you next hour."

Hearing the last caller disconnect, Gil spoke up. "Monica? Are you still there?"

"I am," the young woman from Berkeley County answered.

The Executive Director ran his left hand through his wavy locks of blonde hair. He was in his early thirties, with the faintest signs of crow's feet emerging around the corners of his wide-set blue eyes. "I take it you understand the gravity of this situation."

"Certainly." To Dave, her voice sounded remarkably calm and controlled.

"How many sample precincts do you guys still have to recount?"

"Just three more," Monica responded.

Gil nodded. His eyes were cold and steely. "Governor Royal carried your county big on Election Day. With the shenanigans going on down in Williamson, we'll need all the help you can give us. What's the chance the net difference there will end up over 1 percent?"

"One hundred percent," she declared flatly.

Gil's lips peeled back, revealing a dangerous-looking smile. Dave's eyes widened as he listened to their conversation, captivated.

"That's what I was hoping you'd say," Gil said. "I'm counting on you, Monica. I *need* you to come through for me. You know what it's at stake."

"And *you* know I'm your go-to girl, Gil," she fired back. "I always have been, ever since we were at WVU and you were College Republican chairman. Have I ever let you down?"

"No," he conceded, his smile turning warm. "No, you haven't."

"Well, I won't let you down today, either. If the Democrats want to fight dirty, I won't abide by the Geneva Convention either. If they want a war, by God, they'll get a *war*."

Gil laughed aloud. "That's my girl!"

"I'll be in touch," Monica announced crisply. The line went dead.

Dave shook his head and absent-mindedly ran his index finger around the inside of his ear. "Do you mind telling me what *that* was all about?"

Gil stared at him, saying nothing. His blue eyes might as well have been hidden behind sunglasses. "We appreciate the help you guys from D.C. have given us the past few weeks," he diplomatically began. "The resources you've brought to bear on our post-election proceedings have been invaluable, they really have."

"But ..."

Gil smiled thinly. "But we're more competent fighting in the trenches than you guys give us credit for. And we have a hell of a lot more at stake in this election than you realize."

Dave's eyes narrowed. "Why do you say that?"

Gil sighed and took a seat. "We know what the perception is of our state party. You guys think we couldn't deliver a friggin' *pizza*, let alone an election."

Dave chuckled. "I suppose there's a little truth to that."

Gil clasped his hands together. "And by-and-large, I'd say our poor reputation is well-deserved. We've been bankrupt at least twice I can remember, and we consistently rank at the bottom of state parties when it comes to our fundraising."

Dave paused, choosing his words carefully. "It's left a lot to be desired over the years."

"Well, those of us who have been busting our asses, trying to actually *recreate* a two-party political system in West Virginia – because we really haven't had one in over forty years – are sick and tired of having nothing to show for it. And helping Governor Royal win this election would advance our efforts tremendously."

"Care to explain how?"

"Let's see," Gil responded defiantly. "For starters, it might convince Luke Vincent he's not the damn *czar* of this state. Bloodying his lip would be *extremely* gratifying. It might also convince people that it isn't always a losing proposition being a Republican in West Virginia.

"You grew up here, Dave. A lot of times you feel like you're just banging your head against the wall and that a man would have to be either a masochist or a dyed-in-the-wool true believer to register as a Republican in this state. Maybe both. Seeing people like us get down in the trenches with the Democratic establishment, slug it out and actually come out *on top* for a change? Now *that* would be a real shot in the arm for the state party.

"There's a small, hardcore group of Republican activists here that are tired of getting kicked in the teeth by the Dems. We're *tired* of never wielding power. We're *tired* of begging for table scraps when the Legislature distributes money for projects around the state. We're *tired* of being an afterthought in drafting legislation and setting the state's agenda.

"Most of all," he concluded, a fierce look of determination in his eyes. "We are sick of watching young people leave West Virginia because there are no jobs here, and we're sick of not being able to do anything about it. I mean, this state has low crime, beautiful scenery, friendly people and one of the lowest costs of living in America. But no *jobs*, because the Dems have been calling the shots here for a century and, in the process, they somehow managed to drive our state's economy into the ground. And, in my opinion, those things won't change unless we can convince people that joining the GOP and electing Republican officials is a viable alternative."

"Great campaign speech," Dave wryly commented. "But what does it have to do with our current situation?"

Gil exhaled. "You know that movie, 'A Christmas Story?'"

"Sure. Ralphie wants to get a BB gun and all that jazz."

Gil snapped his fingers. "Exactly. Remember the scene where Ralphie finally flips out and beats up the bully that had been picking on him?"

"Yeah?"

"Well, people like me and Monica Boley – the girl up in Berkeley County – we feel like Ralphie in that scene. We're fed up with being pushed around by bullies like Governor Vincent. And we've reached the point where if it takes fighting dirty to win this election ... Well, we're ready to kick 'em in the nuts and say to hell with the consequences."

CHAPTER 48

MARTINSBURG, BERKELEY COUNTY, WEST VIRGINIA
MONDAY, NOVEMBER 24, 12:20 P.M.

Monica Boley strapped on her seatbelt and turned the ignition key. Glancing in the rearview mirror, she put her blue Mercedes convertible into drive and turned onto King Street. "When we get back from lunch, the Commission will recount the ballots from Precinct Number 40." She enunciated her words slowly and precisely, maintaining an iron grip on her composure. The last thing she wanted was for her twin brother to think she did not have the situation under control.

Marcus sat wide-eyed in the passenger seat, absorbing everything she said. "The one in Hedgesville. I know." He softly patted the palms of his neatly manicured hands on his thighs.

Monica slowly nodded, but kept facing forward. "That's when we have to make our move, Marcus. Time is running out."

Her brother's cheeks were puffed up, filled with air. Still absent-mindedly patting his thighs, he blew a large breath through his pursed lips. "I know, I know. But are you *sure* we have to do this? What if we get caught?"

"We won't," she said with an unmistakable air of confidence. "Our plan is sound. We analyzed every step, and we've executed the plan flawlessly. Want to review it again?"

"Yes. Just one more time. I want to make sure we haven't overlooked anything."

Monica sighed. Throughout their lives, her brother had been the likeable, conservative one. Smart, but not an overpowering intellect. Handsome, but not perfect-looking like a Hollywood movie star. Incredibly *nice*, a real-life Eagle Scout who would help old ladies cross the street. But *very* averse to risk. The kind of poker player who would fold every hand unless he had at least three-of-a-kind.

Monica knew her brother and respected him deeply. His many undeniable virtues had served the young politician well. He had just completed the second year of his term as Berkeley County Clerk and was widely praised for doing his job effectively. He cultivated the right relationships, joined the right clubs, attended the right church, married the right woman and lived in the right subdivision. But there was one, very important attribute Monica knew he lacked and feared would prevent him from attaining his highest political aspirations:

A killer instinct.

Monica, on the other hand, was quite cognizant of her own steel-tempered ruthlessness. It was a trait she had nurtured since elementary school, when another little girl had tried to install herself as the "queen bee" of their class. For some unknown reason, Monica had awakened one day and decided that she just did not *like* the girl. So she had patiently undertaken a plan of action that systematically alienated the girl from every other member of the class. Her Machiavellian plan had been so successful that the little girl's parents pulled her out of the school district for her emotional well-being.

From that one experience, Monica learned what it felt like when she set her mind on a goal, established a plan of action to achieve it, and then met with success. And she quickly learned that she *loved* that feeling.

The world, as viewed through Monica Boley's eyes, was quite black and white. Pro-life, pro-business Republicans were good. Pro-union, pro-choice Democrats were bad. And United States Senator Melanie Wilson was as bad as they came: A bunny-hugging, illegal immigrant-coddling, gun-controlling, Bible-burning, baby-killing menace to America's national security. So when pre-election polls indicated that the race in West Virginia was too close to call, Monica had painstakingly crafted a scheme that she viewed as Jonathan Royal's little personal "Break Glass In Case Of Emergency" safety measure, even though his campaign knew nothing about it.

"What printing company sold the optical scan ballots your office used in this election?" she asked. Her tone of voice sounded like what one might use whilst petting a jittery rabbit.

Marcus exhaled. "Duffey & Gould. Their office is down in Beckley."

"Who is the company's sales rep that serviced your account?"

"Heather Anatakis," he replied. "Your sorority sister from WVU."

"What did you tell Heather was wrong with the *first* batch of ballots Duffey & Gould sent to your office in October?" Monica brushed her shoulder-length blonde hair behind her right ear with her fingertips. Glancing at her brother, she noted his posture had relaxed a bit.

"That the ovals weren't aligned properly," Marcus dutifully recited, as if reading from a memorized script. "The scanning machine wouldn't read them."

"Right," Monica coaxed. "So what did you do?"

"I asked her to send us another batch of ballots with the same serial numbers, but to make sure the ovals were aligned right this time."

"And she did that, correct?"

Marcus nodded. "Yes. Three days later."

Monica casually flipped her turn signal and turned left onto Foxcroft Avenue, heading toward the throng of restaurants there.

"And where did your office buy the blue seals used to lock up the ballot boxes?" she asked, turning the steering wheel counterclockwise and crossing through traffic.

"From Heather's company, again. They sell every kind of election material an office like mine needs, except for the actual voting machines."

"And what did you do when your office received those seals?"

Staring straight through the windshield, the Berkeley County Clerk subconsciously smacked his lips. "I opened the box and confirmed the seals were in good order."

"What else?" she prompted.

"I wrote the serial numbers down on a piece of paper and gave the list to you."

"Yes, you did," Monica agreed. "And unbeknownst to you – *right?* – I contacted the sales rep for the little firm in Shanghai that Heather told me manufactures those seals. And I ordered two more batches of those seals – in the *same color*, with the *same serial numbers* – which they shipped to a mailbox I rented at a shipping store in Winchester, Virginia. Correct?"

"Correct," Marcus parroted.

Monica maneuvered her Mercedes into a parking space. Shutting off the engine, she calmly removed her sunglasses and turned to face her brother. "Once the results were reported on Election Night, I took a printout from your office home with me where I had stashed the first batch of ballots from Duffey & Gould. And what did I do then?"

"You filled in the ballots with a pencil."

"No, Marcus. That's like saying the Sistine Chapel is 'a church ceiling some Italian guy painted.' It doesn't do justice to the labor and devotion involved in creating that masterpiece. What *I* did, dear brother," Monica explained testily, "is sit at my dining room table for two straight weeks, hunched over a mountain of ballots with a box of number two pencils, *recreating the entire election*. Eighteen hours a day, for fourteen straight days, I meticulously shaded ovals on almost *38,000* ballots. And I took great care to make sure that the results for *every other race* on the ballot were essentially unchanged, while comfortably widening Governor Royal's margin of victory in the presidential election."

The young woman's eyes flashed with pride. She raised her right hand so that Marcus could get a good look at its mangled and bruised appearance. "Do you think I *enjoyed* doing that to my hand? Do you think I *enjoyed* spending hours studying how those optical scanning machines worked, so that I could improperly shade hundreds of Senator Wilson's ballots in such a way as to make this story believable? Do you think I did all that for my fucking *health*?"

"No," he replied sheepishly.

"You're damn right, I didn't! But I did it anyway, because this country *needs* Jonathan Royal to be our next president. I did it because we both know that if we didn't do *something* to protect his interests, those sorry, corrupt, inbred pieces of shit from the coalfields would find some way to steal this election.

"And have you heard about what's going on down in Mingo County, Marcus?" she continued ranting. "The Democrats have *magically* found *hundreds* of new votes for Senator Wilson, and as of this very moment, Governor Royal might actually be *behind* in the vote tally. And less than an hour ago, the folks at his campaign headquarters said Berkeley County is our only hope to hold on to victory in West Virginia.

Marcus gulped. "Really?"

Monica took a deep breath and nodded solemnly, consciously softening the look in her eyes. "Really," she replied, lowering her voice almost to a whisper. "We – you and I, Marcus – are *literally* the last ring of defense between Melanie Wilson and the White House. We can't sit back and let them steal this election. We have a moral obligation to stop them."

Marcus stared into his twin sister's face for a few moments, contemplating her words. Monica returned the gaze unwaveringly. She knew she had said everything she needed to say.

Finally, he relented. "I know you're right. But I'm still scared out of my mind."

Monica reached over and gently patted her brother's cheek. "I know you are. But you have nothing to worry about. If this thing blows up, I'll take the heat. You didn't know anything at all about my actions. Your only crime was to leave the keys to your office at the courthouse lying around where your diabolical twin sister could grab them.

"It's not your fault that the County Commission left your office in the old courthouse annex instead of moving it to one of the newer buildings with better security systems. Who could have predicted that a formerly law-abiding pharmaceutical sales rep like me would be so devious as to single-handedly use her loving brother's keys to gain access to his storage room, cut the locks off 20 ballot boxes and replace the stacks of unused ballots inside them with ingeniously forged replacements? Hmmm?"

Marcus chuckled nervously. "That *does* sound pretty preposterous."

"Of course! So don't sweat it. Just watch for my signal whenever you open a new ballot box the rest of the day."

"What kind of signal?" Marcus asked. "Are you going to use sign language like Grandma taught us when we were kids?"

Monica shook her head emphatically. "No. Someone else who knows how to sign could catch us and we can't run that risk. We'll have to use something more simplistic . . . If my arms are crossed, pull the stack of original ballots out of the box to be recounted – those are the ones stacked on the *left* side as you're looking down from the lock side of the box.

"But if I'm standing there with my hands on my *hips*, you should grab the stack of ballots from the *right* side of the box. In that case, flip the original ballots over face down, which will reveal the 'spoiled' label I stuck on the transparent plastic wrapper they're stored in when I cut the locks off and put my forged ballots in there."

Marcus sighed and nodded. "Okay. I'm with you. You've not led me astray yet."

Monica smiled proudly. "And I never will. Stick with me, Marcus, and you'll end up in the Governor's Mansion someday."

CHAPTER 49

WEST VIRGINIA STATE CAPITOL
CHARLESTON, WEST VIRGINIA
MONDAY, NOVEMBER 24, 1:45 P.M.

Vincent and Bowen huddled in front of a plasma TV in the governor's private office that was tuned to CNN. Seven of the network's reporters were posted at courthouses around the state, conveying returns to the world.

Suddenly, the ticker tape scrolling across the bottom of the screen changed colors from red to blue. A new caption materialized above the scrolling results, which read:

"BREAKING NEWS: WILSON OVERTAKES ROYAL IN WV"

Bowen leaned backwards at the waist, balled up both of his fists and emitted an unrestrained war whoop. Vincent beamed and clapped his hands, still watching the coverage. On the other side of the door, shrieks of joy wafted through the Governor's Office suite.

Vincent turned up the volume with the remote. "The final results from Braxton County are in," the anchor woman excitedly announced. "Senator Wilson has gained an additional thirty-five votes there. That development, coupled with the stunning news from Mingo County earlier today, has given her the lead."

Vincent remained transfixed on the TV, rubbing his mouth and chin with his palm. "How big is the lead? Tell us."

"According to our calculations," the anchor said. "Senator Wilson is now leading Governor Royal by the miniscule margin of eleven votes." Her eyes widened and she let out a deep breath, sagging in her seat slightly. "Could things *possibly* get more dramatic than this?"

Bowen heartily slapped Vincent on the back. "How do you like *them* apples?"

Vincent grinned and raised an eyebrow. "I'd like 'em a lot better if it was the end of the day. But I feel better right now than I have in a long time."

"And we haven't finished working our magic yet," Bowen added. "Yeah, we're still in for a rocky ride, but doesn't it feel good to be in the driver's seat for a change?"

Vincent nodded, a satisfied look in his eyes. "If you're not the lead dog, the view never changes. And I like the view from this angle just fine."

CHAPTER 50

WEST VIRGINIA REPUBLICAN HEADQUARTERS
CHARLESTON, WEST VIRGINIA
MONDAY, NOVEMBER 24, 3:15 P.M.

"So it all comes down to two counties," Dave mumbled, staring out the window overlooking the heart of downtown

Charleston. People who lived and worked in the non-political "real world" – bankers, plumbers, secretaries and nurses – walked past the headquarters without a second glance. Totally focused on their own affairs, their minds were far from the recount. Dave could scarcely comprehend what it must be like to live in such a sheltered, happily-insulated kind of world.

On days like this, he suspected it was fantastically … *normal.*

Gil circled the conference table, lost in his own thoughts. "What did you say?" he asked.

"That it's hard to imagine after all the fundraising and debates, redeye flights from the West Coast, opinion polls and blah blah blah blah *blah*, this whole election is going to come down to what happens in two little counties in West Virginia."

"Mingo and Berkeley," Gil said. "One's in the southern coalfields and the other's a six-hour drive away in the Eastern Panhandle. It's crazy."

Dave shook his head. "Unbelievable," he said softly.

Gil stepped over to the whiteboards. Scanning the results, his eyes batted back and forth before resting at the bottom of the last whiteboard. Two entries scribbled in black read, "Royal 375,155. Wilson 375,169." To the right of those was an entry written in red: "-14."

Today's recounts largely had gone off without a hitch. As a result, all the team's other reps had reported their final results and went home, while Monica Boley and Spence remained in contact from Martinsburg and Williamson.

The phone rang. Gil speed-walked over and hit the speakerphone button. "Hello?"

"Hi, Gil," Spence said. "We just finished another precinct down here."

"I'm hoping you have some *good* news to report for a change."

Spence sighed. "It depends on what your definition of 'good' is. The recount of Red Jacket is over, and we only lost another two votes there."

Gil's face turned red. "Well, I don't know what they taught you in Mingo County, Spence. But digging ourselves deeper in a hole would never fall within the definition of 'good' I learned here in Kanawha County." His teeth were clenched and his eyes simmered.

"Maybe not," Spence replied tersely. "But Kanawha County actually *elects* Republicans from time-to-time, Gil. And in places like Mingo County – where Republicans are *never* elected, and those crazy enough to run don't *dream* of doing better than losing by a two-to-one margin – keeping the damage that low is borderline miraculous."

"All right, fellas," Dave loudly interjected. "We're all under a lot of stress, and you both need to chill the hell out. Spence ... how many precincts are left to go there?"

The faint sound of heavy breathing came over the line. "Only eight. And there haven't been any major surprises since that nasty Gilbert precinct."

"All-in-all, things could be much worse when you consider how outnumbered we are down there," Dave conceded. "But the other precinct with memory card problems is still floating around out there."

"Matewan. You don't need to remind me. Every time they pull out another box, I'm afraid it's Matewan, and I almost piss myself."

"Don't strain your bladder. That will be the last one they count."

"Why do you say that?"

Gil glanced over at Dave, and by the look in his eyes, he had an epiphany. "Because they don't want us to know how many votes they'll gain there," Gil said. "They want to wait until the last second to play their hole card so we don't have time to react to it."

Dave smirked and pointed his finger at Gil, like a professor pleased with his star pupil. "Exactly. I bet you'll see Democrats working on the recount down there suddenly taking more bathroom breaks or smoke breaks. Doing whatever they can to delay things, so *they* can see how things unfold in Berkeley County before the Matewan precinct gets recounted."

"Come to think of it," Spence noted. "The County Clerk *has* been giving them more breaks lately. It all makes sense now."

"All right, Spence. Make sure you guys scream bloody murder every time they try to take a break. Speed up the process at every turn. We might not be able to stop those bastards from stuffing the ballot boxes in Mingo County. But we can force 'em to put their cards on the table before we lay down ours."

"That's right," Gil chimed in. "Eight precincts remain in Mingo County. There are still *fifteen* to go in Berkeley County."

"Well, heck," Spence said. "Even a kid from the boondocks like me can understand that math. Consider it done."

BERKELEY COUNTY COURTHOUSE
MARTINSBURG, BERKELEY COUNTY, WEST VIRGINIA
MONDAY NOVEMBER 24, 3:40 P.M.

"Would you bring the ballot box from Opequon Elementary?" Marcus Boley asked. A deputy clerk scurried through a back door and returned with the box. Hoisting it onto a large, World War II-era metal table, the deputy clerk stepped aside and made room for his boss.

Marcus grabbed the blue lock that was fastened through a hinged latch on the box. Unlike most locks, however, this one had no keyhole; purposefully designed to be used only once, a white serial number was printed where the keyhole should have been. Once fastened in place, bolt cutters were required to remove it.

"884325," he declared loudly, displaying the serial number so the campaign reps could examine it themselves. Having done this kabuki dance 56 times without any problems, the campaign reps still double-checked their records to confirm the lock's serial number matched up with the one fastened to this precinct's ballot box after the canvass.

For the 57th time, the serial numbers matched. The reps nodded, signaling assent for the recount to continue. Clutching the lock, Marcus used bolt-cutters to snip its metal arch and removed it from the latch. Casting the now-worthless lock aside, he lifted the lid and glanced at his twin sister who was standing along a wall to his right.

Monica's hands were on her hips, and although she appeared to be in deep conversation with another woman, she tore her eyes away long enough to catch her brother's gaze. In that moment, Marcus *felt* Monica's strength and willpower pour into him. *She says the greater good demands we break the law. I believe her.*

Without Monica's encouragement and shrewd guidance, Marcus knew he wouldn't have had the courage to *run* for county clerk, let alone actually win the race. He owed his political fortunes – past, present and future – to Monica. He would trust her with his life. And as he reached down into the ballot box, subtly flipping the stack of actual ballots upside down while retrieving the stack of forged ballots, the fears that gripped him during lunch faded away.

If Monica says it can be done, it can be. Come what may, we're in this thing together.

Marcus handed the ballots to the recount team. The campaign reps glanced down at the serial number imprinted on the first ballot in the stack, confirmed it matched their notes, and stepped back from the table. The recount team then took the ballots, one Democrat and one Republican examining each ballot to ascertain the voter's intention.

"Royal," one man announced. By remaining silent, the other ballot examiner ratified that opinion. The other two members of the bipartisan recount team dutifully scribbled a hash mark on their tally sheets, which would be reconciled periodically through the process until every vote was counted and the precinct's results were re-tabulated.

Marcus breathed a silent sigh of relief. *One more trial down, only fourteen more to go.* Turning away, he closed his eyes and prayed their luck would hold out.

CHAPTER 51

WASHINGTON, D.C.
MONDAY, NOVEMBER 24, 5:15 P.M.

Tyson Vasquez sat behind his sleek mahogany desk, leaning toward the speakerphone. Yuri Petrenko stood across from him with his arms folded and his brow furrowed.

"What's going on in Berkeley County?" Vasquez loudly asked. "Their numbers are making me nervous."

"Me, too," Bowen's voice echoed from the speaker. "They're gaining ten or fifteen votes a precinct on us. That strikes me as odd, but our folks on the ground think it's all aboveboard. They say the kid who's the county clerk up there is a pretty straight arrow."

Vasquez frowned. "That's what people said about Ted Bundy."

"I don't disagree," Bowen said. "But if the guy's pulling anything on us, we haven't figured it out yet. Some people think the scanner at the central office may have been overly sensitive on Election Night, detecting votes for Wilson that aren't visible on the actual ballots."

"Are any of the other races affected?" Vasquez asked.

"Don't know. No other races are being recounted. We're the only game in town today."

Vasquez reclined his ergonomic chair and sighed, folding his hands across his trim stomach. "Even so, between your handiwork with the paper ballots in Braxton and Wyoming Counties and the *corrected* results in Mingo County, we're up about forty votes now."

"That's right," Bowen confirmed. "Sheriff Perkins says there's just one precinct left before they recount the Matewan precinct." The lobbyist let loose a harsh-sounding chuckle. "He says the county clerk really earned her keep today ... She even told the recount teams to take an hour off for dinner to slow down the process."

Vasquez grinned wanly. "Nice, but the guy in Berkeley County did the same thing. The problem is Berkeley County had almost twice as many precincts and three times as many ballots to recount as Mingo County. We can drag things out, but Mingo probably will be finished first."

"Shit," Bowen swore. "Hopefully, though, by the time the recount figures from Matewan are relayed to Martinsburg, it'll be too late for Mr. Straight Arrow to do anything about it."

WEST VIRGINIA REPUBLICAN HEADQUARTERS
CHARLESTON, WEST VIRGINIA
MONDAY NOVEMBER 24, 6:45 P.M.

The black phone rang. Dave knew it was Spence but dreaded taking the call. Matewan was the last precinct to be recounted in Mingo County, and the news was unlikely to be good.

Gil looked positively nauseous. He stared at the phone until it rang a second time, then hesitatingly activated the speakerphone. "Break it to me gently."

"It's bad, guys," Spence said mournfully. "Real bad. I ran out to call you the moment the returns were final. We just lost another 115 votes."

Dave swore under his breath. Gil pounded the table and screamed, "Fuck! That puts us down 160 statewide with only four precincts left in Berkeley."

"Thanks for being so quick," Dave interjected. "We need to relay this info to the Panhandle immediately. Keep your phone handy."

Dave disconnected the phone and looked at Gil. "Call Monica *now*. The sooner she knows what happened in Williamson, the better."

BERKELEY COUNTY COURTHOUSE
MARTINSBURG, BERKELEY COUNTY, WEST VIRGINIA
MONDAY NOVEMBER 24, 6:50 P.M.

As she hung up, Monica Boley felt the chilling grip of fear for the first time in her life. Part of her realized that every time she gave Marcus a sign, she was measurably increasing the odds her felonious scheme would be uncovered. What she found far more surprising, however (and thus, more difficult to control), was the fear her carefully executed plan might *fail*.

Failure was something unpleasant that less capable people experienced and learned from. Greatness was her destiny; not failure! The idea that she could dedicate herself to a goal and still fall short was, in a word, *inconceivable*.

She shook her head quickly from side-to-side and took a deep breath. After briefly contemplating the prospect of failure, her iron will re-emerged.

Perhaps one day down the road, your mouth will be filled with the bitter taste of defeat. But today, failure is not an option.

Four precincts left, and they were down 160 votes. Running figures in her mind, she sought a way to overcome that deficit without creating undue suspicion. For a brief, terrifying moment, she found herself unable to recall precisely *which* four precincts remained, let alone how many votes for Governor Royal each contained.

Subconsciously, Monica sensed someone was staring at her. Narrowing her eyes, she slowly scanned the courtroom from left-to-right. With a shock, she realized Marcus was gazing at her expectantly from the front of the room. Standing in front of a ballot box, his right hand held bolt-cutters. Seeing the hopeful yet anxious look in his eyes, her mental fog evaporated.

She winked and put her hands on her hips.

CHAPTER 52

WEST VIRGINIA REPUBLICAN HEADQUARTERS
CHARLESTON, WEST VIRGINIA
MONDAY, NOVEMBER 24, 7:35 P.M.

"Something must be wrong," Gil muttered. "Monica's not answering her phone."

Dave was facing away from Gil; his attention glued to Fox News where talking heads discussed the drama unfolding in Martinsburg. "Maybe she's got her hands full right now," Dave dryly said. "Besides, we'll probably find out what happens quicker just watching TV."

Gil pulled up a chair. Aside from the ticker tape scrolling along the bottom, a gray outline of Berkeley County's borders on a white background took up the bulk of the screen.

The anchor sounded grim. "For those folks just joining us, here's what we know so far."

"The only county still conducting its recount is Berkeley County," he explained. "Explosive growth fueled by its close proximity to the nation's capital has helped this once rural area become the second most populous county in West Virginia. Only three precincts remain: Trinity Lutheran Church, Back Creek Valley Elementary School, and The Woods Resort."

The graphics disappeared from the screen, replaced by the anchorman's serious-looking visage. "Mr. Boley just announced the official recount results from the Arden United Methodist Church precinct, where Senator Wilson has suffered a net loss of 41 votes, shrinking her current statewide lead to 119."

"Phil Maxwell is on the scene for us in Martinsburg," the anchor segued. "Phil, what can we expect from these remaining precincts?"

A handsome, rugged-looking man with a fine head of dirty blond hair appeared on the screen, positioned in front of the county's red brick neoclassical courthouse. The building's shining gold-painted dome, adorned with the state seal and topped with a hexagonal steeple, was framed in floodlights over his right shoulder.

The reporter laughed and responded, "Expect the unexpected. It seems the machine used to tabulate the county's optical scan ballots was experiencing a slight malfunction on Election Night, causing it to credit Senator Wilson with votes she did not actually receive. This glitch has affected the results in some precincts, but not all, and there doesn't appear to be any rhyme or reason as to how much the results were affected.

"Local observers tell me these three precincts historically tilt Republican. However, Senator Wilson performed better than expected in two of those precincts on Election Night. The million-dollar question is: Was that result an illusion created by a mechanical glitch?"

WEST VIRGINIA STATE CAPITOL
CHARLESTON, WEST VIRGINIA
MONDAY NOVEMBER 24, 8:50 P.M.

Governor Vincent remained holed up in his private office, watching CNN with Dick Bowen. Their exuberance had given way to excruciating suspense and anxiety.

Marcus Boley handed a paper to his deputy before turning from the cameras. As the deputy approached the bank of microphones stationed 30 feet away from the recounting area, the camera briefly focused on Boley as he grabbed the last metal ballot box from the back table.

"The teams have finished recounting the ballots in Precinct Numbers 46A and 47," the deputy announced. In her late fifties, she had shoulder-length silver hair and she was wearing a navy blue skirt and a white blouse. A red ribbon adorned her lapel.

"In Precinct Number 46A, Governor Royal received 328 votes, while Senator Wilson received 203 votes. Those figures represent a net gain of 46 votes for Governor Royal. In Precinct Number 47, Governor Royal had 262 votes, while Senator Wilson received 295 votes. Those figures represent a net gain of one vote for Senator Wilson.

"Up next is our last precinct from The Woods Resort. That precinct has 784 ballots and we hope to be finished in about an hour. Thanks for your patience."

The deputy stepped away from the microphones, and the talking heads immediately began pseudo-analyzing the latest results.

Vincent muted the TV and asked, "Where do we stand?"

Bowen tapped on a pocket calculator with his thick fingers. His tongue protruded from the side of his mouth and his eyes narrowed. With one final flourish, Bowen raised his head. "We're up 74 with just one stinking precinct to go."

Vincent exhaled, unfastened the top button on his white dress shirt and loosened the knot in his royal blue silk tie. "Thank God! I can't take much more of this."

"I bet the whole *country* feels that way."

CHAPTER 53

ST. MARYS, PLEASANTS COUNTY, WEST VIRGINIA
MONDAY, NOVEMBER 24, 10:05 P.M.

Rikki lay in her king-sized cherry sleigh bed, reading the latest Nicholas Sparks novel. A brass lamp by her bed illuminated the book, while the TV across the room aired CNN.

She knew Sparks' books were formulaic but loved them nonetheless. *So what if they're predictable?* They tugged at her heartstrings in a good way, and they never failed to restore her faith in the innate goodness of human beings. Compared to the bitterness and rancor of the election saga, she welcomed the uplifting romantic respite his novels delivered.

Rikki had cheered the news when Senator Wilson took the lead in West Virginia. Although the state's voters sometimes fell under the sway of Republican presidential candidates, Rikki thought Wilson's progressive platform had been appealing enough to break that trend.

Raising her eyes to the TV, she saw Marcus Boley approaching the media. Resting her book face-down on the bed, she turned up the volume with the remote.

The camera zoomed in on Boley, and Rikki saw he held a single sheet of paper in his hand. "I apologize for the delay in reporting these last figures to you, but as the ballots from Precinct Number 48 were being recounted, a heated debate broke out between a few of our recount workers, which took some time to resolve."

Rikki snorted. *From CNN's earlier footage, it looked more like a fistfight than a debate.* Passions had flared quite angrily, and one of the workers had stormed off in a purple-faced rage before being coaxed back to the table.

"It's past 10 o'clock," Boley continued. "I'd like to thank our recount teams for their hard work. Their task was long and thankless, but essential to maintaining the public's faith in the integrity of our election process."

Way to pat yourself on the back there, Mr. Boley, Rikki observed cynically. *Why don't you do us a favor and get on with it?*

"The final results from The Woods Resort are as follows: 520 votes for Governor Royal; 243 votes for Senator Wilson, constituting a net gain of 136 votes for Governor Royal.

"The results of the recount have been officially certified by the County Commission. The final totals are 21,340 votes for Governor Royal versus 12,036 votes for Senator Wilson, reflecting a net gain of 210 votes for Governor Royal."

Boley exhaled slowly, and Rikki noted that his hand clutching the vote tallies was trembling. Suddenly imagining what it felt like to be plucked from the obscurity of Berkeley County and thrust upon the global stage, Rikki felt a pang of sympathy for him.

"Again, thanks for your patience today," he concluded. Then he smiled wearily. "I don't know about you, but I can't wait to get home and get a good night's sleep for a change."

Boley turned to walk away from the assembled journalists. From out of nowhere, an angry woman interrupted his exit. "I don't know how you could possibly sleep at night!" she screamed. "Not after you Republican bastards have stolen another election!"

Boley abruptly froze, his hands dangling at his side, balled into fists. The woman's personal affront had been captured on film for posterity, and Rikki immediately recognized that, for better or worse, the name of Marcus Boley likely would be reviled by Democrats for generations, linked forever to the hotly-debated results of this recount.

At the far right of the scene, Rikki saw a lone woman who bore a small resemblance to the county clerk. In her early thirties, the woman's blonde hair was cut shoulder-length, and the look on her face reflected an almost indescribable mixture of pride and pain.

"Come on, Marcus," Rikki thought the woman whispered. "It's time to go home."

Boley did not turn to face his accuser. He somberly marched away from the cameras. As he approached the young woman, she gently placed her hand on his shoulder. After shooting a wounded yet defiant glance toward the media, she turned and followed Boley out of the room.

Transfixed by the scene, it took Rikki a moment to realize the ticker tape scrolling at the bottom of the screen had morphed from blue to red. The caption above it read:

"BREAKING NEWS: WV RECOUNT OVER. ROYAL BACK AHEAD BY 62."

Rikki shook her head sadly, turned off the television and picked up the book again, hoping Nicholas Sparks might alleviate the anger and aching in her heart.

CHAPTER 54

CHARLESTON, WEST VIRGINIA
TUESDAY, NOVEMBER 25, 7:30 A.M.

Dave sat in the hotel lounge, attacking his syrup-drenched waffles with fork and knife. Raising a cold Diet Coke to his lips, he felt a hand slap his back. Gazing into his blind spot, he saw Gil Dean wearing a huge smile.

"You look like you got a good night's sleep," Dave quipped.

"Oh, yeah!" Gil said enthusiastically. "I slept like a baby. How about you?"

"For the first time in recent memory, I actually slept through the night."

"Mind if I join you? I was hoping to ask for a favor."

"Sure thing," Dave answered. "What can I do for ya?"

Gil let out a deep sigh and took a seat cattycornered from Dave. "I got a call from Monica at six this morning. She's pretty torn up about the beating Marcus is getting in the press. I was shocked by her emotional state, to be honest. I've known her for years, and I've never seen her get this upset about *anything*."

Dave leaned back in his chair and crossed his arms. *"Really?"*

Gil nodded. "She's hardcore, Dave. She makes Margaret Thatcher look like Mother Theresa. What you heard from her yesterday morning ... That was no act."

"Wow. That's pretty impressive. A little terrifying, too."

"Yeah, well, she was a blubbering mess this morning. She didn't tell me what happened, but I'm *certain* Monica was the driving force behind finding those extra votes for Governor Royal. And she's wracked by guilt and self-loathing now, worried that her help may have destroyed her brother's life."

Dave nodded sympathetically. "So what do you want me to do?"

"Give her a call," Gil replied. "Show her Governor Royal and his inner circle know of her dedication to the cause. That would go a long way towards bucking up her spirits."

Dave cut off a chunk of waffle and took another bite. "Done. Anything else?"

"Martinsburg's just about an hour from D.C. Why don't you make arrangements to have lunch with her. She's a pharmaceutical sales rep, but politics is her true passion. Maybe you could find her a job with the new administration.

Dave chewed on both the waffles and Gil's suggestion. "Every new administration needs its share of true believers. Without those foot soldiers pushing its agenda through the permanent bureaucracy, no new initiatives get implemented. Tell you what: I'll meet with her and gauge her interest in joining our team. Lord knows we'll need to hire countless 'Under Secretaries' and 'Deputy Assistant Secretaries' come January."

Gil smiled broadly. "Excellent." Then, staring down at the unadorned ring finger on Dave's left hand, he added, "And for the record, she's a real knockout. Unattached, too."

Dave took a sip of Diet Coke and almost choked. "Thanks, but no thanks," he coughed. "Margaret Thatcher was a hell of a prime minister, but I'd bet her husband had a *miserable* home life. Can you imagine what it was like around their house when he forgot to take out the trash?"

Gil smirked. "Don't jump to conclusions. You can't always judge a book by its cover."

Dave scowled. Just as he began to respond, he saw Tyson Vasquez pontificating loudly on TV. Glancing around, he saw no one else watching the broadcast, so he leapt up and repeatedly pressed the volume button before returning to his seat.

Vasquez stared into the camera. "We feel confident that once we share our evidence demonstrating the Republicans' countless acts of fraud and intimidation in West Virginia, Senator Wilson will emerge victorious."

Dave laughed loudly, shoveled another bite of waffles into his mouth, and shook his head amusedly. "Good luck with that," he cracked.

Gil's brow furrowed. "What do you mean?"

Dave cocked his left eyebrow and grinned. "Because unlike Tyson Vasquez, I've actually *read* West Virginia's laws on post-recount election contests. And the moment their lawyers do the same, they're gonna crap their pants."

CHAPTER 55

ARLINGTON, VIRGINIA
TUESDAY, NOVEMBER 25, 8:45 A.M.

Senator Wilson and her Beltway advisors circled around a table in her national campaign headquarters. Other key players around the country, including Vincent and Bowen, were connected to headquarters via secure videoconferencing.

Susan Mathis, the campaign's lead lawyer in West Virginia, looked grim.

"We may have a problem," she said solemnly.

"Of course we have a problem," the campaign chairman snapped. "Unless we overcome this deficit, Royal's going to be our next president. That's a *huge* problem."

The lawyer's jaw muscles tightened. "I'm talking about a more specific problem."

"And what would that be, Susan?" Senator Wilson asked.

"Technically speaking, we may not be able to contest the results of this election."

"*What?!*" Tyson Vasquez shouted. "Why not?"

Mathis remained stoic. "Because state law doesn't specifically provide a mechanism for a losing presidential candidate to contest the results after the recount is completed."

"How's that possible?" Vincent asked.

The lawyer sighed. "It sounds preposterous, I know. But my office emailed the relevant code sections to you this morning and I'll put the section headlines onscreen for you now."

With the click of a button, her face disappeared from the screen, replaced by an outline of the section headlines from Chapter 3, Article 7 of the West Virginia Code:

CHAPTER 3. ELECTIONS.
ARTICLE 7. CONTESTED ELECTIONS.

§3-7-1. Contests for state offices and judgeships; procedure.

§3-7-2. Procedure of Legislature on contest for office of governor.

§3-7-3. Contests before special court; procedure; enforcement.
"Where the election of secretary of state, auditor, treasurer, attorney general, commissioner of agriculture, or of a judge of the supreme court of appeals, or of a circuit court, is contested, the case shall be heard and decided by a special court..."

§3-7-4. Contests of seats in Legislature; notices and procedure.

§3-7-5. Depositions; subpoenas; time; tie vote decision.

§3-7-6. County and district contests; notices; time.

§3-7-7. County court to hear county and district contests; procedure; review.

§3-7-8. Correction of returns; extent.

§3-7-9. Costs in election contests.

A minute passed before Mathis spoke again. "Those are the only nine Code sections that deal with election contests. Does it seem like something is missing?"

Evan Rothman, the campaign's general counsel, suddenly gasped. "Oh, my God. There's no provision for the contest of a *presidential* election."

"Precisely," Mathis stated. "And that's our problem in a nutshell."

CHAPTER 56

ST. MARYS, PLEASANTS COUNTY, WEST VIRGINIA
TUESDAY NOVEMBER 25, 10:35 A.M.

Jack laced up his boots, heading for a meeting with a farmer he hoped would grant McCallen Resources a right-of-way across his land to service its wells on adjoining properties. Standing up, he heard the telltale beep heralding his receipt of a new email message.

Knowing the farmer was a cantankerous geezer, Jack's first instinct was to delay looking at the email until after their meeting. Then he realized Petromica should have received his production logs the day before, and *nothing* was higher on his priority list than the Petromica deal.

McCallen stomped toward the office, his boots loudly smacking the hardwood floor with every step. Sitting down at the computer, he opened the message:

Due Diligence, Part II
From: alex.beria@petromica.com
To: Jack@mccallenresources.com
Date: Tues, 25 Nov 10:31 am
Attachment: royaltyaffidavit.doc

Dear Mr. McCallen,

Thanks for getting me the production logs and expense breakdown so quickly. While our eggheads review them, please sign the attached affidavit attesting that MR is not delinquent in paying any rentals or royalties on its leaseholds and return it via email. If you have any delinquencies, fix them or give me a breakdown so we can account for those debts at closing.

Thanks for everything and I look forward to working together.

Sincerely,

Alex

Jack mumbled profanely, printed the attachment and headed for his meeting.

WEST VIRGINIA STATE CAPITOL
CHARLESTON, WEST VIRGINIA
TUESDAY NOVEMBER 25, 11:45 A.M.

"We have to let them know by noon," Bowen said.

Vincent stood by the window and stared at the Capitol lawn. "I know. I'm thinking."

Bowen tightened his lips and twiddled his thick thumbs. Finally, Vincent turned from the window. "We want to steer clear of Mingo, Braxton and Wyoming, right?"

Bowen snorted. "I wouldn't want some judge reopening *those* cans of worms."

Pacing the room with his arms crossed, he raised his right hand and stroked his chin. "And we want to include Berkeley County, so we can shovel around in their graveyard."

Bowen nodded. "Especially if we get the right judge. Which shouldn't be a problem."

Vincent came to a stop. "Fine. If our contact in the Circuit Clerk's office will play ball with us, we'll put Berkeley on the list. But there are two Republican judges on the bench in that circuit, and I don't want one of *them* handling our case."

"Unless you want it to die a quick death," Bowen quipped bitterly. "What other counties are you considering?"

"Mercer and Monongalia," Vincent replied. "We carried Mercer County, it has a sizeable black population, and the judges are friendly with me at the moment. Monongalia has WVU. Surely we can find 60 college kids to swear their rights were infringed on Election Day."

Bowen jotted down notes. "Good choices. I'll pass the word to Tyson. Hopefully, at least one of these judges will give us another bite at the apple."

Vincent sighed. "It'll be tough with just one work day before Thanksgiving. Then the courts are closed until Monday, December 1st. Time is running out."

Bowen tapped his pen on the scratch pad. "Never say, 'never.'"

CHAPTER 57

PLEASANTS COUNTY COURTHOUSE
ST. MARYS, PLEASANTS COUNTY, WEST VIRGINIA
TUESDAY, NOVEMBER 25, 4:30 P.M.

"Hey, Rikki … Is your secretary around?"

Rikki looked up and saw Jack in her doorway, clutching a manila folder. His work boots were caked with mud. "Maybe. What nightmare are you dropping on us now?"

"No nightmares from me today. Just an affidavit I need notarized."

Rikki set aside the West Virginia Code book she was scanning and stood up. "We can help with that. I think she's across the hallway."

He cleared a path and followed her next door where three women were quietly gossiping. Jack smiled. "All right, ladies, break it up! What are ya'll whispering about, anyway?"

The circuit clerk grinned conspiratorially. "I was just saying I'm so glad those lawyers fighting over the election haven't descended on our courthouse like a plague of locusts. From what I'm hearing, others around the state aren't so lucky."

Jack crossed his arms. "Do tell."

"Well, you know circuit court clerks don't have to be lawyers or anything. We just process paperwork, stamp everything that's filed and put documents where they belong. When the judge – or anybody else, for that matter – wants to know what's going on in a case, we hand him the file and let *him* figure it out."

He chuckled. "Makes sense to me."

"Some types of pleadings we see all the time," she said. "Complaints, answers, appeals from DMV decisions suspending someone's driver's license, etc. That stuff is common. We could process it in our sleep. But occasionally, someone files something we've never seen before. In that case, we'll ask colleagues in other counties for advice. Worst case scenario, we can call the Supreme Court's administrative office, and *they* can tell us what to do."

The woman shook her head like she was whisking eggs with it. "Well, Senator Wilson's lawyers apparently dumped something on those poor folks in Berkeley County this morning that stumped everyone. *Nobody* knew what to do with it, not even the folks with the Supreme Court. No one's ever seen anything like it."

Rikki's light green eyes sparkled. "*Oooooh*. Now you have my attention. What was it?"

"The lawyers called it a 'Notice of Contested Election Slash Petition For Writ Of Mandamus,'" she carefully replied. "The courts in Morgantown and Princeton received fairly identical documents."

"State courts?" Rikki asked.

"Yes. Circuit courts in Monongalia, Mercer and Berkeley counties."

Jack's brow creased. "So what in the world will they do with those things?"

229

She shrugged. "No clue. The Berkeley County judge is hearing it tomorrow at ten. The Republican lawyers are up in arms about it, too. They say he doesn't have jurisdiction."

"I need to call Dave and get the inside scoop," Jack said. "That sounds crazy."

Rikki's back stiffened, but she tried to act nonplussed. "Well, I for one hope they look into what happened last night in Martinsburg. It sure looked shady the way those votes for Royal materialized at the last second under the *watchful* eyes of his lapdog, Marcus Boley."

Jack guffawed. "Yeah, right. And those knuckle-draggin' redneck Democrats guarding Mingo County's ballot boxes were sweet little choir boys, huh?"

Rikki glowered at him. "*This* is why we should *never* discuss politics, Jack."

Grinned from ear-to-ear, he chuckled loudly. "Ah, hell, Rikki ... You're the one who started it. I'm just saying the folks on your side ain't as innocent as you'd like 'em to be. Lighten up a little!"

Rikki folded her arms over her breasts, clenching her jaw. "Let's agree to disagree, Jack. I'm still hoping Senator Wilson will find a way to win this thing."

Jack smirked playfully. "Pardon my French, but if you hope in one hand and shit in the other, which one do you think will fill up first? And besides, the polls are on *our* side. People are sick of this election. They want it to be *over*. The polls show 63 percent of the public wants your girl to throw in the towel and let everyone move on."

Rikki's pale green eyes flashed. "Maybe the polls from Fox News. But the poll I saw this morning showed half the people are suspicious of West Virginia's final results. *Half!?*"

Jack shrugged. "Just shows you can't please a bunch of granola-crunching Yankees."

Rikki shut her eyes and shook her head violently. "All right! I've had it! We're going to drop the politics right now, or you can get your affidavit notarized elsewhere!"

He threw his arms up in surrender. "Okay, okay! As soon as Martha notarizes my affidavit, I'll drag my Cro-Magnon self out of here. I promise."

Still gritting her teeth, Rikki jabbed her finger at McCallen. "Not another word or I swear I'll rip the damn thing up." With that, she stormed across the hall to her office.

Watching her leave, Jack chuckled but said nothing. He knew better than to disregard her warning, and he valued the affidavit too much to push her limits. A minute later, he quietly slipped downstairs with the notarized affidavit, repressing the urge to let out a belly laugh.

CHAPTER 58

CHARLESTON, WEST VIRGINIA
TUESDAY, NOVEMBER 25, 9:15 P.M.

Dave poured over the opposition's lawsuits to contest the state's final election results with a chilled pint of Guinness in his hand.

"I thought you said they couldn't do this," Gil grumbled.

Dave's nose turned up. "They *can't*. But I never said they couldn't try."

Dave's cell phone rang and he plucked it from Gil's dining room table. "Anderson here."

"Hey, Dave. It's Mack Palmer. Did you get that stuff my office sent you?"

"We're going through it now, but at first glance, it just looks like a lot of whining to me."

Laughter reverberated in Dave's ear. "Good synopsis. Now do you want me to give you my *legal* opinion or my *practical* opinion about these pleadings?"

"Both."

"From a legal standpoint, I don't think there's much there. They raise some interesting points, but the fact remains that the statute *does not* permit them to contest this election. If Melanie Wilson had run for Berkeley County Magistrate, the statute would give her that right *and* – most importantly – it identifies who has the authority to rule on her case. I mean, even if they're right and we cheated like hell on Election Day, who would be empowered to take evidence on the voter intimidation they've alleged? Hmmm? With all the other offices outlined in the statute, the legislature at least designated *somebody* to make the final decision. But not when it comes to a presidential election."

"That was my thought," Dave said. "The statute gives *no one* that right, but it doesn't describe the procedures for contesting a U.S. Senate race either. How does that affect things?"

"I don't think it does at all," Palmer replied. "Back when these laws were enacted, the Legislature still appointed our U.S. senators. Individual citizens didn't have any say in the matter, and that didn't change until 1913, when the Seventeenth Amendment specifically authorized each state's voters to directly vote on their senators. And, as you know, individual citizens *still* don't get to directly vote in presidential races."

"Right," Dave said. "On Election Day, we technically voted for slates of electors nominated by the political parties' state executive committees last summer. Those five people are the ones who *actually* elect the president and vice president when they cast their ballots in the Electoral College on December 15th."

"Given those facts," Palmer expounded, "it's my opinion the Legislature simply dropped the ball here. As far as I know, no U.S. senate race in state history has been close enough to warrant a contest proceeding. Neither has a presidential race. The election contest laws have been on the books for 150 years, and it's my bet *no one ever thought to update those laws* to provide a way for losing candidates in those races to contest the results."

"Unbelievable," Dave said.

"Now for the practical side of things," Palmer continued. "Two of the three judges presiding over these cases are, in my opinion, pure sycophants of the governor. He appointed one to the bench and raised gobs of money for the other. The third is fairly well-regarded as both independent and fair-minded, but I'm sure the Dems would agree with the sentiments expressed by that noted philosopher, Meat Loaf … *'Two out of three ain't bad.'*" Trying to sing, Palmer sounded like a bull that only made it halfway through the castration process.

Dave winced and held the phone from his ear. "Mack, I respect the hell out of you, but please don't sing near me again. That made me want to jam an ice pick in my ear."

"Sorry. Nevertheless, even though the law might not be on their side, the lay of the judicial landscape is. I'd assume at least one of those judges will find some basis for giving Wilson a chance to contest the results."

Dave sighed. "I agree. In that case, go ahead and prepare the paperwork to get this thing in front of the state Supreme Court ASAP. Time is of the essence, and money is no option."

Palmer laughed. "That's my kind of client! And that's why I have four lawyers hyped up on Red Bull and NoDoz, plus three very surly paralegals, working on it right now. Once we receive a judge's order directing that a contest proceeding be commenced, we'll tweak our paperwork accordingly. Within an hour of receiving such an order, our appeal will be filed."

Dave smiled. "That's music to my ears, Mack."

"And that's why you guys pay me the big bucks."

CHAPTER 59

BERKELEY COUNTY JUDICIAL CENTER
MARTINSBURG, BERKELEY COUNTY, WEST VIRGINIA
WEDNESDAY, NOVEMBER 26, 10:05 A.M.

Judge Olivia Barkwell's cherry wood dais sat in front of an old brick wall that had been incorporated into her thoroughly modern courtroom. "So what are you saying?" she asked pointedly. "Do you mean that citizens who were disenfranchised by illegal intimidation on Election Day have no recourse under the law?"

The young female attorney representing Royal shook her head. "Not at all. The persons responsible for such threats could be prosecuted *criminally* for their actions, or the victims could file civil suits to recover monetary damages for their emotional pain and suffering. But state law *does not* permit them to contest the results of an election on those grounds. Under the law, only the *candidates* for certain offices – not including candidates for president – have standing to contest an election result. And if the Legislature had intended to provide either presidential candidates or individual voters with such a remedy, it could have done so." The woman shifted her weight to her right foot. "Senator Wilson bears the burden of proof here, Your Honor. She must identify some legal basis for this Court to determine both *who* is entitled to contest a presidential election in West Virginia and *what entity* has the authority to hear that evidence. Unfortunately, she can do neither."

The attorney sat down and Judge Barkwell turned to opposing counsel. "Any rebuttal?"

A sharply-dressed African American man in his early forties stood up, deftly tugging his French cuffs. "Very briefly, Judge. Senator Wilson and 53 registered voters of this county have laid out a compelling factual basis for their claims. Our affidavits show many voters were harassed and intimidated on Election Day. Moreover, the circumstances surrounding Governor Royal's last-minute gains during Monday's recount seem *questionable* at best. All-in-all, Shakespeare's line from Hamlet probably best summarizes this situation:

"'*Something is rotten in the state of Denmark.*'"

He paused, giving the judge a moment to digest his words. "The Legislature never intended to deny presidential candidates like Senator Wilson the same right to contest an election that it has given candidates for other offices. Any such oversight would be unconstitutional, and to the extent state law does not provide Senator Wilson with an adequate remedy to address these issues, we'd urge this court to use its inherent powers in equity to create one." He then sat down.

Judge Barkwell slowly rotated her chair, rocking it slightly in the process. Her eyes were fixed on the courtroom's rear wall. "This is a very peculiar case," she said. "On the one hand, I'm troubled the Legislature has not given us much guidance here.

On the other hand, I am *deeply* troubled that West Virginians' constitutional rights may have been infringed on Election Day. Just holding individual wrongdoers responsible for their actions, either criminally or civilly, does not seem likely to deter such illegal acts in the future. To minimize the chance this will ever happen again, this court's ruling must remove the temptation to tamper with our election results. And those other remedies would not accomplish that goal."

Judge Barkwell shuffled and restacked the papers on her desk. "Accordingly, I find that Senator Wilson may prosecute her contest of this election. But because the Legislature did not identify what particular entity should conduct such a contest, this court will use its powers in equity to convene such a proceeding itself."

Governor Royal's lawyer stood up, her mouth open.

"The court notes your objections, counsel," the Judge added.

"Thank you," the attorney said. But she looked like someone had poured vinegar in her mouth. "When does the court propose to start the contest proceeding?"

The Judge sighed. "We're in uncharted waters here, folks. The statute requires losing candidates to provide a detailed description of the basis for the contest within 10 days of the election's certification. The winning candidate would then have 10 days to respond to that notice. But we simply don't have that kind of time."

Wilson's lawyer stood again. "We can give you our information by the end of the day, Judge, along with a proposed order reflecting your rulings from today's hearing."

The Judge nodded. "Good. Governor Royal must provide a written response no later than noon on Monday, which is December 1st. The contest proceeding will begin at 8:30 the following morning. Any witnesses you wish to call and any exhibits you want to introduce as evidence will need to be here then."

"Which brings me to the last issue raised in our petition," Wilson's attorney said. "Custody of the ballot boxes, the poll books, and the optical scan ballots themselves."

Sitting in the third row of the courtroom, Monica Boley's heart skipped a beat. *Oh, God. Please don't let this be happening. <u>Please</u>.*

The Judge rubbed her chin. "I understand why you want the Sheriff to seize those items and preserve them for the contest. But West Virginia Code section three dash four-a dash ten vests the *county clerk* with custody of those materials 'except when in use at an election or when in custody of a court or court officers *during* contest proceedings.'

"The contest begins at 8:30 sharp on Tuesday December 2nd," Judge Barkwell continued. "Mr. Boley shall maintain custody of the election materials until that time when he shall deliver them to my courtroom. From that time until the contest is over, *whenever* that may be, my bailiffs will exercise responsibility for safekeeping those items."

Monica felt a wave of relief wash over her. *You have six days to figure out a way to dispose of the incriminating evidence in those ballot boxes. You can do it.*

Wilson's lawyer wrinkled his nose. "I'll include that language in my order, Judge."

"And make sure you give it to opposing counsel and obtain her signature before sending it to me," Barkwill said. "I want everyone to sign that order before I enter it."

The lawyer nodded. "I have my laptop with me, Judge. If opposing counsel can stick around, I'll pound out an order in no time."

The Republican lawyer stood up. "I'll remain here as long as necessary, Judge. We want that order signed and entered as soon as possible."

The Judge barked a short laugh. "I'm sure you do. The sooner it's entered, the sooner you can race down to Charleston to file an appeal with the Supreme Court."

Royal's attorney smiled pleasantly. "We all do what we have to do, Judge. If you had ruled the other way, I'm sure my worthy opponent would be doing the same thing."

CHAPTER 60

WEST VIRGINIA REPUBLICAN HEADQUARTERS
CHARLESTON, WEST VIRGINIA
WEDNESDAY, NOVEMBER 26, 12:15 P.M.

Dave slid his pizza bread to the side. "I'm too nauseous to eat," he announced in a disgusted tone. "I swear to God, this election is going to be the death of me."

Gil smirked. "What's the matter, Dave? Too much excitement for ya?"

"My idea of excitement is riding a roller coaster: You know how long it will last, and the whole thing is on rails so no matter how fast it goes, you know it's under control. *Neither* of which is true here."

Gil chuckled. "Just sit back and enjoy the ride. This amusement park will close soon and you can get back to your mundane life inside the Beltway."

"That day can't come soon enough for me."

The door swung open, and Mack Palmer charged through it. "The judge in Mercer County ruled against us, too. That makes us oh-for-three today."

Gil pounded the desk. "Great. Do you have any *good* news to offer?"

Palmer clenched one eye shut and bobbed his head from shoulder-to-shoulder, processing the question. "If there's a silver lining, the judge in Monongalia County didn't convene his own contest. He said the presidential election was analogous to a statewide race like attorney general instead of other positions elected by residents of individual counties. Thus, he ordered a three-member 'special court' be convened next Tuesday to conduct the contest. That panel will consist of one person designated by each of the two candidates and a third appointed by the governor."

Gil's jaw dropped. "*Vincent* would appoint the tie-breaker? That's the *good news?*"

Dave snapped his fingers. "A-*ha!* If all three contests don't follow the same procedure, they're violating the terms of the Supreme Court's decision in <u>Bush v. Gore</u>."

Palmer nodded. "*There's* your silver lining. One reason the Supreme Court put a stop to Florida's post-election proceedings in 2000 was the lack of 'uniformity' among the procedures enacted by different counties. Now we have two judges doing one thing and a third doing something completely different. It strengthens our arguments."

Gil shook his head. "No wonder the public can't make heads-or-tails of this crap."

CHAPTER 61

PLEASANTS COUNTY COURTHOUSE
ST. MARYS, PLEASANTS COUNTY, WEST VIRGINIA
WEDNESDAY, NOVEMBER 26, 2:30 P.M.

Rikki heard a knock at her door. Glancing up, she saw Jack smiling sheepishly.

"Have you forgiven me for pushing your buttons yesterday?" he said.

Rikki pursed her lips and exhaled through her nose, staring holes through him. "I've *told* you politics are off-limits, haven't I?"

Remaining tight-lipped, Jack nodded. "I'm sorry. I just got carried away when you started badmouthing Marcus Boley. I've met him, and I'm telling you, he's a good guy."

"Maybe. But even good guys do bad things sometimes; especially in politics. That's all I was saying."

"Fair enough, counselor. I'll try not to get your goat anymore, and we'll just 'agree to disagree' as you put it."

Rikki smiled widely. "Aw, Jack ... You know the quickest way to warm my heart is to quote *me*, because that means you know I *was right*."

Jack chuckled. "On that one small point anyway."

"So what brings you here, Jack? I'm sure apologizing isn't all that's on your agenda."

"Right again, counselor. Beria emailed me a draft contract for the Petromica deal. Nothing's final, of course, until they complete their 'due diligence' investigations."

Jack grabbed a chair and scooted up to Rikki's desk. Lifting his beat-up leather briefcase onto her desk, he unlatched the lid, pulled out an inch-thick document and dropped it on her desk. "Here it is."

Rikki thumbed through it. "Dear Lord! This looks horrible! I hope you're not expecting *me* to read this whole thing!"

"Sure I am. You're my lawyer, aren't you? And Petromica wants our response by the close of business on Monday. Beria's email said something about a 'non-disclosure agreement' I have to sign before they'll even discuss the deal any further."

Rikki stared back at him, wide-eyed and slack-jawed. "Jack, tomorrow is *Thanksgiving*. I do *oil and gas*, not mergers and acquisitions, plus I just took office as the county prosecutor. Throw in that Schoolcraft lease cancelation suit of yours, and my plate is completely full. There's no way I could review that thing before Monday, and there's no way I could get someone else to look at it any sooner due to the holiday. You need more time. See if they'll give you until next Wednesday, at least."

McCallen frowned. "I don't know. They seem eager to get this deal finalized. What I'll probably do is just nod it on through at this point. Before I actually sign a purchase agreement, I'll have you rustle up someone to go over it with a proctoscope. Your pre-nup guy did a great job, so I trust you'll find me a good mergers and acquisitions guy, too."

Rikki reclined her chair. "So how *is* the home life going for you?" she asked, imbuing her words with compassion instead of gawky curiosity.

Jack's mouth tightened. "*Schizophrenic* would be a good word to describe it."

"Sorry to hear that. Let me know if I can do anything."

"Thanks, Rikki. I appreciate that."

Jack put the contract in his briefcase and rose to his feet. "And on that note, I'll take my leave. Tell your mom I said, 'Hi,' and you guys have a Happy Thanksgiving."

"You, too, Jack. I'll try to find someone to review that contract on Monday, and you buy some more time. That thing might be thicker than the Kyoto Protocol."

McCallen's eyes twinkled devilishly. "Leave it to a granola-cruncher like you to bring up the Kyoto Protocol. I thought politics were supposed to be off-limits."

Rikki acted like she was looking for something to throw at him. "Get out of here, Jack, before I bean you upside the head."

The oilman ran out the door. As he rounded the corner and entered the stairwell, Rikki heard his laughter bellowing with each step.

WEST VIRGINIA REPUBLICAN HEADQUARTERS
CHARLESTON, WEST VIRGINIA
WEDNESDAY, NOVEMBER 26, 4:45 P.M.

"Yes, Mom," Dave said into his phone. "I'll be there for Thanksgiving dinner. No, I don't know when I'll make it ... It depends on what the Supreme Court does with the appeals we filed this afternoon."

His phone beeped, and he saw Palmer was calling on the other line. "Mom, I gotta take this call. I'll call you as soon as I know what's going on. Love you, too. Bye."

Dave flashed over to the incoming call. "Talk to me, Mack."

"We have a stay of execution, my friend. The Court voted four-to-one to hear our petition. They've ordered the three lower courts to halt their respective contests."

"Hot damn! So when will they rule on our petition?"

"Don't know, but they put it on the quickest rocket docket I've ever seen. All parties must submit written briefs by noon on Monday, and oral arguments are on Tuesday, December 2nd at eleven."

Dave whistled. "Wow. You weren't joking. That's quick!"

"They know the clock's ticking. The federal 'Safe Harbor Provision' expires seven days after oral arguments. This whole fiasco must be over by December 9th or West Virginia could lose its right to cast ballots in the Electoral College altogether."

"Well, you've made my day," Dave said. "I'll spread the word. You have my cell if you need me over the weekend."

Palmer chortled. "Yeah, and I have your parents' number, too. So don't pretend you have no cell service up there because I'll track your ass down regardless."

"I won't. Now I can drive to Saint Marys tonight."

"Well, enjoy the breather while you can," Palmer said.

Dave quickly called his mom back. The thought of her homemade cranberry sauce was already making his mouth water.

CHAPTER 62

VIENNA, VIRGINIA
THURSDAY, NOVEMBER 27, 12:35 P.M.

Yuri Petrenko was sprawled on his couch with a bottle of beer watching the day's first NFL game when his phone rang.

Carefully inserting his Bluetooth headset into his mangled ear, he answered, "Hello?"

"Good afternoon, Yuri. This is Tyson. How's your Thanksgiving going?"

"Good," Petrenko replied, still watching the game. "What can I do for you?"

"Bowen's on the line and I've conferenced us all together. You there, Dick?"

"Yeah, I'm here," Bowen said.

"Dick doesn't think our odds of influencing West Virginia's Supreme Court decision next week look too good. Dick, could you explain?"

Bowen cleared his throat. "Our five Supreme Court justices are politicians in their own right who have gone through grueling statewide campaigns to win those elected seats. All the skeletons we know of are fairly common knowledge and won't elicit much fear in the justices."

Petrenko sighed and muted the game. "Give me their names. I'll see what I can dig up."

"That's what we hoped," Bowen said. "First, we have Sam Willoughby. W-I-L-L-O-U-G-H-B-Y. Generally a middle-of-the-road guy, he's originally from Wheeling. He was the only justice who voted *against* accepting Royal's petition."

Petrenko scribbled the info down. "Got it. Next?"

"Chief Justice Andrea Reddick. R-E-D-D-I-C-K. She's a judicial conservative. Comes from Huntington and old family money."

"Reddick," Petrenko repeated. "Okay."

"Third is Scott Turner from Lewisburg, the lone Republican on the Court. Even though I doubt he'd vote our way *this* time, we'd still love to get some dirt on that sanctimonious son-of-a-bitch. It could come in handy later."

"My only goal is to win this election," Petrenko coldly retorted. "I don't care what you do with this information afterwards. Who's next?"

After a brief moment of silence, Bowen continued. "Next is Don Gammalo. G-A-M-M-A-L-O. He's from Clarksburg and has a big pro-union background. But he's a wild card."

Petrenko's brow furrowed. "How so?"

"He got beat in the Democratic primary by a more pro-business candidate. The Chamber of Commerce dumped gobs of money into his opponent's campaign, and Don kinda blames Governor Vincent for his loss. Let's just say he still has some hard feelings towards us."

"Gotcha," the Russian stated. "And last up, we have ..."

"Brock Lilly, a Democrat from Beckley. L-I-L-L-Y. He's another wild card, in that he didn't run for re-election. Between the 14 years he spent as a circuit judge and the 12 years he just finished on the Supreme Court, he has enough time to retire. And that's *exactly* what he's doing January 1st, so he never has to worry about running for election again."

Petrenko finished his notes. "We'll see what comes up."

"Thanks," Vasquez said. "And by the way…How are your other projects going?"

"Too early to tell, but I'm optimistic. I'll keep you in the loop."

"Excellent," Vasquez said. "Happy hunting and I'll talk to you later."

"*Hasta.*" Hanging up the phone, he turned up the volume in time to hear Detroit's crowd go wild over an interception returned for a touchdown.

Sinking into his sofa, Yuri placed his notes on the coffee table and took another drink of beer. *I can dig up dirt on hillbilly judges later. Right now, there's a game on.*

CHAPTER 63

CHARLESTON, WEST VIRGINIA
THURSDAY, NOVEMBER 27, 3:55 P.M.

Wearing an apron, Governor Vincent ladled mashed potatoes onto a white Styrofoam plate. "There you go, ma'am," he said, smiling. "You have a Happy Thanksgiving."

Years ago, a blue-collar entrepreneur began hosting a holiday dinner for Charleston's less fortunate. When he died, he left a trust fund with enough money to carry on the tradition. Now the dinner had grown so big that West Virginia's elites fought over the honor (and free publicity) associated with acting as servers for the event.

With his shift ending, the governor kept a close eye on the whereabouts of another server. Justice Don Gammalo had participated in the dinner for twelve years. As Gammalo shed his apron and started saying his good-byes, Vincent subtly began making his own exit.

The governor rarely escaped from such functions quickly. People wanted to shake his hand, bend his ear, get an autograph or have a picture taken. Today, though, he had carefully crafted a strategy to minimize those delays. Turning from the serving line, he surreptitiously dialed Bowen, waited five seconds and hung up. He then walked into the kitchen to shake hands with the cooks who had prepared the feast.

"Thanks for your hard work," he said, gripping one hand after another. "Wonderful job."

Suddenly, his phone rang. "Pardon me," he whispered, answering the call. "Hello? Yes. Okay, then ... I'll be right there."

The governor hung up with notable flourish. "I'm afraid I have to cut this short, folks. I'm needed back at the Mansion. Keep up the good work and God bless you."

With that, he waved goodbye and stepped through a side door into the church parking lot; his Secret Service detail close behind. Quickly glancing around, he saw Justice Gammalo ambling toward his aged Jeep about thirty yards away.

"Hey, Don!" Vincent called. "Wait up a second."

Gammalo stopped and turned around. Seeing Vincent walking toward him, the jurist's eyes narrowed and his mouth twisted sourly.

Vincent trotted to Gammalo's position while his bodyguards maintained a respectful distance. "I've been meaning to catch up with you for a few weeks, but I haven't had time. Things have been so hectic since the election."

Gammalo peered up beneath bushy gray eyebrows at Vincent. "I wouldn't know. My election cycle ended after the primary in *May*, thanks to you."

Vincent feigned injury and innocence. "Don! I didn't have anything to do with your race. I swear!"

"Ha! My opponent's campaign contributors list had your fingerprints all over it. I may have been born at night, but I wasn't born *last* night."

Vincent sighed, spreading his arms with his palms up. "Look, Don, I know you think I supported the other guy, and we've been friends for thirty years. You supported me the first time I ran for the Legislature, and I don't want there to be any bad blood between us. I just wanted you to know some friends of mine have endowed a professorship at WVU's law school. We've discussed it, and I think you'd be the perfect candidate for that position. You have a lifetime of experience to share with students, and you'd have a very comfortable salary. It would be a win-win for everybody."

Gammalo clenched his jaw. His brown eyes blazed. "You're right, Luke," he said slowly. "I *did* support you in that first race. And you stabbed me in the back because your new friends at the Chamber of Commerce dislike some of the opinions I've written from the bench."

The old jurist took a deep breath and pulled his gloved right hand out of his coat pocket. "You used to stand for the working man, Luke," he said, jabbing his finger into the governor's face. "*That's* why I supported you when you first ran for the Legislature."

Gammalo paused, his eyes burrowing into Vincent. "But somewhere along the way, Luke, you *changed*. You don't support anyone but *yourself* now. And if I were you, I'd take a long hard look in the mirror and try to figure out how that happened." The Justice turned and strolled away. "By the way, Luke," he shouted over his shoulder. "Your friends can keep that professorship. I'd rather have a clear conscience than a cushy job any day of the week."

Vincent found himself at a loss for words. He wanted to defend himself, to change the old man's mind and influence his vote in the appeal. But as he watched Gammalo slowly walk toward his old Jeep, the governor was utterly speechless.

CHAPTER 64

PLEASANTS COUNTY, WEST VIRGINIA
SATURDAY, NOVEMBER 29, 6:45 P.M.

His two sons grew louder and rowdier as kickoff drew near for the WVU/Pitt game. Jack knew Tabatha would start yelling if he let the ruckus continue, so he quickly reviewed his email to Beria one last time:

Re: Draft Contract/Due Diligence, Part III
From: Jack@mccallenresources.com
To: alex.beria@petromica.com
bcc: OGMLawyer@hotmail.com
Attachment: enviroaffidavit.doc

Hello Alex,

Thanks for sending the purchase agreement. My lawyers need more time to review it due to the Thanksgiving holiday, but I will respond by next Wednesday.

As indicated in my affidavit, MR is in good standing with the state and federal environmental agencies. There are no environmental claims against MR, and I don't believe any of our other leaseholds are in danger of lapsing due to non-development.

Once my lawyers give their OK, I'll sign the non-disclosure agreement and fax it to you. I trust Petromica now has everything needed to finish its 'due diligence.' It was time-consuming to gather those documents & I hope we finalize this deal soon.

Have a good weekend!

Jack

"What's taking so long to close this deal?" Tabatha asked pointedly. She stood behind him, peering over his shoulder at the computer screen.

Jack literally jumped an inch in the air. "Holy shit! Where did you come from?"

"From in there," she answered, motioning with her head toward the family room. "I came to tell you that if you don't want to find your boys chopped up into little pieces and shoved under the house, you need to get in there and start cracking down on them."

"They're just excited about the game," he bristled. "If we win tonight, we'll probably play for the national championship! This is huge!"

Tabatha snorted. "I've heard *that* before. WVU always finds a way to lose, and this year is no different."

Jack clicked and sent his email. Standing up, he turned and faced Tabatha. "That's the beauty of college football: Anything can happen on any given Saturday, and true fans always find a way to believe in their team."

Tabatha leaned back and cackled. "What a crock of shit. And only someone as naïve as you would say such a thing."

Jack felt his face flush. "What do you mean?"

"The world is full of winners and losers, Jack. It's that simple. The Ohio States and Floridas of the world are winners. The WVUs of the world are losers. No matter how hard they work or believe their dreams will come true, they always choke."

She paused, examining Jack closely, and his neck hair rose. He had seen this malicious spark in her eyes before, and he realized she was about to turn on him like a rabid dog.

"Come to think of it," she added. "WVU reminds me a lot of *you*, Jack. And I bet this Petromica deal goes down the shitter, too. But then again, I've been married to you so long I'm used to it now." She closed with a short, bitter laugh.

Jack's hands were balled into fists and his heart pounded in his chest. "People will be here any minute," he said very deliberately. "So go upstairs, turn on the Lifetime channel, and stay in the bedroom until the game is over and everyone is gone. Because if I see your face down here the rest of the night, I don't think I'll able to control myself."

Tabatha pursed her lips. "Don't worry, Jack. I'll stay *well* out of your hair tonight. The last thing I want to see is a bunch of grown men crying over a football game." Strolling away casually, she laughed again, leaving the echoes of her heels wafting behind her.

The musical doorbell interrupted Jack's fury. He glanced at his watch. It was 6:58. Closing his eyes, he filled his lungs with air then slowly exhaled.

After composing himself, Jack walked to the front door and opened it. Dave Anderson stood beneath the porch light with a mischievous smile and a twelve pack.

Jack stood aside and made a sweeping, inward motion with his right arm. "Come on in. The game will be starting any minute."

Dave stepped inside. "You want me to put these in the fridge?"

"Yeah," Jack replied. "Right after you pull out two of 'em for us."

They strolled down the hallway into the kitchen. Walking past the family room, Jack peered in and saw his two sons lying in the floor, facing the big screen TV. WVU's players were on the field wearing white jerseys with gold pants, lined up for the opening kick.

"Let's move it, Dave!" he yelled. "They're kicking off!"

Glass bottles loudly clanged against one another, then the refrigerator door slammed shut and Dave jogged into the family room. He handed Jack a beer. "I didn't miss anything, did I?"

"Not yet," Jack replied, sitting on the couch. Dave followed suit.

Pitt's kicker booted the ball. Arcing down, it landed in the outstretched arms of WVU's return man who sprinted behind his wall of blockers, blowing past defenders until he was tackled violently at the 40 yard line.

Logan and Brandon cheered loudly, kicking their sock-clad feet against the carpet. Jack uncapped his bottle and extended it to Dave. "Cheers, my friend."

Dave clinked bottles with his mentor. "Let's Go, Mountaineers! Win this one, and it's on to the championship!"

Feeling a sense of contentment, Jack nodded. Gazing around the room at his two sons and his former protégée, he felt both nostalgic and optimistic.

To hell with Tabatha, he thought with a smile. *Maybe she's too bitter to believe dreams can come true. But everyone else here knows better.*

APPALACHIAN POWER PARK
CHARLESTON, WEST VIRGINIA
SATURDAY, NOVEMBER 29, 8:30 P.M.

Governor Vincent ambled through the club suite to the restroom. Entering a stall, he was draining his bladder when his cell phone vibrated.

Flicking twice, he flushed the toilet with his foot and redressed. His phone indicated he had received a new multimedia message.

Vincent sat on the toilet. WVU had just taken over on downs and he felt confident no one would walk in the john while the Mountaineers' offense had the ball.

Tabatha's message read, "Don't you miss Pleasants County hospitality?" Sensing danger, he quickly lowered the volume and took a deep breath.

As the video started, his stomach dropped. Tabatha was outstretched on a bed, wearing a lacy black bra and matching thong panties, while black thigh-high hose covered her long legs. "Why don't you come here, Mr. Governor?" she playfully asked, motioning sensuously with one finger for him to approach. Her words were almost inaudible, but he could follow along by combining his memories with a little lip-reading.

Vincent's image appeared, taking a position by the bed. Recognizing his baby blue golf shirt and khaki pants, he suddenly remembered this tryst: It had occurred the previous summer in a St. Marys motel room, during his trip to the annual Bass Festival.

He watched Tabatha unbutton his khakis, sliding his pants and underwear down his legs. Prostrating herself on the bed, she took him in her mouth. As the scene unfolded, he felt frozen, unable to tear his eyes away.

Two minutes later, Vincent watched himself slowly remove Tabatha's panties and part her legs, positioning himself for entry. She moaned, her long red hair flailing across the sheet as her fingernails dug into his chest. Then he regained control of his senses and shut off the video.

In a split-second, he had a plan. Tapping a carefully worded response, he put away the phone and walked over to the sink.

Washing his hands, he poured cool water on his face and examined himself in the mirror.

This all will be over very soon.

CHAPTER 65

PLEASANTS COUNTY, WEST VIRGINIA
SATURDAY, NOVEMBER 29, 9:40 P.M.

Jack stared at the TV from the edge of his seat. Dave nervously rubbed his palms together. They were waiting for WVU's offense to retake the field after using its last timeout.

"Come on," Dave softly pleaded, rocking back and forth. "We need six here."

A huge bear of a man sitting to Jack's left cried, "Put the ball in the end zone, damn it!" With a thick, dark brown moustache and bushy beard, he was wearing one of the shiny navy blue jerseys WVU wore for most home games.

Jack frowned and elbowed the man in the ribs. "Daggone it, Bart! Watch what you're saying! Your nephews are young and impressionable."

"Sorry, brother. You know what Mountaineer games do to me."

Jack shook his head sadly. "Yeah, I know." Then he jammed a finger into the soft side of his brother's gut. "If I was you, I'd worry more about all those *bacon cheeseburgers* you're eating. If you don't lose some weight, the Mountaineers are gonna give you a coronary."

"That's what I keep telling him!" Bart's wife exclaimed. "I'm waiting for him to keel over one morning as he's climbing up on his tractor."

"All right, Melinda! All right!" Bart McCallen conceded. "I'll start taking better care of myself, I swear." Turning his eyes skyward, the grizzly-looking man declared, "Lord ... if You help our boys pull this game out of their keister, I promise I'll start living better. I *swear!*"

Logan hopped up and down. *"Come on*, Mountaineers!!!"

WVU's players began approaching the line of scrimmage at Pitt's 32 yard line. The defenders scurried around the short side of the field in blue jerseys with gold numbers and blue pants. The graphic at the bottom of the screen read:

"PITT 28   WVU 24   0:09   4th & 7"

Two WVU players lined up wide on the left side of the ball with another two spread out near the far hash mark. The quarterback and tailback stood in the backfield, and the quarterback barked out calls, struggling to be heard over the roaring Pittsburgh crowd. Slashing his right hand down toward the ground like a knife, the quarterback tensed, preparing for the snap. Recognizing the signal, the center raised his head and hiked the ball.

Then all hell broke loose.

The quarterback rolled to his left, clutching the ball in his reliable left hand, while the tailback sprinted in the opposite direction. The two receivers on the right side ran downfield, breaking off into their respective routes, as did one of the receivers on the left.

The second player who had lined up on the left sideline, however, had trotted in motion prior to the snap. When the ball was hiked, he swiftly changed his trajectory and swung wide to the right, sprinting into the backfield. As the quarterback and the receiver drew close to one another, the quarterback deftly made a one-handed backwards pitch with his left hand, safely delivering the ball to the receiver as he bolted past him, heading the other way.

"That's the backup quarterback!" Dave yelled. Sensing a trick play, everyone screamed.

Several Pitt defenders froze, trying to react. One receiver ran a flag pattern, breaking toward the right sideline near the 10 yard line, while the other receiver on that side ran a skinny post toward the back of the end zone. After initially running straight downfield, the receiver who had lined up on the left side changed course, running a mirror-image skinny post. In the meantime, the tailback ran to the 5 yard line and curled back toward the line of scrimmage.

The defensive backs maneuvered swiftly, blanketing the receivers. In the melee, however, no one remembered to cover the starting quarterback, who had sprinted down the left sideline on a fly pattern and was frantically motioning for the ball.

As a linebacker dropped out of coverage and came charging toward the backfield, the backup quarterback came to a dead stop, turned his body 45 degrees toward the left side of the field and uncorked his cannon arm, heaving the ball to the back corner of the end zone. A Pitt cornerback, suddenly recognizing the gap in coverage, tried to race toward the uncovered white jersey flying downfield at the 10 yard line, but it was too late. The backup quarterback's rocket throw hit the starting quarterback perfectly in stride, right on the numbers.

"Touchdown West Virginia!" the announcer screamed. Jack hooted and pumped his fist in the air. Logan gave Dave a high five. Brandon was running in place excitedly when Aunt Melinda snatched him, thrust him up in the air and smothered him with kisses. Jack's teary-eyed brother, Bart, pointed at the ceiling and shouted, "*Thank you, Jesus! Thank you!!*"

In the time it had taken the play to develop, the game clock had run down to triple zeros, and white-jerseyed Mountaineers were hugging one another, rolling around on the turf. As the cameras focused on the dejected faces of two stunned Pitt players, everyone in Jack's family room began to chant, "We want *Florida!* We want *Florida!* We want *Florida!*"

Jack slipped out to fetch another round of beers for himself, Dave and Bart. As he approached the kitchen, the sound of Tabatha's voice stopped him cold.

"*Yes!* He wants to see me *next week!* I don't know how I'll arrange it, though. I'll have to start plotting now."

His head started to spin. *Someone wants my wife to sneak off and meet him?* As he shifted his weight from one foot to another, the hardwood planks beneath him creaked.

"Hold on just a second, Betsy. From all the screaming going on, something big must have happened. Plus, I think someone might be coming."

Jack placed his hand on the wall, steadying himself. *Think quick! Act like you heard nothing.*

As the footsteps grew closer, Jack pulled himself erect and smiled. *There is a time and a place for everything. Once you get to the bottom of things, then you can confront her.*

Rounding the corner, Tabatha almost crashed right into him and she jumped backwards. "What are *you* doing out here?"

"Celebrating because those so-called losers from WVU just beat Pitt, and I'm grabbing some beers to help us celebrate."

Tabatha scowled, silently studying him. "Well, you guys need to settle down. I can hardly hear what Betsy's saying."

Jack smiled thinly and slid past her. "I'll snag these beers and get right on it."

"Are you being *sarcastic?*"

Jack shut the fridge. "Not at all," he said, taking a sip of the beer.

As he moved back toward the happy ruckus in the family room, Jack subtly brushed against her. "Tell Betsy I said, 'Hi.'"

CHAPTER 66

PLEASANTS COUNTY COURTHOUSE
ST. MARYS, PLEASANTS COUNTY, WEST VIRGINIA
MONDAY, DECEMBER 1, 9:45 A.M.

"So you made it back to D.C. in one piece?" Jack asked, speaking into his phone.

"Yeah," Dave replied. "I got home just in time to watch WVU get screwed over."

Jack sighed. "I can't believe Oregon slid around us in the polls."

"It hurts, but Oregon stomped USC in the Pac-12 championship while we didn't even cover the spread on Pitt. As much as it hurts, we have no one to blame but ourselves."

Jack sighed again, heavier. "Well, that's enough about football. Do ya think Royal is gonna pull it out in Charleston tomorrow?"

"I think the law's on our side, but it's gray enough for four Democrat justices to rule against us. We're hammering out an appeal to the Supreme Court in D.C. just in case."

Jack smiled wanly. "I know what you mean. That's how I'm viewing my personal life."

"Oh, yeah?"

Jack shook his head mournfully. "I'm pretty sure Tabatha is screwing around on me. I'm meeting with Rikki to figure out how to get her phone records." Prolonged silence ensued. "Dave? You there?"

"Yeah, I'm still here. I guess I didn't realize Rikki was your lawyer. You've never mentioned that, and it just took me aback."

"Democrat or not, she's the best oil and gas lawyer around. Plus, it always helps to be on good terms with the county's prosecutor."

"Oh, I know," Dave said quickly. "She's brilliant and persuasive, not to mention stubborn. Those are traits you look for in a lawyer; I just didn't realize she was *your* lawyer."

Jack paused. "It's strange, but Rikki and I were just talking about you not long ago."

"Why? How'd *my* name come up?"

"I don't remember. But I told her I thought it was a shame you guys drifted apart. You were such good friends growing up and all."

"Did I mention she was *stubborn?*" Dave asked dryly.

"We both know that. But for some reason, I think she might be softening a bit with age. Call me crazy, but I think she might actually be cordial if you run into her again."

Dave chortled. "She's always been *cordial* towards me, Jack. But her cordiality is always packed inside a big blast of cold."

Jack mulled it over. "Maybe that's not the right word. I think she might be *receptive* to burying the hatchet with you."

Suddenly, static erupted. "I'm going through a dead zone on my way to Martinsburg!" Dave yelled. "I'll call you back."

"Okay! Talk to you later!" The line went dead.

Jack climbed out of his truck and, taking care to avoid rain puddles in the parking lot, he walked into the courthouse and climbed the stairs to Rikki's office.

"Hi, Jack!" Martha cheerfully greeted him. "She's waiting for you."

He nodded and walked back to Rikki's private office. "Hey, counselor! Thanks for seeing me on such short notice."

Rikki laughed loudly. "I'm *always* seeing you on short notice. At least this time you had the good manners to call first. What's up?"

Jack shut the door and sat down. "It's Tabatha. I'm at the end of my rope. I'm sure she's cheating on me."

"What makes you think so?"

"I overheard her telling a friend that some guy sent her a text message, wanting to see her this week," he replied. "She sounded like some boy-crazy seventh grader and I'd like to check out her phone records to see who she's screwing around with. How can we do that?"

Rikki pursed her lips and reclined her chair. "What cell phone company does she use?"

"I don't know," Jack answered. "There's the phone I gave her through my company, and then there's another one she guards with her life. No clue where *that* came from."

Rikki nodded. "Do you still have that power of attorney she signed last year?"

"The one authorizing me to sign her name on documents at our real estate closing?"

"Yes. But she actually signed a general power of attorney authorizing you to basically stand in her place and exercise *any* right or power on her behalf. Execute contracts, sign deeds, borrow money, communicate with third parties, etc."

Jack's eyes widened. "*Really?* I could use that to get her cell phone records?"

"Phone records, emails, you name it. When you request copies of her documents with that POA, the recipients are required to turn them over as if she had requested them herself."

He smiled. "Let's do it."

"You don't need *me* to do anything," she replied. "You're the one she appointed as her attorney-in-fact. You can do it yourself."

"But you know the legalese to make sure they actually turn them over. Plus, I don't want them to mail those records to me … Tabatha might get to them before I do, and that would alert her to what I was doing. I'd rather have those companies mail everything to you."

"I hadn't thought about that," Rikki acknowledged. "In that case, bring me that POA. I'll whip up some cover letters requesting her records. You'll sign the letters, but they'll direct that the records be returned to me as your lawyer. Sound good?"

Jack nodded and stood up. "Sounds great. I'll bring it in this afternoon." He walked out of the courthouse wearing a twisted smile.

So Tabatha thinks she can sleep around behind my back and get away with it? She's in for a rude awakening.

MARTINSBURG, BERKELEY COUNTY, WEST VIRGINIA
MONDAY DECEMBER 1, 11:55 A.M.

Dave inhaled a spoonful of *pasta e fagioli*. "I'm impressed. This place is great."

Monica Boley smiled, softly stabbing her Caesar salad. "The chef who owns it is from Florence. The food here is as good as anything you'll find in D.C. or New York."

Studying her face, Dave was struck by how attractive she was. Her thin nose and rounded cheekbones, combined with lush lips and imperfect-but-straight teeth, gave her a unique and appealing look. Her blue eyes sparkled with intelligence, and her wit was unmistakable. For a woman so relatively young, she seemed exceptionally mature and well-grounded.

Maybe Gil was right. Maybe I shouldn't be so quick to judge the contents of this book just because it has Margaret Thatcher's name on the cover.

"Speaking of D.C.," Dave segued. "Would you be interested in working for the new administration? Assuming we hold on and win this thing, someone with your problem-solving talents would be very useful in Washington."

Monica's smile widened and a mischievous glint flared in her eyes. "I'm *very* interested in discussing positions you think might be suited for me. I agree I'd be useful, and problem-solving is just one of my *many* talents."

Dave's face flushed and he nearly spit out his soup laughing. "I have no doubt. Are there any areas of the government you find particularly interesting?"

"The White House itself," she immediately replied. "Surrounded by all that history *and* working in the Executive Branch's nerve center. That would be amazing. But if you want to shove me away in the Department of Agriculture or something, I'd respectfully decline. No offense, but I'd rather work as a drug rep in Martinsburg than die of boredom."

Dave leaned back, folding his arms across his chest. "Wow. You don't beat around the bush or think small, do you?"

"What's the point? You want my help to accomplish something important, I'll be there with bells on. But if you just want me to fill a vacancy on the payroll, I'm not your girl."

Dave chuckled. "Something tells me you and I will get along just fine."

Monica cracked an easy grin. "I agree."

CHAPTER 67

WEST VIRGINIA SUPREME COURT
CHARLESTON, WEST VIRGINIA
TUESDAY, DECEMBER 2, 11:02 A.M.

Sitting in a stately walnut chair in the West Virginia Supreme Court's courtroom, Mack Palmer stared at his surroundings.

The carpet was dark red and the 30-foot-high ceiling consisted of rectangular stained glass openings. Five black leather chairs were positioned equidistantly behind the Court's massive walnut bench that extended almost the entire 40-foot width of the room. The walls were slabs of white Vermont marble, and tall marble columns stood around the perimeter, positioned atop black Belgian marble bases and capped with Ionic volutes inlaid with gold leaf.

A much smaller table sat in front of the bench with a small lectern on it. Three walnut chairs sat on each side of the lectern, which served as the demarcation line for opposing lawyers arguing cases before the Court.

The intercom buzzed, jerking Palmer back to reality. Seated at a small desk beside the bench, the Court's Clerk (a highly-regarded attorney himself) solemnly intoned, "The Justices of the Supreme Court of Appeals of West Virginia."

On cue, four men and one woman in long black robes stepped into the chambers, passing through thick, 20-foot-high burgundy drapes behind the bench and solemnly took their seats.

"The first case on the docket this morning is Number 38916," the Clerk announced. "State ex rel. Royal v. The Honorable Olivia Blackwell, Judge of the Circuit Court of Berkeley County. This case has been consolidated with Mr. Royal's petitions appealing orders from the Circuit Court of Mercer County and the Circuit Court of Monongalia County, originally assigned Docket Numbers 38917 and 38918."

Palmer stepped forward and placed his notes on the lectern while two other attorneys from his firm sat down to his left. Susan Mathis and her team took seats on the opposite side. Palmer adjusted the microphone, took a deep breath and raised his eyes.

"Good morning," he opened with a smile. "May it please the Court. I'm Mack Palmer, and I represent Governor Jonathan Royal. These petitions for appeal were filed to …"

"We know why your client's petitions were filed," Justice Willoughby snapped. "Why should we grant the relief he's seeking?"

Palmer gritted his teeth and gripped both sides of the lectern. *I hate the way they tear into you like a piece of meat without letting you even start into your spiel.*

"We believe the law does not accord Senator Wilson the right to prosecute a contest of the presidential election, let alone in the way she has chosen. The West Virginia Code does not provide for such a proceeding, and there is no way to ascertain what body – if *any* – would be vested with jurisdiction over such a contest."

The five justices stared impassively at Palmer, weighing his words.

Justice Brock Lilly said, "I agree the Code does not *specifically* describe how such a contest would be conducted, but doesn't the language of Article Seven, Section Three governing other statewide elections offer us a *blueprint* for a presidential contest? I mean, didn't the Court in Monongalia County get it right when it directed a three-person special court to preside over the contest?"

Palmer's stomach dropped, but he kept smiling. "No, Your Honor. Because in creating the special courts authorized to govern contest proceedings in those other races like for attorney general, the Legislature designed a fair process for the contestants, which cannot exist in this case.

"Section Three establishes a special court consisting of one person appointed by the contesting candidate, one person appointed by the declared winning candidate, and a third person appointed by *the governor* of the State," Palmer continued. "We think the Legislature used that setup because the governor was presumed to be impartial in that he wouldn't be running for any of those offices. It should be noted the Legislature specifically established a different contest proceeding for gubernatorial races under Article Seven, Section Two, vesting the *Legislature itself* with jurisdiction over those contests."

Palmer paused. "In this case, the special court would not be impartial because Governor Vincent is, in essence, a party to this litigation. When President Bush appealed the Florida recount decision to the U.S. Supreme Court in 2000, his running mate – Dick Cheney – was also a named petitioner. In fact, we suspect the petitioners intentionally omitted Governor Vincent's name from the circuit court pleadings because they wanted to create the impression he has no real interest in these contests' outcome. Which, of course, is patently false.

"Allowing Governor Vincent to designate the third member of the special court would make a mockery of the Legislature's intent to establish an impartial statewide election contest," Palmer continued. "It would let him stack the deck in favor of Senator Wilson and it would forever taint the legitimacy of the special court's decision. It's simply unworkable."

Justice Gammalo broke the brief silence. "It seems like the Legislature screwed the pooch on this one."

Chuckles erupted throughout the chamber. Justice Willoughby shot his colleague a sharp look. Palmer grinned and said, "That's what we think too, Your Honor."

Chief Justice Andrea Riddick reclined in her chair. "But if we don't let Senator Wilson contest the election results, aren't we countenancing voter fraud and intimidation? If the people who suffered that abuse can't contest the election results, don't the bad guys win?"

Palmer shook his head from side-to-side. "Not at all, Your Honor. As we pointed out in the lower court, those 'bad guys' could still face prosecution or civil liability for their actions. But two wrongs don't make a right, and letting Senator Wilson prosecute a contest the Legislature hasn't authorized would just complicate things. Put bluntly, it would jeopardize the state's ability to cast its five ballots in the Electoral College because there's virtually no chance these contest proceedings, and the inevitable appeals, will be completed before December 9th."

The Chief Justice looked down the bench in both directions, informally polling her colleagues. Seeing no more questions, she said, "I believe we understand your position, Mr. Palmer. Thank you. Now we would like to hear from Senator Wilson's attorneys."

Palmer took a seat while Mathis approached the lectern. "As I'm sure the Court realizes, we strongly disagree with the positions expressed by Governor Royal's counsel."

Justice Turner, the only Republican justice, barked a sarcastic laugh. "Imagine that."

Mathis ignored the barb. "We don't believe the Legislature intended to deprive West Virginians of their right to challenge a presidential election outcome resulting from fraud and intimidation."

"Whoa, whoa, whoa!" exclaimed Chief Justice Riddick. "Aren't you putting the cart before the horse, counselor? I don't see anything in the Code that vests ordinary citizens with the right to contest *any* West Virginia election. From my reading, it appears only losing *candidates* can prosecute an election contest."

"And technically," interjected Justice Lilly, "isn't it true that Senator Wilson wasn't even a candidate on the ballot? I mean, her *name* was printed on it, but according to the Code, people were actually voting on slates of electors nominated by the state political parties. Right?"

"Facially, that might appear true. But everyone realizes that's just a creative fiction. When people shaded in an oval or pressed a touchscreen button beside Senator Wilson's name, they expressed their desire for her to become our next president. The

Electors merely formalize that decision when they convene on December 15th."

"I beg to differ, counselor," Justice Turner responded. "The Electors do not *formalize* anything. Even though they may be *pledged* to vote for their party's candidate when the Electoral College convenes, they are free to disregard that pledge and vote for anyone they want when the time comes."

Justice Willoughby, the only justice who voted against accepting Royal's appeal, stepped into the fray. "Nevertheless, I think this legal distinction is lost on the average voter. Given that fact, how does Senator Wilson propose to conduct this election contest, if we were inclined to allow one to go forward?"

Mathis momentarily glanced down at her notes. "We believe, as Justice Lilly mentioned earlier, that the special court created under Section Three for other statewide races provides a good blueprint. Although we know Governor Vincent would appoint someone completely independent to serve as the third member of the special court in this case, we recognize the need to guard against even the *appearance* of impropriety.

"As such," she continued. "As described in the *amicus* brief filed by the governor's private counsel, he is willing to defer to this Court's judgment in making such an appointment. If this Court permits Senator Wilson to prosecute a contest, he has requested you give him the names of three judges who possess the competence and integrity necessary to serve on that special court, and he will fill the third position with one of those nominees."

The Chief Justice folded her hands together on top of the bench. "We noted that offer in his brief, and it is a gracious one. But wouldn't that just create a whole new set of problems?"

"I agree," said Justice Turner. "That would violate the separation of powers. The governor would be abrogating the executive branch's appointment power to the judiciary."

"Not exactly," Mathis retorted. "He would be filling a position on a *court*, and our state constitution vests all judicial power with this Court. It makes sense for him to *consult* with the Court before making such an appointment, while reserving the final decision for himself."

Justice Turner's face reddened. "But the Code gives this Court no say in that process! Why not ask WVU's head football coach for his opinion on the manner? After all, he's mentioned in those Code sections as many times as we are: *None*."

"I have a question," interjected Justice Gammalo. "Are there no federal laws governing presidential election contests?"

Mathis shook her head. "No, your Honor. I'm afraid not."

Gammalo shook his head in disbelief, then silence ensued. Seeing no further questions from her colleagues, Chief Justice Riddick smiled at Mathis. "It's definitely an interesting case. Thank you both for appearing today. We'll take this case under advisement and make our ruling as expeditiously as possible."

Mathis nodded, gathered her notes and stepped away from the counsel's table. Her two associates followed suit, as did Governor Royal's legal team.

"Next up on the docket," the Clerk announced. "We have Docket Number 38874, the case of Mann v. Micilcavage." As he did so, the reporters in attendance tried to look dignified while hastily exiting the room.

PLEASANTS COUNTY COURTHOUSE
ST. MARYS, PLEASANTS COUNTY, WEST VIRGINIA
TUESDAY, DECEMBER 2, 11:40 A.M.

Jack signed his name to the letters addressed to telephone companies and Internet service providers. Rikki faced the computer, watching live streaming video of the oral arguments.

Jack glanced up wearing a puzzled look. "Did that guy just say 'Michael *Cabbage*'?"

"Huh?"

"Never mind. Hey, I'm almost finished here. Can I check my email?"

Rikki slid him the laptop. "Sure. Help yourself."

McCallen signed the last letter, flicked his wrist and flexed his fingers. "I have to hand it to ya, Rikki, you sure are thorough. I bet every cell phone company in the state is getting a copy of that letter."

"They certainly are, Mr. McCallen. We're leaving no stone unturned."

Jack smiled. "That's what I like to hear, counselor."

Rikki gathered the signed letters. "Go ahead and check your email. I'll give these letters to Martha so they get mailed today."

As she walked away, Jack logged in to his account. Spotting a new message from Alex Beria, he quickly opened it:

Final Preparations!
From: alex.beria@petromica.com
To: Jack@mccallenresources.com
Date: Tues, 2 Dec 10:45 am

Hey Jack,
Thanks for faxing me the non-disclosure agreement. Our 'due diligence' guys have finished their work and we hope to close the deal on Thursday.

Now that you have signed the non-disclosure agreement, we will send you the Trade Secrets Protection Addendum (TSPA) mentioned in the purchase agreement I sent you. As you know, MR will be obtaining access to some of our most valuable trade secrets, especially our horizontal drilling methods that allow gas to be extracted from the Marcellus Shale cost-effectively.

Our horizontal drilling technology is so valuable we have never attempted to patent it, because just filing the necessary applications with the government would allow our competition to see how we do it. Thus, we guard that technology by keeping it 'in-house,' just like Coca-Cola has treated its 'secret formula' by locking it in a vault for over 100 years.

The matters outlined in the TSPA are an essential part of our agreement to invest in your firm. If you do not agree to those terms, this deal will not close. Period.

The TSPA will be hand-delivered to your office tomorrow at noon. Once it is signed, call the courier on his cell phone and he will pick it up and return it to our regional headquarters in Reston. The courier is staying at a hotel in Parkersburg Wednesday night, and he will return to Reston no later than 5:00 p.m. on Thursday, with or without the signed TSPA. Again, the TSPA is such a vital part of this deal that we must have the signed original in our hands before proceeding to closing.

The TSPA's terms are straight-forward and self-explanatory.

As long as you sign off on the terms of the purchase agreement and the TSPA, we will wire the first installment payment to MR's account on Friday morning.

Call or email me if you have any questions.

Alex

Jack re-read the message three times, then signed out of his account and walked into the reception area. "You guys need anything else from me?"

"Nope," Martha answered. "That's it. I'll mail those letters out this afternoon."

Putting on his coat, he turned toward the door. "Tell Rikki I'll call her tomorrow."

"Will do. You have a good day."

As he left the courthouse, he wondered what the hoopla over the Trade Secrets Protection Addendum was all about.

Surely it couldn't derail this deal. Right?

CHAPTER 68

WASHINGTON, D.C.
TUESDAY, DECEMBER 2, 4:10 P.M.

Dave was slurping down Chinese food when he received a text from Palmer:

The decision is out. See attachment. Looks good but might not be the last word. Read it and call me in about 45 minutes to discuss.

Dave clicked on the attachment and began reading the Court's decision. The enumerated notes at the beginning summarized the ruling:

1. Neither the United States Constitution nor the West Virginia Constitution vests the citizens of this state with a fundamental right to vote for candidates seeking

election to the office of President of the United States. *See* U. S. Const., Art. II, §1.

2.   In elections for presidential electors in this State, the names of the candidates for president and vice president of each party are to be placed beside a brace with a single voting position, so that a vote for any presidential candidate is a vote for the electors of the party for which the candidates were named. *See* W.Va. Code §3-6-2(d)(1).

3.   The West Virginia Legislature's power to select the manner for appointing the State's electors is plenary; it may, if it so chooses, select the electors itself. *Bush v. Gore*, 531 U.S. 98, 102 (2000) [quoting *McPherson v. Blacker*, 146 U.S. 1, 35 (1892).]

4.   The West Virginia Legislature has not created any mechanism whereby an interested party can contest the results of the statewide election for presidential electors. *See* W.Va. Code §3-7-1, *et seq.*

5.   The West Virginia Legislature has not granted individual voters, or candidates seeking the office of President of the United States, with the right to contest the results of this State's election for presidential electors. *See* W.Va. Code §3-7-1, et seq.

6.   The Legislature, after granting the franchise in the special context of Article II, can take back from voters the power to appoint electors. *See McPherson v. Blacker*, at 35 ("[T]here is no doubt of the right of the legislature to resume the power at any time, for it can neither be taken away nor abdicated") (*quoting* S. Rep. No. 395, 43d Cong., 1st Sess.)

7.   Any procedure which might be subsequently enacted by the Legislature to govern the contest of this State's election for presidential electors must contain safeguards to ensure the completion of such proceeding

273

in time to obtain the benefits of the so-called 'safe harbor provision' found in federal law. *See* 3 U.S.C. §5.

As Dave scanned through the document, his initial enthusiasm began to wane. Quickly, he dialed Mack Palmer's mobile number.

"Hello?"

"My head hurts now," Dave quipped. "Have we finally won this election or not?"

"Well," Palmer said hesitantly. "For the most part, yes. *But…*"

CHAPTER 69

WEST VIRGINIA STATE CAPITOL
CHARLESTON, WEST VIRGINIA
TUESDAY, DECEMBER 2, 8:15 P.M.

Vincent stalked the floor, his brow furrowed and his hands clasped behind his back. Bowen sat across from him, listening and jotting down thoughts as the conference call continued.

"Forgive me," Vincent said, "but are you saying we could *still* win?"

"It's a long shot, but, yes," Susan Mathis replied. "Time is running out, though."

"Could you explain how?" Senator Melanie Wilson asked.

"The Court took great pains to limit the scope of its ruling. The four justices who joined in the decision were uncomfortable letting Senator Wilson contest the election results where the Legislature had not specifically authorized any particular body to preside over such a contest. However, if you read between the lines, it's as if Justice Lilly was telegraphing how such a contest could be enacted and implemented. Even on very short notice."

"Again, Susan," the nominee said, a tone of frustration creeping into her voice. "We don't have all night here. Can you cut through the legalese and cut to the chase?"

Mathis paused. "The federal 'Safe Harbor Provision' indicates every state in the Union has the absolute power to pass legislation dictating how its electoral votes are cast. That decision is left up to each individual State's legislature, which is how Maine and Nebraska are allowed to divvy up their electoral votes based on the popular vote totals in their individual congressional districts instead of giving them all to the statewide winner."

"Interesting," Bowen mumbled, too low for the speakerphone to pick up.

"Specifically," Mathis continued. "It is the law that's in effect on *December 9th* that governs how West Virginia's electoral votes are cast, *not* the law in effect on Election Day."

"Are you friggin' kidding me?!" Vincent exclaimed.

"Not at all, so long as the law in effect on December 9th provides for the 'final determination of any controversy or contest concerning the appointment of all or any of the electors of such State, by judicial or other methods or procedures.' If so, the 'Safe Harbor Provision' indicates that the law in effect on December 9th 'shall be *conclusive*, and *shall govern in the counting of the electoral votes* as provided in the Constitution, and as hereinafter regulated, so far as the ascertainment of the electors appointed by such State is concerned.'"

"So let me get this straight," Vincent prefaced. "The Legislature can wipe out the results from Election Day by passing a new law? It would be like the election never even happened?"

"Although some constitutional law professors have taken that position, I personally wouldn't go *that* far. But if the Legislature were to convene in special session and pass a new law vesting itself with the authority to convene as a court of contest and take evidence on the issues of voter fraud and intimidation, it could do so. And so long as that procedure was completed no later than December 9th, the Legislature's determination of that issue would be final, and it would govern how West Virginia's votes in the Electoral College are cast."

Silence ensued as everyone contemplated the scenario proposed by Mathis. Fifteen seconds later, Vincent broke the spell. "That's just *crazy!* I can't see it happening. The people in this state would go absolutely bat shit if I tried pulling a stunt like that."

"Then we'll have to make it look like it's not *your* idea," Bowen interjected. "I'll get someone in the Legislature to float a trial balloon for us. See how people react. If we spin it so it looks like the Legislature is just trying to correct its oversight, maybe people will buy it."

Vincent's jaw muscles twitched. "Let me be clear about this folks," he intoned slowly. "I'd love to win this election. But I will not jeopardize my ability to govern this state effectively during my second term. You guys can leave West Virginia in your rear-view mirror if a stunt like this collapses. I can't." Vincent's chest was heaving, his face pinkish. "And I'll be *damned* if I'm going to wind up with the citizens of this state burning me in effigy because they think I'm a sore loser who doesn't know when to quit. I'll *personally* concede this election before I let that happen to me."

"Trust me," Bowen assured. "We'll float the trial balloon, and if it looks like it's going over like a turd in a punch bowl, you can shoot it down yourself. Just give me two days."

Vincent's eyes burned, but he remained silent. Bowen pleaded, "Two days. That's it."

The governor took a deep breath and nodded reluctantly. "Two days. If the public gets behind this idea, we'll run with it. Otherwise, I'm pulling the plug."

Bowen nodded, before loudly adding, "In the meantime, Tyson, keep exploring our other options. If we can't muster enough support to warrant a special legislative session, assume our chances of winning West Virginia's five electoral votes are over and proceed accordingly."

"I read you loud and clear," Vasquez responded.

CHAPTER 70

PLEASANTS COUNTY, WEST VIRGINIA
WEDNESDAY, DECEMBER 3, 12:00 P.M.

Jack sat on the couch, thumping his palms on his thighs and staring at the front door.

I'm as nervous as I was the night Logan was born. I can't believe I'm about to close a deal worth 25 million bucks!

Through the frosted glass, a shadow approached the door. Then the musical doorbell rang. Jack rose and opened the door with a practiced air of nonchalance. "Yes?"

A man wearing a dark suit, white dress shirt and silver silk tie stood on his doormat. Darkly-smoked sunglasses rounded out his look. "Are you Jack McCallen?"

"I am. Can I help you?"

The courier held a cardboard envelope atop a clipboard. As he flipped the envelope over, Jack noticed an iridescent metallic strip was affixed across the envelope's flap. The messenger reached into his pocket, pulling out a small ink pad and a snazzy-looking pen. "Press your right thumb against this ink pad, affix your thumbprint to this document and sign your name below it."

"Why?" Jack asked, bristling.

"Rules are rules."

Jack begrudgingly complied. "Thank you," the courier said. "My card's inside the envelope. Call me once you've signed it, and I'll come pick it up. If I don't hear from you by five o'clock tomorrow, I'll return and take the package back to Reston with me."

"So you're just gonna hang around Parkersburg, waiting to hear from me?"

The man smirked. "Buddy, these guys are paying me a *lot* of money to babysit that thing. If they want to pay me to sit around playing with my balls, I ain't complaining." With that, he walked away. "Don't forget. Five o'clock tomorrow or whatever deal you made is off."

Jack nodded and watched the man get into a polished-looking black luxury car and drive away. As the car disappeared, Jack shut the door and walked into the office with the envelope.

The kids were in school and Tabatha was out running errands – or *screwing* somebody, he realized bitterly – so Jack was home alone. Sitting at his desk, he tore open the envelope, shredding the iridescent strip in the process. Reaching inside, he was surprised by how thin the document was: Only three pages long.

As first, it was mostly boilerplate language. *The parties of the first part, Jackson P. ("Jack") McCallen and McCallen Resources, recognize the interest of Petromica in maintaining the confidential nature of proprietary information, Trade Secrets (as defined in the Trade Secrets Act, 18 U.S.C. 1905 and the Virginia Trade Secrets Act, Virginia Code §59.1-336,) and other business and commercial information of the Company (collectively, "Proprietary Information"). Proprietary Information shall include without limitation, information relating to the businesses, operations, customers, financial affairs, industry practices, technology, know-how, intellectual property, confidential techniques, copyrights, patents, trademarks, blah blah blah.*

Jack read that he and his firm would be subjected to hideous legal ramifications if they dared divulge any of Petromica's Proprietary Information to third parties, including any of the contents of the TSPA itself. By its terms, the TSPA required Jack to cooperate with Petromica in protecting the secrecy and integrity of its Proprietary Information, even requiring him to refuse to comply with any court orders demanding that he disclose such information unless he first received Petromica's written permission to do so.

I don't know about that.

Reaching the top of the third page, Jack suddenly froze. *Oh, my God. This can't be happening. Please, God. Let me wake up.*

Suddenly, he realized with crystal clarity that Sections Seven, Eight and Nine of the TSPA constituted the crux of Petromica's offer. It spelled out, in no uncertain terms, what it expected in return for its investment:

7. **Additional Services.** McCallen covenants that on the fifteenth day of December this year, in furtherance of his services on behalf of Petromica, he will present himself at the Office of the Governor of the State of West Virginia at the appointed time for presidential electors to cast their ballots, at which time he will cast one (1) vote for Senator Melanie Wilson for the office of President of the United States, and

one (1) vote for Governor Luke Vincent for the office of Vice-President of the United States.

8. Conditional Re-conveyance of Shares. In the event McCallen performs the Additional Services outlined in Section 7, Petromica shall re-convey to McCallen all of the stock shares in McCallen Resources which it has purchased pursuant to the Stock Purchase Agreement executed contemporaneously by the parties, said shares to be re-conveyed free and clear of any and all liens and encumbrances, and McCallen Resources shall be entitled to retain the purchase money tendered by Petromica in connection therewith.

9. Reservation of Right To Cancel Purchase Agreement. In the event McCallen fails to perform the Additional Services outlined in Section 7, Petromica shall have the sole and exclusive right to cancel the Stock Purchase Agreement without any penalty whatsoever, thereby declaring the same to be null and void *ab initio*.

With quaking hands, Jack laid the document down on his desk. Covering his closed eyelids with his right hand, he shook his head and fought back tears.

I should have known it was too good to be true. What in God's name am I going to do?

CHAPTER 71

RED CARPET LOUNGE
CHARLESTON, WEST VIRGINIA
WEDNESDAY, DECEMBER 3, 3:00 P.M.

Bowen sat at a secluded booth, swirling his scotch-and-soda. Located just blocks from the State Capitol, the bar's ambience was unspectacular, but it had long been a popular watering hole for sundry politicians, bureaucrats and lobbyists.

"So what are people saying about this 'special session' idea?" Bowen asked.

The man on the other side of the booth loosened his necktie and chuckled. "Does the phrase 'eat a bag of shit' mean anything to you?"

"The legislators are that supportive, eh?" Bowen quipped.

His companion shrugged. "Everybody's just tired of hearing about it, Dick. This has been dragging on for a month, and you can't turn on a TV without *drowning* in the coverage. We've had our fill, and people aren't eager to stick out their necks on this thing."

Bowen sighed. "That's what I was afraid of. It's a damn shame, too, considering how close we are to pulling ahead and winning this thing."

The other man laughed uproariously, causing the waitress to glance over at their booth. She shook her head and resumed wiping down another table about 20 feet away.

"*Close* only counts in horseshoes and hand grenades, my friend."

Bowen drained the last of his drink and motioned the waitress to bring him another. "Thanks for reminding me."

WASHINGTON, D.C.
WEDNESDAY, DECEMBER 3, 3:35 P.M.

"Any word on whether Vincent will call a special session?" Dave asked, holding his cell phone.

"God knows he wants to," Gil replied. "But Vincent didn't get elected governor twice by being *stupid*. Maybe one-third of the Legislature would follow his orders, but the rest want nothing to do with it. People are burning up the phone lines to their delegates and senators, letting them know there'll be hell to pay if they keep dragging this out."

Dave grinned. "Nice. If that's the case, there's a fat lady somewhere, getting ready to sing. Before long, we might need to break out the champagne."

Gil chuckled. "From what I understand, there's a young lady in Martinsburg who would welcome an invitation to join you for that bubbly."

A quizzical look crossed Dave's face. "Care to shed some light on that comment?"

"Let's just say Ms. Boley enjoyed your lunch on Monday," Gil answered. "And she was *particularly* pleased you look younger in person than you do on TV."

"Sheez. Do I really look that old on the tube?"

"Well, you don't look like you need a *walker*. But…"

"I get your point. So did Monica say whether she'd work for us when the dust settles?"

Gil laughed. "Oh, yeah! If you're serious about offering her a position inside the White House, she'd jump on it. And if that position coincidentally involved working with a certain dapper rising star from the Mountain State, even better."

Dave smiled widely. *Maybe I'm going to like this 'working for the President' gig.*

CHAPTER 72

PLEASANTS COUNTY, WEST VIRGINIA
WEDNESDAY, DECEMBER 3, 4:30 P.M.

"Come on, Dad!" Logan yelled. "It's gonna be dark soon!"

Jack stared uphill at his two sons, who were 30 yards ahead of him on the hiking path behind their house. Like partially-unleashed balls of energy, the boys stared back impatiently, begging him with their eyes to move faster.

"Settle down, guys. The sun doesn't go down for another half-hour. We have plenty of time to get to the top of the hill."

Logan exhaled like it required all his forbearance to keep from running downhill and kicking his dad in the shins. Jack's younger boy, Brandon, let out a loud laugh. "I thought you were in shape, Daddy!"

Jack clenched his teeth. "Daddy's fine. He just had a rough day today. You guys keep going; I'm right behind you."

By focusing on his breathing and taking longer strides, Jack kept pace with the boys. As they strolled along the leaf-covered path beneath the barren limbs of overhanging trees, Jack watched his sons interact with one another. Smiling and joking, they reveled in hiking through the woods with their dad as if they didn't have a care in the world.

If only I could be so lucky.

Ten minutes later, they reached a clearing at the top of the hill enclosed by an old black wrought-iron fence. The boys raced the last 50 yards. Jack interlocked his hands behind his head and swallowed big gulps of air, hoping his breathing would soon return to normal.

Scattered around the clearing were twenty headstones of various sizes, shapes and ages. The McCallen clan had called Pleasants County home for close to a hundred years, and Jack's grandfather had set aside this patch of land as a family cemetery so that those who so desired could remain close to home even after their time in this world had ended.

Jack ambled toward his father's grave out of habit. Duke had been dead five years, but the old man had been overjoyed to see Jack produce two healthy sons capable of carrying on the family name. Recalling the pride in Duke's eyes when he had held Brandon for the first time, as two-year-old Logan stood by his bedside, made Jack smile wistfully.

I could give my boys the _world_ *with 25 million bucks in my pocket. They wouldn't worry about a thing the rest of their lives.*

Jack bent down and gently wiped the dust and brittle leaf fragments from his dad's flat black marble grave marker. Reading his full name and birth and death years reminded him how fleeting life is. Seeing the letters, "CPO, USN" engraved on the marker caused memories of the petty officer's many war stories to come rushing back.

The last line on the marker read simply: "Proud Patriot. Loyal Husband. Loving Father."

Jack traced a finger over the inscription, thinking back to his childhood when Duke led him by the hand up this path. They would come to the cemetery, and his dad would spend hours telling him stories about the loved ones in these graves. In the process, his father practically brought those bones to life, helping Jack understand where he came from and who he was.

Glancing at the far end of the cemetery, Jack watched Brandon and Logan take turns tossing pebbles at a small obelisk marking the grave of his Uncle Frank. He knew they meant no disrespect – just another little way of competing with one another, seeing whose aim was better – and the sight made him grin.

Suddenly, Jack's mind flashed back to a conversation he had with his dad when he was in high school. He was mowing lawns to earn extra money, supplementing the small pay Duke gave him for doing odd jobs at McCallen Resources.

Returning home one day, Jack discovered an elderly woman had accidentally paid him with a twenty dollar bill instead of a five. Gleefully contemplating how he could impress a local girl with his unexpected bounty, Jack naively shared the news of his good fortune with his dad.

Jack still remembered the look that came over Duke's face. "Son," his father had said with a patient, yet firm tone. "Let me tell you something. Money is not a bad thing. Life's always a little easier if you don't have to worry about where your next meal is coming from.

"But money is dangerous. It changes people and makes good people do bad things. So as you're sitting there, thinking about where you might spend that extra 15 dollars, let me give you one more thing to think about." Duke paused and took a drag off his Marlboro Red. "If you spend all the money in your wallet, you can *always* go out and get more money with a little bit of hard work. But once people have reason not to trust your word, it's damn near impossible to get that trust back." Eyeing Jack closely, Duke softly added, "Don't you think your family's reputation for honesty is worth more than 15 dollars?"

McCallen gently patted his father's marker, shut his eyes and exhaled. *I hear you, Dad. I hear you.*

Looking across the clearing, Jack saw the last faint rays of sunlight disappearing in the west. "Okay, guys. Let's head home. Your mom should have dinner ready when we get there."

Brandon and Logan each threw one last pebble at Uncle Frank's gravestone before running toward him. Shutting the gate, Jack put one hand on each of his two boys' shoulders and began walking downhill. "But what do you say we take our time getting down there?" he added.

CHAPTER 73

PLEASANTS COUNTY, WEST VIRGINIA
THURSDAY, DECEMBER 4, 11:00 A.M.

Hurrying to her hair appointment, Tabatha barreled into Jack's office looking for her earrings. *The boys must have been playing with them or Jack put them somewhere stupid!*

Pilfering through Jack's desk, a shimmering metallic object distracted her. Her curiosity piqued, she picked up the cardboard envelope with the metal strip that caught her eye. Seeing a document inside, she opened it up and read it. *Figures! That stupid son-of-a-bitch must have forgotten it. He'd forget his head if it wasn't attached to his body.*

Carrying the TPSA, Tabatha clip-clopped her way into the family room and angrily hit the speed-dial number for Jack's cell phone.

"Hey," Jack greeted. "Good morning. How are you?"

"Did you *forget* something when you left this morning?" she asked accusingly.

Five seconds of silence ensued. "I don't think so. Why? Did you find something?"

"Just this paper you need to sign so Petromica will send us 25 million dollars."

"Ohhhh," Jack said slowly. "*That.* Well, honey ... You see ... There's a problem with that document and it looks like the deal is off. I told Petromica an hour ago."

"*What?!* Why did you do that?"

"Look at section seven on the last page."

Tabatha quickly flipped to it. "The one that says, 'Additional Services?'"

"That's the one."

Tabatha mouthed the words to herself as she read. Raising an eyebrow, she smirked. "*So?* What's the problem? You can cast that electoral ballot for whoever you want!"

Jack stuttered. "Are you kidding? I've been a Republican my whole life! I was elected to the State Senate three times because people know who I am and what I stand for. How could you suggest I forget all that and vote for the Democrats in the Electoral College!?"

Tabatha scoffed. "Uh ... Because Petromica will give you *25 million dollars* to do it. And besides: Senator Wilson carried Pleasants County on Election Day! For all you know, the only reason she didn't win West Virginia outright is because of some stuffed ballot boxes in Berkeley County."

When Jack remained silent, Tabatha sensed an opening. "Come on, baby. Think how that investment will help our company. We can drill into the Marcellus Shale! Think of the financial security we could give Logan and Brandon."

Jack sighed deeply. "I know, Tabby. I've agonized over it. But I can't do it. That money is dirty, and I know it. I wouldn't be able to live with myself. I'll just have to find another way to hold things together until the Schoolcraft suit is resolved."

"And how do you plan to do that, Jack?" she screamed. "Nobody will loan you any money, and we can't keep throwing money down a rat-hole to that towel-head lawyer of yours! You don't have any other options! You *have* to do this!"

"No, I *don't*. We'll have to tighten our belt and put our faith in God. With a little more work, we can always make a little more money."

"And by 'tightening *our* belt,' you mean cutting the money you give *me* each month."

"We'll *all* need to be a little more frugal," Jack said.

"Well, fuck that!" she yelled. "I'm already pissed I have to sit around and watch Betsy and all the other girls go to the spa when they want and take off to New York for weekend trips because you say we don't have enough money for me to join them. *I've had it, Jack!* This isn't the life I signed up for when I agreed to marry your ass, and something has to give!"

"You're damn straight something has to give!" Jack screamed. "You think *you've* had it? You're lucky I haven't strangled the life out of you yet! I bust my ass to keep this company afloat, and all you do is sit around and bitch that your life isn't *easy enough*."

Tabatha rolled her eyes. They had been through this a thousand times. If Jack had wanted his wife to work outside the home and bring in additional money, he should have married another woman. She was sure there were plenty of *homely* girls who would have jumped at the chance to spend the rest of their lives married to Jack McCallen under those circumstances.

As it was, however, he married *Tabatha Pettigrew*, the hottest woman in the entire Mid-Ohio Valley. And a wife like that came with a price tag.

"As I've told you before, Jack, that's not my problem," she said coldly. "You knew what you were getting into when you married me. If you wanted low maintenance, you should have married someone else. I take pride in looking good for you. Looking good for you is *my* job. I work hard at it. So don't cry to me because you're working hard to live up to *your* end of the bargain and provide me with the lifestyle I deserve. You made this bed ... You have to lie in it."

"The hell I do," Jack shot back. "Not any more. I've put up with your shit long enough and *I'm out of here.*"

Tabatha's eyes widened. "What do you mean?"

Jack let out a deep breath. "It's *over*, Tabatha. Our marriage is *over.* I've given and I've given, and it's never enough for you. I can't take this shit any more. I want a divorce."

Her knees weakened and she gingerly sat on the couch. "You can't be serious."

"I am. I'll swing by this afternoon and pack a few things. I was going hunting with Bart on his farm on Saturday anyway, so I'll just take some clothes and stay there all weekend. You keep the boys the next few nights. We'll sit down and discuss things on Monday."

Remain calm, Tabatha told herself. *The pressure from this change in the Petromica deal has him teetering on the edge. You know every button he has and how to push them. Buy some time and think of something.*

"I'm sorry, honey," she whispered, remembering to sniffle. "I didn't mean to upset you. Just take a few days and don't make any rash decisions. We'll sit down on Monday and try to work things out. Okay?"

Jack exhaled. "All right. I'll come by around two this afternoon to pick up my stuff before the boys get home from school. Make sure you're not around when I get there."

"I won't be. And Jack ..."

"Yes?"

"I really do love you."

Jack paused a moment, then responded, "I'll talk to you on Monday."

The line went dead.

Tabatha sank into the couch, clutching her phone in one hand and the TSPA in the other. *This can't be happening! There must be __something__ I can do to turn this around!*

Sitting on the sofa, her blue eyes danced back and forth as she pondered her dilemma. Moments later, a faint smile etched itself on her face.

Glancing down at the letter from Petromica, Tabatha punched numbers on her phone, took a deep breath and composed herself.

"Mr. Beria? This is Jack McCallen's wife, Tabatha. I think my husband has made a *foolish* decision to reject your company's offer, but we *may* be able to salvage the deal ..."

CHAPTER 74

WEST VIRGINIA STATE CAPITOL
CHARLESTON, WEST VIRGINIA
THURSDAY, DECEMBER 4, 8:00 P.M.

"So what's the verdict?" Tyson Vasquez asked.

Bowen stood alone on the State Capitol's steps, facing the Kanawha River. Clutching his phone to his ear, he puffed on a cigarette. "Down for the count. Despite threats, promises, horse-trading and ass-kissing, there will be no special session."

Vasquez swore. "You predicted that, but I hoped you'd find a way to ram it through."

"I gave it hell. Governor Vincent will issue a statement tomorrow at ten, thanking the legislators who supported the idea but admitting we'll have to wait and deal with it in January."

"Do me a favor and have Luke call Senator Wilson tonight to personally advise her of this decision. She'll appreciate hearing it from the horse's mouth, so to speak."

Bowen threw his cigarette butt down and stomped it with his shoe. "Consider it done. And unless you have something up your sleeve I don't know about, we're about out of cards."

Vasquez paused. "We're exploring some options. Nothing you need to worry about right now, plus things are changing by the hour. If I think you can help, I'll let you know."

Bowen gritted his teeth. He hated not being in the loop, but that was politics: In one day, out the next. "Well, give me a ring if you need *anything*. The thought of coming this far only to fall short makes me want to scream. Or puke. Or get shit-faced beyond recognition."

"That feeling is pretty widespread around here."

SUNNYVALE, CALIFORNIA
FRIDAY, DECEMBER 5, 2:00 P.M.

Well, this is unusual. And where in the hell is St. Marys, West Virginia, anyway?

He plugged in the woman's name and noted she had an account with the Internet service provider who employed him. So his first means to disregard such requests was unavailable.

Next, he examined the language describing *what types* of information were requested. One look caused him to scowl:

> Please provide me with copies of all "documents" pertaining or related to this account. "Document" means every writing or record of every type and description that is or has been in your possession, custody, or control or of which you have knowledge, including but not limited to

correspondence, memoranda, tapes, computer files, facsimiles, voice recordings, or any other reported or graphic material in whatever form, including copies, drafts, and reproductions. "Document" also refers to any other data compilations from which information can be obtained, and translated, if necessary, by you through computers or detection devices into reasonably usable form.

Finally, he pored over the authorizing document enclosed with the request to see if there were any limitations that might justify rejecting the request for information:

That I, Tabatha McCallen, do hereby make, constitute and appoint my husband, Jackson P. "Jack" McCallen as my true and lawful attorney-in-fact, for me and in my name and stead, to. . .

14. Generally act as my attorney or agent in relation to all the foregoing and as to any and all other matters in which I may be interested or concerned; on my behalf execute all such instruments, and **do all such acts and things as fully and effectually in all respects as I myself could do if personally present. . .**

Rats!

Begrudgingly, he burned a DVD copy of all the requested files currently stored on the company's servers. With a click of the mouse, he generated a 'please find enclosed' letter and dropped it into an envelope with the DVD. Clicking the mouse again, he printed one of the ISP's standard "verifications of authenticity."

With a sigh, he walked across the hall and handed the verification to a secretary. "I need you to notarize this for me."

"Wow," she said, with raised eyebrows. "Somebody found a golden ticket, huh?"

He grimaced. "Sometimes, you can't find a reason to tell them to go away."

The woman signed and stamped the verification. "Oh, well. Better luck next time."

CHAPTER 75

PLEASANTS COUNTY, WEST VIRGINIA
SATURDAY, DECEMBER 6, 4:45 A.M.

Jack sat at his brother's kitchen table with a plate of scrambled eggs and a cup of black coffee. "The one thing I hate about hunting is you have to wake up so damn early."

His brother, Bart, grinned at him. "It's worth it, though."

Jack smiled back. "I can't deny that. Between everything at work and the election crap, I didn't think I'd get out in the woods at all this year."

Bart shook his head in amazement. "That's why I said you could keep that damn oil company. I'll stick with farmin'. There's no way some *job* would keep me from deer hunting."

"All I can say is, 'Thank God for small miracles,'" Jack said. "Today's the last day of rifle season, and with any luck, I'll finally break my dry spell."

"What's it been now … three years?"

Jack scowled. "Four."

Bart leaned back and stroked his beard. "Well, brother, I think today's your lucky day. You're due for some luck, and now that you're finally getting rid of that anchor you've been married to all these years, I think your luck's about to change."

Jack tensed. "Now, Bart. I haven't made up my mind about that just yet."

"Ha! Tell that to somebody who didn't grow up with you! You can tell yourself that if it makes you feel better. Hell, you may even *believe* it. But once you're in the woods, surrounded by silence and at peace with the world, you'll see divorcing her ass is the right thing to do."

Jack's gaze narrowed. "Ya think?"

Bart nodded with certainty. "Trust me."

Jack sipped his coffee, glancing at the clock. "All right, Ann Landers. We need to head out so we're in our tree stands before daylight."

Bart stood and stretched. "Since I've already got two this year, Jack, I'm gonna help you break your dry spell. I'll circle around the back side of the ridge and run a few bucks towards you from that pine thicket they like to bed down in."

Jack smiled widely. "You're a hell of a man, Bart."

"What are brothers for?"

Fifteen minutes later, wearing their cold weather gear and blaze orange, their rifles were slung over their shoulders and they were walking downhill from Bart's farmhouse toward the open field where they hunted as boys with their dad. Bart tapped Jack on the shoulder and silently motioned he was breaking away to circle widely around the deer's typical sleeping area.

Jack waved and continued easing downhill toward his tree stand. A thin layer of snow that fell the afternoon before had frozen overnight and crunched softly beneath his footsteps. The crisp morning air filled his lungs and he found himself energized with growing anticipation.

Deer were drawn to a small creek that ran along the back side of Bart's meadow, and the acorns that fell from old oak trees lining the field's perimeter offered the animals plentiful food. Fresh tracks Bart spotted in the wet ground the previous evening told them deer had crossed here recently, further heightening their confidence.

Reaching the same oak tree at the far right corner of the field where he had hunted for forty years, Jack smiled and nodded contentedly. He quietly ascended the old tree, using two-by-four boards nailed into the trunk as rungs, until he finally climbed into his portable tree stand about 15 feet above the ground. Unlimbering his rifle, Jack tried to get comfortable and settled in to await the break of dawn.

Over the course of the next hour, stars slowly faded from the pitch black sky and the first faint whispers of light began filtering into the woods, allowing Jack to be on guard for signs of motion around him. Against the white backdrop of the fresh snow, Jack knew he soon should be able to pick up movement of deer from several hundred yards away, once the sky grew brighter. Remaining as motionless as possible, Jack was enveloped by silence and smiled peacefully.

Everything will be okay, he thought with a smile. *Finally.*

As much as he loved Tabatha, Jack knew he could not spend another night under the same roof with her. She had borne him two wonderful sons, and he would always love her for that. *But if I don't walk away now, I'll end up killing her. And I can't let my boys go through something that horrible. As hard as a divorce will be for them, it will be better in the long run if Tabatha and I go our separate ways.*

As the darkness continued to fade, Jack saw the first signs of life emerging around him: The swaying shadows of trees and brief glimpses of squirrels hopping playfully along the ground beneath him. With every passing minute, Jack's view of the meadow grew clearer, though it remained partially obscured by intermittent banks of fog floating above the ground.

Just as the world around him was almost fully lit, Jack heard something rustling in the trees lining the far side of the meadow. If Bart had driven the deer from their thicket, they would be expected to emerge in that area. Steeling his body, he focused on the trees. Then a muscular ten-point buck ambled his way through the ghostly wisps of fog and into the meadow.

Filling his lungs with the crisp morning air, Jack eased his rifle onto his right shoulder and smiled from ear-to-ear. Peering through the scope, he watched the buck slowly stride toward the middle of the fog-shrouded field about a hundred yards away.

Steady. Just a few more feet and this dry spell will be history.

As Jack disengaged the safety switch and prepared to pull the trigger, serenity washed over him. After four years without bagging a buck, he had no doubt his luck had changed.

The laws of physics are immutable and uncaring. The muzzle velocity of a bullet fired from a typical hunting rifle is about 2,800 feet per second. By comparison, sound waves creep along at 1,129 feet per second. The difference between the two speeds explains why State Senator Jack McCallen never heard the gunshot that propelled a bullet through his skull, scrambled his brains and ended his life.

CHAPTER 76

PLEASANTS COUNTY COURTHOUSE
ST. MARYS, PLEASANTS COUNTY, WEST VIRGINIA
MONDAY, DECEMBER 8, 1:05 P.M.

"They say it was probably an accident," Martha said softly.

Rikki silently stared at her secretary. A bottle of Visine and a box of tissues sat nearby. "Well, we haven't had a murder here in thirty years, so that would make sense. But still ..."

"I know. Jack calls you on Friday saying his deal with that company had fallen through *and* he was meeting with a lawyer in Parkersburg to get divorce papers drafted ..."

"And the next day he's dead," Rikki added. "What are the odds of that happening?"

Martha nodded. "What are you going to do?"

Rikki shrugged. "The Sheriff's Department is investigating. They'll call us once the ballistics tests are back."

Martha folded her arms across her chest. "And where was Tabatha Saturday morning?"

Rikki's face soured. "Bart heard the gunshot go off about 7:30. At that time, Tabatha was cooking breakfast for their two boys *and* talking on the phone to her friend, Betsy. We may have to send her phone company a subpoena to confirm her story, of course."

"Of course," Martha agreed. "Speaking of which ..." She leaned into her office and grabbed a padded envelope from her desk. "This was in the P.O. box at lunch."

Addressed to "Jack McCallen c/o Sarika D. Gudivada, Esq," Rikki noted it came from Tabatha's email provider. She opened the envelope and extracted a jewel case with a disc, along with two pieces of paper. "This DVD supposedly has all the documents and files we asked for."

"Good God!" Martha exclaimed. "How long will it take to go through that stuff?"

"No idea, but shut the door and hold my calls. I'm looking for a needle in a haystack."

WEST VIRGINIA ROUTE 2
BELMONT, PLEASANTS COUNTY, WEST VIRGINIA
MONDAY, DECEMBER 8, 4:50 P.M.

"Thanks for picking me up at the airport, Dad," Dave said.

The older man nodded but kept facing forward, both hands on the wheel. "Your mom would have divorced me if I didn't. And with dinner almost ready, I didn't want to tick her off."

Dave chuckled. "Well, I appreciate it. Traffic was a nightmare between D.C. and the little airport where I house the plane. And I forgot to call and give you my ETA until I was in the air, so I had to wait until I landed in Parkersburg. Sorry."

"Save the apologies for your mom, son: She's the one who was scrambling to get dinner ready on a moment's notice. If you weren't flying in for Jack's funeral, I'm sure I'd be eating something from McDonald's tonight."

"Glad I could help out," Dave quipped, grinning and shaking his head in amusement.

As the car motored north on Route 2, they approached the hulking Willow Island Station, a coal-fired power plant on the Ohio River. With the sky darkening behind the plant, white lights blinked atop the plant's smokestacks and cooling towers.

"Every time I drive past here, I think about The Accident," Dave said.

His father nodded. "51 men died in the blink of an eye when the scaffolding on that cooling tower collapsed. Just goes to show how fleeting and fragile life truly is."

"Yeah, and it's the same thing with Jack. I mean, I just watched the game with him a week ago and now he's dead. Unbelievable."

"Speaking of which," his dad said. "I got a call from the guys at the Lodge today. They need warm bodies to give Jack a Masonic funeral, and they hoped you and I could help out."

Dave grimaced. "It's been ages since I did one of those. Hell, I can hardly remember the last time I sat in a Blue Lodge meeting."

"Well, the Lodge is aging, Dave. There are less Masons around than there used to be. You may be rusty, but you have a good memory. You'll be fine with a little practice."

Dave sighed. "All right. If that's what Jack wanted, I'll help send him out right."

"He would have appreciated it. Things have been ugly around the McCallen clan the past few days."

"Oh, yeah? How so?"

"Well, take this funeral for instance. Tabatha wanted to have Jack cremated until Bart heard about it and went berserk. He apparently told her there would be *two* funeral services if Jack wasn't buried in their family cemetery. She eventually caved, but not graciously."

Dave stared at his dad, gape-mouthed. "Dear Lord! That cemetery meant the world to Jack! How could she have even thought about putting him to rest somewhere else?"

"Well, David," his dad replied dryly. "It would have been cheaper to have him cremated than interned in a nice coffin, and Tabatha's a royal bitch. Need I say more?"

CHAPTER 77

CHARLESTON, WEST VIRGINIA
TUESDAY DECEMBER 9, 8:15 A.M.

CHARLESTON, WV (AP) – The fallout from the death of State Senator Jack McCallen (R-Pleasants) continued this morning, when the West Virginia Republican Party appointed his replacement as one of the state's five presidential electors.

The party's Executive Committee has appointed McCallen's widow, Tabatha, to fill that position. At July's state convention, Mrs. McCallen was one of five Republicans designated as an "alternate" elector. Although typically an honorary title, party leaders felt her appointment was the best way to honor McCallen's memory following his death.

Visitation will be from 6:00 to 8:00 p.m. this evening at the Sweeney Funeral Home in St. Marys. The funeral service will be held at noon tomorrow at the Pleasants County High School Alumni Center followed by a private burial service at the McCallen Family Cemetery.

- excerpt from wvgazette.com

WEST VIRGINIA STATE CAPITOL
CHARLESTON, WEST VIRGINIA
TUESDAY, DECEMBER 9, 1:30 P.M.

The name and number on Luke Vincent's smartphone kept staring back at him. Although his stomach was churning, he knew he had to extend his condolences.

Tabatha McCallen is a widow and a presidential elector. Dear God, this has gotten messy!

Vincent raised the phone to his ear and steeled himself.

"Hello?" the sultry voice answered. Her throat sounded raw.

"Hi, Tabatha," he opened softly. "How are you doing?"

The widow sighed. "It's been tough. The boys are taking it hard. They miss Jack so much and they just seem so ... *angry* about it all."

"It'll take time, but kids are stronger than people think. They'll always miss their dad, but I'm sure they'll go on to lead remarkable lives. Just look at JFK's kids."

"But they had Bobby and Teddy Kennedy and the whole Kennedy clan to look after them. Who do my sons have? Jack's brother, *Bart?* He's a doofus small-town farmer without an iota of ambition! A fat load of good *he'll* be."

Vincent sighed, looking for positive sentiments. "Everything happens for a reason."

"That's what I keep telling myself. I hope things will get better once the funeral is over and the shock fades."

"Well, your family is in our prayers. And if you need anything, don't hesitate to call."

"Thanks, Luke. Maybe I'll do that once things settle down. We need to talk anyway."

The governor grimaced. *Just what I need. She actually took that offer <u>literally</u>.* "Okay, then," he said. "You have my number. Take care and keep your chin up."

"Thanks for the call, Luke. I'll talk to you later."

Vincent hung up. Biting his lip, he stared out the window. *Jack's death is liable to make her even crazier. I better treat her with kid gloves until she gets on her feet again.*

CHAPTER 78

SWEENEY FUNERAL HOME
ST. MARYS, PLEASANTS COUNTY, WEST VIRGINIA
TUESDAY, DECEMBER 9, 7:00 P.M.

The line of people waiting to pay their last respects stretched down Second Street from the funeral home past city hall. Huddled beneath umbrellas in their winter coats, people quietly chatted while patiently waiting their turn to pass Jack's coffin and say goodbye.

Standing in the drizzle near the entrance, Madhani Gudivada said, "It's nice to see so many people here. It shows you how well-respected Jack was."

Rikki propped the door open. "That he was, Mom. That he was."

Entering the foyer, Rikki noted the place was totally packed, as expected. Two men around Jack's age embraced one another by the guest registry, slapping each other on the back. Their tight-lipped wives shook their heads, sympathizing with their husbands' grief.

Sheriff 'Silent' Doug Vaughn approached Rikki, holding his black broad-brimmed hat in his hands. "Evening, Rikki. Evening to you, too, Mrs. G."

"Hello, Sheriff," Rikki replied. "How's everyone holding up?"

Sheriff Vaughn raised his left eyebrow, accentuating the inch-long scar below his sightless eye socket. "Bart's holding up, but he has his moments. Tabby, though, I can't get a fix on. One second she's sobbing uncontrollably and the next, she's laughing it up and holding court. Then again, she's *always* been crazy, so who's to say she's acting any weirder than normal?"

Rikki clenched her jaw and nodded as the line kept advancing toward the casket. "How about Brandon and Logan?"

The sheriff snorted. "Your guess is as good as anybody's. They've hardly been seen since the accident. Tabby claims they're inconsolable and says she didn't bring them tonight because they couldn't handle it."

"What does Bart think about that?"

"I'm just glad I haven't had to lock Bart up for killing his sister-in-law," Vaughn replied. "He about lost it yesterday when she started talking about cremation."

Rikki's eyes flared. "Thank God I kept a copy of Jack's will. When Bart told me what she planned to do, I almost cried. It boggles the mind she could be so heartless and spiteful."

"That's Tabby for ya. Speaking of Jack's will, I took a gander at it after Tabby brought it in to be probated. I noticed he named you the executor of his estate and trustee over everything he left for the boys. That must have pissed the little widow off."

"Oh, yeah," Rikki answered. "She didn't care for that at all." Glancing around furtively, her voice almost dropped to a whisper. "Jack couldn't *totally* disinherit her under the law, but by putting his company's stock in a trust, he kept her from getting her gritty hands on it. If Tabatha could sell that stock now, do you think Jack's sons would ever see a dime of that money?"

The sheriff's face ticked. "Not now that you've spelled it out for me. Glad to hear Jack had his head screwed on straight."

Passing through the doorway, they entered the parlor where Jack's coffin lay. Glancing ahead, positioned squarely where the line turned at a right angle to walk the final 40 feet toward the coffin, Rikki saw Dave Anderson and her stomach fell through the floor.

Oh, God. I've managed to avoid him for all these years. How could I have not realized he would come home for Jack's funeral?

Dave wore a sharply-tailored black pinstriped suit over a white dress shirt and black silk tie with white and gold diagonal stripes. Facing the front of the room, he stood to the side of the coffin-bound traffic, chatting amiably with the school board president.

"David!" Madhani exclaimed. Turning her head to the right, Rikki watched in horror as her mother began waving like a madwoman at her childhood sweetheart. Hearing his name, Dave glanced toward them and broke into a big smile.

"Momma G!" he responded, opening his arms wide. "How have you been?"

Madhani bounced out of line and headed toward Dave before Rikki could get a word in edgewise. She watched helplessly as her mother bounded over and threw her arms around his broad shoulders.

Grinning from ear-to-ear, Dave hugged her tightly. As Rikki watched them embrace, the scene seemed to unfold in slow motion. Still clasping his arms around Madhani, Dave opened his eyes and trained them directly on Rikki.

Staring into Dave's green eyes, she could not breathe. Transfixed in his gaze, she saw no animosity or resentment. His eyes seemed warm, yet filled with sadness.

You can't avoid this moment any more. Just walk over, be cordial and say, 'Hello.' It will be over in no time, and you can go about your business. He'll be back in D.C. tomorrow.

"Go on over there, Rikki." She glanced up and saw Sheriff Vaughn looking down at her. "I'll hold your place in line."

Rikki nodded and walked slowly across the room. As she closed to a distance of about five feet, she felt her right hand extend toward Dave. "Hi there," she said simply.

Hearing her daughter's voice, Madhani spun out of the embrace and stared at Rikki wide-eyed. Dave glanced down at the proffered handshake and then looked into her eyes.

"After not seeing you for 15 years," he said very softly. "I hope you'll at least let me give you a hug."

Rikki bit her lower lip and silently nodded twice. Dave drew closer and wrapped her in his arms; his right arm draping down her left shoulder, enveloping the side of her neck, while his left arm curled around her rib cage.

Feeling his arms wrap around her, Rikki struggled to control her emotions. The rage and heartache she had carried for so long pounded in her chest, demanding to be given voice. *How could you leave me to face Daddy's death alone? When I needed you the most, you were so far away! Of all people, David, how could you have done that to me?*

With her face perched so closely to his neck, Rikki caught a whiff of his aftershave. As quickly as it had flared, her rage subsided. In its wake came a cascade of long-buried memories:

A fiercely competitive debate they had waged in high school civics class, each asserting their respective political philosophies. She lauded the universal tolerance preached by Dr. Martin Luther King, while he passionately defended the doctrines of self-reliance and individual property rights championed by Ronald Reagan.

The tingling sensation she had experienced when the two of them sat together in the school library one day, studying for a chemistry exam.

Lying in bed talking on the phone with him for hours on end, struggling to keep from laughing so loudly because she knew it would wake her parents and evoke her father's wrath.

The pride she had felt when she strolled into the prom on his arm. And the time Dave had threatened to deliver an ass-kicking to a blowhard at the mall who loudly questioned the propriety of their romantic relationship due to her dark skin and allegedly "mongrel" ethnicity.

The hunger and passion that churned when they ripped off their clothes in the backseat of his Camaro, clumsily exploring their sexuality for the first time.

The comfort she felt holding his hand, sharing her dreams and fears as they lie awake at night in his college bed before making love yet again.

The complete, unabashed confidence she felt at the age of 22, when the world was an unpainted canvass, merely awaiting the colorful barrage of their brushes. *Nothing* was impossible. *Nothing* was out of their reach.

The look on Daddy's face the morning he died. How I felt when he asked me, "Where's David?" and I had to tell him, "He's in Charlottesville, finishing his finals."

The ashen look on Dave's face, after he had rushed into her father's hospital room in Morgantown only to learn he had arrived too late to say goodbye. The tears he had shed while literally on his knees, pleading for forgiveness, as she turned her back and walked away from him, vowing never to speak to him again.

Then, as Dave relinquished his embrace and stepped back, Rikki suddenly heard Jack's voice drift through her mind: *"It's a damn shame that a good man like Dave could spend his entire life paying for one bad decision, and that a good woman like you might never be able to find it in her heart to forgive him for being less than perfect."*

Rikki closed her eyes and breathed in through her nose.

Okay, Jack. I give up. You're right. You win.

"It's good to see you, Dave," she said, and was surprised by how honest the words sounded. "It's been a long time."

*   *   *

No screaming, no cussing, no crying, Dave noted cautiously. *And unless I was hallucinating, she actually said she was happy to see me.*

Satan must be strapping on ice skates because Hell has frozen over.

Still shaking off shock, Dave smiled. "Yes it has been. Better late than never, I say."

Rikki giggled. "Leave it to you to put a positive spin on things." Her voice sounded wry yet cheerful. "How have you been?"

"Busier than a one-armed man hanging wallpaper. But other than that, I can't complain."

Rikki rolled her eyes. "Good Lord! I accused Jack of channeling *you* recently. Now I think it's a two-way street."

Dave guffawed. "Jack was a damn good man with a great outlook on life and a great sense of humor. I'm gonna miss the hell out of him."

Rikki nodded, a sad look in her pale green eyes. "Me, too. It seems so unfair, you know? Just when he seemed on the verge of hitting some big new wells, something like *this* happens."

Dave quickly glanced around the room. "And from what I understand, he was kicking Tabatha to the curb, too."

Rikki gasped. "Where did you hear that?"

From the look on her face, Dave knew she still couldn't keep a secret to save her life. "Jack and I were pretty close. We watched the game at his house last Saturday, and the tension was so thick you needed a chainsaw to cut it." He chuckled loudly. "I didn't need to be a rocket scientist to figure *that* one out."

Rikki pursed her lips and shook her head in a gesture Dave knew was intended to feign disgust. "Some things never change. Even after all these years, you're *still* a smart ass."

Dave grinned proudly. "Guilty as charged, Madam Prosecutor."

At that moment, Dave saw Sheriff Doug Vaughn staring at him with an amused look. "Hey, Sheriff!" he exclaimed with a wave. "Glad to see Pleasants County has someone on the job keeping a *good eye* on things." He winked and cracked a devilish grin.

The sheriff barked a quick, hearty laugh. "Rikki's right. You *are* still a smart ass. I'll never understand why your daddy never beat that out of you."

Dave shrugged. "He probably figured it wasn't worth the effort."

Silent Doug grinned. "He was probably right, too. How's D.C.?"

"Like I told Rikki, I've been so busy lately I can barely remember what it looks like. But I can't complain."

Dave deftly positioned himself between Rikki and the sheriff, as the line crept toward Jack's coffin. Leaning his face between the two, he assumed a more serious tone of voice. "So tell me something, guys. What do you *really* think happened to Jack?"

Rikki looked at the sheriff, who did not bat an eye (good *or* fake). "We don't know yet, Dave," Vaughn said. "We're still waiting for the ballistics results, but I smell a rat."

Dave nodded. "I think we all do. When I saw him ten days ago, Jack was excited about his firm getting a big investment from some foreign company. Bart says that deal fell through last week. But Tabatha says everything's still moving forward." He scanned their eyes. "You know anything more concrete?"

"That's the first I've heard of it," Vaughn replied.

Dave turned to face Rikki. "What about you, Rik?" he asked, using her old high school nickname. "You were Jack's lawyer. Did he mention anything about this deal to you?"

Rikki's jaw muscles tightened. "You're asking me to violate the attorney-client privilege. You know I can't do that."

"Your client is *dead*, Rikki," Dave shot back. Seeing a spark of defiance flicker in her eyes, he softened his words. "And the privilege only applies to *secrets* and *confidences*. Is that company's *identity* something Jack would want you to guard after his death?"

Through narrowed eyelids, Rikki's gaze bore into Dave, making him feel like an ant writhing under a magnifying glass in the summer sun. "Probably not," she said slowly, and Dave breathed a sigh of relief. "Without discussing the deal's specifics, the company that inquired about forming a partnership with McCallen Resources was called Petromica."

Dave felt his chest tighten. "Are you absolutely sure about that?"

Rikki looked at him quizzically. "Without question. Petromica."

Dave placed his hand over his mouth, realizing it had dropped open.

"Why do you look like you just saw a ghost?" Rikki blurted. "What's going on?"

Dave shook his head, gathering his senses. "Have you heard of Dmitri Mazniashvili?" he asked. Rikki nodded; Sheriff Vaughn shook his head negatively. "The guy who *creatively liberated* some of the former Soviet Union's oil and gas reserves back in the day … The guy whose mission in life is to keep Jonathan Royal out of the White House. *That* guy?"

"Yeah?" Rikki replied. "What does *he* have to do with this situation?"

"He owns a controlling interest in Petromica."

Her eyes widened. Then a woman began wailing pitifully.

Turning around, Dave saw Tabatha standing by Jack's closed casket. Wearing a black dress and sheer black hose, her left hand rested on the coffin. A shorter woman with wavy bleach-blonde hair and a PermaTan rubbed her back.

"How could he have left me like this, Betsy?" the widow sobbed. "Oh, God! This is so unfair! What am I going to do without Jack?"

Nice, Dave thought cynically. *She'd make a great instructor for Histrionics 101.*

Approaching the casket, Dave saw two framed photographs at its head. One was a large family portrait that obviously was taken at a professional studio. In it, Jack stood behind Tabatha, who was seated with Logan to her right and Brandon to her left. The boys were cheesing it up while Tabatha donned her patented, pageant-plastic smile. Jack, on the other hand, smiled wearily and looked … *resigned* more than anything else.

The second photo was an informal 8x10. Standing at the 50 yard line of Mountaineer Field, Jack beamed from ear-to-ear as his hands rested on the shoulders of his two equally happy sons. All three wore blue and gold WVU football jerseys. Jack's gold ball cap was emblazoned with a navy blue "Flying WV" logo, and the boys had matching logos painted on their cheeks. The dead man's face reflected pure joy.

Tabatha slowly looked up from the casket. Recognition dawned in her eyes and she stepped toward Dave with her lower lip quivering.

"Oh, Dave," she said, throwing her arms around his neck. "I'm so glad you could make it. Jack always thought of you like a brother. It means a lot that you're here."

Dave felt himself recoil at her touch, yet the floral smell of her perfume dizzied his senses. Her body felt both soft and firm as she embraced him.

My God! She's like a succubus or something! This is terrifying!

Dave counted to three and then diplomatically pulled away. "I'm so sorry for your loss, Tabatha. If you or the boys need anything, just say the word."

Tabatha smiled and sniffled. "Thanks, Dave. That's so sweet. I know it's going to be rough, but if things get really bad, maybe I'll give you a call and cry on your shoulder a bit."

Dave bit his tongue, hoping his face looked duly sympathetic. "Keep your spirits up, Tabatha. We'll be praying for you guys."

The widow smiled and patted him on the cheek. "Thanks. I'll be talking to you."

Dave quickly stepped aside to make room for his fellow well-wishers. Sheriff Vaughn entered the breach and extended his right hand in a coldly formal fashion. "Jack was a good man. The whole county shares your loss." Then, without giving her an opportunity to respond, he nodded curtly and walked away.

Madhani Gudivada took Tabatha's right hand in both of hers and patted it tenderly. "Your husband has been a blessing. I pray God will comfort you and help your boys to become strong men like their father."

Tabatha's face looked like she had been forced at gunpoint to lick a cat's anus and then act like it tasted like strawberry ice cream. "Thank you for coming," she said, quickly slipping her hand from Madhani's grasp.

Watching the scene unfold, Dave saw Rikki's eyes momentarily flash with anger. Then, he watched in amazement as she somehow dissipated that hostility and stepped forward with a smile to offer Tabatha a hug. "Take care, Tabby. If you need anything, call."

Tabatha patted Rikki on the back three times before parting. "I'll do that. In fact, I'll stop by to see you on Thursday, once things start to slow down."

Rikki looked puzzled. "Anything in particular you want to talk about?"

"Yes," Tabatha replied. "What you plan on doing with the 25 million dollars Petromica is investing in my company. I know some of it will be invested in new wells, which is fine. But some of it must be released to me, so the boys and I can be financially comfortable for once. That's what Jack planned to do, and I see no reason for those plans to change."

Rikki stared at the widow and her mouth involuntarily twitched once. "I understand. Could you see me at 2:00?"

Tabatha loudly sighed. "Actually, I thought we should get together earlier in the day. We really need to address this situation and the sooner, the better."

Rikki's left hand dangled by her side, and she flexed her fingers before clenching them into a fist. "11:00 is the earliest I could see you. Starting at 9:00, I have magistrate court hearings every 15 minutes."

Tabatha's mouth tightened. "Then, I suppose it will have to be 11:00."

The prosecutor donned a smile. "Excellent. I'll see you then."

Tabatha watched her walk away before turning her attention to the next person in line. Rikki casually headed toward the exit.

"What are you doing tomorrow morning?" she whispered as she brushed by Dave.

He fell in behind her. "Nothing 'til 11:30. Why?"

"Meet me at the courthouse at 8:00. Something strange is going on, and since you know more about this Petromica outfit than I do, there are some things I should show you."

CHAPTER 79

PLEASANTS COUNTY COURTHOUSE
ST. MARYS, PLEASANTS COUNTY, WEST VIRGINIA
WEDNESDAY, DECEMBER 10, 8:45 A.M.

Rikki navigated through the contents of the DVD from Tabatha's email provider. Dave pulled up a chair and stared at the monitor intently, his eyes darting back and forth.

"What format are these files in?" he asked, lifting a can of Diet Coke to his lips.

"The emails are pdf files arranged in chronological order. One directory has her outgoing messages while another has incoming messages. Any attachments to those emails are in their original format: Word documents, jpegs, etc."

Dave nodded. "Anything incriminating? Or that at least support Jack's suspicions she was cheating on him?"

"Actually, I haven't found anything linking her to anyone else. Lots of inane messages to and from her girlfriends, some of which *insinuate* she was accepting solicitations from potential paramours, but no confessions or hotel reservations or anything. Maybe we'll have better luck when her cell phone records come in.

"I did find *this* little message peculiar, though," Rikki added, clicking on one of Tabatha's outgoing emails:

Hi, Alex!
From: NaughtyTabbyKat@yahoo.com
To: alex.beria@petromica.com
Date: Fri, 5 Dec 1:12 pm

Hi Alex!

I really enjoyed our conversation today and I still think the objections Jack raised regarding the Addendum are nonsense. Certainly not enough to quash the deal.

I'll try to talk some sense into him this afternoon, then I'll call you to let you know whether we can move the original deal forward, or whether we will need to pursue the alternate plan we discussed this morning.

By the way, I thought your voice on the phone sounded very sexy this morning. ;-) Maybe even a little exotic. :-) Are you as handsome in person as you look in that pic on the website? LOL

Tabby

Dave snorted. "Nice screen name. Any other messages involving this Beria character?"

"Not that I know of," Rikki answered. "But I have no way of knowing what transpired after the ISP responded to our request at 2:10 p.m. last Friday."

Dave absentmindedly tapped his index finger on the tip of his nose while scrutinizing the email to Beria. "Any idea what this 'Addendum' is?"

Rikki's nose crinkled. "No. My guess is it was part of the stack of paperwork Petromica sent Jack in connection with this deal."

"Do you still have copies of that stuff?"

"Unfortunately not. I'm no mergers and acquisitions expert, plus he didn't bring it to me until the day before Thanksgiving. I told him we'd need to find someone else to review it."

"Did you?"

"Yeah. I sent him to a guy up in Morgantown. I'll call him and see if he could overnight those documents to me; if he still has them, that is."

Dave leaned back in his chair and rubbed his chin, staring out the window. "Jack didn't tell me much about his business. But I do know he was frustrated he had leaseholds atop the Marcellus Shale yet couldn't raise the cash to drill into it. 25 million bucks is a lot of cash! What language in that Addendum could Jack have found so objectionable?"

"I don't know," Rikki responded. "But I aim to find out."

Knuckles rapped loudly on the open door behind them. Turning around, Rikki saw Sheriff Vaughn standing in the doorway holding a manila folder. "Good morning, guys. Figured out who killed Jack yet?"

"Not quite," Dave answered. "I thought that was *your* job."

Vaughn ambled in, smiling pleasantly. "It is. But it looks like you two geniuses are fixing to do it for me."

Rikki sighed. "We're reviewing Tabatha's emails. I hoped Dave could shed some light on Petromica or see things from a new angle. Unfortunately, all he's really done is rant about how this Mazniashvili character is the slimiest good-for-nothing dog on the planet."

Dave shrugged, clearly unaffected by the jab. "What do you want me to say? He has more money than God and desperately wants to keep living in a New York City penthouse rather than end up in an execution video like Saddam Hussein. I'd put *nothing* past him."

"He also happened to make his fortune in the *oil and gas* business," Rikki retorted. "Petromica seems like a legitimate company that would have a legitimate reason to invest money in a company like Jack's that has valuable leaseholds but lacks the money to fully develop them. On paper, the two companies seem like a match made in heaven."

"Thus," Dave said, turning to Vaughn, "in the absence of evidence one way or the other, we're at a standstill."

"Well, that's where I come in," Vaughn responded. "Rikki, do you want to know what our investigation has uncovered? Or would you rather me come back when you're alone?" He motioned toward Dave with his head.

Rikki exhaled. "Go ahead. I might not agree with his politics, but Dave's a smart cookie and two heads are better than one. Maybe he'll see something we might otherwise overlook."

Vaughn nodded. "All right. The autopsy results confirmed what we already knew. The cause of death was having his brains blown out. The bullet in question was standard .308 NATO ammo, commonly used in several hunting rifles. We'll know more specifics once the state crime lab in Charleston finishes looking at it."

"Do you know where the shot came from?" Dave asked.

"We think so," Silent Doug answered. "The trajectory from Jack's wounds indicates the bullet was fired uphill from a position out in the woods, all the way across another clearing on the far side of Bart's meadow. About 700 yards from Jack's tree stand."

Dave whistled. "That's either one hell of an accident or one hell of a shot."

Vaughn squinted his good eye and cocked his head sideways. "It's *possible* someone could have taken a shot at a deer in that other clearing and missed. But it looks suspicious."

Rikki nodded solemnly. "Did you guys find anything else out there?"

The sheriff opened his folder. "By the time we got to the scene, the snow had melted off, so we didn't find any good shoeprints. No spent casings either. All we found at the spot where we think the shot came from was a crumpled-up candy wrapper, and God only knows how long it had been there."

Vaughn shut the folder. "We'll know more once we hear from the crime lab and when Jack's email provider responds to our subpoena. That's it for now."

Rikki stood up and extended her hands skyward, stretching. "All righty then. Thanks for the update, Sheriff. If we find anything interesting, we'll let you know. Keep up the good work!"

Silent Doug shot her a crisp salute. "Will do. You guys have a good day. Dave ... I'll see you at 11:30."

The sheriff left her office and Rikki's brow furrowed. "What's going on then?"

Dave sighed. "We both got drafted to participate in the Masonic funeral rites at Jack's gravesite. We're meeting a half-hour before the service so we know what we're doing."

"Ah. I see."

Rikki strolled across the room and peeked out the doorway. "You know, Dave, I really like the sheriff, but something about him has just freaked me out since we were kids."

"Like what?"

"I don't know. I mean, he seems honest and as nice as can be. Maybe it's just the way his one eye is always looking off to the side. I've never known exactly how that happened, and it kinda creeps me out. For all I know, he lost his eye in one of those twisted secret rituals you Masons conduct twice a year in a cornfield under a full moon."

Dave let loose with a belly laugh. "You've been reading too many conspiracy books, Rikki! Trust me, the truth is a lot simpler."

"Oh, really? And I suppose you know how the sheriff actually lost his eye."

"Sure. It's not like anyone was sworn to secrecy. It's just something he prefers not to talk about. I think he's afraid it might come across like he's bragging about it."

Rikki sat at the conference table, motioning for him to follow suit. "Mr. Anderson, you have my undivided attention."

Dave smirked and sat down cattycorner to her. "All right." Taking a deep breath, he dramatically opened by saying, "Quite simply, Douglas MacArthur Vaughn is a *badass*." He paused, contemplating his next words. "He was a hell of an athlete in school; first-team All-State at linebacker. And right after graduation he enlisted in the Army, despite the fact we were neck-deep in Vietnam at the time.

"He was a model soldier. Went through Special Forces school, earned his Green Beret, and pulled two tours of duty in 'Nam. In fact, his team was one of the last units we pulled out, just before Saigon fell to the commies."

Pausing for breath, he glanced at Rikki, who was listening with her pale green eyes open wide. Sensing that his audience was captivated by the story, he continued.

"When he got home from 'Nam, he arrived in town wearing his dress greens, his Green Beret, and a patch over his left eye. His first night home, a bunch of his buddies took him out drinking, including my uncle, who told *me* about it. And later that night, after getting a bellyful of booze, Silent Doug finally told them about his eye."

Dave leaned forward, resting his elbows on the conference table and sipped on his Diet Coke. "His team was conducting covert ops against Viet Cong supply depots in areas of Laos held by the Pathet Lao communists. One night, his unit attacked a depot and was surprised to find a bunch of Soviet 'advisors' there."

Rikki leaned forward, her mouth slightly agape.

"The ensuing fight was brutal: Small arms fire and hand-to-hand combat. The sheriff matter-of-factly described what happened, saying he lost count of how many people he killed just trying to get out alive.

"With all hell breaking loose around him, he was in the process of dragging an injured comrade to the landing zone for their Huey helicopter. Just as he threw this dude in the chopper, one of the Soviets slung a grenade, and the sheriff got hit with shrapnel. He was bleeding like a stuck pig and screaming his head off, but somehow crawled into the chopper as it took off.

"When he finally regained consciousness, he was in a hospital bed in Japan, missing an eye. He won the Distinguished Service Cross for his actions in that engagement, which is just one rung below the Congressional Medal of Honor and about as high of an honor any mortal is likely to get without actually *dying* for our country."

"Wow," Rikki said breathlessly. "What an amazing story."

"Yeah," Dave agreed. "After that one night drinking with his buddies, he's apparently never said another word about what happened. And, as a side note, ol' Silent Doug has had a bad case of the ass about Russians ever since."

"*Russians?*"

"Yeah," Dave reiterated. "He hates their guts. I think he's watched *Rocky IV* about a thousand times. Probably jerks off to it."

Rikki laughed aloud. "You are one twisted puppy," she said, shaking her head.

"I know. I have this terrible fear it's going to come back and bite me some day when I least expect it. God knows if the sheriff heard me say he jerked off to a Stallone movie, he'd probably rip off my leg and beat me to death with it."

"Well, why don't we keep that as our own little secret," Rikki suggested.

"That sounds like an *excellent* idea."

CHAPTER 80

NEW YORK CITY, MANHATTAN
WEDNESDAY, DECEMBER 10, 12:45 P.M.

NEW YORK CITY (AP) – The grassroots political action group Strike Back has called for members of the Electoral College to defy the final election results from their states and "vote their conscience" when casting their presidential ballots on Dec. 15.

Now that the so-called "Safe Harbor" deadline of Dec. 9 has elapsed with no change in West Virginia's election laws, the presidential hopes of Sen. Melanie Wilson (D-CA) appear bleak. Despite having won 41,000 more votes than Gov. Jonathan Royal (R-NC) nationwide, Wilson likely will join Al Gore, Samuel J. Tilden and Grover Cleveland as the only presidential candidates in American history whose popular vote victories failed to earn them Electoral College majorities.

Dmitri Mazniashvili – the billionaire who is Strike Back's largest contributor and who has largely funded a separate pro-Wilson super PAC – criticized West Virginia's failure to investigate allegations of voter intimidation and election fraud: "How can the American people have faith in the integrity of their elections when citizens are denied their fundamental rights? When an antiquated institution like the Electoral College arbitrarily and repeatedly thwarts the will of this country's citizens, it is time for that institution to be abolished."

Gov. Royal's campaign spokesman scoffed at such suggestions. "The Founding Fathers' wisdom has stood the test of time. The Electoral College is another example of the checks and balances enshrined in our Constitution, and these calls for presidential electors to violate their legal and moral responsibilities demonstrates that Strike Back's views are far outside the mainstream."

Royal's spokesman added, "Mr. Mazniashvili's suggestion that presidential electors betray the voters' trust demonstrates he has no respect for the rule of law. The President-elect remains committed to extraditing this felon to stand trial for his crimes in his native country, and the sooner that task can be completed, the better."

- excerpt from FoxNews.com

CHAPTER 81

McCALLEN FAMILY CEMETERY
PLEASANTS COUNTY, WEST VIRGINIA
WEDNESDAY, DECEMBER 10, 12:45 P.M.

About 50 people attended Jack's graveside ceremony in his family cemetery. Aside from the footpath leading from Jack's home, a gravel roadway ran from the back of the cemetery down the other side of the hill to the main road. A black hearse sat by the gated entrance with its back doors open as the crowd milled around the newly opened grave, waiting to say goodbye.

Rikki and her mother stood side-by-side toward the rear. Tabatha sat on a padded red velvet chair directly beside Jack's grave. Only the neckline of her relatively modest black dress was visible beneath her tailored black wool overcoat, and a sheer widow's veil covered her face.

Sitting stoically to her right was Jack's oldest son, Logan. Wearing a black suit, his thick dark hair was neatly combed and parted to the side as he stared vacantly at his father's coffin. His younger brother, Brandon, fidgeted in the chair to Tabatha's left with his jaw clenched shut. His red hair was disheveled, and his balled fists rested on his thighs.

Eight men clad in dark suits approached the grave in a somber, single-file line, forming a semi-circle around it with one man positioned at the head of the casket and another at its foot. Matching white lambskin aprons, immaculate in appearance, were strapped across their midsections, and their hands were covered with thin white gloves.

The elderly gentleman standing at the head of the casket solemnly removed the black felt fedora covering his crown. His full head of hair was as white as his gloves, and after scanning the crowd to confirm it was time to start the service, he took a deep breath and began delivering the message he had committed to memory perhaps four decades earlier.

"Brethren and Friends," he began in a clear, baritone voice. "It has been a custom among the Fraternity of Free and Accepted Masons from time immemorial, at the request of a departed Brother or his family, to assemble in the character of Masons and, with the solemn formalities of the Craft, to offer up to his memory, before the world, the last tribute of our affection."

Rikki watched in amazement as the old man delivered his speech without any notes whatsoever. The other six Masons, including Sheriff Vaughn, Dave Anderson and his father, stood silently with their hands by their sides, listening intently.

"Our Brother has reached the end of his earthly toils," the white-haired man declared. "The brittle thread which bound him to earth has been severed, and the liberated spirit has winged its flight to the unknown world. The silver cord is loosed; the golden bowl is broken; the pitcher is broken at the fountain; and the wheel is broken at the cistern. The dust has returned to the earth as it was, and the spirit has returned to God who gave it."

As the speech continued, Rikki found herself staring at Dave as he dutifully played his role in the ceremony. His green eyes occasionally strayed from the elderly speaker and fell upon Jack's boys, and Rikki watched him try to maintain an outward appearance of calm self-control. But his watering eyes belied his true emotional state, as did his occasionally trembling lower lip. As she watched Dave struggle to master his grief-stricken heart and bend it to his will, Rikki suddenly felt a surprisingly intense urge to rush to his side and comfort him.

What in the world is going on with me? What's with all this sentimentality I'm feeling? Am I losing my mind?

The old man's voice drew Rikki back to reality. "But we have learned of the Great Architect of the Universe," he asserted with a nod. "We know that in the Universe all is order; although His design is too huge for any mortal eye to comprehend. But if the Great Architect is there, why should we care that we can see no more than our own small piece of the work?"

The speaker paused, casting his gaze across the crowd. "We know the great building is clear in the Master's mind, and it is growing toward completion. Our apparent confusion is only the gathering of the material out of which the structure shall rise complete in its beauty and perfection. We can do *our* work and bear *our* burden and even endure the pain of disappointment and loss if we have learned to trust in *Him*. That trust turns the bitter drop to sweetness."

Suddenly, the old man's eyes fixed on Rikki, and her heart skipped a beat. "Friendship is refreshment and sweetness as we pass this way," he said with a patient smile. "It is much to feel that, wherever we are, we have *friends*. Although human companionships are temporary in this world of change, let us cherish the comfort they provide, and let us find the strength to forgive our friends when their actions have caused us pain, just as we ask the Great Architect to overlook those instances when our own handiwork has failed to comply with his perfect commands."

Rikki felt a lump in her throat and she suddenly had trouble seeing the old man's face. *Didn't Jack say something like that to me a while back? That carrying around anger can't be good for me? That being imperfect should not be an unforgivable sin?*

The speaker turned to Jack's widow and sons. "Our entire fraternity surrounds his loved ones with the assurance of its affection. We offer the support of our sympathy, the comfort of our faith, and the inspiration of our hope, that they may look beyond this hour of grief through the opening portals of the infinite. Let us be unceasingly grateful for every God-given virtue, which the life of our Brother expressed, and let us be comforted and sustained by the assurance that life goes on unbroken and uncorrupted, and that God alone is the life and light of men."

With a nod to Dave's father, the old man turned his body at a 45 degree angle, facing the Masonic semi-circle. Mr. Anderson took one step toward the speaker and handed him an apron that appeared identical to those the Masons were wearing.

"This Lambskin, or white leather apron," the man explained, laying it on Jack's casket, "is an emblem of innocence and the badge of a Mason. It reminds us of that purity of life and conduct so essential to gaining admission into the Celestial Lodge above, where the Supreme Architect of the Universe presides."

A second Mason approached and handed the old man what looked like a big fern leaf. Grasping it his gloved hands, the speaker tenderly placed it beside the apron atop the casket. "This Evergreen is an emblem of our faith in the immortality of the soul," he declared. "By this we are reminded that we have an immortal part within us which shall survive the chilling blast of death and, springing into newness of life in realms beyond the grave, shall never, *never* die."

The old man turned his attention to his counterpart at the foot of the casket and gave a nod. The other Mason returned the nod, took one step toward the coffin and bowed his head.

"Most Glorious God," the man began. "Pour down Thy blessing upon us, and strengthen our solemn engagements with the ties of sincere affection! Endue us with fortitude and resignation in this hour of sorrow, and may the present instance of mortality draw our attention toward Thee. Enable us to look with eyes of Faith toward that realm whose skies are never darkened by sorrow; and after our departure, may we be received into Thy everlasting kingdom, to enjoy the just reward of a virtuous and well-spent life.

"Amen."

As she opened her eyes at the end of the prayer, Rikki heard the other seven Masons intone as one: "So mote it be!"

The old man at the head of the gravesite smiled peacefully and placed his fedora back on his head. Gazing around at the crowd, he announced, "This concludes our service. May God grant his loyal servant, Jack McCallen, the eternal peace and joy he so richly deserves, and may God bless you all."

With that, the lead Mason strolled over to offer his condolences to Tabatha and the boys while the crowd dispersed. Rikki watched Bart McCallen walk up to Dave and wrap him in a bear hug. With clenched eyes and flaring nostrils, Dave pounded the palm of his right hand against the man's back twice and said, "I'm so sorry for your loss, Bart. You need anything at all … *anything* … you give me a call, and I'll be there for you."

Bart loudly sucked air through his mouth, trying to control his breathing. He gripped Dave tightly and fought back tears. "It's not *fair!* Those boys *need* their dad, damn it! How can they grow up to be *men* when the only role model they're gonna have around the house is *Tabatha*, for God's sake?"

Dave pulled away from Bart and stared him square in the eyes. "They still have their Uncle Bart. You know the kind of men Jack would have taught them to become. You *are* the kind of man Jack would want them to become. *Don't give up.*" Dave placed both of his hands on Bart's arms and gave them a slight shake. "No matter how hard she tries to make it on you and the boys, Bart, don't let her beat you down. Those boys are sharp as tacks. Soon enough, if you keep reminding them of the ways Jack taught them right from wrong, they'll be able to look around and figure out who's doing right by them and who isn't."

Bart pursed his lips and blew a big breath out his nostrils. With moist eyes, he glanced at his nephews and nodded. "You're right. I can do this. It's what Jack would have wanted."

"And it's what Logan and Brandon *deserve*," Dave added.

Bart hugged Dave again and said, "You're a good friend, Dave. Thanks for talking some sense into me."

Dave lightly patted Bart on the back. "Any time."

Bart drew away from Dave and his wife, Melinda, subtly put her hand inside the crook of his elbow. "Thanks for everything, Dave," she said softly. "Now if you'll excuse us, we need to get home and start moving on with our lives. We can't grieve forever."

"You guys take care."

Bart and Melinda waved goodbye, walking toward the gate and the line of cars that had circled around the cemetery and faced back toward the main road. As Dave watched them leave, Rikki approached and stood just behind his right shoulder. "Hey. How are you doing?"

Dave glanced at her and exhaled. "That was tough. Wading back into the crossfire of Beltway politics will feel like a vacation."

Rikki nodded. "When are you headed back?"

"First thing in the morning. The transition team meets at noon tomorrow, and with this protracted election battle, we're way behind schedule in getting his administration organized."

"Well, be careful going home. I'll get word to you if there are any new developments in Jack's case."

Dave smiled wearily. "Thanks, Rik. I appreciate that. I know it's way beyond the call of duty for you."

Opening his arms, he asked, "So can you give me one more hug for old times' sake?"

Rikki rolled her eyes and leaned in to his proffered embrace. Feeling his arms wrap around her gently, she placed her hand on the middle of his back. *Life is too short*, a voice whispered in her head. *And you may never pass this way again.*

As they separated, Rikki looked at Dave's face, examining it searchingly. Although a tad worse for the emotional wear of the graveside service, he actually looked surprisingly serene. And for some strange reason, Rikki suddenly realized she did not want her time with him to come to an end just yet. "So what are you doing for dinner this evening?" she casually asked.

Dave shrugged. "Probably heating up leftovers. Mom has choir practice tonight, so Dad and I are fending for ourselves."

"Well, I have a better idea."

He looked confused. "What's that?"

"Why don't you stop by my place? One of my clients owns a beef farm, and he gave me a big box of steaks for Christmas. I could throw two on the grill, and we could kick back, have a few beers, and do some catching up. After all," she added with a grin and an elbow to his ribs. "It's only been ... What? Fifteen years or so?"

Dave chuckled. "Give or take a few days."

"So what do you say?" Rikki asked, folding her arms across her chest and shivering slightly. "It's getting cold out here, and you know I don't deal well with the cold. My ancestors were sweltering in a hot river delta while yours were snowshoeing across the Scandinavian tundra, buddy boy."

He laughed aloud. "Fine. What time?"

"How about six? And do you even know where I live?"

Dave scoffed. "Of course. This is *Pleasants County* we're talking about; everybody knows where *everybody* lives around here! Plus – aside from an oil and gas lawyer who charges *way* too much money for her services – there aren't a whole lot of people around here who could afford that sweet spread you have overlooking the river."

Rikki scowled. "I'm not even going to respond to that. You bring the beer and I'll provide the steaks. Deal?"

"Deal. See you at six."

CHAPTER 82

ST. MARYS, PLEASANTS COUNTY, WEST VIRGINIA
WEDNESDAY, DECEMBER 10, 7:20 P.M.

Dave reclined and extended his legs. "Holy cow! That was an awesome meal, Rikki."

She grinned mischievously. "Of course it was," she replied snarkily. "Would you expect anything less from me?"

"Ha! Who do you think you're talking to? I still remember when my exotic-looking girlfriend lured me into inviting a bunch of my UVA classmates over for dinner, assuring me she could cook homemade Indian food as good as her Momma's!"

Rikki smiled widely and giggled. "Oh, my God! I can't believe you still remember that debacle!"

"How could I forget watching you freak out after you burned everything to a crisp? Then I had to rush to an Indian restaurant and bring back Styrofoam boxes of food we could pawn off as *your* creations." Dave cackled so hard his whole trunk shook. "I can't believe they actually fell for it!"

"Personally," Rikki added. "I loved it when your friend said, 'This girl of yours sure is a great cook,' and you shot back ..."

"She sure is *something* all right," they said in unison, then burst into laughter.

Dave grabbed his empty beer bottle and shook it lightly. "I think I could use a refill."

Rikki slowly stood up. "Me, too. Let me take that and I'll get us two more."

"Much obliged."

Rikki strolled into the kitchen, dropped the two empties into the recycling bin, and grabbed another round. Returning, she playfully brought a cold bottle into contact with Dave's neck.

"*Whew!*" he exclaimed, bolting upright. "That's freezing!"

Rikki grinned and handed him the bottle as she sat down. "I couldn't resist."

Dave sipped the beer. Gazing around the house, he nodded approvingly. "This is a nice place, Rikki. Awfully big for one person, but beautiful, nonetheless."

"Well, I'm not moving any time soon, and it's big enough for Mom to move in when she can't take care of herself anymore." She grinned again, devilishly. "Plus, if I ever find a man smart enough to handle me, he can move his pretty little self in here, too."

Dave chortled. "That's a tall order there, Rikki. Personally, I'd be happy if I could find someone I get along with. Someone who might not necessarily *understand* my quirks but at least could smile, shake her head, and accept me the way I am."

Rikki clanked Dave's bottle with hers. "That's a nice way to put it. I might steal it."

"I'm happy to share it with you," he said. Then, the look in his green eyes turned more serious. "I figure that's the least I could do, considering how I ..."

The sentence hung unfinished, as if he didn't know what else to say.

How I wasn't there to hold you when your dad died. How I foolishly believed him when he said his condition was stable enough for me to finish my finals.

How I failed to live up to your expectations.

"It's okay," Rikki said softly. "I understand."

Dave's lips tightened. After studying her face, his posture relaxed and he nodded. "You have no idea how many times I've *prayed* I'd live long enough to hear you say that." Closing his eyes, he exhaled deeply. "Thank you."

Rikki felt her mouth twitch. "We were young. We made mistakes. I was just *so hurt* you weren't with me when Daddy passed away, and forgiveness isn't one of my strong points."

Dave snorted and smiled wanly. "That's the understatement of the century."

"I'm just sorry I held on to that grudge for so long. Spending time with you the past few days has made me remember what great *friends* we were, even before we started dating. And I'm sad I let that bitterness linger because it stole fifteen years of friendship from us."

Dave's eyes glowed and he smiled. "I've missed *laughing* with you, Rik. More than anything, I've missed our mental jousts and hearing your laughter."

Rikki put her hand on his. "Well, I'm happy we finally buried the hatchet. If nothing else, that has helped dull the sadness the past few days."

"Jack was a good man," Dave reflected wistfully. "I'm gonna miss the hell out of him. And I hope to God when you guys catch who killed him, whatever happens to him – or *her* – makes waterboarding look like getting a wedgie."

"Do you *really* want to go into that?" Rikki asked testily. "Because I'd be happy to debate *your* party's abominable decision to add torture to America's foreign policy arsenal if that's how you want to spend the rest of the evening."

"No thanks. I just dug out of one big hole, and I'd rather not push my luck."

CHAPTER 83

PLEASANTS COUNTY COURTHOUSE
ST. MARYS, PLEASANTS COUNTY, WEST VIRGINIA
THURSDAY, DECEMBER 11, 10:55 A.M.

While awaiting Tabatha, Rikki reviewed Jack's will again. Knowing the widow was likely unhappy about the way Jack had structured his estate, Rikki wanted to be prepared to answer any questions (and thwart any objections) she might raise.

The stairwell door opened and then Tabatha asked the secretary, "Is she ready for me?"

"I don't know," Martha replied. "I'll check."

Tabatha sighed loudly. A moment later, Martha stepped into Rikki's office with a wide-eyed look that said, *Wow! What a bitch!*

"Mrs. McCallen is here to see you," Martha said chirpily. But her words were undercut by her accompanying motion, acting like she was sticking her finger down her throat.

Rikki smiled. "Send her in."

Martha ambled back through the doorway. "Ms. Gudivada can see you now."

Tabatha strutted into the office and sat down, daintily crossing her right leg over her left.

"So how can I help you, Tabatha?"

"I need to know your plans for distributing part of Petromica's investment in my company to me and the boys," she replied, twirling her high-heeled foot.

"Well, Tabby," Rikki began. "*Technically*, McCallen Resources is not *your* company. When he died, Jack owned the whole company, aside from any shares he may have agreed to sell to Petromica, and his shares will pass through his estate. And according to his Will, that stock is to be held in trust for you and the boys until Brandon turns 25."

"I *know* what the Will says," Tabatha retorted. "It says the *stock* has to be held in trust. But it doesn't say Petromica's investment money must be kept in trust, does it?"

"No," Rikki admitted. "But that money was *derived* from the stock, so it must remain in trust, too."

Tabatha's eyes narrowed. "I've already met with Barry Glassman," she said menacingly. "*He* says that if the beneficiaries of the trust think the trustee is unreasonably refusing to disburse trust proceeds to them, they could have the trustee removed."

Count to ten. Don't lose your cool but stand your ground.

"Any trustee who acts unreasonably could be removed by a court," Rikki continued. "But since Jack hasn't even been dead a week, it's only prudent for me to thoroughly investigate the firm's financial situation before deciding whether the beneficiaries' interests would be served by disbursing any sales proceeds. With oil and gas prices so high now, it might be smarter to invest that money in more new wells."

Tabatha smiled dangerously. "And if one of those multi-million-dollar wells ends up a dry hole, the beneficiaries could sue the trustee who made that investment over their objections for malfeasance of duty. Right?"

Five, six, seven, eight, nine, ten. Breathe.

"We can cross that bridge when we get to it. But I'm not jeopardizing the long-term viability of the trust."

Tabatha's face reddened and a vein bulged on her forehead. "I've had my doubts about your competence for years," she spat. "Having seen you operate in person now, you've done nothing to alleviate those concerns."

Breathe. Breathe.

"I'm sorry you feel that way, Tabatha."

"But before I do anything rash, I want another lawyer to look over what's been happening in that Schoolcraft lease cancellation suit. So as a beneficiary of this trust, and a true *owner* of that stock, I direct you to copy your file in that case and forward it to Mr. Glassman so his firm can advise me as to whether it is appropriate for you to keep handling that case."

"*What?*"

"Now that you are trustee for our stock in McCallen Resources," Tabatha said, "it might be wiser for another lawyer to handle the company's litigation. Otherwise, it would be like you were representing yourself. And I've heard that a lawyer who represents himself ..."

"Has a fool for a client," Rikki finished, before pausing. "That's understandable. I'll have Martha copy the file, and I'll draft a report for Mr. Glassman explaining the current status. He's handled oil and gas cases, so hopefully we can bring him up to speed quickly."

Tabatha looked smug. "Well, I'm thankful you aren't *always* difficult to deal with. Maybe there's hope for you yet."

Six, seven, eight, nine ...

Rikki glanced down at her watch. "Unfortunately, I have to cut this short as I have another hearing downstairs. But I'm glad we sat down and went over things. I'll call Mr. Glassman when the Schoolcraft copies are ready."

Tabatha slung her purse over her shoulder. "I'll tell him to expect your call by the end of business tomorrow."

What an arrogant bitch! Like this is my only case! But the sooner it's done, the sooner she'll be out of my hair. Breathe ...

"That should be fine," Rikki said, opening the door. "You have a good day."

Tabatha smirked. "I certainly will."

As the widow strutted away, Rikki stepped into the conference room to regain her composure. The stairwell door slammed shut and Martha said, "That woman is a royal class shrew in need of a butt-kicking."

Rikki gritted her teeth. "If she doesn't watch out, she's gonna get one."

CHAPTER 84

CHARLESTON, WEST VIRGINIA
THURSDAY, DECEMBER 11, 11:55 A.M.

Governor Vincent's phone rang. He looked at the viewscreen and saw it was Tabatha.

Oh, God. What now?

Vincent pressed a lever and the limo's privacy glass went up. "Hello?"

"Hi, Luke," she said sweetly. "Is it a bad time?"

"Not at all. How are you doing?"

"I'm doing great. Now that I'm talking to the most powerful man in the world, that is."

He chuckled uneasily. "I wouldn't say that, but I appreciate the sentiment."

"At this moment, Luke, you *are* the most powerful man in the world," she reiterated.

Vincent's brow creased. "And why would you say that?"

"One word from you could make Melanie Wilson the next president."

NEW YORK CITY
THURSDAY, DECEMBER 11, 7:30 P.M.

Yuri Petrenko held an old-fashioned glass. Mazniashvili's face was joyous, and the billionaire raised his own glass.

"To victory!" Mazniashvili cheered.

Petrenko smiled wanly and tossed back the vodka. "To Operation Aristocrates. It was a brilliant plan, *vozhd.*"

Mazniashvili raised his right index finger and waved it back and forth. "No, no, no. I had an *idea*. You, Yuri ... You gave it *life*. Without you, I might still be looking for a new country to call home."

Petrenko knew better than to disagree. As ruthless as Mazniashvili was when provoked, his generosity to loyal underlings was legendary. *And I would not object to receiving that generosity. Not one bit.*

"So can I ask you one question?" Petrenko asked.

Mazniashvili nodded magnanimously. "Fire away."

"Why did you call it, 'Operation Aristocrates?'"

The billionaire grinned. "Ah ... *That*." He lit a cigarette. "In ancient Greece, in what became known as the Second Messenian War, the region called Arcadia was allied with the Messenians against the Spartans and others.

"As the two sides prepared for a major battle, the Spartan side bribed the Arcadian king to reveal his allies' plans. Through this duplicity, the Messenians and their allies were slaughtered at the ensuing battle, their entire army virtually destroyed."

Mazniashvili took a drag, and the cigarette glowed orange. "Upon learning of the king's treason, the Arcadians stoned him to death. His family, too.

"The name of that greedy, unlucky Arcadian king was Aristocrates," he concluded.

"Ah," Petrenko said. "An appropriate name, indeed."

CHAPTER 85

PLEASANTS COUNTY COURTHOUSE
ST. MARYS, PLEASANTS COUNTY, WEST VIRGINIA
FRIDAY, DECEMBER 12, 9:55 A.M.

Rikki sat at her desk, holding a digital voice recorder. Documents from the Schoolcraft case were piled beside her.

"I expect the plaintiffs will primarily argue the lease should be cancelled because McCallen Resources failed to fully develop the leasehold's mineral resources," she dictated. "Some evidence supports this theory: The production logs indicate only a marginal amount of gas passed through the wellheads during the past three years.

"As an aside, Jack may have recently conveyed a 49 percent equity stake in MR to a firm called Petromica, LLC. Although I thought Jack had backed off the deal, his widow claims he changed his mind. I have no signed documents corroborating this assertion. Thus, I suggest you discuss that issue with Mrs. McCallen."

That money-grubbing bitch, Rikki silently added.

"In the alternative, you could contact Petromica's point man and request copies. Here is his contact information ..."

Someone knocked on the door. Craning her neck to stare over her shoulder, she saw the local officer from the West Virginia Division of Natural Resources. "Could I borrow your Code book for Chapter Twenty?"

"Sure," Rikki said. "It's on that bookcase. Help yourself."

"Thanks," the DNR officer replied. "I need to file a criminal complaint against two guys who poached a buck this morning."

"Didn't deer season end last Saturday?"

"Yep. That's why they're being charged with illegal hunting out-of-season."

"Well, keep up the good work." She then rotated around to resume her dictation.

"Damn, Rikki!" the DNR man exclaimed. "You've only been on the job three weeks, but you're really on top of things! How did you find out about *that* guy?"

She turned to face him, looking puzzled. "What guy?"

He pointed toward her computer screen. "*That* guy. I gave him a citation last Saturday for hunting without a permit."

Rikki looked at the screen and a chill went down her spine. He was pointing to Petromica's press release for its hiring of Alex Beria. She had accessed it to give Tabatha's new lawyer Beria's contact information.

"He said he accidentally washed his license and would bring me proof it was valid," the DNR officer said, still flipping through the book. "I ain't seen him, though, so I guess he needs to be arrested, too."

Rikki tried to look calm. "Are you sure this is the same guy?"

The officer chuckled. "Hell, yeah! Ain't too many guys wandering around, missing half an ear. Plus, his teeth were like that guy's ... so white, it was like he painted and bleached 'em."

Breathe. One, two, three ...

"So where did you run into him?"

"He was coming out of the woods about six miles up Mount Carmel."

That's just two miles from Bart's farm.

Rikki pursed her lips and nodded. "What side of the road was he on?"

The man's face scrunched up. "As you head up Mount Carmel from Route 2, he was coming out of the woods on your right."

Bart's farm is on that side of the road.

"Hmm," Rikki mumbled. "Do you remember what time you ran into him?"

The man's face reflected curiosity. "Is this '20 Questions' or something?"

"Indulge me."

He grinned. "All right ... I think it was around 8:30."

An hour after Bart thinks the shot that killed Jack was fired. Plenty of time to walk two miles through the woods to a getaway vehicle.

"Could you bring me your file on this incident?" Rikki asked. "I'd like to compare it to my notes on this guy."

"Sure," he said, shrugging. "You're the prosecutor."

Yes, I am, for better or worse. Dear God, I hope I'm not in over my head here.

WASHINGTON, D.C.
FRIDAY, DECEMBER 12, 11:15 A.M.

Jonathan Royal's transition team sat around the conference table, discussing potential cabinet appointments. Randolph Stephens sat at the head of the table, as befit his status as one of the Republican Party's elder statesmen.

"Next up we have Treasury," Stephens said. "Do we have the final background checks?"

Dave calmly shuffled through his papers. "I emailed them yesterday afternoon. Printed copies should be in the briefing packet, too."

"Good," Stephens said gruffly. "There's just 39 days until the Inauguration, people. The sooner we get these background checks back, the sooner Governor Royal can figure out who he wants serving in his Cabinet. We don't want any surprises."

Dave's phone vibrated. Holding it beneath the table, he opened his inbox.

"A few of us are coming to D.C. tonite 2 catch a comedy show," the text from Monica Boley read. "Wanna join us?"

Dave repressed the urge to grin, fearing it might draw attention. He used his thumb to quietly hammer out a response.

"Beers and laughs sound good. What time and where?"

The elder statesman's face turned red. "God damn it!" Stephens screamed. "Defense is the most important vacancy and you still haven't interviewed those people?" He shook his head in disbelief. "You've had those names almost a week!"

Man. He's really tearing that dude a new one. Thank God that's not me!

As his colleague stammered an excuse, Dave's phone vibrated again.

"1140 Conn Ave b/w L & M, @ 8:30."

Dave mentally calculated how long it would take him to wrap up the meeting, get home, eat, shower, get dressed and get to the club.

"I'll meet u there. I'll let u know if anything changes."

Dave glanced at Stephens and was glad to see his blood pressure had dropped. Aside from the screw-up with Defense, the man seemed fairly satisfied with their progress.

"Energy Department," he announced. "And if there's a bunny-hugger on your list, I'm gonna punch you in the throat."

Yet another pleasant day in the nation's capital, Dave thought with a smirk.

CHAPTER 86

PLEASANTS COUNTY COURTHOUSE
ST. MARYS, PLEASANTS COUNTY, WEST VIRGINIA
FRIDAY, DECEMBER 12, 1:00 P.M.

"Hold my calls," Rikki said. "I need peace and quiet to finish reviewing this stuff."

"What if it's the Sheriff's Office?"

"If it's about Jack's death, fine. Otherwise, I'll call them back."

Martha nodded. "Okay. Good luck!"

"Thanks," Rikki replied, shutting the door.

For three hours, she had agonized about her conversation with the DNR officer. His file confirmed (much to her chagrin) that he had issued a citation to one Aleksandr Sergeivich Beria.

Funny. No wonder he goes by Alex. I had no idea he was Russian.

When questioned, he had given a Virginia driver's license with a Falls Church address.

Petromica's regional headquarters is in Reston. Isn't that near Falls Church?

The citation indicated Beria was 33 years old, stood six-feet-two and weighed 230 pounds.

Sounds like a well-built fellow. I wonder what happened to his ear.

Prodigious internet research led Rikki to articles confirming that Petromica was largely owned by Mazniashvili.

The same guy Jonathan Royal wants to extradite. The same guy who publicly called for presidential electors to switch sides.

Rikki slowly rocked back and forth, staring out the window at the decrepit refinery next to the courthouse. The more she thought about the situation, the more she did not like it.

Last Friday, Jack said the Petromica deal was off. What could have changed his mind? And why can't I find this Addendum mentioned in Tabatha's email to Beria?

She sighed and rubbed her temples. Then a startling thought crossed her mind, causing her to gasp.

What if that Addendum had to do with Jack switching his vote in the Electoral College? And if he refused, someone would have wanted to keep that proposition private.

Thinking about Jack made her eyes water. Republican or not, he was a good man who would never betray his convictions by switching sides.

Even though Melanie Wilson would be a better president than Jonathan Royal could ever dream of being. Jack might not have agreed, but I _know_ it's the truth.

Then, Rikki's thoughts led her to a place that made her blood turn cold.

Jack would have refused to switch his vote. _Tabatha_, on the other hand...

A quick Internet search yielded five stories. Four had been published in the last few days, but the fifth was from the West Virginia Republican Party's convention last summer, designating Tabatha as one of their five alternate electors.

Would Mazniashvili have known about that? Or is Tabatha smart enough — and heartless enough — to cook up a scheme where he got the Electoral College vote he wanted, while she got a big bag of money and a dead husband?

Rikki quickly answered that question in the affirmative. But thornier issues remained: For instance, even if her worst suspicions proved true, could the county's police officers crack a murder case in 72 hours? The Electoral College convened on Monday.

Probably not, but stranger things have happened.

And since she fervently believed America would be best served if Melanie Wilson became its next President ...

Why should I even <u>try</u> to stop Tabatha from voting for her on Monday? Don't bad things sometimes happen to good people because God has a greater plan we can't see or understand? Didn't that old Mason at Jack's funeral say something like that? Who can say God didn't use Tabatha's machinations and Jack's death as a means to put Melanie Wilson in the White House?

She was strongly tempted to delay investigating her suspicions. If they could build a case against Tabatha, Beria and/or Mazniashvili for murder next month, what would it matter? The criminals would still go to jail, while the country would get a better president. Everyone would win.

And if I try to stop their little conspiracy, wouldn't they put a bullet in my head like they did Jack's? What's one more dead body to these people?

As she absentmindedly fingered her pen, her eyes were drawn to a framed photograph on her desk. It was a 5x7 picture taken when she was six years old. Perched atop her father's right thigh, her feet dangled between his legs. Rikki smiled and softly brushed her fingertips across the glass. In the picture, her dad's black hair was neatly parted and devoid of gray. Never a fashion expert, Dr. Gudivada wore a green bowling shirt and black Bermuda shorts. Even more appalling, he wore sandals and black socks that stretched almost to his knees.

Studying his face, she was struck by the serenity in his eyes. Sure, he looked happy; and proud, too, balancing his daughter on his lap. But he exuded an enviably peaceful glow that was instantly recognizable.

Throughout her life, Rikki's father had been her ethical role model. When he said he would do something, he did it.

Although tactful, he would express opinions that ran contrary to general wisdom if he felt they were warranted. And when a child needed medical treatment, he gave that patient the best care he could, regardless of the parents' ability to pay. While he may have earned less money than many of his peers, he probably slept a lot better.

He looks serene, because his conscience is clean.

For some reason, she recalled an incident from the seventh grade. She had just started junior high school and her intelligence was widely regarded. Another girl in her class — popular but not smart and a bully, to boot — had been successfully pressuring Rikki to share her homework, and she brought the situation to her father, asking for his advice.

Dr. G had listened carefully to her dilemma. "You know, daughter, when I was a little boy in India, we had a saying, 'The person who holds the ladder is just as guilty as the thief.' If you are letting this girl cheat off of you, you are just as guilty as she is. Plus, you're not doing her any favors. How will she learn to do her math problems if you keep doing them for her?"

She recalled how fear had gripped her. "What if she gets mad and beats me up, Daddy?"

Her father had smiled patiently and stroked her long black hair. "Doing the right thing sometimes comes with risks, child. A wise man once said, 'All that is required for evil to prevail is for good men to do nothing.' That holds true for beautiful young ladies, as well."

Staring at the picture, Rikki desperately wished she had the benefit of her father's wisdom today. *He would know what to say. He would know what to do.*

Then, a profound sense of calm settled over her. The anxiety that had previously saturated her thinking gave way, unexpectedly, to clarity and tranquility.

I took an oath to uphold the Constitution when I became the prosecutor of this County. Not just those parts I like, but the whole thing, even though I might not agree with it. Everyone has their burden to bear, and some lucky or unfortunate few are given an important role to play.

For better or worse, I now know both my burden and my role.

Rikki pulled out her cell phone and made the call she knew destiny demanded she make.

The die is cast. Let's roll.

CHAPTER 87

FLYING M FARMS
NEAR COMUS, MARYLAND
FRIDAY, DECEMBER 12, 2:55 P.M.

"Back already?" the proprietor of the private airfield asked.

"I'm afraid so," Dave replied. "What can I say? I'm suddenly feeling important."

As he submitted his flight manifest and prepared to jump in his Cessna, his phone rang. It was Jonathan Royal.

"Good afternoon, Governor," Dave said.

"Your message sounded like you were about to have a coronary. What's going on?"

"I'm flying back to West Virginia. We may have a faithless Elector on our hands."

After a moment of silence, Royal asked, "What do you need?"

"You can't do anything right now. It's a miracle I know anything at all, and the woman who asked me to help investigate the situation is both stubborn and prideful. And a Democrat."

"No offense, but that's one fucked-up state you came from, where a Democrat is warning *you* about one of our Electors going rogue on us."

Dave chuckled. "You don't know who I'm dealing with. She's one-of-a-kind. In any event, I have to tread very carefully. I *might* be able to convince her to let me bring our resources to bear, but if I suggest that too early, she could easily tell me to climb back on my plane and get the hell out of her sight.

"She never likes to admit she needs help," Dave continued. "*Especially* from a stinking Republican and particularly not from *me*. I know, without a doubt, she believes or at least wants to believe she can handle this situation alone. And bringing in helicopters full of Republican operatives, turning them loose on her little county, will not promote her continuing cooperation."

"So who the hell is she?" Royal asked.

Dave sighed. "She's the prosecutor in Pleasants County, and she thinks someone killed Jack McCallen because he wouldn't turn traitor and cast his electoral ballot for Senator Wilson. She thinks his replacement may be in on the fix.

"Oh, yeah, she's also my ex-fiancé."

Royal chortled. "If my presidency wasn't hanging in the balance, I'd say that is the single most ironic, hysterical, fucked-up thing I've ever heard in my life. After everything I've went through to get elected, you're saying my fate is in the hands of a woman that *you pissed off at some point in the past?*" He laughed caustically. "Unbelievable. If that's the case, you need to get down on your knees, kiss every square inch of her ass, and beg her to marry you."

"I did that a long time ago," Dave grumbled. "It didn't turn out so well."

"Then let her kick you in the balls, if that's what she wants! I can't afford to have even one Elector go south on me. If this ends up in the hands of Congress, I'm probably cooked."

"Trust me, I know. I'll try to get to the bottom of this. And I'll try to convince her to let us play a bigger role in the investigation."

"Why don't we send some people in anyway?" Royal bristled. "It's a free country."

"Two words: *Prosecutorial discretion*. She's not a big fan of yours, and if she thinks we're pushing her to do something she hasn't decided to do on her own, she'll get riled up. After all, even if a crime was committed, she could easily sit on it until after December 15th. She's holding all the cards, and we can't force her hand. We have to play by her rules."

Royal sighed loudly. "Fine. I don't like it, but I don't *have* to like it. I'll keep my fingers crossed and put my faith in you and The Big Guy Upstairs. Call me."

The desk attendant motioned at the flight paperwork. Dave nodded and signed where indicated. "I will. Talk to you later."

Hanging up, Dave walked across the tarmac with his suitcase, tapping buttons on his phone. "Have to take a raincheck tonite," he typed to Monica Boley. "Sorry. Duty calls."

Strapping into the Cessna, he suddenly remembered to call his parents.

"Hello?" his father answered.

"Hey, Dad! I've had a change of plans. Could you meet me at the airport in 90 minutes? I'm on my way back home."

"Homesick already?"

"It's a long story."

CHAPTER 88

PLEASANTS COUNTY COURTHOUSE
ST. MARYS, PLEASANTS COUNTY, WEST VIRGINIA
FRIDAY, DECEMBER 12, 3:30 P.M.

I wonder what dirty secrets might be hidden in here, Rikki thought to herself.

Staring at her monitor, she browsed through the files from Tabatha's cell phone company, focusing on the calls made between December 4th (the day Jack's deal with Petromica apparently disintegrated) and December 8th at 3:05 p.m. (when the disc was burned).

On December 4th, Tabatha called Jack at 11:05 a.m. The call lasted 12 minutes, and then she immediately called a 703 area code number and spoke for 20 minutes.

703 is a Virginia area code. It covers the Northern Virginia suburbs of D.C.

There were five calls between Tabatha and this 703 number on December 4th and 5th. The longest was on Friday around 2 p.m., lasting 31 minutes. At 10:30 on the morning Jack died, an incoming call lasted just three minutes. Four additional calls to/from that number occurred on December 7th and 8th.

Who were you talking to, Tabatha?

Rikki logged into her email account and scanned through her inbox. Locating the first email from Beria that Jack had forwarded to her, she re-read it.

Beria's cell phone number is (703) 925-1420. She double-checked Tabatha's cell phone records. *Bingo. Same number.* On a hunch, she went through Tabatha's calls and found none were to or from Beria before December 4th.

Hmm … interesting.

Returning to her own email inbox, Rikki reviewed the emails between Jack and Beria, looking at the documents that were attached to each, hoping to find this so-called Addendum.

No such luck. I don't even see the purchase agreement in here. Maybe Jack just printed it off and brought it in the day before Thanksgiving.

A loud ring interrupted her thoughts. Scowling, she answered the phone. "Hello?"

"Sorry to bother you," Martha said. "But this call is from the Virginia DMV. I thought you'd want to take it."

"Absolutely. Patch it through."

A man's voice came over the line. "Is this the prosecutor?"

"Yes," Rikki replied. "Thanks for calling me back. I take it you received my fax."

"I did, and I have some bad news for you."

Rikki's brow creased. "What's that?"

"Our database indicates we've never issued a driver's license for anyone by the name of Aleksandr Sergeivich Beria."

"What about a non-driver's license state identification card?"

"That answer would be *nyet*, as well," the bureaucrat cracked.

Rikki sighed. "So if someone had shown one of our officers a Virginia license with that name on it …"

"Fake. As a four-dollar bill."

"Shoot! Thanks anyway. Could you fax me a letter confirming that?"

"Within the hour and the certified original will follow via snail mail."

Very efficient. "Wonderful," Rikki said. "Have a great day."

She hung up and immediately dialed the Sheriff's office.

"Sheriff's Department," the receptionist answered.

"Hi, Lucy. Is the Sheriff around?"

"He's out in the hallway jabbering at somebody. Hold on."

The receptionist put her on hold and country music began to play. Thirty seconds later, Sheriff Vaughn picked up. "Hey, Rikki. Whatcha need?"

Rikki smirked. *Getting right to the point, as always.* "Could you come help me draft a search warrant for Jack's cell phone and email records? I've only been on the job three weeks, and I don't want to make any rookie mistakes."

Vaughn chuckled. "Good thinking, Madam Prosecutor. I'll be right over."

The line clicked dead, and five minutes later, Silent Doug walked into her office. "So whatcha got cooking here, Rikki?"

"Sheriff, I don't know what's going on, but I think Dave might be right: It's looking like the guy from Petromica may have been involved in Jack's death."

At that moment, Dave walked in, smiling ear-to-ear. "I must have died and gone to heaven, because I think Sarika Gudivada just admitted I might be *right* about something."

Rikki scowled. "Quit crowing. I told you that on the phone. Why else would you be standing here with that stupid grin on your face?"

Still grinning, Dave lightly elbowed Vaughn in the ribs. "Did you hear someone spotted that boy from Petromica in the woods near Bart's farm on Saturday?"

The sheriff cast his good eye toward Rikki. "Is that true?"

"As much as it pains me, yes it is."

"And I bet Virginia's DMV has no record that a license for *Aleksandr Sergeivich Beria* was ever issued, huh?" In saying the name, Dave gave his best impression of a Russian accent.

"A *Russian*?" Vaughn asked with a tone of disgust. "In *our* woods?"

Rikki nodded. "Yes. And again, the smug bastard to your left is correct ... a DNR officer cited a guy by that name for hunting without a permit on Saturday two miles from Bart's farm. The guy's license apparently was fake."

Vaughn shook his head rapidly. "So are we talking about a *real* Russian with a fake ID? Or some Joe Schmo using a fake ID with a Russian name on it?"

Rikki shrugged. "Could be either. We just don't know."

The Sheriff's face twitched. "Give me that Roosky's name. I'll run an NCIC report on him to check for criminal records."

Rikki handed him a folder. "Just have Martha make you a copy of the entire file."

Vaughn smiled dangerously. "Excellent. Gun-toting Rooskies in the woods of Pleasants County do not make me very happy. And I'm not very nice when I'm unhappy." Then he bolted out the door like a man on a mission.

CHAPTER 89

VIENNA, VIRGINIA
FRIDAY, DECEMBER 12, 5:30 P.M.

Petrenko was watching ESPN and eating a sandwich when his phone rang. "Hello?"

"How are you, Yuri?" Dmitri Mazniashvili asked.

"Not bad. And you?"

"Not good," the billionaire answered.

Yuri sat up straight. "What's wrong?"

"I just got a call from AIS. Are you *sure* there were no loose ends with Aristocrates?"

"Almost certain of it. Why?"

"Some law enforcement officials in West Virginia are asking questions about a certain Aleksandr Sergeivich Beria. Virginia's DMV ran that name through its database and the local sheriff's department just ran an NCIC report on it."

Petrenko winced. "Shit. Maybe someone found McCallen's emails."

"I'd be *greatly* displeased if our hard work fell apart now. I don't take failure lightly."

That's like saying Adolf Hitler was a man who didn't take Jews lightly.

"Don't worry, *vozhd*. I'll fix it."

"Good. Have a good evening. I'll be following your progress closely."

The line fell silent. Petrenko shut off the TV and trashed the rest of his sandwich.

Mazniashvili did not get to the top of the food chain by tolerating failure. And thinking about his likely reaction to failure in this situation made Petrenko sick to his stomach.

CHAPTER 90

PLEASANTS COUNTY COURTHOUSE
ST. MARYS, PLEASANTS COUNTY, WEST VIRGINIA
FRIDAY, DECEMBER 12, 7:05 P.M.

Dave and Rikki sat on opposite sides of her desk, each staring at a laptop, combing through Tabatha's phone records.

"Even if we can't link them with Jack's death yet," Dave theorized, "can't we charge them with bribery?"

Rikki scrunched her face. "It'd be hard. They'll claim the $25 million is just an investment. It's the perfect cover story. Unless this Addendum calls for Tabatha to switch her vote, we have no evidence that's their deal. What's more, until Tabatha casts her ballot for Senator Wilson on Monday, we can only *speculate* she has been bribed."

"And from my standpoint," Dave said. "Waiting until Tabatha has given Wilson the vote she needs to forge a tie is unacceptable. It'd be too late to stop it and keep Mazniashvili from getting what he wanted: A 'Get-Out-Of-A-Firing-Squad Free' card."

"Good point," Rikki said. "Plus, bribery only carries a jail term of one-to-ten and a fine up to fifty grand. I bet Tabatha would think that's a small price to pay for 25 million."

"If she can get her hands on it, since Jack died and left you in control of his company."

Rikki grinned. "That *was* pretty far-sighted of him, huh?"

Dave cocked an eyebrow. "And people say *I'm* the paranoid one. If nothing else, this situation shows that just because you're paranoid doesn't mean people aren't out to get you."

They briefly stared at one another in silence before resuming their work.

Scanning through the disc, Dave clicked on a folder entitled "MMS," and a chronological list of files appeared. Clicking the first one, sent at 2:45 p.m. on January 28, revealed a short message from Tabatha that read, "c u in the room @ 4:30. im waiting 4 u."

The message had an attachment entitled, "IMG_1224.JPG." Dave opened it and exclaimed, "Holy crap! Check out this picture she sent with one of her text messages!"

Rikki scurried around the desk. Gazing over his shoulder, she saw a digital photograph of Tabatha McCallen standing in front of a mirror in a cream corset, matching G-string and thigh-high stockings. Wearing a seductive smile, Tabatha held a cameraphone in her hand.

"What number did she send that message to?" Rikki asked.

Dave pointed to the number and scribbled it down. "That one."

"Did she send any other messages to it?"

"I don't know," Dave replied. "Let's find out."

Scanning through the files in the MMS folder, Rikki tapped on his shoulder. "There's one," she said. "November 29th at 8:31 p.m."

"That was during the Pitt game," Dave said. "She was upstairs alone while we watched the game in Jack's family room."

Dave opened the message. It read, "Don't you miss Pleasants County hospitality?"

"I think we've found Tabatha's paramour," Rikki said. "I wonder what titillating little tidbit she sent him this time."

The attachment was entitled, "bass_fun1.mpg." Dave leaned back in his chair to watch the festivities.

The videoclip showed Tabatha lying on a bed in a room with wood-paneled walls.

Dave grew visibly excited. "Hey! That looks like a room from the motel here in Saint Marys!"

"What makes you think so?"

He smiled mischievously. "You apparently don't recall our senior prom as fondly, or as vividly, as I do."

Rikki felt her face flush. *If my skin wasn't so brown, I'd probably be turning beet red right now.*

Clad in black lingerie, Tabatha looked at the camera and said something while making a seductive 'come hither' gesture.

"Did she say something about a *governor*?" Dave asked.

Then the digital image of Luke Vincent appeared on-screen.

"Oh, my God," Rikki softly uttered as the scene unfolded. "I don't believe it."

Dave emitted a war whoop. "Hot damn! Vincent is a *dead* man!"

"Whoa, whoa, whoa!" Rikki interjected. "This doesn't prove anything."

"It proves Vincent is a lying piece of shit that cheats on his wife."

"That's beside the point! Yes, he may have been less than faithful …"

"From the way he keeps thrusting himself into Tabatha and the sounds she's making, I don't think there's any *doubt* he's been unfaithful."

Rikki sighed loudly. "But that doesn't prove he had anything to do with Jack's death."

Dave stared at her, slack-jawed. "Are you *kidding* me?! He was boning *Jack's wife!* He stands to become vice president if Jack's out of the picture because his mistress will cast the decisive ballot in the Electoral College! I don't see how you can look at this video, knowing what has transpired, and not *assume* Vincent is up to his eyeballs in this plot."

Rikki glared. "What the man has done in his private life is wrong. But that's between Vincent, his wife and God, and it has nothing to do with his fitness for office."

Dave started to attack that assertion, but stopped himself cold. *She holds all the cards here, and we have to play by her rules.*

Gritting his teeth, he exhaled softly. "Okay. I promise I won't rush to judgment if you'll remain open-minded that Vincent *may* be guilty of more than marital infidelity here."

Rikki eyed him closely. "On one condition."

"What is it?"

"You promise not to reveal the existence of this video to anyone," she said. "I gave you access to these files because I *trusted* you and hoped you could help me get to the bottom of Jack's death. If our investigation thwarts this plot and costs Melanie Wilson the presidency, I can handle Democrats calling me a traitor. If that's the price I pay to uphold the Constitution, as screwed up and illogical as it may be, so be it. But I will *not* be able to sleep if you betray my trust and use this information to humiliate Luke Vincent and destroy his marriage, because his wife is a sweet woman and she doesn't deserve to be treated like that."

Staring into her pale green eyes, Dave saw she was deadly serious. But the video's publication alone would likely end this plot and keep Tabatha from serving as an Elector.

After 15 years of not speaking to you, she has finally forgiven you. Would you really be willing to throw that all away just to win an election?

CHAPTER 91

1140 CONNECTICUT AVE. NW
WASHINGTON, D.C.
FRIDAY, DECEMBER 12, 8:00 P.M.

As Tyson Vasquez nursed his gin and tonic, waiting for the comedians to take the stage, his eyes were drawn to four attractive, professionally-dressed women in their early thirties sitting about five feet to his right.

"So where's this new guy you've been gushing about?" a brunette asked playfully. The question was directed toward a blonde with shoulder length hair.

"Dave had to fly back to West Virginia this afternoon," the blonde replied. "He wouldn't say much except that an Electoral College voter may have been bribed to switch sides."

Vasquez kept sipping his drink while listening more closely. *Dave? I wonder if that's who I think it is.* He turned toward them with an easy smile. "You're not talking about Dave Anderson, are you?"

The blonde smiled back. "Maybe. How do you know Dave?"

A-ha. That's what I thought.

"He did some lobbying for us. Great guy." Vasquez stuck out his hand. "I'm Tyson Turner. And you are?"

"Monica Boley."

Boley? What are the odds?

Vasquez squinted an eye. "Say ... didn't I see somebody in the news a while back by the name of Marcus Boley?"

Her eyes lit up. "That's my brother. He supervised one of the county election recounts in West Virginia."

I knew those bastards were up to something in Berkeley County. Now to prove it!

Vasquez smiled. "Small world! So did you say Dave is flying to West Virginia today?"

She seemed to stiffen, but kept smiling. "Yeah. There's some political stuff going on."

Clamming up on me, are we? That's okay, Monica. You've said enough already.

"That sounds like Dave," Vasquez remarked, then glanced at his watch. "Well, I hate to run, but I have dinner plans. The next time you see Dave, tell him Tyson sends his regards."

"I will. Have fun!"

Vasquez threw a twenty down and casually left the club. Buttoning his wool great coat with one hand, he used his other to make a call.

"Hello, Yuri? This is Tyson. We have a situation ..."

CHAPTER 92

PLEASANTS COUNTY COURTHOUSE
ST. MARYS, PLEASANTS COUNTY, WEST VIRGINIA
SATURDAY DECEMBER 13, 10:10 A.M.

Rikki rubbed her forehead while brushing up on the law governing search warrants:

> "To constitute probable cause for the issuance of a search warrant, the State's affidavit must set forth facts indicating the existence of criminal activities which would justify a search. <u>State v. Hlavacek</u>, 185 W.Va. 371, 407 S.E.2d 375 (1991)"

> "Probable cause is defined as facts sufficient to support a reasonable belief that criminal activity is *probably* taking place or knowledge of circumstances indicating a fair probability that evidence of a crime will be found. It requires *more than a mere 'hunch,'* but less than proof beyond a reasonable doubt."

Rikki exhaled. Their current evidence just wasn't enough to get a search warrant for Tabatha's house.

And in Pleasants County, word would spread like wildfire if we tried to get a search warrant and failed. Then Tabatha would just destroy any evidence she might still have.

No, Rikki glumly realized. Without additional information, they were stuck.

The phone on Martha's desk rang. Rikki went next door and answered it. "Hello?"

"Hey, Rikki. This is Sheriff Vaughn. I can guess why you're working on a Saturday."

"I'm certainly not here for my health. What do you have?"

"There was nothing under Beria's name in NCIC and the only fingerprints on the DNR citation were the officer's. Apparently Beria wore his gloves the whole time they were talking."

Rikki sighed. "That figures."

"I have another idea," Vaughn said. "The FBI's biometrics unit is in Clarksburg. They can access the feds' database of facial photographs, national driver's records, and immigration records. Maybe they could run Beria's picture through their database."

"That's a great idea!"

"The problem is, today's Saturday and nobody is in the lab."

"Super," she said sarcastically. "So much for that idea."

"Don't throw in the towel yet. I go fishing with a guy who works there, and I hope he'll do us a favor."

"Would it help if I drove over there and showed him some cleavage?"

Vaughn chuckled. "Probably wouldn't hurt." Then he paused. "That's a joke, Rikki. I didn't mean anything by it."

She giggled. "Well, I'll use 'em if I have to. That's the least I could do for Jack."

"I'm sure he'd appreciate it. I'll be in touch."

360

Three hours later, Rikki and Dave met for a status update.

"We should receive Jack's emails by 5:00 today," Rikki said. "With any luck, they'll include the purchase agreement or this mysterious Addendum."

Dave looked puzzled. "How can you get access to *Jack's* emails but you *can't* get a search warrant for Tabatha's?"

"Because Jack is dead. Dead men have no constitutional rights, and the State must determine whether his death was criminal or accidental. Moreover, as executor of Jack's estate, I'm authorized to obtain his records. Tabatha, on the other hand, is quite alive and protected by the Fourth Amendment. Thus, the State cannot access her private records under these time constraints without a search warrant."

"Which requires 'probable cause,' huh?"

"Yep. And the circumstantial evidence alone doesn't rise to that level."

"Why can't you just use that Power of Attorney again?" Dave asked.

"Because Jack is *dead*," Rikki shot back. "When Tabatha signed the Power of Attorney, she authorized *Jack* to do certain things on her behalf; not me. The POA does me no good."

Dave scowled. "What a pain! We're almost certain Tabatha has been bribed, and there's not a damn thing we can do because we can't *prove* it. But how can we prove it if we can't get access to her house or her email?"

"It's a catch-22," Rikki admitted.

The sound of footsteps approaching caused them to turn around just in time to see Magistrate Chuck Flowers stride into view. "I'm not interrupting anything, am I?" Flowers asked with a grin.

"Nah," Rikki said. "I'm catching up on my backlog, and Dave graciously agreed to help me chip away at it while he's in town."

"Well, that's thoughtful," Flowers remarked. "I wouldn't be here on Saturday afternoon, myself, if not for a mental hygiene petition. Some nut has voices telling him to cut his penis off with a steak knife. Now I'm supposed to figure out what to do with him, and I don't think the Supreme Court would appreciate me asking him if he needs any A-1 sauce."

"Probably not," Rikki chuckled.

Flowers stuck his hands in his pockets. "I just figured I'd stick my head in and see what was up. You kids have fun. I'll be downstairs dealing with crazy people if you're bored."

"Thanks, Your Honor," Rikki called. A moment later the stairwell door slammed shut.

"I wonder why we didn't hear that door open earlier," Dave said.

"Probably because he was being sneaky," she replied. "He may be a good Democrat, but he's kinda *shifty*, if you know what I mean."

Dave shrugged. "Seemed nice to me."

"Yeah? Well, Luke Vincent appointed him to that position when another magistrate retired. Does that change your opinion?"

"He's a lying, malevolent piece of cow dung, then. I'll ask the sheriff to keep his one good eye on him."

Rikki laughed loudly. "Twisted, twisted, *twisted*. What am I going to do with you?"

Dave cocked an eyebrow. "I'm just happy you're *talking* to me again. Anything beyond that is gravy."

*   *   *

Magistrate Flowers walked into his office, locked the door behind him and picked up his phone. After four rings, a man gruffly answered, "Hello?"

"Dick Bowen? This is Chuck Flowers up in Pleasants County. How ya doing?"

"Not bad. To what do I owe the pleasure of this call?"

Flowers leaned back, hoisting his loafers onto the desk. "I just overheard an interesting conversation in our prosecutor's office. I don't know what's going on, and I don't *want* to know what's going on. But if anyone you know is trying to influence Tabatha McCallen's vote on Monday, they should know what I overheard."

"I'm all ears."

CHAPTER 93

MARTINSBURG, BERKELEY COUNTY, WEST VIRGINIA
SATURDAY, DECEMBER 13, 2:25 P.M.

"The wife and daughter are away for the weekend," Vasquez said. "That means the Boy Wonder is the only one home."

Petrenko nodded. "It's still daylight, but I say we go for it."

"I agree," Vasquez said.

As Petrenko reached for the door handle, his phone started playing the *Deliverance* theme. Vasquez looked confused.

"It's Bowen calling," Petrenko explained as he answered the call. "Hello, Dick."

"Howdy, Yuri. I've got a bone to pick with you. You have a minute?"

"Now's not a good time. Can I call you back?"

Bowen mumbled something, then said, "It'll only take a minute, goddamn it."

Petrenko clenched his jaw. "Fine. You have 60 seconds. Go."

"If Senator Wilson's campaign is still conducting operations in West Virginia, they'll be more likely to succeed if I know about them, as I have access to certain resources that might remain unutilized if I'm outside the loop."

"What's he saying?" Vasquez asked impatiently.

Petrenko hit the mute button. "He's whining and wants to know what's going on."

Vasquez scoffed. "Ha! Everything he's touched has turned to shit. The hillbillies should step aside and let the Big Boys handle things." Yuri nodded and unmuted the phone.

"The prosecutor thinks Tabatha McCallen has been bribed to vote for Senator Wilson on Monday," Bowen continued. "I need to know if that's the case. The prosecutor's a Democrat, and I could call her and tell her to back off."

"I appreciate your offer to help," Petrenko asserted. "But access to our current operations is on a strictly 'need-to-know' basis. Unfortunately, you don't meet that definition right now. If we decide your expertise in managing the local officials is needed, we'll call."

Bowen mumbled something again, a tad harsher this time. "It's your dance card. I'm just trying to help. Don't come crying if things go wrong."

"I've been forewarned." Petrenko hung up and turned to Vasquez. "You ready for this?"

Vasquez nodded. "As ready as I'll ever be."

"Then let's hit it. As the rednecks say, *'Time's a'wastin!'*"

ST. MARYS, PLEASANTS COUNTY, WEST VIRGINIA
SATURDAY, DECEMBER 13, 3:30 P.M.

Rikki stretched out on her couch, facing the television. Her mother walked in and gently rubbed Rikki's forehead. "How are you feeling, daughter?"

Rikki smiled wearily. "A little run down. But all things considered, not bad."

Madhani walked around the couch. Rikki lifted her legs, giving her a place to sit. "As tired as you are, you haven't been this lively and happy in a long time. This new job must agree with you."

Rikki pondered the question. "That's part of it, but I think it may also be due to how much I'm enjoying spending time with David again. It's so strange, but I didn't even realize how much I had missed hanging out with him and laughing until he reappeared in my life."

Madhani beamed. "Have you told him how you feel?"

Rikki shook her head. "No. What would be the point? So much has happened between the two of us, and it's been years since we dated. Besides, once this case is over, he's heading back to D.C. to become Jonathan Royal's chief of staff or something. It's not like he'd come back to St. Marys just for me."

Madhani patted her daughter's thigh. "You'll never know if you don't ask."

Rikki pursed her lips but said nothing. The awkward tension was punctured when the phone rang. The prosecutor swung herself off the couch and answered it. "Hello?"

"Madam Prosecutor," Sheriff Vaughn greeted. "I'm looking out my back window and I see your car in the driveway. Why aren't you at the courthouse fighting crime?"

Rikki chuckled. "Settle down, neighbor! I'm taking a break. Have you run down your buddy at the FBI?"

"Well ... I've got good news and bad news."

"Give it to me."

"The good news is he's willing to help us out. I'll shoot you his email address so you can send him that picture."

"Okay. And the bad news is?"

"He won't be back in town until tomorrow afternoon," Vaughn said. "In the meantime, keep your eyes peeled for Rooskies and let me know if you see any lurking around."

"I don't think I have to worry about anybody coming after me, Sheriff."

"Don't be so sure," Vaughn shot back. "Never put *anything* past a Roosky."

"Aye-aye, sir!" Rikki giggled.

"And stop hanging around Dave so much. I think that smart ass is rubbing off on you."

CHAPTER 94

11 SUNNYSIDE CIRCLE
MARTINSBURG, BERKELEY COUNTY, WEST VIRGINIA
SATURDAY, DECEMBER 13, 4:45 P.M.

"You're not as stupid as you look," Vasquez sneered. "It took you a while to come clean about stealing this election, but I'm glad you wised up and cleared your conscience."

Marcus Boley lay in a pool of his own vomit, moaning and coughing and clutching his testicles piteously. Petrenko kicked him in the crotch again for good measure. Marcus promptly cried out and dry-heaved again.

"No marks to the face," Vasquez softly told Petrenko. "We want the world to know Mr. Boley is making this statement *voluntarily*. Isn't that right, Boy Wonder?"

Marcus wallowed on the kitchen floor, struggling to breathe. Once oxygen returned to his lungs, he sobbed loudly but nodded.

"Good," Vasquez said, strolling into the dining room. "Bring him in here and put him in front of the camera. We want this done quickly."

Petrenko roughly grabbed Boley and dragged him into the dining room. Kicking him in the small of his back, Petrenko said, "Get up and sit down. *Now*."

Boley slowly stood and Petrenko pushed him down into a chair at the head of the table. A digital camera connected to a small, sophisticated-looking microphone faced him.

Vasquez returned with a wet washcloth, a hairbrush, a towel and a freshly-pressed golf shirt. "Clean yourself up. It's show time."

Once Marcus was deemed presentable, Vasquez sat down within arm's length of the camera. Petrenko burned holes into Boley with his eyes and cracked his knuckles.

"Are you ready to unburden your soul?" Vasquez asked wryly.

Boley glared at him, but nodded, placing his right hand on the table in front of him. It appeared to be fidgeting nervously.

"No funny business," Petrenko warned, as he tapped the pistol holstered beneath his left armpit. "Just spill your guts and we're out of here."

Vasquez held up his finger, drawing Boley's attention. After focusing the camera, he hit the remote and pointed directly at Marcus. "We're rolling," he mouthed.

"My name is Marcus Boley," he said, his right hand quaking slightly as he pointed to his chest with his index finger, then slowly moved both of his hands downward and rested them on the table. "I am the Berkeley County Clerk. By my actions, I have illegally influenced the presidential election results, causing Governor Royal to be credited with hundreds of votes that were not cast. In so doing, I have thwarted the will of West Virginia's voters and stripped Senator Wilson of five electoral votes she should have won."

Vasquez de-activated the microphone with the remote. "I'm impressed. You *are* a quick learner. Now explain exactly how you deceived everyone, and we can let Congress decide how to deal with this mess."

"And don't forget, Boy Wonder," Petrenko spat. "No doctors, no cops, no calls to 911. You can't remember *anything* about the people who recorded your statement. Deviate from that script an inch, and not only will you watch me kill your wife and daughter; I'll also tie down your sister, jam a gag in her mouth, then spend a week ass-raping her until she bleeds to death or dies from dehydration, whichever comes first."

Right hand continuing to twitch, Boley's lower lip quivered and he nodded twice.

"Now then," Vasquez said. "Where were we?"

CHAPTER 95

ST. MARYS, PLEASANTS COUNTY, WEST VIRGINIA
SATURDAY, DECEMBER 13, 7:05 P.M.

"Your move, David."

Dave scanned the chessboard, trying to figure out what trick his father had up his sleeve. *Why in blazes did he move that rook over* <u>*there*</u>? Delicately fingering his knight's head, Dave hesitantly lifted it from the board and moved it to another position without actually letting go of the piece. Seeing his dad begin to smirk, Dave reconsidered the move.

"You've been spending a lot of time with our new prosecutor," his dad said without looking away from the board. "How's that going?"

Dave scowled and asked, "What are you trying to do? Throw me off my game?"

"Like I'd need to *cheat* to beat you," his dad guffawed.

Finally deciding he could safely move a bishop without imperiling his king, Dave did so. "It's been good. She's so witty and gregarious. We have a lot of fun together."

His dad nodded, moving a knight toward the middle of the board. "That's important. Everyone eventually gets old and fat. Life's more tolerable if you enjoy the company of the person you're with. God knows you never had that with your ex-wife."

"You don't have to remind me," Dave muttered, staring at the board. *What the hell? What's he trying to pull with that knight?* "I'm just glad that long national nightmare is over."

Glancing over at his dad, Dave noticed he seemed to have virtually no stress in his life. *Did that stem from choosing the right mate? Or was he just lucky enough to be born that way?*

"Tell me something, Dad."

"Okay," his dad replied, his fingers dancing atop a pawn.

"When you were dating Mom, did you ever do anything stupid?"

His father cocked an eyebrow. "Well, son ... *Stupid* is a relative term. One man's stupidity is another man's highest level of intellectual functioning."

"You know what I mean. Something you look back and say, 'That was *boneheaded!*'"

"Well, would you consider breaking up with your mom 'boneheaded?'"

Dave gasped. "Are you kidding me?"

"I'm afraid not. You see, we'd been dating about six months. I was young and feeling trapped, so I told her I needed my space and broke up with her."

"Wow," Dave remarked. "I had no idea."

"Well, fathers don't typically brag about their own stupidity. In any event, your mom handled it very maturely. No crying or screaming like a lot of women; she graciously wished me luck and went on her merry way."

"So what happened to bring you guys back together?" Dave asked.

"Well, I'm many things, but *stupid* isn't one of them. Usually, that is. So it didn't take me long to realize I'd made a terrible mistake. I mean, I missed your mom so much I *ached* to be with her. The problem was, by the time I figured it out, she was already dating someone else."

"No way. Who was it?"

Dave's dad frowned. "That's not germane to the point of this story, which is to address your question about whether I've ever done anything 'boneheaded.'"

"Point taken," Dave conceded. "Please continue."

"So I was feeling sorry for myself, wishing I hadn't acted so hastily. I hoped she would forgive me and take me back, but I was terrified that if I asked, she might say *no*."

"That would have sucked. There would have been no Dave running around!"

"That's right," his dad noted dryly. "Everything always revolves around you, huh?"

"Forgive me for viewing this story through the prism of my own self-existence."

His father rolled his eyes. "Eventually, I mustered up the nerve to walk that plank because I realized I'd look back and regret it if I didn't have the guts to *try*."

"Way to go, Dad!"

"I convinced her to meet me after school one day, and I begged her to take me back. And after letting me twist in the wind a few seconds while she glared at me, your mom busted out laughing and said, 'I *wondered* when you'd finally realize what a good thing you had.'

"And the rest is history."

Dave leaned back with his arms folded across his chest. "That was a great story, Dad. Thanks for sharing it with me."

His father grinned, slid his black queen forward diagonally and declared, "Checkmate."

Dave's eyes frenetically dashed back and forth across the chessboard, seeking an escape from the trap his dad had laid with the knight and rook.

Well, shit. The old man outsmarted me again!

371

CHAPTER 96

CHARLESTON CENTRAL BAPTIST CHURCH
CHARLESTON, WEST VIRGINIA
SUNDAY, DECEMBER 14, 11:30 A.M.

Luke Vincent sat on the front pew with his left arm comfortably draped around his wife's shoulders when a deacon stepped to the pulpit.

"Reverend Hall is on our mission trip to Peru, and our guest speaker today is Reverend Dennis Mincer. I've heard him preach many times, and I'm sure you'll enjoy his sermon today."

A short man with a bad comb-over and a brown moustache stepped forward, shook the deacon's hand and then stood behind the pulpit.

"Friends," he began with a heavy drawl, "I want you to know how blessed I feel to be sharing the Word of God with you today."

Vincent eyed the pastor suspiciously, trying to figure out if he had seen the man before. *Something about this guy seems familiar.*

"As you know," the preacher continued, "Williamson's much smaller than Charleston. When I was growing up in the hollers of Mingo County, I'd always get excited when my parents would take us to Charleston. It was *The Big City* for us, and as far as we were concerned, we might as well have been going to New York City."

The preacher smiled warmly and a few people chuckled. "And when I was a seminary student, I wanted to preach in a big church after graduation. I was *good* at preaching. Soon enough, I figured I'd have my own TV show, spreading the Gospel around the world. I convinced myself any congregation would be lucky to have me as a preacher."

A-ha! Vincent realized. *This guy looks like Tim Conway's character, Dorf!*

The preacher smirked and shook his head. "Of course, that was *my* opinion. My daddy used to say: 'Dennis, if I could buy ya for what you're worth and sell ya for what ya *think* you're worth, I'd be a rich man.'"

A wave of laughter swept through the congregation. Looking around, Vincent saw people smiling, paying close attention.

Wow. This guy might be nerdy-looking, but he really is good at what he does.

"My biggest problem," the pastor confessed. "Was I wasn't a good listener. I was *awfully* good at listening to myself, but not so good listening to what *God* was trying to tell me." The preacher paused, allowing that notion to sink in. "Ever since The Fall, people have been weak and frail. Prone to selfishness, stubbornly clinging to our prejudices and scornful of God's discipline; to watch us in action is to *marvel* at God's patience and unconditional love." He lightly gripped the lectern with both hands. "In his first letter to Timothy, Saint Paul opined that the love of money is the root of all evil. And while I'm not smart enough or godly enough to quibble with Saint Paul, I think we bring many of our problems upon ourselves by thinking we know best instead of submitting our will to the Lord's."

"Amen," Donna Vincent whispered, nodding her head and smiling.

"The way I look at it, our persistent desire to chart our course, to do what *we* want instead of what *God* wants, is an example of Satan using our flawed nature to subject us to temptation."

The pastor smoothly swept his gaze toward Vincent. The governor was startled by the weighty presence of the man's eyes, and the sermon's seemingly personal turn.

"Temptation comes in many forms," the preacher said, his eyes fixed on Vincent. "When we should be exercising, we're tempted to be lazy. When we should be sharing our good fortune with others, we're tempted to keep it for ourselves. When we should be faithful to our spouses, we're tempted to pursue illicit trysts and satisfy our carnal urges. And when we should accept responsibility for injuring those we love most, we want to shift the blame elsewhere."

The preacher inhaled. To Vincent, it seemed he was focusing his energies squarely on him.

"Examine this list and ask yourself this," he thunderously challenged. "When confronted by such temptations, can you identify even *one* instance where man's shortcoming is not based on a desire to nurture his own selfishness instead of heeding the will of God?"

Silence permeated the sanctuary. Standing before the congregation, the preacher slowly scanned the room before smiling wanly. "I didn't think so."

Vincent felt his wife gently place her hand on his thigh. Glancing over, he was struck by how Donna glowed with a peaceful sort of beauty.

From my first campaign when I had to sit down at a spaghetti dinner with the Knights of Columbus, she was right there with me.

When I had to climb into a dunking booth for a school fair on a cold afternoon in November, she was right there with me.

When I ran for State Senate the first time and <u>lost</u>, she was right there with me.

She gave birth to our children. She comforted them when they scraped their knees. When they needed help with homework, she gave it because I was usually politicking somewhere.

When I've needed help, love, encouragement or support, she has always given it to me. If I lived a thousand lifetimes, I could never find another woman so giving and selfless, and I have repaid her kindness and love by lying down with another man's wife whose body is beautiful but whose soul is dark, calloused and empty.

I am a fool.

Vincent looked up. The preacher smiled at him and nodded.

"Though we're stubborn and self-destructive, we still have hope. In First Corinthians, Chapter Ten, Verse 13, Saint Paul wrote, 'No temptation has seized you except what is common to man. And God is faithful; he will not let you be tempted beyond what you can bear. But when you are tempted, he will also provide a way out so that you can stand up under it.'" Reverend Mincer paused. "We're all children of the flesh, subject to temptation. But we can resist temptation if we ignore that selfish voice in our heads and seek God's assistance. We must recognize the people and situations that cause us to falter and avoid them. Because no temptation, however seductive, is worth the pain it causes or the risk it poses to our souls."

Luke Vincent closed his eyes, hoping no one would see them watering. As the preacher closed out the service, Vincent knew what he had to do.

It will probably cost me the vice presidency, but it's the right thing to do. For once, I'm going to do what's <u>right</u>. I can only pray God will help me live with the consequences.

CHAPTER 97

PLEASANTS COUNTY PARK
ST. MARYS, PLEASANTS COUNTY, WEST VIRGINIA
SUNDAY, DECEMBER 14, 1:40 P.M.

The sun shined through the empty trees overlooking the small park positioned on the edge of St. Marys. The temperature was up in the fifties, as Dave and Rikki began their hike.

"So what job will you get if Governor Royal ends up winning?" Rikki asked.

Dave shrugged. "Possibly chief of staff, but more likely a 'counselor to the president' position like Karl Rove had."

Rikki's face turned sour. "Don't end up like *that* dirtbag, plotting and scheming behind the scenes like Rasputin."

He rolled his eyes. "The man was a genius. The press and the Dems hated him because he was *effective*. Don't believe everything CNN spits out."

Rikki playfully pushed him. "I don't. But you could use a little less Fox News, yourself."

"Touché."

They slowly ascended the path, snaking through the woods in a direction running parallel with the Ohio River, walking past a few picnic shelters. "So why not attorney general?" she asked, her voice rising above the sound of their footsteps hitting gravel.

"I've never really practiced law on a full-time basis. Jonathan needs an AG with hard-core, real world legal experience. He can find somewhere else to stick a political hack like me."

Rikki's phone rang, and she answered the call. "Hello?"

"Good afternoon," Sheriff Vaughn said. "I have big news for you."

"Ooooh! I like the sound of big news."

"My buddy ran Beria's picture through the biometrics database. We got a match."

"Fantastic! What do we know?"

"His real name is Yuri Petrenko," Vaughn replied.

"Yuri Petrenko," Rikki repeated, staring at Dave.

"He came here five years ago, obtaining permanent resident status after his employer sponsored his immigration application," the sheriff said. "The company was Assurant Information Systems."

Rikki nodded and relayed the information to Dave.

Dave's lips tightened. "Yet another Mazniashvili outfit. Credit reports, data mining, even the voting machines used in Mingo County."

"Prior to coming to the Land of Freedom and Opportunity," Vaughn continued, "Comrade Petrenko served with distinction in the Motherland's military. The Spetsnaz, actually, where the most ass-kicking Rooskies end up. No humanitarian missions to Somalia for him! I'd bet he had at least a little sniper training, too."

Rikki's eyes widened. "You're probably right. Thanks for the update. I'll re-examine things in light of this information and call you later."

"That's fine. I'm at home watching the Steelers game and eating a couple dozen of the chocolate chip cookies my wife is baking for her book club meeting tomorrow." He barked a quick laugh, and Rikki thought she heard his wife nagging in the background. "Call me." Then he hung up.

"So what do you think?" Dave asked.

"We need to do some more research if we want to get that search warrant."

Dave nodded. "Let's get a move on then. We'll just walk straight through the graveyard and down Barkwill Street to the courthouse. Five minutes, tops."

Rikki punched him lightly in the arm. "You act like I didn't grow up here!"

"Sorry. I'm still not used to being around you without flinching. My bad."

376 MAPLETREE LANE
MARTINSBURG, BERKELEY COUNTY, WEST VIRGINIA
SUNDAY, DECEMBER 13, 2:35 P.M.

"Just who do you think you are, buddy?" the man asked. "I'm watching the game!" He stood on the front porch in a Washington Redskins sweatshirt and gray sweatpants.

Tyson Vasquez did not blink. "I have evidence of a crime and time is of the essence. I won't entrust it with anyone but the elected Sheriff of Berkeley County, and that means *you.*"

The man eyed Vasquez suspiciously. The former congressman was holding a DVD.

"Suit yourself," Vasquez said. "But when this disc hits CNN tomorrow, you'll be the national laughingstock, not me."

The sheriff snatched the disc. "Fine," he growled. "But you're staying right here while I watch this thing, and unless there's something *earth-shattering* on it, I'm hauling your ass to jail even if I have to make up something."

Vasquez calmly smiled. "Then I have nothing to worry about."

CHAPTER 98

BERRY HILLS COUNTRY CLUB
CHARLESTON, WEST VIRGINIA
SUNDAY, DECEMBER 14, 3:00 P.M.

Vincent grabbed his putter and stepped up to the ball. Gently rocking his arms backwards, he softly swung through the ball, but it hooked slightly, missing the hole. Shaking his head, he ambled toward the ball.

"That's a gimme," Bowen yelled from the cart. He was sprawled across the seat with a cigar in one hand and a beer in the other.

Vincent scooped his ball from the green, and then trudged to the cart like a death row inmate heading to the electric chair. Secret Service agents trailed nearby.

Bowen took a drag from his cigar. "You're playing like shit today, Luke. Something on your mind?"

Vincent stepped on the cart's parking brake and drove forward. "You could say that. I have to deal with Tabatha tonight, and I'm dreading it. It won't be pretty."

"Why tonight? And why won't it be pretty?"

Vincent sighed. "She made me a proposition on Thursday: If I'd agree to leave my wife, she would switch sides and cast her Electoral College ballot for me and Melanie."

"Holy shit! That's great! We can still win this thing!"

Vincent's eyes smoldered. "It's not great! It's *horrible!* I don't want to get divorced; I *love* my wife!"

"You don't have to actually *do* it. Just *tell* her you'll do it. And after she casts her ballot tomorrow, you can tell her you changed your mind."

The governor laughed caustically. "*Right*. Like she'd take that lying down. She'd be on the front steps of the Capitol, passing out her videos and telling everyone with a microphone that I took advantage of her grief-stricken ass by promising to leave Donna in exchange for her vote."

Bowen frowned. "So what are you supposed to do?"

"She's driving down to Charleston tonight," Vincent replied. "She's staying where she always does – the hotel that Marco Zakarias owns – and she said that as long as I come to her room and 'make love to her' tonight, she'll switch her vote. She says she'd give me a year to actually leave Donna. You know … move to D.C. and then say the stress of the job had caused us to drift apart, etc. She had the whole thing planned out. It's terrifying, really."

Vincent shut off the engine. "I'll call her on my way home and tell her I can't go through with it. Dick, I can't even have sex with her again. The thought of laying a finger on her makes me want to puke. I can't bear the thought of doing that to Donna anymore."

He sighed. "All I can do is throw myself at Tabatha's mercy and hope she won't drag Donna into it. I doubt it will accomplish anything, but it's all I have left."

Bowen stared into the distance and finished his beer. "I wouldn't say that."

BERKELEY COUNTY JUDICIAL CENTER
MARTINSBURG, BERKELEY COUNTY, WEST VIRGINIA
SUNDAY, DECEMBER 14, 3:30 P.M.

The Berkeley County magistrate stuck with weekend duty was Ernest Powell. A crusty retired policeman, he originally ran for magistrate to combat boredom. With his law enforcement background, Powell had a "friendly" disposition toward requests from the men in blue.

"What do you have here?" he asked, peering at the document the sheriff had given him.

"It's a request for a search warrant, Your Honor."

Powell smiled. "And who's the unlucky sap getting served?"

The sheriff stiffened slightly. "It's, uh … the County Clerk, Your Honor."

Powell's face shot up. "Marcus Boley? What for?"

The sheriff frowned. "We think he stuffed the ballot boxes during the recount. Hard to believe, but we have a video-taped confession. He described the whole operation in detail."

Powell whistled and signed the warrant. "I'll be damned. Never *dreamed* Marcus would do something like that. Hell, he grew up here – used to be an Eagle Scout even."

"Well, we think he was encouraged to do it by some big shot with Royal's campaign. The guy was raised in West Virginia, too. His name is Dave Anderson."

Powell's nostrils flared. "He'd better never come to Berkeley County, or I'll throw him *under* the jail."

The sheriff put the signed warrant in his pocket. "Once we look in the ballot boxes, we'll probably be back with a warrant charging him with conspiracy to commit election fraud."

The magistrate smiled menacingly. "I'll look forward to seeing it."

PLEASANTS COUNTY COURTHOUSE
ST. MARYS, PLEASANTS COUNTY, WEST VIRGINIA
SUNDAY, DECEMBER 14, 4:15 P.M.

"So what do you think?" Dave asked.

Rikki scowled at the West Virginia Code book, hunched over her desk and rubbing her temple. "I think I'm getting a headache. How about you?"

"My brain feels like it was jammed in a blender. And with no criminal law experience, I'm probably not much more helpful than a chimp."

Rikki giggled. "If nothing else, you're good comic relief. I'm truly glad you're here."

Dave smiled and folded his arms across his chest. "Me, too."

She turned to the Code again. "I know we'd get a search warrant if the other magistrate was on duty. There's plenty of circumstantial evidence against Tabatha, if it turns out Beria – I mean, *Petrenko* – shot Jack."

"So why wouldn't Magistrate Flowers give us one?" Dave asked, incredulous.

Rikki pursed her lips. "I think he'd give us one for *Petrenko's* records or residence. He was near the crime scene with a rifle and a fake ID after their $25 million deal went sour. But we don't have that much against Tabatha. She has an airtight alibi, and she probably couldn't shoot a rifle to save her life."

"I wouldn't bet on that. She's one cold heartless bitch."

"But even her one email to Petromica doesn't show they were plotting to kill Jack! She thought Jack's decision to spike the deal was foolish but that they could salvage the deal."

"Or *maybe* they would need to '*pursue the alternate plan*,'" Dave clarified.

"It was carefully worded," Rikki said. "Unlike the videoclips she sent Vincent."

Dave sighed. "It's a shame we can't arrest her for being a no-good dirty whore."

Rikki nodded sympathetically. Then her pale green eyes lit up, and she began to smile. "You know what? You might be on to something."

CHAPTER 99

11 SUNNYSIDE CIRCLE
MARTINSBURG, BERKELEY COUNTY, WEST VIRGINIA
SUNDAY, DECEMBER 14, 5:30 P.M.

The sheriff stood on Marcus Boley's porch with two deputies. Doorbell chimes echoed from the house but no one answered the door. "Maybe he's in the shower or something. But we have a search warrant, so let's go in."

The door was unlocked, and they walked in single-file. The sheriff motioned the deputies to draw their weapons and follow him into the next room.

Entering the room, they smelled puke and shit and blood before they even saw the body.

Marcus Boley's corpse lay in the floor with a pistol in his right hand. Chunks of brain and blood littered the far wall, and though he was wearing pants, the unmistakable stench of feces indicated he had lost control of his bodily functions.

A deputy sprinted into the kitchen to puke. The other pointed to the table. "What's that?"

Looking where the man pointed, the sheriff saw a sheet of paper bearing Times New Roman print. It was splattered with tiny, pinkish drops of blood mist.

The sheriff leaned down, examining the document without touching it. "Looks like a suicide note. I guess Marcus couldn't handle the guilt."

"But we found nothing wrong in the ballot boxes," the non-puking deputy said.

The sheriff shrugged. "He must have disposed of the evidence. Oh, well. Let's get the crime scene kit out. We're in for a long night."

CHAPTER 100

PLEASANTS COUNTY COURTHOUSE
ST. MARYS, PLEASANTS COUNTY, WEST VIRGINIA
SUNDAY, DECEMBER 14, 6:10 P.M.

"Maybe I'm stupid," Dave said. "But since we have grounds to arrest Tabatha, why don't we *just go do it?*"

Rikki sighed, exasperated. "This isn't the movies, David! Once the sheriff charges her with a crime, what happens next is up to the magistrate on duty *when the charges are filed.*"

"Okay. So this guy Vincent appointed is on duty now ..."

"Magistrate Flowers."

"So what? He can't dismiss the charges. Your case is airtight."

"Doesn't matter. Remember, the magistrate could handle this complaint two ways. He *could* issue a warrant for her arrest, directing she be hauled in to answer the charges ..."

"I wasn't *always* asleep in criminal procedure class," Dave protested.

"On the other hand, he could just issue a summons, directing her to voluntarily appear and answer the charges at some future date."

Dave's eyes widened. "Ah! That would suck."

"To put it mildly. Flowers could easily refuse to issue a warrant on this misdemeanor. And if that's the case ..."

"She'd still get to vote in the Electoral College tomorrow."

"Precisely. Her appointment is final. If she's at the Capitol tomorrow at noon, she gets to cast that ballot."

"What happens if she doesn't show up?"

Rikki thrust a book at Dave. "Here it is. Chapter Three, Article One, Section Fourteen. See for yourself."

Dave turned to the relevant section:

> "§3-1-14. Presidential electors; how chosen; duties; vacancies; compensation.
> . . .If any of the electors so chosen fail to attend at the time appointed, the electors present shall appoint an elector in place of each one so failing to attend, and every elector so appointed shall be entitled to vote in the same manner as if he had been originally chosen by the people. . ."

Rikki waited for him to finish. "If she's not there at noon, the other four electors will appoint someone to take her place."

Dave sunk into his chair. "Wow. Okay, I'll call Gil Dean to make sure a dependable replacement is on standby. Then I'll call my good old buddy, the Mayor of Charleston."

Rikki looked at Dave, curious. "You're good buddies with Booz Hancock?"

"Well ... He's a Republican, and Gil introduced us."

"That guy's a loose cannon," Rikki said. "Why do you have to talk to *him* tonight?"

"Even if we get an arrest warrant for Tabatha, who would serve it on her if she's already in Charleston?"

"Oh. Right. I hadn't thought of that."

"Think how huge the Capitol is. If word gets out she's a wanted woman, Vincent's crew will try their damnedest to delay service of the warrant until *after* the ballots are cast."

"That's another one I overlooked," Rikki said. "You see: I told you there was a reason I've been keeping you around here."

Dave grinned devilishly. "And I thought you just wanted some eye candy around the office."

You haven't been hard to look at, for sure, especially when you smile like that.

Silent Doug walked in on cue, holding a chocolate chip cookie. "Don't flatter yourself, Dave. If she wants eye candy, she can stop by the Sheriff's Department." Biting into the cookie, he sucked in his paunch and straightened his posture.

"Coming back to my point," Rikki segued, handing the criminal complaint to Vaughn. "Because I'm afraid Flowers won't issue an arrest warrant, I asked the sheriff not to file the complaint until 9:00 tomorrow morning when Magistrate Irwin's shift begins. And *she*, on the other hand, has politics more to your liking."

Dave's face brightened. "She's a Republican?"

"Dyed-in-the-wool. She thought Jack walked on water and it turned her stomach to see Tabatha treat him like dirt. She'd probably deny bail altogether if the law didn't prohibit it."

Dave chuckled. "Sounds like my kind of woman!"

This Sheriff looked up, slack-jawed. "I don't mean to question your judgment, but is that *all* we're charging her with? I didn't even know it was against the law."

"That's it for now. But when we see Magistrate Irwin in the morning, we'll ask her for a search warrant, too."

"Ah!" Vaughn said. "Ostensibly to gather additional evidence on the initial charge ..."

"But crafted so you can seize anything that incriminates her for more serious crimes."

Vaughn nodded and signed the document. "I like it. I'm heading home for dinner, and I'll meet you in Magistrate Court tomorrow morning at 9 a.m. I'll bring a search warrant with me."

"I think I'll go home and get something to eat, too," Rikki said. "Dave ... You care to join me, say around eight?"

"Does a fat baby fart? My mom's at her evening church service and McDonald's doesn't sound appealing to your humble, unpaid assistant. See you then."

CHAPTER 101

BERKELEY COUNTY SHERIFF'S DEPARTMENT
MARTINSBURG, BERKELEY COUNTY, WEST VIRGINIA
SUNDAY, DECEMBER 14, 7:30 P.M.

Monica Boley's eyes were bloodshot. Her shoulder-length blonde hair was disheveled and frayed as she struggled to digest the news that her brother was dead.

It's my fault. He was such a sweet, innocent, upstanding man, and I dragged him down in the mud where he didn't belong. Now he's dead. Oh, God! What have I done?

The sheriff gave her a bottle of water and sat down. "You gonna be okay?"

She stared across the table. *He must think I had something to do with it. It's time to man up and change his mind.*

"I'm in shock, but I need to see the video. I refuse to believe Marcus 'stole' the election. And I definitely don't believe he committed suicide. Even if he did what you say, he loved his wife and daughter too much to put them through that hell."

The sheriff silently nodded. His eyes did not blink. "It must be hard. Maybe seeing the video will help you make sense of it all."

He double-clicked the laptop's touchpad and spun it around to face Monica. The clip began playing and she leaned toward the screen.

Marcus's image appeared onscreen. Looking distraught, he stared at the camera as he spoke. But the look in his eyes struck her as ... *wrong.*

And what's going on with his hand? His fingers are flopping all around the table.

"My name is Marcus Boley," he haggardly said, pointing to his chest with his right index finger. Then he slowly moved both hands downward, fingers spread slightly apart, and brought them to rest on the table. "I am the Berkeley County Clerk. By my actions, I have illegally influenced the presidential election results, causing Governor Royal to be credited with hundreds of votes that were not cast. In so doing, I have thwarted the will of West Virginia's voters and stripped Senator Wilson of five electoral votes she should have won."

The audio dropped and then the video jerked, as if the camera had been paused. Five seconds later, the monologue resumed.

"I pursued this course after speaking with David Anderson, Governor Royal's campaign liaison in West Virginia," Marcus said, running his forefinger across his chin before returning his right hand to the table in its former position.

What?! He's never talked to Dave! What's going on here?

Then, the realization hit her like a cold washcloth to the face and she struggled for breath. Their maternal grandmother had been deaf and she taught both her grandchildren sign language at an early age. *We decided not to use sign language during the recount, but it looks like he's trying to send a sign here!*

Watching her brother's hands, she instantly recognized the word he was communicating.

Helpless.

"Rewind this! I need to watch the whole clip again, but turn the volume down a little."

The sheriff looked puzzled but complied. As the clip played, Monica watched Marcus' hands instead of listening to his words. The message revealed was dramatically different.

"My name is Marcus Boley," he began.

He's pointing to his chest, which means, "I am ..." Then he moves both hands downward and leaves them lying on the table. " ... Helpless."

As Marcus described Dave's role in the scheme to steal the election, he subtly ran his right index finger across his chin.

That means he's speaking out of the side of his mouth. That statement's a lie.

"Throughout this process," Marcus said, sweeping his right index finger across the table from left to right a few inches, then shifting the position of his thumb so that it looked like the hammer of a gun in relation to the barrel shape of his finger.

They. Guns.

"I received updates from a staff member regarding the recount figures being reported from Mingo County," he said, pointing to his chest again. This time, after placing both hands palms down on the table, he subtly shifted them to the right and flipped his right hand over, palm up.

Monica gasped and started sobbing.

I am helpless. Dead.

As the video played on, Marcus stared into the camera like a robot, impassively reciting words Monica knew he had been forced to say. His left hand remained motionless, palm down on the table while his right hand slowly twisted into carefully camouflaged sign language letters.

INNOCENT DO NOT BELIEVE LIES.

Monica wiped away tears and clamped down on her rising rage with an iron will.

I don't know who killed him, but I know he didn't kill himself. Now I have to convince these people Marcus was framed so they can start figuring out who murdered him.

"Before you jump to any conclusions, Sheriff, could you have someone who understands sign language watch this video? I think you'll be shocked at what they tell you."

CHAPTER 102

ESQUIRE HOTEL
CHARLESTON, WEST VIRGINIA
SUNDAY DECEMBER 14, 8:20 P.M.

Tabatha lounged in bed watching a movie on Lifetime. Wearing a peach silk camisole and matching French-cut panties, a bag of microwave popcorn and a glass of wine sat on the bedside table to her right.

The movie's heroine had learned that her supposedly devoted husband was actually a convicted murderer living under an assumed name in California after escaping from an Alabama prison. Making matters worse, he was living a double-life, spending half his time with another wife he maintained in a city two hours north.

You should have known better, sister. Men are dogs. You need to use them before they can use you. Get leverage on them and never give it up.

The lying dog begged the heroine for forgiveness. "She means nothing to me, I swear! I just married her because she got pregnant and she wouldn't let me see my son otherwise."

Don't believe him. Act like you believe him, then clean out his bank account before his other wife beats you to it. Take care of Number One first. Everyone else can fend for themselves.

The phone rang. Tabatha answered without even looking away from the TV. "Hello?"

"Sorry to bother you, ma'am, but you have a visitor down here," a husky male voice said.

Tabatha sat up, smirking. "Oh, really? Who is it?"

The caller paused. "Someone from the Capitol, ma'am."

A-ha. How very thoughtful of you to drop by, Mr. Governor. I knew you couldn't resist the chance to tap this again.

Swinging her pedicured feet to the floor, she smoothed her camisole. "Tell him I need five minutes to freshen up. After that, you can send him up. The door will be propped open."

"I'll let him know."

Tabatha hung up and walked into the bathroom, toting the bag of popcorn with her. Throwing it away, she quickly brushed her teeth, put on some lip gloss and sexed up her hair.

There. You look absolutely edible. Now you can give the governor some of that pussy made of sunshine God gave you. Then he'll remember why it's *good to keep Momma happy. Because if Momma ain't happy, ain't <u>nobody</u> happy.*

As she walked out of the bathroom, preparing to provocatively drape herself on the bed, the door creaked open, then shut. She donned her best studio-perfect smile, and just as she turned toward the door, she heard three quick, heavy steps ominously rolling toward her.

The collision knocked her to the floor. She landed with one arm trapped beneath her.

What's happening?!

It felt like a Volkswagen was parked on top of her. Thick, gloved hands clutched at her hair, ripping her head backward.

"If you scream, I swear to *God* I'll fucking kill you," the man said, grabbing a fistful of hair with one hand and rolling her onto her back. Then he slipped his humongous fingers from her hair and began gripping them tightly around her throat.

Oh, God! I can't breathe! Help! Somebody help!

Tabatha clutched at her throat to no avail. The massive bald man on her chest brushed her hands aside while closing his grip on her windpipe even tighter. Wearing black denim jeans and a matching long-sleeved mock turtleneck, he looked old but was as strong as a bear. "I know you've been paid a lot of money for your vote tomorrow, you fucking cunt. That vote is the *only* reason you're still alive. Do you understand me?"

Wide-eyed, Tabatha kept squirming, desperately trying to hurl her attacker off her chest.

Get off! Can't breathe! Oh, my God!!!! Help!!!!

"You better get real smart, real quick, Tabatha," he growled. "I'm not talkin' to hear my fuckin' head rattle! Do you want to live another five minutes or not?"

Wordlessly, she nodded emphatically though he was jamming the back of her head into the carpet and pinching her trachea shut.

"Good. Then listen closely, because you only get one chance to get this right."

Tabatha stared into the man's eyes and was terrified by what she saw there. Unshakable, dark, cold, pitiless, non-negotiable *rage* stared back at her as the Lifetime movie played through the television's speakers.

"You *will* vote for Melanie Wilson and Luke Vincent tomorrow at noon," the man said flatly. "You can keep every fucking penny you've been paid to prostitute yourself that way, I don't give a shit. Enjoy it. But you will *never* speak to Luke Vincent again. I could live with you screwing his brains out as long as you were discreet. But for you to have the fucking *gall* to use that against him – threatening to tell his wife about it and then trying to bribe him to leave his wife in exchange for the vice-presidency ..." The man sneered, using his grip on her windpipe to jostle her head. "That's unforgivable. You're *way* out of your league here, Little Missy. Stupid, greedy sluts like you have been gang-raped and left floating dead in a river for less than that."

Tabatha feared she was losing consciousness, as her brain vainly screamed for oxygen. She wanted to sob, but her lungs were empty. Lying on the floor with this monster on top of her, she realized she was very much in danger of dying. Her lips trembled uncontrollably and she felt the hot sensation of urine trickling down the backs of her thighs.

"Do I make myself clear?"

Tears welled in her eyes. She nodded like her life depended on it.

"Good," the man spat, easing his grip on her throat. "Because if you *ever* try to contact Luke again, or speak of your affair to *anyone*, I will hunt you down and do vile, mortifying things to you. I will treat you like the unspeakable whore you are. And then I will kill you."

With that, he let go of her throat and kneed her once in the stomach. As she doubled over in pain, gasping for air, he stood up, casually walked over to the door and exited the room.

As oxygen re-entered her lungs, Tabatha laid crumpled on the floor in her own urine. The sound of hysterical screaming filled the room. Then she realized she was the one screaming, and she clapped her hands over her mouth as she stared around the room through tear-filled eyes.

Oh, God, oh, God, oh, God! I have to call the police! No, I can't call the police! He'll find me. He'll kill me. He'll kill me. He'll kill me.

Rising from the floor, she flung herself onto the bed and cried uncontrollably with her face planted in a pillow, muffling the noise.

Think, Tabby! Think! You've got to get control of yourself! Think!

CHAPTER 103

ST. MARYS, PLEASANTS COUNTY, WEST VIRGINIA
SUNDAY, DECEMBER 14, 8:50 P.M.

Three slender candles lazily burned atop the coffee table. Rikki reclined on one sofa arm holding a glass of red wine. Wearing a pink cotton sweater and light blue jeans, her feet were curled beneath her as she watched Dave sitting at the other end of the sofa. As he stared into the gas logs, the flames' shadows flickered across his face. Instrumental music from the Big Band era softly flowed from the stereo speakers.

As she studied her ex-fiancé's profile, Rikki smiled faintly. His green eyes sparkled, hinting at the intelligence she had long admired and found desirable. The gray flecks scattered through his short-cropped brown hair gave him an air of maturity, and the youthful cocksureness that used to grate on her nerves at times had been replaced with an aura of gravity and serenity.

No one has ever accused him of lacking self-confidence. But he seems more humble *now, and that combination of confidence and humility is downright sexy.*

The sound of upbeat saxophones filled the room and Dave grinned widely. Glancing at Rikki, he bopped his head and snapped his fingers in beat with the music. "I love this song! It reminds me of my grandparents."

"What is it?"

"*Little Brown Jug.* Glenn Miller Orchestra. It's just … *catchy.*"

God, it takes so little to make him happy. He's like a kid at Christmas all the time.

Rikki sighed. "How you can be so aloof, knowing what we're facing in the morning?"

Dave shrugged, still bopping. "No sense worrying about what we can't control. There's nothing else we can do tonight, so why worry about it?"

It must be nice to be so carefree. Care to bottle some of that attitude for me?

Rikki raised her wineglass. "Here's to stopping Tabatha in her tracks tomorrow."

"Here's to *you,*" Dave responded. "For having the courage to seek justice for Jack, even though you think Melanie Wilson should be President. You're a brave, amazing woman."

The prosecutor bit her lip. "You're too kind. I'm just doing what my father would have expected me to do. But thanks for acknowledging my dilemma."

Rikki took a sip of her wine. Its sweet, yet somewhat tart taste filled her mouth as she pondered the strange twists of fate that had brought her to this moment.

I'm sitting here drinking wine with my ex-fiancé. It should feel bizarre, but it just feels ... right.

The stereo played the finishing flurry from *Little Brown Jug* and, after a few seconds of silence, the haunting clarinet intro to *Moonlight Serenade* began to play. Dave sat his wineglass down and extended his left hand across the couch, palm up. "Care to dance, Rik?"

Rikki's stomach dropped. As if in a dream, she took his hand and stood up, allowing him to guide her to the middle of the floor. Dave wrapped his right arm around the small of her back, grasped her right hand in his left, and they slowly began moving in rhythm with the song.

Following his lead, her pulse slowly quickened. Softly rubbing her left hand against his muscular shoulder, she tilted her face toward his cheek and got a whiff of his aftershave. The scent made her smile, as did the feel of his hand holding her close without forcibly pulling her against him.

God, this feels right, she thought. Closing her eyes, she leaned closer as they slowly rotated again, and she felt Dave's fingertips softly nudge into the small of her back.

Then, as the hypnotic tones of the muffled brass instruments played on, she felt his lips press gently against her cheek. Consciously attempting to control her breathing, Rikki subtly turned her head to the right, and his lips softly made contact with hers.

The kiss went on, slowly at first. Opening her mouth slightly, she felt his tongue delicately explore the inside of her full lips. After two more circles on the dance floor, Rikki felt Dave put his left hand on her cheek and the passion from their kiss built in her chest.

"I have missed you *so much*, Rikki," he whispered between nibbles on her lips.

Her breathing sped up and she ran her long fingers through the short tufts of hair on the back of his head. "I've missed you, too," she said breathily. "God knows I wanted to forget you ever existed, but being in your arms just feels so *right*. I'd be lying if I said it didn't."

Staring into his green eyes, Rikki saw a hunger she vividly remembered. It was matched by the longing growing inside her.

Three soft claps sounded from the dining room. Turning her head, she felt her knees buckle as she saw a tall, muscular man with a blond crew-cut standing there. Bright white teeth peeked out from beneath his sneer, and the lower half of his left ear was missing.

"Wow," Yuri Petrenko said caustically. "How touching. What a shame it took 15 years to reach this point."

"How do you know that?" Dave demanded, squaring his shoulders and placing himself between Petrenko and Rikki. "And how did you get in here?"

Oh, God, Rikki realized, *I left the doors unlocked.*

Petrenko laughed. "You know AIS. We know *everything* about *everybody*. I could recite your wedding date, your divorce date, her dad's date of death, yada yada yada. All that really matters is this goody two-shoes girl of yours started sniffing around Jack McCallen's unfortunate demise, *and* she left her backdoor unlocked tonight. Not a good combination of decisions. It seems she has this mistaken belief that people are inherently good and trustworthy."

Dave cast a sour glance over his shoulder at Rikki. "Nobody's perfect," he muttered.

Petrenko reached down to his belt, unsheathing an eight-inch-long blade that shimmered in the firelight. "If it's any consolation, I do feel guilty butting in like this. Part of me wanted to wait until after the humping was over to kill you both, but I couldn't risk waiting any longer."

"Hey!" Rikki blurted. "What makes you think there was going to be 'humping' going on here tonight anyway?"

"Please! *Moonlight Serenade?* That nostalgic crap isn't playing by accident, lady."

Suddenly, the floorboards between the front door and the living room creaked. Looking to her left, Rikki saw Silent Doug Vaughn standing there in a blue WVU sweatshirt, gray cotton sweatpants and gray felt slippers, holding an empty Purex measuring cup. The flames from the fireplace reflected off his glass eye while menace flared in his flesh one.

"If I was you, Roosky," he said slowly. "I'd put down that knife and stop badmouthing Glenn Miller. You're under arrest for burglary, and you don't want me to add anything else."

Petrenko sneered and shook his head in disbelief. "What's this? The local neighborhood watch hero making a citizen's arrest? You're in *slippers* for God's sake!"

Vaughn wiggled the glass measuring cup. "The wife's baking cookies for her book club meeting tomorrow morning. It's Sunday night and the grocery is closed, so she sent me next door to borrow some sugar from Rikki. I heard the music playing and figured she didn't hear me knock, so I let myself in."

"You left the *front door* open, too?" Dave asked, incredulous.

"This is the safest place in the world!" Rikki replied. "We leave our doors unlocked all the time!"

"Quit jabber-jawing and get your asses behind me right now," Vaughn growled. Dave and Rikki quickly complied while Vaughn slowly stepped toward Petrenko. "I'm trying to talk some sense into your visitor before he does something stupid he'll end up regretting."

Petrenko laughed so hard Rikki thought he might pee himself. "Listen, Grandpa. There's no chance those two will be alive tomorrow. You've got a lot of balls, and I *really* don't want to have to gut you, too. So why don't you just walk out of here … Tell your wife the prosecutor was asleep and she'll need to finish baking her cookies tomorrow."

Vaughn snatched a grey velour throw from the loveseat and wrapped it around his left forearm. "You've never met my wife. She makes Stalin look like Gandhi. I'd rather take my chances with *you* than walk back in that house without sugar."

Petrenko sighed and shifted the knife, gripping it with the blade protruding from the pinky side of his right hand. "Suit yourself," he said, bouncing toward Vaughn like a boxer emerging from his corner.

The sheriff stood still with his hands dangling at his sides. Petrenko lunged forward, throwing a right-handed punch and the blade flashed in the firelight. Vaughn nimbly moved his left foot back a half step, using his thickly-wrapped left forearm to brush aside the punch just as he jabbed Petrenko in the face with the Purex measuring cup. The blow jolted the Russian off-balance, leaving him wide-eyed and gape-mouthed.

Awestruck, Rikki watched Vaughn move like a whirling dervish. Sliding his left hand under Petrenko's right forearm, he crashed his right elbow down on the Russian's tricep, causing the knife to shoot violently from his grip. Vaughn then reared back and smashed the glass cup into Petrenko's face, causing it to explode. Discarding its shattered remnants, he pummeled the man's face five more times with his bare fist. Petrenko crumpled onto the floor in a dazed and bleeding mess before losing consciousness.

Vaughn quickly solidified his grip on Petrenko's now knifeless and lifeless right hand and forearm, extending them away from his body, backwards and behind his head. Bringing his knee down on the middle of Petrenko's back, he forcefully pushed the man's face down into the carpet, balancing his weight between Petrenko's skull and back to keep him immobilized.

"Dave," he said calmly, panting slightly. "Make yourself useful and grab this bastard's legs for me. Rikki, go fetch my flex-cuffs out of the cruiser. *Now!*"

Dave kicked the knife away before pouncing on Petrenko's legs. Rikki paused briefly to slip on Birkenstocks then rushed out the front door. A minute later, she returned with a fistful of two-foot-long plastic straps. Vaughn hauled the dazed Russian's hands behind his back. "Do me a favor: Strap a cuff on his wrists and pull it tight. Not so tight that you cut off the blood flow, but too tight for him to weasel out of it."

Rikki swiftly looped a strap around Petrenko's wrists, tightened it, and fastened it into place with a stainless steel barb. She repeated the process with a second strap for good measure.

"Good," Vaughn said. "Cuff his ankles, too, and strap his ankles to his wrists. I'll keep my fat ass on him so he can't wiggle around."

Dave sat on the back of Petrenko's knees, holding his ankles with a white-knuckled grip, but his face was sweaty and pale. Moaning loudly, Petrenko began kicking against Dave's grip.

Rikki quickly threw a set of flex-cuffs around his ankles and tightened it until it almost cut into his skin.

The sheriff examined Rikki's handiwork and smiled. "Okay, Dave. You can get up now. That stupid Roosky ain't goin' nowhere."

Petrenko thrashed wildly against the restraints, gritting his blood-spattered white teeth. Veins popped out on his forehead and arms. It did not matter.

"Whatcha have to say to Grandpa *now*, you Roosky motherfucker?!" Vaughn screamed. He had a crazed smile and an even crazier look in his one good eye. "Huh? Does the cat have your tongue, you Communist cocksucker?! Tell my wife she'd have to wait until tomorrow to bake her cookies, my eye!

"Oh, yeah!" he ranted, spit flying from his mouth. "Speaking of eyes! Did you get a good look at my *fucking eye*, you son-of-a-bitch? You know what it's like driving when you can't check out your blind spot because *the whole left side of your head is a fucking blind spot?* I probably have your fucking daddy to thank for that 'going away present' I brought back from Nam." Grimacing, he kicked Petrenko in the throat. "Don't I, you sorry fucker?"

"You really shouldn't strike your prisoner," Rikki whispered from the side of her mouth. Petrenko hacked and coughed so hard it sounded like his trachea had collapsed.

"He was resisting arrest," Vaughn shot back. "Wasn't he, Dave?"

"Hell yeah, he was! Kick him again!"

Standing above the prisoner, his gray felt slippers in the man's face, Vaughn's chest heaved up and down and he stared down at Petrenko hatefully. "You're lucky this lady is kinder than I am. *Personally*, I'm inclined to drive your ass down to the river, throw you in it and be done with it. You're under arrest for burglary, assault, brandishing a deadly weapon and resisting arrest. For now."

Petrenko glowered but said nothing. Then the sound of Donna Summers' hit, *She Works Hard for the Money*, blared from the cell phone clipped to his belt.

Rikki bent down, stared at the phone and smiled. "Well, what do you know? Why's Tabatha McCallen calling you at this hour?"

"Probably clamoring for her 30 pieces of silver," Dave said.

CHAPTER 104

ESQUIRE HOTEL
CHARLESTON, WEST VIRGINIA
SUNDAY, DECEMBER 14, 9:45 P.M.

After feeling trapped in a nightmare where the silence was only broken by her own screaming, Tabatha finally emerged from that haze and looked at the clock. It was 9:45. With quaking hands, she made a call on her cell phone.

Four rings. Five rings. Come on, dammit! Answer!!!!

The call rolled into voicemail and Tabatha yelled, "Alex! Where are you?! This is my third call! Someone broke into my hotel room and tried to kill me and I can't find you! What am I supposed to do if that monster comes back? *Tell me!!*"

With watering eyes, she cupped a hand over her quivering lips. "The first half of the money was wired on Friday. I know the second half isn't due until tomorrow afternoon, but I almost *died* tonight, damn it! I'm changing the plan."

She took a deep breath and continued. "If the rest of the money is not wired to my account before noon tomorrow, you can shove that precious Addendum up your ass.

"It's not up for discussion, it's not negotiable. Call me."

Tabatha hung up and collapsed on the bed. Then, remembering she was covered in dried urine in the same room where some maniac had almost killed her, she leapt up and deadbolted the door. Stripping off her soiled lingerie, she threw them away and jumped in the shower.

As cool water ran down her face, she soaped up her body and scrubbed like she was possessed. *If I ever see the son-of-a-bitch who choked me again, I'll blow his head off. And if those bastards at Petromica don't want to wire me the rest of the money before I cast that ballot, tough shit. What will they do? Sue me to get the first half of their bribe back?*

CHAPTER 105

PLEASANTS COUNTY COURTHOUSE
ST. MARYS, PLEASANTS COUNTY, WEST VIRGINIA
MONDAY, DECEMBER 15, 8:45 A.M.

Standing outside the courthouse in the same clothes he had worn the previous day, Dave twisted his torso, grimacing. "My back is *killing* me from sleeping on the sheriff's couch last night."

"You think I liked sleeping in his daughter's old bedroom?" Rikki asked. "I lay there all night wondering whether I was more freaked out by Petrenko trying to kill us or all the old Strawberry Shortcake stuff around me."

Dave chuckled wearily. "Makes me glad I was on the couch. But I think Petrenko feels worse than both of us. I bet he's still coughing up teeth after the beating Silent Doug gave him!"

Rikki shook her head in awe. "You told me he was a badass. You weren't kidding."

On cue, Vaughn strolled around the corner with a dejected-but-defiant-looking Petrenko waddling two steps ahead in ankle cuffs. Guiding the Russian by his wrists, which were cuffed behind his back, Vaughn yanked the handcuffs roughly, causing Petrenko to wince. "Do you think the magistrate will give us any grief for waiting eleven hours to drag in this piece of trash?"

"Did you follow my suggestions?" Rikki asked.

"Word-for-word. We read him his Miranda rights and immediately tried to question him at the station. He lawyered up, so we put him in a cell under video surveillance. Then Doc Lacy came in and patched up his face while we searched his car and phone and typed up paperwork."

"Then we're fine," she said. "The purpose of the delay wasn't to extract a statement from him and the video shows he was given medical treatment before arraignment. He was left alone, without interrogation or harassment, while law enforcement executed the search warrant."

"Did you find anything interesting during the search?" Dave asked.

Vaughn grinned dangerously, sending chills down Rikki's spine. "Aside from that pistol, there were tracking slips for ten heavy packages shipped to the Mingo County Sheriff right before the recount. Six missed phone calls and a text message from Tabatha demanding that he 'wire the rest of the money' to her account by noon or 'the deal is off'."

"Nice," Dave observed.

Rikki pursed her lips. "Did you put that info in our request for a search warrant for Tabatha's home and records?"

Vaughn proudly tapped a neatly-folded document tucked in his chest pocket. "Yep."

Dave's cell phone beeped. Looking at the screen, he looked confused. "What the hell? This text supposedly was sent last night at 8:30. Why did I just receive it?"

Vaughn chuckled. "Cell phone service is pretty sketchy down in our subdivision. Looks like you found that out the hard way."

"Marcus is dead," the text message from Monica Boley read. "Shot in head 2 look like suicide. U are accused of using him 2 fix election. Whoever killed him wants 2 frame u."

The color faded from Dave's face and he leaned against the courthouse wall.

"Dave! What's wrong?" Rikki asked.

"Someone has murdered Marcus Boley. Shot in the head to look like a suicide. She says someone has accused me of conspiring with Marcus to fix the election."

Petrenko's jaw muscles tightened but he said nothing.

"Who accused you of that? And who is *she?*" Rikki asked.

Dave's cheeks pinkened. "His sister, Monica. She didn't say who accused me, but she thinks whoever killed him made the accusations."

Rikki studied his face. "Is it true?" she asked softly.

Dave's face flashed with anger, resentment, pain, disbelief. "I can't believe you'd even ask me that, Rik! I'd do almost anything to help Jonathan win this election, but I damn sure wouldn't break the law!"

Then why does Marcus Boley's sister have your cell phone number?

He seemingly read her mind. "Monica's very bright, ambitious and a Republican in her own right. The state party asked me to interview her for a job with Jonathan's administration. If we win, that is. And that thought makes Mr. Petrenko and his boss damn unhappy."

Vaughn twisted the prisoner's wrists enough to make him wince. "I wondered why he had a file on Boley in his car! I bet Berkeley County's boys will want to look at his pistol, too."

Petrenko's face remained impassive, but his restrained hands were balled into fists.

A tall silver-haired woman climbed out of a maroon Ford Focus and approached them.

"Glad you all are so punctual," Magistrate Irwin announced with a smile. "I like starting my shift with a bang! So what do we have?"

"For starters," the sheriff said. "This dumbass burglarized Rikki's home, threatened her life and attacked me."

The magistrate scowled, wagging a finger at Petrenko. "Shame on you! What else?"

"We're filing charges against Tabatha McCallen," Rikki said, "and we have a search warrant for you to sign in that case, too."

Irwin's eyes narrowed. "Charging her with what?"

Rikki handed her the complaint. Irwin adjusted her glasses and read it. Reaching the section that described the nature of the alleged crime, her blue eyes sparkled and she suppressed a giggle. "Wonderful! Come right in, and we'll finish the paperwork so you can transport this man to the regional jail and move forward with your case against Mrs. McCallen."

"*Jail?*" Petrenko asked in a high-pitched voice. "Aren't you going to set bail and give me a chance to post it?"

Irwin heartily guffawed. "You broke into the prosecutor's house and attacked the sheriff, and you want *me* to grant you bail? You must think I'm even stupider than you are."

GOVERNOR'S MANSION
CHARLESTON, WEST VIRGINIA
MONDAY, DECEMBER 15, 9:05 A.M.

Luke Vincent adjusted his silk tie as CNN played in the background. Contemplating what might unfold put a knot in his stomach tighter than the one around his neck.

If I make it through the day without Tabatha publicly kicking me in the nuts, and without seeing Donna break down in tears before physically kicking me in the nuts for being a cheating bastard, I will get down on my hands and knees and thank God every day for the rest of my life.

"Adding to today's drama are the confusing and conflicting reports surrounding the death of Marcus Boley," the TV reporter explained. "In a video that CNN and other media outlets received early this morning from an anonymous source, Mr. Boley apparently confessed to rigging his county's vote totals to swing West Virginia's five electoral votes in favor of Governor Royal, and initial reports indicated Boley may have committed suicide."

What?! Vincent turned from the mirror and sat down on the bed, facing the TV.

"However, our sources say no other evidence indicates Boley improperly influenced the election. Moreover, we're now hearing that his death may have been a homicide."

Vincent felt his body go numb. *Oh, my God.*

"In the meantime, the world will watch the Electors cast their ballots with bated breath, wondering if Governor Royal will hold onto his projected two-vote victory. From Charleston, West Virginia, this is Sylvia Chan reporting."

Vincent felt the warm touch of his wife's hand on his shoulder. "That's just awful," Donna said. "That poor man."

I just hope Bowen had nothing to do with it. If so, I might as well have shot Boley myself.

CHAPTER 106

PLEASANTS COUNTY COURTHOUSE
ST. MARYS, PLEASANTS COUNTY, WEST VIRGINIA
MONDAY DECEMBER 15, 9:40 A.M.

Petrenko waited for Magistrate Irwin to finish the paperwork sending him to jail until a preliminary hearing on his felonies could be held within the next 10 days. "Could I have my cell phone to make a call?" he asked.

The deputy shook his head gravely. "Sorry. It's been confiscated as evidence."

"But the number I need to call is saved on it!" Petrenko said, exasperated.

The deputy shrugged. "Sorry. Rules are rules."

No bail, no phone. What a crock of shit! It's like I'm in Soviet Russia again!

Nervously tapping his foot, Petrenko tried to remember Mazniashvili's cell number. *Come on! Think!*

In a flash, the number came to him. "Can I at least use the magistrate's phone to make my call?

The deputy handed him the phone. "Sure."

Petrenko cradled the handset between his right ear and shoulder, staring at the keypad as he dialed the number. *1-917-STALIN1.*

After three rings, Mazniashvili answered. "Who is this?" he gruffly asked.

"This is Yuri. I've been arrested, and I need the best lawyers money can buy."

Mazniashvili spat out an unspeakably vile string of Georgian profanity. "How could you have been so careless?!"

I thought that paunchy old man was a pushover. I got overconfident, and now I might have to spend the rest of my life in jail.

"I'd bet this line is monitored," Petrenko replied. "But I'll tell the lawyers about it when they visit me in the North Central Regional Jail. That's the *North Central Regional Jail.* And once those lawyers are lined up, please check on our friend, Aristocrates, because I may be tied up for a while, and she's a little frazzled. I believe she's in Charleston, as is the other friend I told you about. Their contact information is in my email at work."

The billionaire mumbled. "I got it. Remain calm. Help is on the way."

"That's what I'm counting on, *vozhd.*"

WEST VIRGINIA STATE CAPITOL
CHARLESTON, WEST VIRGINIA
MONDAY, DECEMBER 15, 10:15 A.M.

Bowen rushed into Vincent's office, panting heavily. His face was scarlet and sweaty.

"Jesus, Dick! You look like you're about ready to keel over! What's going on?"

Bowen slumped forward, resting on the back of a Queen Anne chair. "I just got the word that an arrest warrant has been issued for Tabatha in Pleasants County. But I forgot to charge my cell phone last night. and it died on me, so I had to race down here to tell you in person."

"What's she wanted for?"

Bowen stood up, gulping for air. "We got problems. I'd suggest you have all State Police units stationed on I-77 between here and Parkersburg be looking for Pleasants County Sheriff's cruisers." He handed Vincent a piece of paper. "Or *that* SUV registered to Sarika Gudivada. Or *that* Cadillac with Virginia plates registered to David Anderson."

"And what should I tell the troopers to do if they see one of these vehicles?"

"Delay 'em. If she's not arrested before noon, I think she'll vote our way today."

Vincent looked like his brains had been microwaved. "What are you talking about? I thought you told her last night I couldn't have anything else to do with her!"

"I did! But I think she has bigger incentives to vote for Melanie Wilson today than your dick. Let's leave it at that. The less you know, the better."

CHAPTER 107

CHARLESTON CITY HALL
OFFICE OF THE MAYOR
CHARLESTON, WEST VIRGINIA
MONDAY, DECEMBER 15, 10:25 A.M.

Mayor Booz Hancock stalked around the fax machine like a caged panther. Nearing sixty, his hair remained black thanks to coloring products he would swear on a Bible he never used. His dress shirt looked like he had found it that morning wadded up on his closet floor.

The contrast between the mayor and his police chief was pronounced. Wearing an ironed blue uniform, the chief's black wingtips were polished to a shine. He sat on the sofa with his hat in his lap, patiently awaiting orders.

"Gil said it should be here any minute," Hancock groused. "If this is so important, why the hell aren't they moving quicker?"

"We're ready to act as soon as it arrives," the chief said calmly.

It was as if he had said *Abracadabra*. The fax machine rang then emitted a high-pitched screech. The mayor squared himself in front of it, rubbing his fingers expectantly.

The moment the first sheet printed out, Hancock snatched it up and read it. "It's about time," he said. The three-page fax came from the Pleasants County Magistrate Court. The "Warrant For Arrest" was addressed to "Any Law Enforcement Officer," and stated:

> "Therefore, you are commanded in the name of the State of West Virginia to apprehend the above-named defendant and bring that person before any magistrate in this County, to be dealt with in relation to these charge(s) according to law. This arrest warrant is to be executed FORTHWITH."

The third page was a black and white glamour photo of Tabatha McCallen. A note at the bottom indicated a digital copy had been sent to the Mayor via email.

Hancock smiled and handed the fax over. "All right, Chief. You know what to do."

"Right. We'll get copies distributed to our units posted near the Capitol entrances."

Hancock nodded once. "And what will the officers say if any Capitol rent-a-cops or, God forbid, actual State Troopers question them? You know … wondering why they're lurking around the Capitol, for God's sake."

"They'll say we received an anonymous tip someone may try to sneak a bomb into the Capitol to disrupt the Electors' meeting," the chief replied. "Our city's police officers are providing an additional ring of security to ensure that doesn't happen."

"Good. And one last thing, Chief: Are you sure these officers can be trusted?"

"When you called me last night, I went through our roster and hand-picked these men. If I can't trust *them*, I can't trust anybody."

Mayor Hancock smiled and smacked his hands together. "Well, get moving then!" Like lightning, he raced around his desk, hammered on his keyboard and printed out a photo of the nefarious Tabatha Pettigrew McCallen. He handed it to the chief, who wheeled out the door. Hancock then whipped out his cell phone.

"Hello, Gil? This is Booz. Yeah, I got that fax. It's under control. Now, then … once we've managed this crisis for Governor Royal, you need to let that son-of-a-bitch know I fully expect Charleston's federal grant applications to go to the top of his administration's to-do list. And he'd better put smiley faces on 'em, too. *Capice?*"

ESQUIRE HOTEL
CHARLESTON, WEST VIRGINIA
MONDAY, DECEMBER 14, 10:35 A.M.

Tyson Vasquez entered the hotel lobby, quickly scanned it, then stowed his sunglasses and made a beeline for the front desk. "I'm here to see Tabatha McCallen," he announced.

The receptionist punched on the keyboard, then looked sad. "I'm sorry, sir, but she's already checked out. Are you Alex Beria?"

I am today, he thought. "Yes, I am."

She bent down then popped up holding a sealed white envelope. "She left this for you."

"Thank you," Vasquez said. He opened the envelope and unfolded the note inside.

> Dear Alex,
> As I said in my email, the second half of the money must be wired before noon today if you people want the deal to go through. No money, no deal. I'll call my bank this morning before I go to the Capitol.
> If you need to reach me, call my cell.
> Tabby

Vasquez returned the note to the envelope, shoving them both into his suit jacket pocket. Whipping out his cell phone, he turned around and headed toward the door.

"Mr. Mazniashvili? This is Tyson. Aristocrates has flown the coop, and she's trying to change the terms of your deal."

CHAPTER 108

MID-OHIO VALLEY AIRPORT
PARKERSBURG, WEST VIRGINIA
MONDAY, DECEMBER 15, 10:40 A.M.

"What is taking so long?" Rikki half screamed.

Dave gripped the Cessna's yoke and took a deep breath. "Once we get clearance from air traffic control, we'll be on the ground in Charleston in 35 minutes."

"We should have just driven," she shot back.

Sheriff Vaughn fidgeted in the backseat, holding a cell phone to his ear. "Uh. Maybe not. My deputy says the State Troopers still aren't letting him back on the road. There's a report someone stole one of our cruisers and they're detaining him until they get to the bottom of it."

Dave cracked an I-told-you-so grin. Rikki harrumphed and stared out the side window.

The plane's inboard radio squeaked. "November-Three-Seven-Six-One-Whiskey, you are cleared for takeoff."

"Roger, Tower," Dave replied, staring through his sunglasses at the runway. "Thanks."

Dave slowly taxied down the runway, aligning the Cessna with the centerline. Gently pushing the throttle forward, the engine and propeller roared ever louder, and he used the rudder pedals to maintain his runway alignment.

"I gotta go," the sheriff said before hanging up.

The plane sped up. Carefully monitoring his instruments, Dave applied back pressure to the yoke when his airspeed hit 55 knots, causing the nose to lift. Rolling forward, he felt the plane exhibit its tendency to turn left, so he applied the right rudder to counter it and then pitched the plane up to 75 knots to climb off the runway.

As they banked higher, the barren, tree-covered rolling hills spread around them in every direction, broken only by sparse patches of mostly middle-class housing and the thin gray ribbon of Interstate 77 that paralleled their course to Charleston.

"Okay, guys," Dave yelled over the roar of the plane. "Hold on tight!"

CHAPTER 109

CHARLESTON TOWN CENTER MALL
CHARLESTON, WEST VIRGINIA
MONDAY, DECEMBER 15, 11:00 A.M.

Tabatha strolled through the boutique, browsing the latest fashions from New York. *Soon enough, price will be no concern, and I'll be able to enjoy everything I've deserved but couldn't afford.*

Selecting a sexy red dress, she held it up and examined herself in a mirror. She smiled, thinking of how it would look on her, and how men would react when they saw her in it.

I'm still hot now. But I'll need some touch-up work in a few years. A little dermabrasion here. Maybe a neck lift and a tummy tuck, too. Birthing those two hellions was murder on my stomach. I'll need to fix that now that I'm officially a free woman again!

Her cell phone rang. *Who's calling me from a 917 number?* "Hello?"

"Mrs. McCallen? Dmitri Mazniashvili here."

Her nose crinkled. *"Who?"*

The billionaire was struck speechless. "Uh. I'm Alex Beria's boss."

Tabatha folded the red dress over her forearm. "Well, it's about time you people got in touch with me! Where has Alex been? Why hasn't anyone called me! And where do you get off sending some goon to my room last night threatening to kill me?!"

"What?!"

"Don't act like you're deaf! I have half a mind to call this thing off, and if I *ever* see the bald son-of-a-bitch who was choking me last night, I swear to God I'll kill him."

"M-M-Mrs. McCallen. I have no idea what you're talking about. But I assure you our organization had *nothing* to do with anyone who may have threatened you last night."

"Oh, he *threatened* me all right! Choked the hell out of me, too! Why, I swear ... "

"Mrs. McCallen!" Mazniashvili said loudly, "I will apply my full resources to determine who assaulted you last night. And when we find that man – as I assure you, we will – I will let you kill him in whatever stomach-churning manner you find most enjoyable. But right now, you and I have an *extremely* important business transaction to discuss."

Tabatha exhaled. "There's nothing really to discuss. If you wire the other twelve-and-a-half million dollars to my bank account before noon, I'll march into Governor Vincent's office and do your bidding. If not, I won't."

"We will get that taken care of, I assure you. But it's taking us a little time to do it."

"Time's a luxury you don't have. You have the routing information for my account?"

"Yes."

Tabatha smiled and her posture relaxed. "Fine. I'll call the bank at a quarter 'til noon to make sure the second installment has arrived. But if the money's not there, you can kiss this deal good-bye and I'll keep the first installment."

"You can't do that!"

"Watch me."

CHAPTER 110

PRIVATE AVIATION CENTER
CHARLES E. "CHUCK" YEAGER AIRPORT
CHARLESTON, WEST VIRGINIA
MONDAY, DECEMBER 15, 11:35 A.M.

Rikki and Dave jogged through the small civilian aviation terminal, as Sheriff Vaughn did his best to keep up, huffing and puffing as he speed-walked behind them.

Rikki grinned. *I guess kicking the snot out of Russians is his forte, not cardio.*

A Charleston Police Department cruiser waited outside the terminal's entrance. Quickly exiting through a glass door, the three walked toward the cruiser.

"I take it you're the three people the mayor wants me to pick up," the twenty-something cop remarked.

"Yes," Rikki replied, climbing into the passenger seat as Dave and Vaughn climbed in the back. "Let's hit it! The meeting starts in 25 minutes!"

The cop slammed the car into drive. "We'll be there in ten," he said, a glint of determination in his eyes. The tires squealed, throwing a trail of smoke in their wake, as the cruiser barreled downhill.

CHAPTER 111

KANAWHA BOULEVARD EAST
CHARLESTON, WEST VIRGINIA
MONDAY, DECEMBER 15, 11:45 A.M.

Driving her black BMW east on Kanawha Boulevard, Tabatha made her way upriver toward the Capitol. Her cell phone lay beside her with the speakerphone on.

"And you're absolutely positive that money is in the account?" she asked.

"Yes, Mrs. McCallen. We don't receive wire transfers of $12.5 million every day. It was deposited into McCallen Resources' account 10 minutes ago."

"And that's the company account I set up last week, right?"

"Yes, ma'am."

Tabatha breathed a sigh of relief. *25 million dollars and a free woman to boot! Life couldn't get better unless I saw that thick-fingered goon who choked me last night jogging down Kanawha Boulevard right now. Then I could run his ass over, and life would be perfect.*

"Thank you very much, Alicia. I'll be in touch."

Tabatha ended the call. Three seconds later, a 202 area code number rang in. She smiled smugly. *Must be another big shot from Petromica, making sure Momma is happy. Because if Momma ain't happy, ain't nobody happy!*

"Hello?"

"This is Tyson Turner from Petromica. The second installment has been wired to you."

"Yes, Mr. Turner, thank you. I've enjoyed doing business with your company."

"Now you must make it to the governor's office in time to vote. Where are you?"

Tabatha glanced at the dashboard. "My GPS says I'm a mile away."

"Wonderful. You just need to drive down California Avenue and enter the Capitol through the governor's parking area in the basement."

Tabatha stiffened in the driver's seat. "I most certainly will not."

"What?! Why not?"

"I'm not the governor's dirty little secret," she said. "He's *not* sneaking me in through the basement. If he wants my vote, he can be seen in public with me for a change. Today, I'm strutting my pretty little ass through a main entrance. And if he doesn't like it, too bad."

The man took a deep breath. "I don't think you appreciate the gravity of this situation. People are trying to keep you from arriving here by noon. You're in danger!"

"Ha! I'm in no more danger now than I was last night, when your goon tried to kill me."

"Mr. Mazniashvili shared your concerns with me. I don't know what happened last night, but we had nothing to do with it."

"Whatever. The bottom line is you people have paid up. If you don't want me rolling around with Luke any more, that's fine by me. He was always a terrible lay, anyhow."

The tension at the other end of the call was palpable. Tabatha relished it. "So what entrance do you plan to use, Mrs. McCallen?"

"I don't know yet," she replied flippantly. "I haven't decided. Just make sure the red carpet is rolled out for me when I get there. After all I've been through, I deserve that much."

She ended the call as she drove past the white marble front façade of the Capitol. Noting that all the parking spaces along California Avenue were filled, she kept driving east on the Boulevard. Seeing a few empty spaces on the westbound side, she made a U-turn and pulled into the first available one.

I deserve that much, <u>at least</u>!

*   *   *

The Charleston police cruiser blew through the stop light, sirens blaring and blue lights flashing, as it turned onto Kanawha Boulevard. "I'll swing around to the East Wing and drop you off right at an entrance."

Rikki glanced down at her watch. Only eight minutes until the Electors met.

The cruiser flew east down the Boulevard past the front of the Capitol overlooking the Kanawha River. The street that ran perpendicular to the Boulevard along the east side of the Capitol was California Avenue, and the cop pulled onto it.

Looking over, Rikki saw another uniformed Charleston cop leaning against the side of the marble Capitol. Standing beside the East Wing entrance closest to the Boulevard, he wore a relaxed smile while talking into a cell phone.

"There she is!" Dave screamed, gesticulating wildly at that entrance. Rikki looked away from the cop and saw Tabatha entering the building. Her long red hair and the stately way she walked left no doubt to her identity.

Their driver honked the horn and squawked a warning blast with his siren. The cop at the entrance glanced over at the cruiser with an inquisitive look.

"Stop that woman!!!" the driver screamed, pointing at Tabatha. Dave, Rikki and the sheriff slung open their doors and raced after her, as did the driver.

The officer at the door sprung into action, his eyes as wide as Frisbees. Hurling open the thick glass-and-steel door, he yelled, "Halt!"

*　　　　　*　　　　　*

Tabatha was twenty feet inside the door when the cop told her to stop. She kept walking down the Capitol's main corridor that ran through the Rotunda and connected its two wings.

Remain calm. Maybe he's not talking to you.

Those delusions shattered when the thick door slammed against the marble surrounding the entrance, and the cop yelled, "The female subject just entered the East Wing and is heading towards the Governor's Office! Requesting backup!"

Kicking off her high heels, she sprinted down the corridor with all the speed her long muscular legs could generate, dashing past oil paintings of the state's governors that lined both sides of the marble hallway.

"She ran cross-country!" Dave screamed. "For God's sake, somebody tackle her!"

Uniformed Charleston city cops raced into the Rotunda from Kanawha Boulevard and the back side of the Capitol, converging on Tabatha from both the right and left, but she ran right by them with her long strides, blowing through the Rotunda.

Fifty more yards! You can do it!

Tabatha flew past the Secretary of State's door, and the public entrance to the Governor's Office loomed twenty yards ahead. Smiling widely, she cranked up the pace with the most energetic finish line kick of her life. Reaching the end of the corridor, as she prepared to turn into the Governor's Office, a burly

Charleston cop flew in and violently tackled her like she was a running back trying to vault into the end zone.

She flailed on the marble floor, trying to dislodge the cop from her back. "Get off me! I have to get in there! Don't you know who I am?!"

The cop's hefty body barely budged, and he remained sprawled atop her. A bevy of other officers quickly reached the scene. Some grabbed her arms and legs, while others formed a human barricade across the Governor's Office entrance.

"Yes, ma'am," the tackler replied with a grin, breathing heavily as he spoke. "You're Tabatha Pettigrew McCallen, and you're under arrest."

"*For what?!*"

An officer in the barricade unfolded a document. "This warrant says you're charged with the misdemeanor offense of adultery."

Rikki rushed up to the pile, squatting down so she could stare Tabatha in the eyes. "For starters. But when we searched your house this morning, we found the Trade Secrets Protection Addendum you signed with Petromica. So by the time we get back to St. Marys, we'll have bribery and accessory before the fact to first degree murder added to the list."

Tabatha lunged at her. "You fucking camel jockey! You don't know anything!"

Rikki smiled menacingly. "Maybe not. But I *do* know the $25 million Petromica wired into that account you set up is now safely in an escrow account owned by McCallen Resources that neither you nor Petromica can access."

"*What?!* You can't do that!"

"Oh, yes, I can. Jack appointed *me* as his company's trustee, and I can do whatever is necessary to protect that money for his heirs. And nothing would be more prudent than to get it away from your greedy little hands. Because if you had anything to do with Jack's death, under state law, *you won't inherit a dime of his money!* Everything will go to his two boys."

The cops lifted Tabatha from the ground, cuffed her hands behind her back and began frog-marching her toward the closest exit.

"What's going on here?" Governor Vincent stood in the doorway to his public reception area, looking confused. A bald man with a massive frame and meaty hands stood beside him.

"*You!*" Tabatha yelled over her shoulder. "I'm not going down alone! If I go down, *you're* going down too, Luke! You've got some nerve having that monster try to kill me last night! As soon as I make bail, I'm gonna track him down and cut his balls off, I swear to God!"

The cops rushed Tabatha outside but her profanity and threats remained audible for at least another 50 yards. Television camera crews circled her like sharks in bloody waters.

Sheriff Vaughn tapped their police escort on the shoulder. "You mind taking me down to Kanawha County's courthouse? I need to be there when she's arraigned so I can argue for a high bail and hopefully drag her crazy ass back to Pleasants County this afternoon."

The cop nodded. "Sure. Let's go."

"Could someone *please* tell me what's going on here?" Vincent repeated, this time more emphatically.

Rikki stepped toward him and extended her right hand. "Mr. Governor, I'm Rikki Gudivada, Pleasants County's prosecutor. You and I need to have a private conversation."

Vincent grew silent and his lips tightened. Finally, he closed his eyes and nodded. "Okay. Let's go back to my office and talk."

As the governor slowly trudged past the receptionist's desk, Rikki turned to Dave. "I'll be right back. This shouldn't take long."

Dave looked over at the bald man who had been standing beside the governor just a moment ago. He was leaning against the doorframe for support and his face looked red.

A State Capitol guard walked up to the bald man from the crowd. Smiling sheepishly, he tugged on his shirt sleeve. The bald man glanced at him and his eyes went wide.

"Hey, Mr. Bowen," the guard said. Looking around furtively, he leaned close to Bowen and asked, "How did your granddaughter like that squirrel you got her last month?"

"*Squirrel?*" Dave exclaimed. His eyes lit up like a Christmas tree.

Bowen clutched his chest and collapsed on the marble floor, shaking violently. Two Charleston cops knocked the guard out of the way, hovering over Bowen's prostrate body. "Somebody call an ambulance! I think he's having a heart attack!"

Dave stepped away, and a crowd of hyped-up Republicans led by Gil Dean swarmed around him. One of them held out his hands, palms up. "So *now* what are we supposed to do?"

Gil stepped into the breach, holding a big green book. "According to the Code, 'If any of the Electors fails to attend at the time appointed, the Electors present shall appoint an Elector in place of each one so failing to attend, and every Elector so appointed shall be entitled to vote in the same manner as if he had been originally chosen by the people.'"

One of the men looked at Gil, who nodded curtly. "In that case," the Elector said, casting a quick glance at the clock on the receptionist's desk, "since it's noon and Tabatha McCallen is not here, I nominate Gil Dean be appointed to replace her."

"I second that motion, Senator Boggess," another blurted.

"All those in favor?" Boggess asked.

"Aye," the four Electors declared.

"The motion carries. Congrats, Gil. You get to cast the fifth ballot. The Secretary of State will explain the actual process, so let's make ourselves comfortable 'til she gets here."

The five Electors, including Gil, strolled across the reception area and sat on various couches and loveseats. Dave followed suit, flopping down on a couch.

"Enjoying the circus, Dave?" Gil asked, grinning.

Exhaling deeply, Dave closed his eyes. "Just wake me when it's over."

CHAPTER 112

CHARLESTON, WEST VIRGINIA
WEST VIRGINIA STATE CAPITOL BUILDING
MONDAY, DECEMBER 15, 12:05 P.M.

Vincent sat down behind his desk. "Have a seat, Rikki. So what do we need to discuss?"

Rikki folded her hands together. "Mr. Governor, I'm here to offer you a plea bargain."

Vincent laughed nervously. "A plea bargain? For what?"

"Adultery. With Tabatha McCallen. We have video of the act in a St. Marys motel room."

With his elbows resting on the desk, Vincent leaned forward. "I'm ashamed and appalled at my behavior. But I don't see why you need to treat it like a *crime*."

"It's rarely prosecuted, but adultery is a crime that's not been repealed by the Legislature. We suspected Tabatha had been bribed to switch her Electoral College ballot, but we didn't have enough evidence to prove it. And in good conscience, I couldn't let Senator Wilson profit from it, so I had to charge Tabatha with adultery to keep her from voting."

Vincent sat wide-eyed, shaking his head. "I had no idea."

"I suspected that might be the case, which is why I'm willing to offer you this deal."

Vincent exhaled softly. "What do you want me to do?"

Rikki paused, processing her thoughts. "If Tabatha won't accept a deal in the murder case, I'll need your testimony to solidify the adultery charge. In exchange for that, and your agreement to enter marriage counseling, I'll grant you immunity on the adultery."

Vincent looked shocked. "That's it?"

"That's it. The video is under seal in the Sheriff's Department. Our criminal complaint did not identify Tabatha's adulterous lover. I know your wife and she is a good woman. I'm disgusted you disrespected her by sleeping around with a tramp like Tabatha. But I believe politicians still have privacy rights, and your wife doesn't deserve to have this crap aired in the press. If you'll take this deal, I'll do everything I can to keep that from happening.

"*However*, if I find out you had anything to do with Jack's death, I will make sure you spend the rest of your life rotting in prison for it."

Vincent's lip quivered and his eyes welled. "You're right. Donna doesn't deserve to be put through that and I thank you for trying to spare her the humiliation." Taking a deep breath, he stood up. "I'll do it."

EPILOGUE

ST. MARYS, PLEASANTS COUNTY, WEST VIRGINIA
WEDNESDAY, DECEMBER 24, 7:00 P.M.

Holding the phone to her ear, Rikki stared out her living room window. Large, wet snow flakes cascaded through the darkness behind her porch light.

"I heard the special prosecutor cut Tabatha a deal," her mother said. "Is that true?"

Rikki sighed. "She pled guilty to bribery and being an accessory to Jack's murder, plus she's testifying against Petrenko. She'll be eligible for parole in 20 years, but she had to disclaim any inheritance from Jack's estate. *And* she had to relinquish her parental rights."

Madhani gasped. "Wow. And she agreed to do that?"

Rikki put on silver hoop earrings as she strolled through the living room in black jeans and a soft red sweater. "She's vain, Mom. She figures she can sweet-talk the parole board into letting her out before she turns sixty. With her good genetics and bedroom skills, she probably thinks she'll still be able to find another sugar daddy."

Kneeling by the couch, Rikki placed three gift-wrapped packages in a large cardboard box. "Mazniashvili is paying a dream team of lawyers to defend Petrenko," she continued.

"With no witnesses and no murder weapon, the State needs Tabatha's testimony to get a conviction. Personally, I think Berkeley County will have better luck nailing him for Marcus Boley's murder."

Madhani harrumphed. "And are they going to prosecute Mazniashvili for *anything?*"

"Well ... the special prosecutor may indict him as an accessory, too, but he's holed up in the UAE right now," Rikki replied.

"The United Arab Emirates?"

"Yes. Mazniashvili says he's needed there to manage his business affairs. But I'd say the real reason is we have no extradition treaty with the UAE."

"Well, I hope David gets President-elect Royal to fix that problem," Madhani declared.

Rikki's stomach dropped. Dave and Royal had met that morning one-on-one. She felt sure Royal had offered him the chief of staff position.

The question is, 'Will he take it?'

"So have you told him how you feel?" her mother asked softly.

Rikki shook her head sadly. "No, Mom. God knows I miss him, but I can't put that kind of pressure on him. I *won't*. Not when this once-in-a-lifetime opportunity has landed in his lap. I'm happy we've buried the hatchet, and I'll treasure our friendship. But I just have to accept that love and marriage weren't in the cards fate dealt us."

A long pause ensued. "It is your life, daughter," Madhani replied. "You are the one who must live with the consequences of your decisions. But your father and I have always urged you to follow your heart. When in doubt, Sarika, *follow your heart!* If not, I fear you will throw away your own once-in-a-lifetime opportunity."

Rikki's phone beeped. Dave's face smiled up from the screen. "Dave's calling on the other line," she said quickly. "I'll call you back."

"Good luck, honey."

Taking a breath, Rikki flipped over to the incoming call and put on a smile. "So what's the deal, buddy boy?"

"Well," he began, "it's confirmed. Jonathan wants me to be his chief of staff."

Her heart sunk. *Losing you once was painful enough. Why did God let me fall in love with you all over again? Just to make me go through the pain of losing you a second time?*

"Congratulations, Dave!" she said, hoping she sounded genuinely excited. But her chest tightened, and she felt like she was going to cry. "What an honor! So when do you start?"

"That's still up in the air. I asked him to give me 24 hours to mull it over."

Rikki's brow creased. "Why?" She thought she heard the muffled sound of a car door shut as Sheriff Vaughn's two coon dogs bayed in the distance. *Silent Doug's kids must have driven in from Charlotte for Christmas.*

Dave paused. "There's another vacancy I've decided to apply for."

His response sounded like an echo. *Gremlins in the cell phone grid?* That distracted thought was interrupted by the musical chimes of her doorbell.

"Hold on a second. Someone's at my door." Carrying the box of gifts across the room, she absent-mindedly set it on the ground to open the door and found herself speechless.

On the other side of her door, she saw Dave.

Standing on her porch in a black wool great coat, he held an envelope in his gloved right hand. Snowflakes gently drifted down behind him, contrasted harshly by the tension on his face. Wordlessly, he hung up his phone and she did the same.

"I've had this card stashed in a drawer for over 10 years, Rikki," he said quietly. Clutching the envelope tightly, he hesitatingly extended it. "The words are as true tonight as the day I wrote them."

Rikki lifted the faded gold seal and opened the envelope. The card's front bore the words, "Thinking of You ..." Glancing up, she saw Dave staring back at her, tightlipped.

Opening the card, she continued reading. Originally blank, it was filled with lines of his own distinctive, almost unreadable handwriting:

You cross my mind every day. I wonder what you're doing and I pray you're happy. Every night, I pray you will forgive me for the pain I've caused you but I don't know if that prayer will be answered.

I can't describe how much I miss talking to you. You were my best friend and confidante, my fellow adventurer and partner-in-crime. No matter where I go or what I do, my life feels empty without seeing your smile and hearing your laughter.

I've loved you from the moment I met you. I still love you with all my heart and I have no doubt I will love you until the day God calls me home. And if miracles happen and you ever feel the sparks of love for me again, know this: I will abandon everything for you. I will run to your side and never leave you again.

Break my heart if you must, but I can't keep my mouth shut any longer. My heart might get broken, but at least I'll go down swinging. I'd rather die loveless and alone than spend the rest of my days wondering, 'What if...'

I probably sound like a pitiful fool or a broken record. I know you've heard this all before, but I'll say it one last time...

I love you, Rikki. My heart <u>aches</u> for you. If you give me another chance, I'll spend the rest of my life making sure you never regret it.

Dave

Looking up from the card she held in her left hand, Rikki was speechless. Dave took a step forward and tenderly took her right hand.

"I'm so thankful you've forgiven me, Rik. But I want more than forgiveness. I want *more* than your friendship." His eyes flitted from right-to-left as he searched for words. "I want to kiss you. I want to hold you. I want to argue with you and laugh with you. I'm baring my soul to you on your porch on Christmas Eve like a lovesick teenager in a bad movie because I *desperately* want to grow old with you. And I can't make a decision about this whole chief of staff thing until I know if there's a chance in hell we could have that kind of relationship again."

"Oh, Dave," she blurted before planting her lips on his. Dropping the card, she ran her fingernails through his graying temples and felt his arms wrap around her back. *Yes, I still love you! How could I not?*

For a long time, Rikki felt like she was in a dream. Smelling Dave's aftershave, she reveled in their kiss as they stood on the porch with the snow falling around them. Then, the realization struck her as cold as the winter air.

He wants me to move to D.C.

Taking a quick step backwards, she brought the passionate kiss to an end. "I can't do it."

Dave's eyes bulged. *"What?!* What do you mean?" Taking a deep breath, he clenched his jaw. "Are you saying you don't love me?"

Rikki felt her lower lip tremble. "No!" she cried. "Of course I love you! But I can't leave St. Marys! I just took over as prosecutor and Mom needs me here and ..."

Dave leaned backwards at the waist and laughed uncontrollably. "Oh, Christ! I'm not *asking* you to leave St. Marys."

"You're not?" she asked, confused.

"God no!" he replied, emitting another loud laugh. Still feeling confused, Rikki watched as he took her hand and knelt on the porch. "I meant what I wrote in that card. If God has graced me with your love again, I will abandon *everything* – even being the White House chief of staff – to be with you *wherever* you choose to be."

Rikki beamed from ear-to-ear. "Really?"

Dave nodded. "Damn straight. You want to stay in St. Marys? You got it." He kissed her hand and laughed aloud as he stood up. "My mom will be thrilled to have me home again!"

"But what in the world are you going to do here?" she asked.

He arched an eyebrow. "Well, I still have my law license. And I seem to recall you're fixin' to hire an assistant prosecutor." He grinned. "Plus, you're gonna need some help running Jack's company. You care if I send you my resume?"

Rikki folded her arms across her chest and shook her head, playfully furrowing her brow. "You look so proud of yourself, Mr. Anderson. Like you think you've thought of *everything* here. But what would you do if I say, 'No.'"

Dave cupped her cheeks with his hands and kissed her softly on the lips. "Then I'd find another job. I might be able to do some long distance political consulting, but I'd dig ditches or flip burgers if need be. As long as I can come home to you each night, I'll still be a happy man."

Rikki laughed, threw her arms around his neck and kissed him again. "You sure are sweet with words, Mr. Anderson. In that case, I suppose I'll say, 'Yes.'"

"*Woo-hoo!*" he exclaimed, lifting her up by the waist and twirling her around once before returning her to Earth. "So how are we gonna break the news to our folks?"

She stepped inside the house and pointed to the box of gifts. "You can make yourself useful by grabbing that box. I was on my way over to Mom's, and you can tag along and make her the happiest little Indian woman in the world. Assuming she doesn't die of a heart attack on the spot, *then* we'll figure out how to tell your parents."

"We've been officially a couple again for less than three minutes, and I already have a 'honey-do list.'" Strolling past her, he patted her once on the butt.

Quick as a cobra, she swatted his trespassing hand. "Isn't that a small price to pay for *moi*, Mr. Anderson?"

Lifting the box from the floor, he turned around and gave her a peck on the cheek as he headed toward the door. "That it is, Ms. Gudivada. That it is."

THE END

ABOUT THE AUTHOR

Brent Wolfingbarger grew up in Belle, West Virginia, and graduated from DuPont High School. He earned his bachelor's degree in political science at West Virginia University before receiving his law degree from the Washington & Lee University School of Law.

After a short stint working for a law firm in Elkins, West Virginia, Brent moved to Charleston and opened his own practice where he spent the next twelve years handling cases in a variety of fields including election law, civil rights, real estate, medical malpractice and oil and gas. He also argued before the West Virginia Supreme Court in extremely complex cases including two election law cases and a medical malpractice wrongful death case involving multiple physicians and drug manufacturers.

In 2006, Brent accepted a position as an assistant county prosecutor, where he spent over five years prosecuting the full spectrum of cases including murder, sexual assault and computer-related crimes. During this time, he actively focused on issues related to the acquisition, analysis and use of digital evidence in criminal cases and he served as a liaison to the West Virginia Internet Crimes Against Children (ICAC) task force.

Brent lives in Washington, DC with his wife and two children where he continues to work as a prosecutor, evaluating complex allegations of fraud committed by health care providers and durable medical equipment companies against the Medicaid program, and prosecuting violent crimes committed against elderly and disabled victims. In this capacity, he regularly works on task forces involving multiple law enforcement agencies, including the FBI, the Department of Homeland Security and the United States Attorney's Office.